M

3 1266 21031 1825

28 DAY BOOK

D1802474

DISCARDED OR WITHDRAWN
GREAT NECK LIBRARY

4/14   1   2013

GREAT NECK LIBRARY
GREAT NECK, NY 11023
(516) 466-8055
www.greatnecklibrary.org

MAY 6 - 2013

Though lovers be lost, love shall not
And Death shall have no dominion

—*Dylan Thomas*

Also by C.E. Murphy

The Walker Papers
Urban Shaman
Winter Moon ("Banshee Cries")
Thunderbird Falls
Coyote Dreams
Walking Dead
Demon Hunts
Spirit Dances
Raven Calls
Mountain Echoes
No Dominion
Shaman Rises (Dec 2013)

The Old Races Universe
Heart of Stone
House of Cards
Hands of Flame

Baba Yaga's Daughter & Other Tales of the Old Races

The Worldwalker Duology
Truthseeker
Wayfinder

The Inheritors' Cycle
The Queen's Bastard
The Pretender's Crown

Anthologies
Don't Read This Book
Dragon's Lure
The Phantom Queen Awakes
Running with the Pack
How to Write Magical Words: A Writer's Companion

& with Faith Hunter
Easy Pickings
A Joanne Walker/Jane Yellowrock crossover

C.E. Murphy

No Dominion

THE WALKER PAPERS: A GARRISON REPORT

A MIZ KIT
PRODUCTION

GREAT NECK LIBRARY

MKP

NO DOMINION

ISBN-13: 978-1-61317-030-4

Copyright © 2013 by C.E. Murphy

All rights reserved. Except for use in any review, the reproduction or utilization of this work in whole or in part in any form by any electronic, mechanical, or other means, now known or hearaver invented, is forbidden without the written permission of the author. The author can be contacted at cemurphyauthor@gmail.com

This is a work of fiction. Names, characters, places and incidents are either the product of the author's imagination or are used fictiously. Any resemblance to actual persons, living or dead, business establishments, events or locales is entirely coincidental.

Cover art by Anne Cain (annecain-art.com)
Photography by Kyle Cassidy (kylecassidy.com)
Tortoise icon by Ursula Vernon (ursulavernon.com)
Editor: Mary Theresa Hussey

cemurphy.net

For my patrons

without whom this book would quite literally not exist

Contents

Magic Hath an Element	13
Rabbit Tricks	29
Petite	46
Forgotten But By A Few	59
No Dominion	79
The Rising Green	309
Band-Aids and Bog-Men	333
Twenty Years After	351

Chronology Notes:

"Magic Hath an Element" takes place at the same time as the opening chapters of URBAN SHAMAN (Book One of the Walker Papers), but is told from Gary's point of view.

Magic Hath an Element

At 7:23 A.M, a leggy brunette climbed into my cab and changed my life.

She was rude, snapping, "Drive," without even lookin' at me. That kinda fare always set my teeth on edge, superior and holier-than-thou. Never judge somebody by how they treat you, judge 'em by how they treat the cabbie.

Still, drivin' paid the rent. "Where to?"

"I don't know. Northwest."

I eyed her in the mirror. There was me, a couple days past seventy-three and pretty hale for a guy that age, with all my hair and teeth I wasn't sayin' either way about, and there was her, twenty-six and pretty in the way women who don't know how well they're put together can be. She wore her hair real short, which I thought most dames should. What with her doin' something on a notepad, scribbling and muttering, I couldn't see her eyes to tell the color. She looked tired, though, like she'd come off a European flight, not just something continental. I said, "Northwest, the airline? It's just a couple feet up the term—"

She snarled, "*To* the northwest." I glared at her and drove. A minute later, as if she hadn't started out rude, she asked a favor: "You got a map?"

No self-respecting cabbie would admit it if he did. "What for?"

"So I can figure out where we're going."

I turned around and stared at her.

"Watch the road!"

Watching the road was for sissies. I twitched the steering wheel and cars merged around us, safe as houses. The fare slumped in her seat, green eyes wide, and got politer: "Do you have a map, please?"

"Yeah, yeah, all right." I threw a city guide over the seat and listened to pages rattle as she shuffled through them. A couple minutes later she said, "Okay, we're going to Aurora."

"You sure? That ain't such a good neighborhood, lady."

"I'm sure. I'm trying to find somebody who's in trouble."

I lifted my eyebrows at her in the mirror. "Good place to start."

She scowled at me. I smiled back, my best patented seen-it-all smile that told pretty young things not to mess with me, and instead of messing, she asked if I had a cigarette. I shook my head. "Those things'll kill you, sweetheart. My wife died of emphysema on our forty-eighth wedding anniversary. You want a smoke, kid, find it somewhere else."

She looked embarrassed, but didn't have the smarts to quit while she was ahead. She muttered, "I'm not a kid," and

I eyed her in the mirror again.

"You're twenty-six, doll. From where I'm sittin' anybody less than fifty is a kid."

Her jaw dropped. "Nobody ever guesses my age right."

"It's a gift. I can tell how old people are."

"Some gift."

"Gets me good tips, especially with women in their forties. I give 'em a big story 'bout how I always get ages right, and then I lie. Works like a charm."

"You guessed my age right."

"No point in lying. I never met anybody who didn't want to be in their twenties. Look, why're you headin' to Aurora, doll? Nothing there but trouble, and you don't look like the type."

"I told you." She put her head against the window. "Somebody's in trouble. I saw her from the plane."

That made my life a lot more interesting. I put my arm over the passenger seatback and twisted to stare at the fare. "You're trying to save somebody you saw from an *airplane*? What the hell, you got some kinda hero complex? How the hell're you gonna find one dame you saw from the air?"

"It's basic math, for God's sake. I got the approximate height and speed we were traveling from the pilot, so figuring out the distance wasn't that hard, and I saw a modern church on a street with only one amber streetlight. If I can find it before the lights go out—"

"Then you'll be the first one on a murder scene." My day was gettin' a *lot* more interesting. The guys back at dispatch would love this one. I was gonna get free coffee for a week off this story. Couldn't let her know I was lookin' forward to whatever came next, though, and it was only God's own truth when I said, "You're nuts, lady, and desperate for thrills."

She snapped, "Like it could possibly be any of your business," which was true enough, but I never met a cabbie who didn't think everything his fares did was his business.

"Relax, sweetheart. A pretty girl like you oughta be on her way home to her sweetie, not—"

"I don't have one."

"With your personality, I can't figure why not."

The fare put her face in her hands. "Haven't you ever just really felt like you had to do something?"

"Yeah, sure. I really felt like I had to marry my old lady when she got knocked up." It wasn't true, but the fare had gotten in my cab, not the other way around. She got whatever story I felt like telling today. That was the beauty of driving fares. Them, me, we were all different every time. "I never felt like I had to go chasing broads I saw from airplanes, though. I got troubles of my own."

"Yeah, well, maybe I've got enough that I need somebody else's to make the load seem lighter."

I grunted, surprised. Usually kids in their twenties were way too young to realize that helpin' somebody else eased their own burdens. I warmed up to the fare even if she was rude, and nodded at the rear-view mirror. "Arright, lady. Let's go find your corpse."

I got the fare to Aurora in record time, even if I had

to say so myself, which I did, because she didn't even say thanks, just looked out the window and said, "Streetlights are still on. We're in time," as I pulled into a gas station. She gave me an unfriendly look in the mirror. "I'm not paying your gas bill, buddy."

"Aurora's a big neighborhood, doll. Maybe somebody knows where your church is."

Her eyebrows went up. "I thought men couldn't ask for directions."

"I ain't askin'," I said with aplomb. "You are."

She got a kind of "well don't that beat all" look on her face, and went to get directions from the skinny kid in the station. She even pulled cash out of her wallet and waved it at him, just like in the movies. If she didn't leave herself enough to cover the fare, I guessed I knew where to come back to get it from. A minute later she came out looking triumphant and said "East three blocks, and if that's not it, he says there's another A-frame church about half a mile southwest of here. Hurry, it's getting light out."

I'd never met a dame as macabre as this one. "What, you want to get your hands in the blood while it's still warm? You need help, lady."

"For God's sake, do you call everybody 'lady' and 'doll'? My name's Joanne, and you're the one hung up on corpses. I'm hoping she's still alive."

"Yeah? You an optimist or just dumb?"

The fare—Joanne—fumbled putting the seatbelt on. All the sassiness went out of her and she turned her face away like a little girl. "You have no right to call me dumb."

She was right. My wife woulda been ashamed of me. "Hey, look, lady. Joanne. You're right. I'm sorry. I didn't mean nothin' by it."

"Yeah, whatever. Just drive."

I shut up and drove. Took about two minutes to head east, but when we turned down the street the kid had directed us to, its streetlights were already out. Joanne whispered, "Fuck," and me, still feelin' like a jackass, offered, "That one's still on." Just one light, ugly and orange against the sky.

Joanne stared at as we went by, then flung herself around in the seat. "Oh my God, that's it! Holy shit, that's it, there's the church! Stop! Stop the car!"

A guy as old as me shouldn't get his heart rate up with excitement like that, but for a second I was just as pleased as she was. I hit the brakes, slamming her around in the back seat a little, then backed us into an empty church parking lot. "Maybe you're not dumb, doll. Maybe you're lucky."

"Yeah, well, God watches over fools and little children, right?" She tumbled out of the cab and me, I put the parking brake on and charged after her. She slowed down and looked back at me. "What, you're coming?"

"You just made me drive from Hell to breakfast, sweetheart. I'm not missin' the grand finale. Besides, I never seen a fresh murdered corpse before."

She muttered, "Have you seen stale ones?" then gave me a look like she was really seeing me for the first time. I was taller than her, not by much, which was sayin' something, as I'm six-foot-two. She got done looking me over and said, "You look like a linebacker."

Now there was a compliment to turn an old man's head. I waved it off, tryin' not to feel too pleased. "College ball, back before it turned into a media fest. It's all about money and glory now."

"It didn't used to be?"

"Nah." I gave her my best grin. "Used ta be about glory and girls."

She laughed, which was a whole lot better than the tight face and almost-crying from a minute ago. Feelin' better about myself, I headed for the church—big A-framed thing, nothin' like the one-room plain wood church I went to when I was a kid—but the fare took off down the parking lot. I bellowed, "Thought your dame was inside!"

"Well, I hope she is! I just want to make sure there's no blood."

"Blood?" I'd been teasing about a corpse, but I sure as hell didn't really want to see one. I bet Joanne didn't either, even if she was hell bent for leather trying to find one.

"If the guy with the knife caught her—"

"What guy with a knife?" This was gettin' a whole lot more serious than it had seemed five minutes ago. I followed the fare down the parking lot, where she was lookin' over the cement. "You didn't mention nobody with a knife."

"Didn't I? I said somebody was chasing the woman—"

"You said somebody was in trouble. You didn't say nothin' about a knife!"

"Oh. Well, there was a knife. A guy with a knife, and he was good, graceful with it, like he'd learned to use it on the street."

She didn't look crazy. She looked kinda like a supermodel, with the long legs and arms and a kinda big nose that made her interestin' instead of gorgeous. I guessed nobody said supermodels couldn't be nuts, though, and if she thought she'd seen all that, a woman and a guy after her and a knife, from a *plane*, then I figured she was nuts. "Lady, you better have 20/200 vision or something."

She stood up from surveilling the parking lot. "I wear contacts."

"Yeah, well, get 'em checked, 'cause you mighta seen a guy from a plane, but you missed the tooth fairy's visit." I stomped past her to prod a bloody tooth another fifteen feet away.

Joanne said "Ew," which was pretty fastidious for a dame lookin' for a corpse. She came past me, looked over the ground, and pointed. "Somebody got cut, too. There's spatter like blood off a knife."

"From your dame in the church."

"Maybe. I hope not."

"Lady, if your broad's in the church, what're we doin' lookin' around out here?"

She wrinkled her nose, and kinda hopefully said "The light's better over here?"

I couldn't help but grin. "That joke was old an' dumb when I was a kid, doll." I threw her a quarter and we both went into the church.

It was worse inside than out. There was nothing homey about the place, nothing welcoming. Christ on the cross hung up there like an accusation above a plain white pulpit and an altar that looked big enough to sacrifice a bull on. Joanne tip-toed like she was afraid to make any sound on the hardwood floors. Me, I wasn't so fussy. A house of God had to be either older than me or have some heart to get respect. I stomped along behind her, making extra sure be noisy and off-set her quiet.

There wasn't a soul in the place besides the two of us, though, which didn't seem too positive for the broad she'd seen. She caught my eye, and, looking none-too-happy about it, said, "I don't know. I thought she'd be here. Hello? Hello?"

Turned out the church had one thing going for it: great acoustics. Joanne's voice bounced to the rafters and rang around up there. She looked up like she could see the words themselves. "Wow. I'd love to sing in here."

"You sing?" Dunno why it surprised me. She just didn't seem like the singing type, not with the crazy gotta-save-the-girl thing she had going on.

She shrugged. "I don't scare the horses."

The way she said it made me think she probably had a great set of pipes and didn't like admitting she was proud of it. People were funny like that. No skin off my nose either way. I took a look under the pews. "Yeah, well, maybe you can sing yourself up a dame, 'cause there's nobody here, Jo."

Her spine stiffened like somebody'd pushed an iron rod up it. "Nobody calls me that but my dad."

"Yeah? What, did he want a boy?"

"Not exactly."

Compared to that, the scarin' the horses tone of voice had been just beggin' me to ask questions. I leaned on a pew, looking her over. Poor kid was all but bristling, waiting for me to push it a little too far. I was a nosy old bastard, but not dumb. "So what do they call you?"

"Joanne. Or Joanie. Sometimes people call me Annie, but not very often."

My back reminded me I was an old man. I straightened up, rubbing the middle, and shook my head. "Not Annie. My wife was named Annie. You don't look like one."

She relaxed a little. "What'd your wife look like?"

"'bout four eleven, blonde, brown eyes. Petite. You gotta be at least a foot taller than she was."

"Yeah. So call me Jo, I guess, if you want."

We ain't gonna be bosom buddies, the undertone said, and I figured she was right. Didn't matter what I called her. But if I was giving her nicknames she didn't like, she probably oughta know my name, at least. I stuck out a hand. "Gary Muldoon."

She glanced at me, then shook my hand. "Yeah, I know. Your license said so. I mean, it said Garrison, but I never met anybody who went by that."

"Me neither. I think my ma saddled me with it 'cause she hoped I'd be President."

Joanne grinned. "President Garrison Matthew Muldoon. Sounds pretty good to me. Except, no offense, but they don't elect guys as old as you anymore."

"And when they did I wasn't this old yet."

Her mouth twitched like a laugh was tryin' ta get out.

"You realize that makes almost no sense."

I leaned against a pew, arms folded smugly over my chest. "You understood."

The laugh almost got out. "So I did."

"Arright then. Look, lady, either there's nobody here or you gotta do your thing and find your dame."

"My thing?"

"You got *some* kinda thing goin' on here. Normal people don't stick their heads out plane windows and see somebody needing rescuing, so do your thing and find her. My meter's still runnin'."

"Oh, great. I hope you take credit cards." She walked all the way to the front of the church and around the pulpit. "Shit."

I jolted off my pew and long-legged it up the aisle. "What? She dead?"

"No." Joanne slumped against the pulpit. "There's nobody here. I really thought she would be."

"Hah. I won't ask for a tip, just for the satisfaction of bein' right."

"Gee, thanks." She shoved off the pulpit and stomped circles around the altar, then leaned on it. "Shit. I really thought she'd be here. Churches are supposed to be sanctuary, or something, you know?"

"About a million centuries ago."

She gave me a dirty look. "Like when you were a kid, you mean." She thumped the altar in emphasis.

It slipped.

Joanne jumped off like the damned thing had bitten

her. I grabbed the pulpit so I wouldn't grab my chest like some wheezy old guy, and we both stared at the open crack where the lid had moved. "...do you believe in vampires, Gary?"

"God damn it, I was tryin' real hard not to think that way."

Her eyes were big as saucers. "Kind of fits, though, doesn't it? Scary church with a crypt, the living dead ris—"

"The sun already rose," I said firmly. "No vampires after dawn, right?"

"There's no such thing as vampires."

She sounded like she was trying to convince herself. She sure as hell wasn't convincing me. "Well?" I demanded. "Are you gonna look in it?"

"Yeah."

I waited a minute. She kept standin' there. "When?"

"As soon as I get up the nerve."

I edged her way and prodded her in the back. She inched forward, feet squeaking against the floor. Had to be wearing rubber-soled boots to make that sound. I looked down. She was, and they were providing plenty of resistance, so I gave her a little more shove.

She glared at me. "You're a big strong man. Aren't you supposed to be plunging into danger before me?"

"I'm forty-seven years older than you, lady, and you're almost my height and in my weight class. And it's your vampire."

That put the kibosh on her goin' anywhere. She turned back to me, all pink-cheeked with offense. "I am not in your weight class!"

Dames, I swear. "How much do you weigh?"

"Isn't it rude to ask a woman how much she weighs?"

"Nah, it's rude to ask how old she is, and I already know. G'wan, look in the coffin."

"Oh. Damn." She took a half-step toward it, mumbling, "I weigh one seventy two," like if we talked about her weight she didn't have to think about vampires.

"No kidding?"

"I'm almost six feet tall. What'd you expect, that I weighed a hundred and thirty? I'd be a stick figure." She peeked in the coffin's tiny gap, then shivered. "Give me a hand with this."

I crept forward, muttering, "I outweigh you by about sixty pounds, doll," 'cause it turned out she was right, talkin' about weight was better than thinkin' about vampires.

"That's why you're a linebacker and I'm not. Push on three. One two three!"

Forget linebackers and weight classes, the shove we provided coulda come from a superhero. The lid shot off the box and crashed to the hardwood floor with a bang that shook the rafters. Joanne lost her balance and fell into the damned crypt.

She landed on another crazy lady tryin' ta get out.

Chronology Notes:

"Rabbit Tricks" takes place shortly after COYOTE DREAMS (Book Three of the Walker Papers).

Rabbit Tricks

TUESDAY, JULY 26, 10:37 A.M.

Allison Hampton made me want to weep in despair.

Nothing in my entire life had prepared me to look as put-together and attractive as she had every time I'd met her. Her thick blonde hair was wrapped in a twist, keeping its weight and heat away from her shoulders. She wore a sleeveless pearlescent shell blouse and above-the-knee slacks-weight shorts that showed off tanned legs and low-heeled strappy sandals that looked both attractive and comfortable.

I looked at my feet. The hem of my jeans rode low over a pair of open-toed black clogs that added a couple of inches to my already considerable height. They were comfy, but they were not sexy. The jeans were new, and low-cut enough that I needed the belt that had come with them, and my green knit tank-top had seemed quite sufficient to an off-duty tour of the police station five minutes earlier, when

Allison hadn't yet arrived. She was wearing dangly gold earrings. My ears weren't even pierced. I was wondering if 93 degree heat was sufficient to excuse me for melting into a sad greasy puddle of comparative unattractiveness when a little girl rocketed from Allison's mini-van and launched herself at me.

"Ossifer Walker! Ossifer OFFICER Walker! Guess what guess what guess WHAT!"

I caught her, grunted, and staggered back, trying not to laugh at her enthusiasm and her mother's dismay. "Hey, Ashley. What?" At least Ashley wasn't dressed to the nines. Then again, she was six. Blue jeans and a pink t-shirt suited her just fine.

"Today is MY BIRTHDAY!"

"You're kidding." I rolled my jaw, trying to get hearing back into my ear, and blinked toward Allison, who nodded ruefully. "Seriously? You're spending your birthday getting a tour of the police station? Well, happy birthday!"

"Inside voice, Ash," Allison said hastily. We weren't inside, but my eardrums were grateful for the comparative modulation of the little girl's voice.

"It's what I wanted! I'm going to be a police ossi*officer* when I grow up. Just like you!" Ashley wriggled all over, rather like a puppy, and slid down my hip. I clutched at her, but apparently down was what she was after, and a couple of seconds later she tore up the precinct building stairs to stand by the doors, all straight and proud.

I turned to Allison. "Don't take this wrong, but you have a sort of peculiar kid."

Allison laughed. "She's convinced policemen are superheroes ever since you got us that ambulance. This is by far the longest she's ever wanted to be one particular thing when she grows up."

"I kind of hope she doesn't outgrow it for a while. She's cute." We let Ashley open the door for us, and I guided them through the building to my boss's office.

Captain Michael Morrison got to his feet with a much more genuine smile than I was used to seeing when I entered his personal space. He always looked good at work—okay, I could have stopped that sentence after 'good' and it would still be accurate—but I'd warned him I was bringing the Hamptons in for their tour today, and the captain had gone to a little extra trouble to look sharp. His silvering hair had had been trimmed, and he hadn't yet abandoned the suit jacket that usually landed on a coat rack or the back of his chair by mid-morning. Allison Hampton's smile went a bit softer and more inviting than I liked, and I bit my tongue hard. Pretty women finding Morrison attractive was none of my business, even if it made me want to break a strap on those expensive sandals of hers.

"Ashley." Morrison offered first the little girl, then Allison, a hand to shake. "Mrs. Hampton."

"Ms, actually," Allison said pleasantly.

"Ms," Morrison said equally pleasantly, and I reminded myself that this was not a good time to suggest they could get a room. God forbid they should actually do it, for one. Morrison came around his desk to lean on it and look down at Ashley thoughtfully. "Seems to me I said something about a case for you to work on, didn't I."

Ashley did the puppy wriggle again, nodding until her hair shimmied like a scarecrow in the wind. "One all for me!"

"As it happens, I've got something for you." Morrison very solemnly offered her a page in a file folder. "We're missing a very important box, Ashley. Did you know that police officers come around to the Seattle schools and talk about safety?"

"Of course I do!" Ashley caroled. Allison's eyebrows went up in disbelieving amusement and she caught my eye to mouth 'no she didn't'. I forgot I was busy hating her and her polished look and her flirty voice, and grinned back.

"Well," Morrison said, still solemnly, "we've lost our box of materials that we bring to the schools. I was hoping you could help us find it. Why don't you sit down and read over the notes we have, and then you and Detective Walker can work on solving the case?"

My grin went a bit foolish. The 'case' had been Morrison's idea to make up for me disappointing Ashley a few weeks earlier. I'd spent half the previous afternoon running around the station setting up clues and the eventual reward of the box for Ashley to discover, and had done it all with a warm fuzzy feeling. I'd spent years with Morrison as my own personal bugbear. I kind of liked discovering he had a squooshy side.

Ashley's smile lit up the room. "Okay!" She flung herself belly-first on the floor and squirmed halfway under Morrison's desk to make herself comfortable. Morrison blinked, first at her, then at Allison Hampton, who'd crouched as soon as Ashley hit the floor.

"She never met a floor she didn't like. Ashley, come out—"

Morrison shook his head. "It's fine. She won't be long."

"Still, I'm so sorry—" Allison stood back up, the better to apologize.

"Hey," Ashley said from under the desk, "there's a rabbit hole under here."

"Really." I bent over, amused, to take a look.

Thing was, there was a rabbit hole under Morrison's desk.

"Uhm." I cleared my throat, hoping for a somewhat wittier bit of repartee to burst forth. None did. "Um, Morrison, can you see that?"

I could hear the exasperated look he gave me. Apparently humoring small children with invented police cases was one thing, but humoring me playing along with rabbit holes was something else.

I couldn't really blame him, truth be told. A little over six months ago I'd gone from an aggravating but extremely skilled mechanic to an extremely aggravating and utterly unskilled shaman. Morrison did not like inexplicable things like the Wild Hunt or banshees turning up in his precinct. Neither did I, for that matter, but I'd come to terms with the fact that it was my job to deal with them.

"No, Walker, I don't see..." Once more, I could all but hear Morrison's change of expression, this time accompanied by the grinding of gears in his skull. After a moment he said, "I take it you do," in an extraordinarily measured voice.

Ashley squirmed further under the desk, calling, "I'm going dooooown!" as she half disappeared into the rabbit hole.

I straightened up, hoping my smile didn't look as forced as it felt. "Boss, if you don't mind us taking over your office for a few minutes, Ashley and I can work out the clues in the map during our adventure in the rabbit hole. Maybe you could take Allison for a cup of coffee over at The Missing O."

"Oh, I couldn't leave you—"

I felt a little sorry for Allison, who sounded as though she really meant it, and who looked suddenly as if coffee with an adult would be manna from heaven. Coffee with Morrison, who was not only an adult, but attractive and nice to her kid, would presumably be...whatever was better than manna. Ambrosia.

I broadened my smile, trying hard to make it look genuine. "Don't worry about it. Morrison's too much of a stickler for time to let a coffee break run more than fifteen minutes. Ashley and I will be fine."

"We'll be fiiiiine, Mooooom!"

Ten seconds later they were out the door, and I dove down the rabbit hole after Ashley Hampton.

I was not in the habit of departing this world—the Middle World—in physical form. I'd spent a fair amount of time over the past six months leaving it in spiritual terms, visiting a whole host of realms—Upper, Lower, Astral, Dream, Dead—but I hadn't once physically crawled down a hole that led somewhere else. On a gut level, I thought Ashley and I were traveling into the Lower World, the plane of demons and power animals and extremely powerful, living mythology. It was the root of the universe to which the Middle World belonged; the Upper World was the branches, people by spirits and, er, well. Power animals and extremely powerful, living mythology.

Ashley, gleeful, shrieked, "There's a raaaabbit! A white raaaabbit! C'mere, bunny! C'mon, Ossifficer Walker! Help me catch the rabbit!"

The part of my brain that was no help at all made me mumble, "It's Detective Walker now, actually." The part that was more helpful connected white rabbits with—well, Alice in Wonderland, as anybody would, but the Alice half of the Hampton Duo was off having a doughnut with Morrison.

Moving on, then. I went from Wonderland to the briar patch, and leggy trouble-making Brer Rabbit. Not for nothing had I spent some of my formative years in Qualla Boundary, the Eastern Band of Cherokee's land trust in North Carolina. One part voodoo god, one part wise man, Brer Rabbit was a trickster, full of foolish cunning.

All of a sudden I really didn't want Ashley to catch the critter she was after. "Ashley, wait up!"

I erupted out of the tunnel in a shower of soft loamy sweet-smelling earth. The world around me stretched flat for an instant, going two-dimensional and awful, then snapped back to a more comfortable three dimensions, though a hint of flatness remained. The sky above was rubbed with red, sunlight pouring down with less intensity than I was used to. The vegetation responded to the light, growing tall and thick but with black edges to the leaves: not sinister, but not normal. I was on a low hillside, above a slow-moving river that ran through the valley bottom.

Ashley scampered off across the landscape, shouting, "Come back, come back, Mister Rabbit! I want to have a tea party!"

A flash of cottontail white stopped and turned around to examine Ashley. I swore and scrambled to my feet, chasing child and bunny at top speed. There were aspects of the astral realms which I could travel at impossible speeds. This wasn't one of them, and by the time I caught up with Ashley and Brer Rabbit, they were seated at a pink-clothed table which, thankfully, did not also have a dormouse and a Mad Hatter in attendance.

Still, a rabbit and a little girl sitting down to tea was really pretty much weird enough. Ashley saw a white rabbit. I saw a brown one, much less cartoony than Disney would have me imagine him, and looking at him gave me the same shiver of awe that the thunderbird and Big Coyote had.

"Well, how do you do, Ossifer Walker." Brer Rabbit, a sparkle in his eyes, tipped his cup of tea toward me in greeting. I didn't like that sparkle at all: it said that like far too many things in the Other parts of the universe, he knew more than he was saying. He'd call me *Ossifer Walker* for Ashley's sake—in fact, the fact that he was talking at all put the whole worldscape solidly in Ashley's view, because none of the primal animal beings that I'd met had talked, previously. For a disconcerting instant I saw through the button-nosed form sitting at the tea table: Saw through it, with the astounding second sight that I still hadn't become entirely accustomed to.

Through that sight, Brer Rabbit was elemental, a thing of spikes and sparks and fractal patterns, chaos embodied. He was every trickster that had ever been, every one that ever would be, and he went back and forward through time as easily as wind blew through leaves. I forced my eyes shut, not that doing so affected the sight, and willed it away. I didn't think human beings, even shamans, were supposed to spend much time contemplating chaos. I was afraid my brain would melt, and I wasn't quite being hyperbolic about it.

My voice came out in a whisper, somewhat less certain than I'd have liked: "How do you do, Brer Rabbit." Less certain and more Southern, which surprised me. Mostly I sounded like I was from Nowhere, U.S.A, due to having grown up Everywhere, U.S.A. as my father drove us around. Once in a while, though, the years in North Carolina came through, and for all that the storybooks spelled it *br'er*, I couldn't help just swallowing most of the letters and turning the word to *bruh*, *Brother*, the way it was supposed to be.

"Won't you sit down and have some tea, Detective Walker?" Ashley poured me a cup without waiting on my answer, and put two small cookies onto a plate for me. I sat down, not so much because I wanted to break bread with

Brer Rabbit as I had no idea what he might do with Allison Hampton's daughter if I didn't. Every story I knew about him danced through my mind, and the rabbit managed to smile at me.

"Now, it won't be the Tar Baby nor the briar patch that looses you of me today, Officer Walker. Nor will it be the tortoise and the hare, nor the scarecrow. We know those tales, you and I, and we will not tell them again here and now." He sounded like that certain style of old Southern gentleman, the ones who say every syllable in slow concentration, though even so, "Tar Baby" was a rolled-out luxurious, "Taah Baybeh".

I picked up my teacup to give my hands something to do. "What is it that you want?"

Affront came into the rabbit's brown eyes. "How can you think I want anything, Officer Walker?"

"You're Brer Rabbit. You always want something." A fragile smile worked its way past the edge of my teacup. "Usually something you shouldn't have."

It took everything I had not to look at Ashley. Brother Rabbit didn't have that same restraint, and glanced her way before smiling at me.

"Did you know it's my birthday?" Ashley beamed at Brer Rabbit, at me, and at the birthday cake which hadn't previously been on the table. "I'm seven today," she added self-importantly. "How old are you?"

"Why, I'm as old as the very hills, Miss Ashley. I'm as old as human dreams. And I did know it was your birthday. If it weren't, you might never have seen that rabbit hole I dug just for you."

"My mommy couldn't see it. Sometimes grown-ups don't see what's there. Except Detective Walker. She sees things. She's a superhero!"

Brer Rabbit looked from Ashley to me and back again. "Is she, now. Well, I have an idea, Miss Ashley. If Officer Walker is so much a hero, perhaps she'll play a little game with me. If she wins, you go home with her, back to the place you call home. If I win, you'll stay with me, here in this magical land."

Ashley chirruped, "Sure!" before I could stuff half the cake into her mouth and silence her. Some superhero I was. She turned her bright little smile on me and lifted a china pot. "Would you like some honey in your tea, Detective Walker?"

"Um." I looked into my undrunk tea. "No, thanks, sweetie. Not right now." Not until after I'd rescued her from a chaos elemental. Ashley shrugged and began cutting pieces of her cake, though she didn't go so far as to offer any to me or Brother Rabbit. I supposed there were limits to what you could expect of a seven-year-old left with a cake and no parental supervision. I turned my attention back to Rabbit, warily asking, "What game?"

"A game of chance," Rabbit said, and it struck me maybe a little too late that for a creature dredged out of Ashley's imagination, he was awfully well-spoken.

"It's not just her imagination I spring from, Officer Walker. She may be hearing something very different from what you hear. Tricks," Brer Rabbit said with a shake of his head. "They're terrible things."

What was terrible in my mind was that one, he appeared to be reading my thoughts, and two, Brer Rabbit generally came out ahead of the other animals in his stories. Being out-smarted by a rabbit didn't seem like a good way to build my shamanic confidence.

Well, said my ever-present sarcastic voice, *you could try remembering your mental shields.*

Glimmering approval turned Brer Rabbit's brown eyes to amber as I belatedly constructed the Enterprise-like shields that Coyote had taught me to build. I really needed to get in the habit of maintaining those things twenty-four/seven. "I do come out ahead," Rabbit agreed, "but so would you, if you were the hero of your own stories."

I stared at him a long moment, unable to stop myself from looking back over the last seven months of my life in that light. Technically, I'd come out ahead, in that I wasn't dead. On the other hand, quite a few other people were. I wasn't all that sure I qualified as the hero of anything.

"Ooh," Ashley said happily. "Carrot cake."

Brer Rabbit sat up, paws tucked to his chest, nose a-quiver, just like the most rabbity rabbit there ever was. He looked avariciously at Ashley, who had managed to smear cream cheese frosting all the way from her eyebrows to her chin. I checked the cake, but there was no face-sized imprint in it. I had to admire the kid's tenacity, in that case.

"Tell you what," I said dryly. "You can have a piece of carrot cake if you let Ashley go. In fact, you can have the whole carrot cake. A nice full round tummy and a nice warm sun to sleep under. What could be better than that?"

Brer Rabbit's nose twitched again and for about a millisecond, I thought it was actually going to work. Then he sank back into his seat, whiskers drooping. "I'm afraid keeping the girl is more important."

"Why?" Nerves suddenly cramped my hands and I was glad I'd remembered to shield my thoughts. None of the stories I'd heard talked about Brer Rabbit stealing children. That was more of an Irish fairy tale.

A thunderous cloud rolled over the sky, cutting out all the light. The Lower World stretched flatter and thinner, like it was trying to hide from something, or, it came to me, as if it was trying to hide something. Me, maybe. Me, or Ashley. My own voice came from far away, pulled into discordant tones by the distorted world: "Who sent you, Bro' Rabbit?"

He wouldn't tell me, but I knew the answer already; knew it as though it had been burned into my bones. There was a creature out there, something the banshee had called Master, and he had haunted me since the day my shamanic powers awakened. I didn't know what he was or what he wanted besides a piece of me, but all of a sudden Ashley Hampton looked like a very tempting piece of bait. I'd followed her into the rabbit hole without a second thought. I'd go anywhere to keep the kid safe. Little girls didn't deserve to get mixed up in my weird-ass world.

Ashley, miserably, said, "I want to go home."

"Oh, but not yet." Brer Rabbit threw off the gloom—literally: the sky lightened again, darkness fleeing before his smooth Southern voice—and I put an arm around Ashley's shoulders protective. "We haven't had our cake yet," he said.

Ashley sniffled. "Okay. But it was more fun before, when we were playing."

"We can play as long as you like," Brer Rabbit promised.

Kids were amazing. Mercurial little monsters, in the depths of despair one moment and happy as larks the next. Ashley brightened right up. "Will you dance with me?"

For a rabbit, he did a surprisingly good job of looking non-plussed. Then he stood, came around the table, and swept Ashley up in his rabbity arms.

The child I had my arm around stayed right where she was.

Carrot cake and honey and a pink table cloth stuck to Brer Rabbit's face and chest and paws.

Ashley grabbed my hand and whispered, "Run!"

We raced back out of the rabbit hole so fast I clobbered my head on the underside of Morrison's desk. Ashley flung herself to the side, eyes wide and dramatic as she gasped at the ceiling. I rubbed my head and spluttered, then finally began to applaud. "How'd you do that, kid?"

"He said Tar Baby wouldn't work, but he didn't say anything about a Honey Baby!" Ashley pushed up on her elbows, eyes still very wide. "I just had to build it real fast while you and him were talking. I pretended real hard that I wasn't doing anything and hoped he wouldn't see!"

"I didn't even see." And I was supposed to be a grown-up who noticed things. "That was brilliant, Ashley. That was fantastic. You're amazing."

She beamed at me, though the expression went away again almost instantly, turning instead to conspiracy. "I think we shouldn't tell my mommy, okay?"

I laughed, a sort of frantic noise in the back of my throat, and fumbled around for her case file. "I think that might be a good idea. How about we go find this instead, so she can be impressed when she gets back?"

Ashley scrambled to her feet and took my hand a second time. "I'm going to be just like you when I grow up, Detective Walker."

I followed her out of Morrison's office, wondering if she just might be.

Chronology Notes:

"Petite" takes place moments after SPIRIT DANCES (Book Six of the Walker Papers) ends. The author feels strongly that you should read SPIRIT DANCES first. *Very strongly.* *looks stern*

Petite

The most infuriating woman I had ever met handed me the keys to her car, kissed me, and walked out my front door.

Every bone in my body said to follow her. Not just to stop her from leaving, but because I lived in a residential neighborhood. She wasn't likely to catch a taxi on my block at four in the morning. Smart money would be on me driving her to the airport. But I stayed where I was, looking at the keys in my palm.

Joanne Walker had never voluntarily handed those keys over to somebody else in her life, and she'd just given them to me.

FIVE YEARS AGO

"Michael. Michael Morrison. It's good to meet you." I'd repeated the same words, the same solid handshake, dozens of times already. Seattle weather was cooperating, pouring sunshine down on a Fourth of July picnic, and it looked like everybody from the Seattle Police Department's North Precinct who wasn't on duty that day had turned up. The man introducing me around, Captain Anthony—Tony—Nichols, was pleased. It was a good opportunity to meet my new team in less formal circumstances than the department building, he said. It would warm them up to me.

I didn't want them warmed up, I'd said. I wanted them to do their jobs.

He'd looked at me, and though he hadn't said it, I'd heard it anyway: *You're young, Mike. Trust me on this.*

I was young, and that was why I wanted formality. Thirty-three was damned young to be taking over as precinct captain. I had the credentials—youth correctional programs in high school, college completed in four years, volunteer services for the department in my free time, top of my academy class, made detective by twenty-five, lieutenant by twenty-eight. Every officer in Seattle knew the only thing I'd ever wanted to be was a cop, and they respected the effort I'd put into it.

My hair had also gone silver by my thirtieth birthday. I wasn't kidding myself: if it hadn't, I'd still be a lieutenant instead of preparing to take over the North Precinct when Tony Nichols retired at the end of the month.

But I was young, which was also why I listened to Nichols. Why I trusted him. He'd been a cop longer than I'd been alive, and he'd been a captain since before I reached double digits. If all I wanted was to be a cop, then I'd be a fool not to learn from men like Nichols. So I was at the picnic in shirtsleeves and slacks, as informal as I would let myself get, even surrounded by men and women in shorts, tank-tops, t-shirts and skirts. Plenty of them were in uniform, too: men—mostly men—coming or going from their shift, but mostly they were casually dressed, and I was a little too formal.

That suited me just fine.

We worked our way through the picnic—this is Bruce, bad hamstring injury sideline him to desk work, that's Ray, real fireplug of a guy, Jenn works Missing Persons, over here is Sandy, yes, he knows his hair is red, not blond—and I'd relaxed enough to accept, if not drink, the bottle of beer someone offered when I first saw her.

She was sitting on the hood of a purple car that had been rolled illegally far onto the grass. A dozen or more big men sat around the vehicle's front end, passing beer and whiskey bottles back and forth, frequently via the woman on the hood. One bottle tipped as it was passed over, and the guy who'd spilled wiped the splash off the car's paint job without thinking about it, like making sure the Mona Lisa didn't get stained. I knew nothing about cars, but the paint job had to be Mona Lisa quality: the purple glowed with an internal shimmer, like someone had layered starlight into it. Its shadows were black and in sunlight the purple looked deep enough to dip your hand into. The only reason I was certain you couldn't really was because she was sitting on it, not sinking in like it half-seemed she should be.

She was as startling as the car. Even from the distance she looked as tall as I was, just under six feet. Her black hair was cropped boyishly short. Aviator sunglasses rested on a beaky nose above a full mouth, and her shoulders were broad and square. She had muscular arms bared by a white tank-top. Not the slender long muscles women got from careful gym regimes, but bulk, real strength, like she did heavy work for a living. Her legs were muscular too, and her bare feet dangled over the car's grill. She made me think of pin-up models, except strong and lean instead of bombshell curves.

"Thought you liked petite redheads."

"What?" I looked away from the woman.

Nichols hid a grin, poorly. "Thought you liked petite redheads. Curvy ones. Seems to be what you date."

Heat built around my collar. "She caught my eye, that's all. Who is she?"

"Joanne Walker. One of our mechanics."

I hated that I said it: "She's a *mechanic*?" She looked like a mechanic's girlfriend. She looked like the luckiest mechanic in Seattle's girlfriend, but like a girlfriend.

"Mm. She rebuilt that car she's sitting on. Calls it Petite."

"Her car has a *name*?" Worse than having a name, it was emblazoned on the license plate, suddenly visible as someone leaned over to get another beer.

"A lot of people name their cars, Mike. Anyway, she put herself through college on scholarships and working at Chelsea's Garage over in the University District," Nelson went on. "I'd seen her a few times. Recognized her when she came in to apply for the Motor Pool job last fall."

"She's hard to miss."

Nichols nodded. "She's half Cherokee. I wanted her to

join the force, but the idea scared her."

I lifted an eyebrow. "She's six feet tall. How can anything scare her?"

Nichols laughed. "She's a kid, Mike. About twenty-three. She doesn't know a damned thing about herself, and she's not ready to stick her head out past what she's familiar with, not yet. She's smart and she's great with cars, and right now that's all she's ready for. I talked her into going to the Academy before she started in the Motor Pool, just in case it woke her up to her own potential."

Twenty-three. Ten years younger than me. Too young, even if she wasn't an employee. I shook my head without knowing I'd done it and saw it reflected in Nichols' eyes. Not just his eyes, but in his expression, too, like he was seeing something I wasn't sure I wanted him to. "Did it? Not if she's one of the mechanics."

"She graduated in the top third of her class. Too proud to do worse, I think, and too cautious to do better. Except in the defensive driving course. They said she was the best driver they'd ever had come through the school. She was a good shot, too, not afraid of guns. But she wanted the Motor Pool when she came back, and I thought it wasn't time to push her. Not yet. So she's down in the garage for now. I'd wondered at first if she'd get along, the only woman down there, but..."

He gestured, encompassing the ring of men littered around the purple car. Walker sat above them like their queen, laughing and passing alcohol back and forth. She leaned over and stole somebody's burger for a bite, then handed it back, and he didn't complain. "Not a problem," I said dryly.

"I think she's their mascot, if you can put mascots on a pedestal. That's most of the Motor Pool over there. You want me to introduce you?"

"Maybe later."

Nichols failed a second time to hide his grin. "Right. Well. I think I'll go grab some of Elise—that's Bruce's wife—some of her potato salad. If they ever invite you to dinner, say yes. Elise is one of the best cooks I'd ever met."

"Will do." I watched Nichols retreat—because that's what he was doing, and without a hint of subtlety—then went back to studying Joanne Walker.

Smart money was on walking away, or waiting for Nichols to come back and put a badge and a formal introduction between us. The woman—the *girl*—was an employee, and I wasn't going to start my captain's career with a score like that against me. I hadn't come this far this fast by making stupid mistakes.

But for some reason I had to see which of us was taller. I was halfway to the gathering at the purple car before I realized it, and then Walker noticed me and it was too late to find another destination.

She slid off the car's hood and stepped over one of the men surrounding it. Long legs and Daisy-May shorts: the man she'd stepped over grinned until he couldn't anymore, and one of the others hit his shoulder in a combination of envy and praise. Walker ignored them and came up to me, stopping a few feet away. I was taller, but only just, and she was barefoot, which put her at the disadvantage.

It didn't seem to bother her. She tipped her aviator shades down, revealing hazel eyes that tended toward green. She looked me over from head to toe and back again, then gave me a slow smile. "Hi. I'm Joanne Walker. Joanie."

The hand she offered me to shake had a beer in it. I tapped my own beer bottle against hers and then took my first drink of the day, because she drank and it seemed the natural, polite, and social-class-appropriate response. "Mike Morrison," I said when we'd both drunk. "Pleasure to meet you."

"You too. You're new, or your car never breaks down. Which is it?"

"New."

"Thought so. Come on, have a drink." She turned away and sauntered back to her crew, stepping over someone else as she approached the car. With me a step behind her, the man didn't have time to appreciate it, which gave me a faint smug satisfaction I had no right to. "Guys, this is Mike. Mike, this is everybody. Nick, he runs Motor Pool, that's Dave, this is Benny, that's Jake—" She ran through another eight or ten names, ending with, "And yes, there will be a quiz."

"Nick, Dave, Benny—" I repeated them all back to her, earning a round of applause from the mechanics and laughing approval from Joanie Walker. She even swept a hand over the purple car's hood in invitation, and one of the mechanics wolf-whistled while another two looked put-out.

Protocol would be dissembling, but I was already past

the end of the rope. I sat on the car's hood, shoe heels braced on the bumper, and Joanne scooted forward to sit next to me and *tsk*. "You always this formal, Mike? Shirt sleeves and leather shoes in the middle of July? You obviously haven't been drinking enough. There'll be another quiz," she added, mock-severely, "once you've had enough to loosen up that collar.

"I'll pass," I promised her.

She arched an eyebrow. "The quiz, or on loosening up?"

"You decide."

Her grin came again, slow and long and amused before she took a pull on her beer that emptied the bottle. One of her crew chortled and Joanne threw the bottle at him, not hard. He caught it and offered an un-credible apologetic look. She slid a glance at me, winked, then shrugged innocently at the guy on the ground.

This was going to be a mistake. I had no business trying to flirt with employees, even if—especially if—they didn't know I was the boss. But it had been a while since a woman had caught my eye as quickly as Joanne Walker had, and even knowing nothing could come of it, indulging was a rare satisfied temptation.

I glanced over my shoulder at the long hood of the car we sat on. It was a classic, and every model of classic car I'd ever known slipped out of my mind. "What is this, anyway? A Corvette? A—" I was only certain of one classic Corvette line, and offered it up: "A Stingray, maybe? 1963?"

Joanne Walker laughed out loud, a bray that sounded delighted, but it faded into jaw-dropped disbelief when she saw I'd meant the question. "Are you serious? Oh my God. You think Petite's a *Corvette*?" She glanced at her crew, most of whom were watching with reserved glee, though the two who'd been irritated by my invitation onto the car's hood were openly grinning already.

Walker, all too clearly egged on by their quiet delight, repeated, "Oh my God," and launched into . "No, Corvettes are curvy, you idiot. I mean, the classic ones are. They came straight out of the fifties, shaped like the women, you know? Hips and boobs, that's what all those curvy wheel wells are, and the Stingrays had a split back window, swear to God they were supposed to look like a woman's butt. Petite's a Mustang, a 1969 Mustang, a muscle car, you moron. Twiggy, not Bettie Page, that's the kind of model she's built on. She's a Boss 305, there were only a few thousand like her made, oh my *God*, a Corvette, *really*? How can you not know this?"

Stiff with embarrassment, I said, "I was never really in to cars," and she choked a laugh. "Dude, apparently not even enough to get laid. Didn't you ever get it on in the back seat of one of these things?"

"How old do you think I *am*?"

Her eyes narrowed in the instant before she blurted, "Oh, God, I don't know, like forty-five?" She didn't think I was anywhere near that old, or she wouldn't have invited me to sit on the Mustang's hood in the first place, but she'd put herself on the spot with her own question, and had to upwardly revise whatever she thought the answer really was. And probably downwardly revise it as well, because I'd asked, and I wondered if she'd mentally come up with an answer anywhere close to the truth.

It still stung, which wasn't any more appropriate than the smugness I'd felt a few minutes ago. "Not quite."

"I guess *not*, if you don't know a '69 Mustang from '63 Stingray. I didn't think that was actually possible for people with Y chromosomes. Ar—oh, hey, Captain."

Nichols walked up, a bowl of potato salad in one hand and a hot dog in the other, and smiled genially around at the Motor Pool crew. "Hi, folks. I see you've met Captain Morrison already. What do you think of him?"

"What do we *think* of him?" Walker crowed

Nichols, as if oblivious to the tone of her voice, went on pleasantly: "I've been introducing him around. I thought it would be good for the precinct to meet my replacement before his first day of work in August."

Blood drained from Walker's face. She looked at me, white with accusation, which was fair enough: I'd all but introduced myself under false pretenses, and I was just about ashamed enough to look away. Just about, but not quite, and she had just enough pride and anger to drown out her horror. We glared at each other, neither willing to back down, long enough to make not just the Motor crew, but even Captain Nichols, uncomfortable.

Walker finally broke the stalemate with a tight smile and a low harsh voice. "Well. Live long and prosper, Captain Morrison."

She looked pointedly at my seat on her Mustang. I got up, stepped through the crew, and walked away thinking I'd never been told to go fuck myself so politely in my life.

NOW

Somehow she'd found a taxi in my quiet residential neighborhood after all. By the time I followed her, she was gone, the street empty but my driveway filled with not just my Toyota Avalon, but the 1969 Mustang Boss that had been the source of years of contention between us.

The car had had a rough year. Almost as bad as Joanne, and unquestionably worse than my own. An arrow had been shot through the gas tank, an ax dragged through the roof, and then a helicopter had winched the vehicle out of an earthquake fissure that had crumpled the back end. Joanne had spent every spare moment and all her spare cash re-restoring the car, even finally putting in the manual transmission she had always wanted to.

As far as I knew, no one but Joanne had driven the car since she'd found it in a barn a dozen years earlier and started the restoration work on it. I unlocked and opened the driver's side door slowly and sat down. The seat didn't need adjustment. Walker and I had proved to be exactly the same height, in the end. I put the keys in the ignition and my hands on the wheel, feeling the shape of Walker's body in the seat and the soft worn spots in the leather from her hands. Faint scent lingered: mostly Irish Spring soap, but with a hint of oil and grease that would always remind me of Walker.

"It's all right, old girl," I finally whispered to the car. "She'll come back to us as soon as she can."

We sat together, two things that loved her, and I fell asleep a little while before dawn.

Chronology Notes:

"Forgotten But by a Few" takes place the same weekend as SPIRIT DANCES (Book Six of the Walker Papers), while Gary is in San Diego.

Forgotten But By A Few

I woke up on the plane with the feeling somebody'd been sittin' on my chest. Ain't a nice feeling, 'specially when a heart attack snuck up on you a year or so back. Well, it hadn't snuck up on me, I'd been witched into it, but when you're lying in a hospital bed with a nurse who don't never say more than two words together at once scowling down at you, whether it snuck up or got sent don't really matter. So waking up with that feeling made me a lot more nervous than it used to woulda, and that was a lousy way to start a holiday weekend.

'course, it coulda just been the warm humid air in San Diego feelin' thick in my chest. Not that Seattle ain't humid, but it just ain't the same. San Diego's got no winter, plenty of sunshine, beautiful women hanging out at the beaches, and one of the best zoos in the world. In the long couple years between my wife dying and me meeting Joanne, I'd wondered why I still lived in Seattle. Now I knew, a'course, but that didn't mean I was gonna miss my St. Patrick's Day weekend with the boys.

And it was getting important to show up every year. The number of us who could make it was shrinking, and not because we couldn't afford to come. Whether we liked to admit it or not, none of us were spring chickens anymore. I was one of the youngsters, and my seventy-fourth birthday had been a couple months ago. Korea had been a long time ago, and nothin' but M*A*S*H re-runs kept it fresh in folks's minds.

Two of my buddies were waitin' for me at the luggage carousel. One of 'em held a sign that said my name in big ugly Army-style stencils: GARRISON MATTHEW MULDOON, with a military rank that hadn't meant anything to me in fifty years. The other guy, Dave Ackerly, had a sign reading ANDERSON COLVER LEE, MASTER SGT. tucked under his arm. Andy was the guy holding my sign, and I had one in my bag that said CORPORAL DANIEL BAE KIM. Sun would have the next one, and the last guy in would have a sign for Ackerly, the first fella in. That sign would say WHERE THE HELL'S THE LIMO, ACK?

We'd been doing this a while. There were rituals. Sometimes it meant we spent about six or eight hours at the airport, waitin' for everybody to come in. Truth was, we could spend our whole weekend in the airport and none of us would care much, except for it was hard to get beer at baggage claim. Mostly it was about seein' each other again, always maybe for the last time. Don't much matter where that happens, as long as you get to say goodbye.

Andy pounded my back while the sign with my name on it jabbed me in the ribs. "Muldoon! You look good, you look great, you look—" He let me go and took a step back. Andy was a little black guy from Alabama whose skinny bones had gotten him out of more tight spots in Korea than any of us could count. He was strong as hell, made up of baling wire and sprung steel, and every time I saw him his eyes had sunk farther into his head. He looked terrible, though I wouldn't tell him that to his face.

"You look great," he said again, except this time he meant it. "What's going on, Muldoon, you got a new girl?"

"Yeah, Andy, a hot young thing who can't get by without me." Funny thing was, it was true, not that he'd believe me. "You're looking good too, old man."

"Bullshit, I look like hell, but that's okay, I been through hell."

Anything else he said was lost as The Ack-Man elbowed him out of the way to shake my hand, then, who were we kidding, offer up a bear hug as big as Andy's. I felt his ribs when I hugged him. Dave was closer to my size, couple inches over six feet, but his muscle had withered away over the years until he was tall and skinny and old. We were all old. It just looked better on some of us than others. We grunted each other's names into each other's shoulders, no sentimentality here, no sir, then stood back and all three of us looked each other up and down, seeing what the past year had done to us.

We were so busy doing that, that Daniel snuck up on us before I got his sign out. He said, "I see how it is," out of nowhere. "You make a fuss for all you white guys, but you don't give a damn about the Korean."

"Man, I am not white!" Andy and Danny had gone around on that one for fifty years and would keep doing it til they were both dead. I scrambled for Dan's sign, held it up, checked it, and flipped it right-side up, putting as big an innocent grin on my face as I could manage.

"You're still a goddamned sneak, Danny." Danny had been our secret weapon, the American-born Korean who walked in and out of enemy territory without ever raising an eyebrow. He was the only one of us without any body scars from Korea. Fifty years later I still didn't know just how deep the other ones cut, the ones on his heart. "Thought your plane didn't get in for another twenty minutes."

"And you're still goddamned blind." Another round of hugs and hand-shakes went around, Dan saying, "Tailwind, we got in early," between greetings. If I looked good, he looked like an anti-aging commercial. He had that luck of the draw a lot of Asians seemed to get, the tight smooth skin over bone structure most women would kill for, and his hair was still black as pitch. He coulda been anywhere from his late fifties to a couple weeks older than God, and I knew for a fact he was the oldest of us, turnin' eighty-three in another week. He stepped free of Ack's hug, then, with a sigh, took his sign from his duffel.

It said WHERE THE HELL'S THE LIMO, ACK?

We all stared at it, hardly understanding. Then the breath wheezed out of me, my chest feelin' as heavy as it had on the plane. "Wait, what the hell, where's Mick?"

"His wife called me this morning. You guys had all left already." Dan was up in San Francisco, the shortest flight any of us had to get to San Diego. My shoulders fell. There wasn't much else Dan had to say, though he went ahead and said it: "He'd been having a hard time breathing the past few days, she said. He went to the doctor, they said he was fine, so he was planning to come up just like always. He went to bed early last night, and when she came to bed..."

"Dammit. *Dammit*." Seventeen of us had come back together from Korea. Time and trouble had taken most of us away, but these five—me, Andy, Dan, Mick and Dave— we'd stuck through. The last three years it had been us five, and just last night it had looked like it would be all five of us again.

Andy had his hand pressed against his chest, same way as I'd had gettin' off the plane. We all looked like we couldn't breathe, and I sure felt like the breath had been knocked outta me. The older we got the less like a crime it felt when one of us died, 'cause there was nothing so bad as a kid losin' out on all those years ahead of him, but that didn't make it easier. One of us muttered, "Son of a bitch," and we all nodded.

"The limo's waiting," The Ack-Man finally said. "Let's go have a drink. It's after five in Korea."

"She's a kid," I said into my beer. Green beer, an Alaskan Amber with food coloring. I'd had enough to drink that I'd stopped tellin' the bozos behind the bar not to color my booze, and we'd all had enough to drink that we'd stopped talking about Mick and were on to our own lives. "She's a mess. Nah. She was a mess. She's growing out of it."

"Lemme get this straight." Dan leaned forward over a cup of tea. Not even in the worst of it in Korea had I ever seen him drink anything stronger than tea. "You've got a twenty-seven year old girlfriend and you think *she's* a mess?"

I couldn't help laughin'. Alla Joanne's friends thought she had somethin' going on with me, but I hadn't figured on my friends thinking I had somethin' going on with her. "Ain't like that, Danny-boy."

"Oh God," said The Ack. "Don't let him start singing. I'm not drunk enough for that. Hell, Mick's not drunk enough for that, and you can bet he's out-drinking the Devil right now."

"The girl's magic," I said to the beer, and my buddies, the guys I'd known a lifetime, all burst out laughing.

"Last time he said that was about Annie." Andy went from grinning to solemn and raised his glass of dark ale. "Miss that lady."

I tapped my glass against his. "Every day. But this girl, Jo, she's real magic. I had a heart attack last year."

That shut them up, three old guys sitting around a boozy table in what woulda been a smoky bar, back in the day. Little bastion of quiet, that was us, all silence and worry on a Friday evening in a pub full of kids. Lotta them were in the military, Navy kids who reminded us of ourselves, 'cept about a million years younger. The Ack still wore his hair in a crew cut, and Andy didn't have any. Maybe we looked ex-military to the kids, or maybe we just looked old and boring. Either way, they left us alone, but when we got quiet it spread out around the bar for a minute. Then The Ack got himself together enough to say, "You never said. What's the cardiologist say?"

"That I got the heart of a twenty-five year old."

Andy, deadpan, said, "Thought you said she was twenty-seven," and all of us laughed again. The kids in the bar relaxed and the noise level went back up. Nothin' like a bunch of old farts to bring down the mood, I guess.

Ack waved Andy's joke off, though. "How's that possible? Don't get me wrong, Muldoon, but you were a smoker. That leaves marks."

"It's the girl. Joanne. The kid's got magic." I looked between my old buddies, then pushed the beer aside and sighed. "Don't give me those faces. You remember the war."

I didn't look at Danny when I said it, but the other two did. His eyebrows beetled at me and I shrugged. "Your culture. Your demons."

"My goddamned demons are the same one every other American kid has," Dan muttered. "Bela Lugosi's Dracula and not meeting Marilyn Monroe."

"You knew what they were called." From anybody outside of this circle, Andy's tone woulda been accusatory. It almost was anyway.

"I didn't know how the hell to get rid of 'em, did I." Danny drained his tea with an emphasis that woulda gone better with a shot of Jack Daniels, but a guy worked with what he had. "I don't want to talk about it."

We all grunted. None of us wanted to talk about it.

None of us ever had, except obliquely. But there'd been something fucked up in the Korean nights, something different from the war. Not worse, but harder to understand. We understood the war. We hated it, we were scared of it, we didn't want it, but we got it. *Stop 'em at the 38th parallel, blast them yellow Reds to hell.* Billy Joel was a kid while me and these guys were fighting that war, but he got it too. War was easy to understand.

The thing that came pressin' down on your buddies, stealin' their breath like cats were supposed to steal babies', the thing that screamed all night like a Korean banshee, the things you didn't quite see from the corner of your eye and died tryin' to chase down, those were harder to understand. Danny'd had names for them, names his Korean-born parents had told him. Stay away from 'em, he'd said, they'll steal your soul and eat your bones.

We'd listened. Our whole damned platoon had listened, even when it meant us sittin' on each other to keep ourselves from goin' out after the sound of a shriekin' baby that just wasn't quite right. We'd listened, 'cause Danny was our secret weapon and there ain't no point in havin' one if you don't use it for all it's worth. But other troops hadn't had him, and a lot of their guys were the kind who went missing in action, no body or explanation to send home to his family, just a flag and an apology.

We lost two guys that way. Reckless Rick, he was always gonna get himself killed one way or another, but we found his body the next day, lookin' drowned when we all knew there wasn't any water for miles. And the other Andy, Dandy

Andy, who the prettiest guy in our unit. Couldn't keep his hands off the girls, or their hands off him. He'd gone off with the most beautiful local girl any of us had seen, and he'd come back in the morning white-faced and shaking. Never said a word, just died by noon, and when the doctors stripped his body to put him in dress greens, he looked like a hundred vampire leeches had gotten to him.

After that everybody listened to Danny, and listened good. He never knew how to stop 'em, just to stay the hell away, so that's what we did. And now, fifty years later, we all sat there starin' into our beers, still tryin' ta stay the hell away.

'cept I'd spent the past fifteen months hangin' out with a girl who wouldn'ta done that, even if it'd been the smart thing to do. Especially if it'd been the smart thing. It didn't matter that they wouldn't believe me. What mattered was trying to make them believe there were people out there who could fight the monsters.

And maybe, just a little, it mattered to me that they learned I was one of 'em. "I *do* wanna talk about it," I said abruptly. "Because didja know every one of us who came back from the war, every single one of us has died of a heart attack?"

They didn't. I could see it in their eyes. Andy rubbed his chest again, makin' me pull a deep breath too, just to make sure I could. "Every one of us, even when we were young. Died of a heart attack in our sleep. That's thirteen heart attacks."

"Lots of people die of heart attacks. You just said you

almost did too."

"Yeah, but—" All of a sudden I felt sorry for Jo. You couldn't just say, "Yeah, but I was witched into it," even if it was true. The poor girl had spent the last year trying to offer up sensible explanations where none existed, and now that I was trying to, it was harder than it looked. "But I had Joanne," I finished.

They laughed at me again. I couldn't blame 'em. "Arright, arright, yeah, I got myself a sweet young thing and she healed my heart. Gotta use that big fat military retirement check for somethin', right?"

Ack-Man snorted. "You can use it to buy me another drink. Mick would've had us all under the table by now. Let's show him he's not forgotten."

There was nothin' to say to that but buy another round, an' hope mentionin' all the heart attacks might get one of 'em curious enough to ask me about it later, when we were all too drunk to see straight. In the meantime we took turns talkin', telling tales about the past year, remembering old friends, and thankin' God we were happy drunks instead of miserable ones. Danny kept us that way by stayin' sober and dragging us out of self-pity when we went that way.

But him bein' sober meant he noticed I wasn't talking much about the past year after all, but about Annie and older times instead. He called me on it, too, after last call and we'd been poured out onto the street by a bunch of kids impressed with how well the old guys held their liquor. We staggered through San Diego toward our hotel, arguin' over who snored worst and should have to bunk together, and Dan stepped up alongside me to say, "So what's with the girl?"

"You don' wanna know. You don' wanna talk 'bout it. You don' wanna...woo. Too much booze. Shoulda shtayed shitting. Sitting. At the bar. Booze woozing. Shick. Ah, hell, Danny, I gotta get shome water. D'ya shee a water fantain? Foun. Tin."

Dan did a good job of not sounding like he was laughing too hard. "In the mall, come on."

"Mall'sh closhed at thish hour."

"It's open-air, Muldoon, come on. You get some water in you, you'll be fine. Never heard of you having a hangover."

"Yesh. Rep. You. *Tay*. Shun. To main...tain."

Dan, grinning, got me pointed toward the mall and found me a water fountain. I leaned on it and drank til my head stopped spinnin'. My gut felt worse with the sloshing, but I could walk again. Danny got me pointed back toward the other two, and we were snickering at me like a couplea school girls when The Ack's voice roared down the street: "Muldoon! *Danny*! Jesus, somebody call 911!"

Out of my head or not, I got my feet under myself and broke into a run, out-pacing Danny. Took maybe half a minute to get back to the other two and maybe half a second to realize The Ack was on his knees beside Andy, who lay sprawled across the sidewalk like a rag doll. I lumbered on, details coming into focus as I got closer. The Ack was in tears. Andy was still breathing, but labored, like it was gettin' harder and harder. Lights were goin' funny, smearing and stretching the way they did in movies to show the viewpoint character was dead drunk. I felt like I was seein' another, messed-up world.

That mess snapped into focus, and I saw a ghost sittin' on Andy's chest.

It looked like a lover bendin' to kiss him, all this smoky black hair trailin' between its face and his. Its mouth was over his, but I could see his breath bein' pulled into it, hungry soft an' sweet. It didn't look substantial, at the same time it looked heavy. It made me think again of bein' unable to breathe when I woke up on the plane, an' for a horrible minute I wondered if I'd had a real narrow escape there.

Then I did the only thing I could think of, and tackled the damned thing.

Now, there ain't no way that shoulda worked, except for the girl in my life. Joanne Walker, the closest thing I ever had to a daughter. Whether my old Army buddies wanted to hear it or not, the girl had magic. Healin' magic, the kind that could make an old ex-smoker's heart as strong and healthy as a teen athlete's three days after he went into the hospital in cardiac arrest. And more than that, the kind of magic that could go into a world of spirits and demons and ask the spirits if any of 'em would be willin' to help an old guy along, to protect him a little an' be there when he needed a little extra strength.

The kinda magic that would bring a tortoise spirit right into my soul, where it mostly rested and waited patiently for the times it was needed. It wasn't until it picked me that I ever learned anything about 'em. Turned out they were symbols of immortality the whole world over, not that I was in any hurry ta live forever. Not that I was in any hurry to die soon, either, so we were both happy with that symbology. An' everybody knew the tortoise won the race, so that was a good thing to have in my pocket too.

What I never knew, though, was that the world over again, tortoises were symbols of somethin' able to protect itself. Made sense, once I found it out, but I never knew it before. And if I'd learned anything 'bout magic from Jo, it was that if a gift has one side, then it's gotta have a flip side.

Somethin' that could protect itself, in my mind, was also somethin' that could fight.

I hit the ghost with two hundred an' twenty pounds of ex-linebacker enthusiasm. Its mouth ripped open like it was screamin', but no sound came out. We rolled together, me and it, until we hit a building wall still warm from the afternoon sunshine, an' it came out on top.

The weight on my chest came back just like it'd done that afternoon. Pressin' down, takin' my breath, but this time my drunk old self saw the ghost leaning in, felt its cold mouth on mine. Saw all kindsa rage and fear in its eyes, and had no idea why. I couldn't move, feelin' like a hundred stones were flattenin' me. It was desperate, trying to crush my life away as fast as it could. Like it was dyin', and I was the only thing gonna keep it alive.

My tortoise flipped itself over, presenting its mottled shell to the ghost. It fell away and my breath came back, even though my head kept spinnin'. I sat up, checkin' myself with my hands. I was still all there, still all breathin'. The ghost spun toward Andy again, and I remembered him actin' like he couldn't breathe all day. "Wait a sec!"

No way I thought the thing would understand me, but it stopped and turned, tremblin' with need. "Wait a minute," I said again. "What's goin' on, what do you want? How the hell can I even see you?"

"See *who*?" The Ack whispered, but Daniel hushed him. The ghost looked between us, haunted bleak gaze, and said something in Korean.

"I don't *speak*—dammit! Danny! What's—" I replicated the sounds it had made best I could, feelin' like a fool. "What's that mean?"

He hesitated. "Are you sure you got that right?"

"No!"

"Because if you did, it's asking for fish soup."

I stared at him. "I don't think life-suckin' ghosts ask for fish soup, Dan. Wait a second. Can you see it?"

"Revenge." The ghost spoke English that time, and its bleak haggard face started changin', becomin' more like a girl than a ghoul. I pinched my fingers against the sidewalk, gettin' ready to run or tackle or whatever I had to, but she said "Vengeance," again, and I figured that was communication, not a threat. "So long," it whispered. The thing's accent was pure Korean, like it'd learned English as an adult. As an adult ghost. Joanne was just gonna love this one. "My family...dead. For them...I slay." She gestured to all of us, and I closed my eyes.

"Somethin' happened in Korea. We, our unit, we killed her family, maybe. Killed her, dammit. I'm sorry, doll. I'm so damned sorry." That was all explanation to my buddies and half a question to the ghost, but I hardly needed to see her nod to know I was right. "You been with us since then? Comin' after us since then? *Danny*?"

"It came back with us," Dan said miserably. "Fifty years ago, it came back with us. I can't see it. Why can *you*?"

"'cause I'm drunk off my ass, an' I been magicked up a lot lately. You gotta be in an altered mental state ta see this shit. Now stop avoidin' the topic an' tell me what you knew."

"Nothing! I just knew something was there, and I never did know how to stop them. Then it disappeared and I thought...I don't know what I thought. I never imagined it was coming after us, Muldoon. I had no idea. Heart attacks. Everybody dies of heart failure in the end. And besides, we were spread all over the place."

The ghost peeled her lips back from black rotting teeth, an' I was glad as hell she didn't have enough breath to stink. "Long hunt." Her ruined face crumpled and she reached out, not to any of us, but toward the sea.

Not the sea. Any idiot coulda seen that, and I wasn't that much of a fool. Toward Korea. Toward her home. "Last blood." She came alive all of a sudden, throwin' off the smoky air an' insubstantiality to look like a real girl. Just a kid with eyes haunted by death, same way as we'd all been back then. She wasn't anybody, not a face burned inta my memory, not one of the regular nightmares that came through the long years to remind us what we'd done. She was just a girl, and we'd prob'ly dropped a bomb or fired a bullet and earned ourselves some'a what the brass called *collateral damage*.

She hadn't been one of 'em, though. I could see it now, the bloody hole in her chest an' the shadow of the knife that had put it there. She'd killed herself to haunt us, an' there was a kinda horrible sick honor in that. "I am so sorry, darlin'. But you been pickin' us off slow, when you coulda taken us all at once at one of these get-togethers. Why's that?"

"Pain."

A laugh that wasn't funny came right from my gut. Pain, for alla us who knew each other and had to watch each other die slow over the years. Thank God the ghost was a kid, 'cause real pain woulda been takin' us all out at once and leavin' our families to cope with the shattered remains of their lives. Still, I said, "Guess we got what we deserved," and a big part of me meant it. "You're hurryin' it up now, though, sweetheart. Why's that?"

Her face collapsed, no more girl, just ravaged wretched spirit. She reached toward home again, speaking in Korean. I ground my teeth an' did my best to make the same sounds. I'd never managed ta learn Spanish, nevermind a tonal language. But I guessed I got it right that time, 'cause Danny started translatin' and what he said made sense: "I need strength to cross the water. I thought I was the last of my family, that all the others had been lost in the war. But I feel it now, even from so far away. My daughter, the baby, she lived, and now she dies. I don't want her to die alone, and I want to lay down my burden when she does. So you must all die now, to end my vengeance and give me strength to cross the water."

"I thought spirits had trouble with crossin' water. Or maybe that's witches. Nevermind. Sweetheart, you got any idea how far that is? You ain't gonna make it. Not even if you press us all dry, there ain't no way you're gettin' across the Pacific Ocean on willpower alone. People been tryin' forever, an' it just don't work."

Turned out that wasn't such a smart thing to say. She whipped toward me, leapin' like a cat. My tortoise hunkered down, ready to take a hit, but Danny got between me and her and started shoutin' in Korean. She slammed into him, but backed off again, listening instead of tryin' ta gobble his soul. I edged toward Andy and Ack, makin' sure they were okay. Andy was still clutching his chest, but he nodded, so all three of us sat there starin' at Danny talk to a ghost. She finally nodded, then looked at me expectantly. "She's noddin', Danny. Whatever you're doin', keep it up."

"I'm taking her home."

"You're what?" Ack and Andy drowned me out, shouting louder and louder about all the reasons that was a dumb damn idea. I started out agreeing with 'em, but I was the one who could see the ghost. The more they shouted, the angrier she got. She got smaller, crouching, and I could just about see her gettin' ready to uncoil and jump on us all.

I reached out an' slapped my hands over Andy and Ack's mouths. "Shut up. Shut up. It's more'n that, ain't it, Danny. She's gonna let us go as long as we shut the hell up. She needs to get home more than she wants revenge."

"Almost more. What I didn't translate was she was saving me for last, Muldoon. Because I betrayed Korea. She didn't care that I was born in America."

"Oh no." I got to my feet, hopin' the tortoise was feelin' up to a real fight. "You ain't goin' off to sacrifice yourself for us. Trust me, buddy, I know sacrifices are bad magic."

"I'm not sacrificing anything. She didn't care that I was born in America. But if she was nodding, she understands what I told her. If she has family left, grandchildren, I'll bring them back here. I'll say that they're mine, from during the war. North Korea's a hard place to live, Muldoon. Her family will have more opportunities here."

"That line woulda worked a lot better back before DNA and paternity tests were possible, Danny-boy."

My old friend, the one whose heart scars I didn't know a damned thing about, gave me a pained smile. "That's not going to be a problem."

I almost didn't get it. Then Ack breathed, "Son of a bitch," and it all came tumblin' down.

"Her name was Lee Sun Soo." Danny watched the place where the ghost stood, but he was lookin' at a memory. "We had been together more than a year. A year, but not many days. I only saw her when I could slip away at the end of an assignment. But it was enough, until her soldier brother came home on leave. He heard me teaching her English, before we knew he had arrived. Someone higher up realized my cover was blown before I even knew it. They snatched me out and bombed her village. So many people died. I thought Sun Soo was one of them. I thought our daughter was one of them."

I shoulda known. I shoulda known, because Jo'd run into ghosts a time or two, an' they always had some kinda strong emotional connection that kept 'em going, usually to people. I shoulda known it wasn't the whole unit, even if it coulda been. I said, "Damn, Danny," 'cause there wasn't much else to say.

"I'll see you guys next year." Dan came back, shook each of our hands, then walked back to Lee Sun Soo.

He couldn't see it, maybe, but I could: smoky black tears on her face, and her hand tucked into his elbow as they walked away together, fifty years too late.

Me an' Andy an' Ack sat there on the sidewalk for a hell of a long time, not one of us quite willin' to look at the others. After a while the sun came up, and a while after that a cop came along to tell us to get our drunk old asses off the street. We got up, dusted ourselves off, and headed for the nearest diner.

"Well, shit," Andy finally said, over bacon and eggs. "I guess maybe I'd better tell you about Brer Rabbit and Big Man-Eater, then."

No Dominion

"No Dominion" begins and ends in the middle of RAVEN CALLS
(Book Seven of the Walker Papers).

You should read Raven Calls first.

CHAPTER ONE

A god, an elf and a shaman walked into a bar.

All right, no, they didn't. They'd walked backward through time, an' so had I, but if I didn't make some kinda joke about it, I was gonna get nervous. A joke was usually enough to throw off oncoming alarm, and it made me figure maybe standing at the Hill of Tara in ancient Ireland, watching the sun start to fall in the west maybe wasn't so strange. Not after a year that included tackling gods and line-blocking demons, not to mention fighting zombies and hunting banshees.

And besides, the whole damned world was lit up with what Joanne Walker called the Second Sight. She was the shaman. Me, I was the cab driver who'd ended up her sidekick. I reckoned most folks would think it oughta be the other way around, what with her being twenty-seven and me seventy-four, but I didn't have magic, just enthusiasm. Not that long ago I hadn't even had that, but Jo had reawakened a sense of adventure I'd thought died along with my wife.

Funny thing was, as soon as I started living again I couldn't remember how to stop anymore. The three years I'd spent being a grumpy old man after Annie's death had faded like they'd happened to somebody else. Good thing, too, 'cause a grumpy old man couldn't appreciate the world the way I was seeing it right now.

I didn't know what the colors meant, only that I could see 'em pouring through the land. Giant pillars like Stonehenge—only wood—made a boundary around Tara. Everything inside 'em glowed blue, the same shade of blue I'd seen Jo call up time and again when she was healing somebody. Here an there, yellow shot up, making for green bursts where it blended with the blue. It all pulsed with life, even down into the ground, where browns and blacks wriggled together like worms and bugs. Right smack in the middle, just a couple dozen feet from where we were standing, shone the whitest magic I'd ever seen. It blasted up from a chest-high stone that had been there in our time, too: the *Lia Fáil*, the Stone of Destiny. Legend had it that when the true king of Ireland touched it, it would scream so the whole country could hear. I reckoned most folks didn't look at it with the Sight, 'cause with Jo's magic flowing through me I could hear the damned thing shrieking inside my head. It was enough to drive a guy crazy.

Or it might be if the elf, the god an' the shaman weren't there to break up the monotony. Truth was, I couldn't hardly look at the god. Cernunnos blazed emerald green against the setting sun's gold, and left a reverse-color imprint on my eyeballs if I looked at him for more than half a second. There were others with him, a few riders of the Hunt on the ground nearby, and more milling about on horses that pranced on streaks of sunset gold in the sky. I recognized one of 'em: a boy who looked about twelve, even though I knew he had to be older than dirt. He was Cernunnos's half-human son, and blazed with the same kinda power, just less intense.

The elf was easier to look at than the kid, even. Nuada of the Silver Hand. I'd read about him, but reading didn't prepare me for a living being who looked like he'd been dipped in molten silver. His left hand was silver, actual living silver metal, and it had some of Cernunnos's green fire to it. The rest of his—his *aura*, that's what Jo would call it—the rest of his aura was earthier, like precious metal veins running through hard stone. He seemed connected to the world in a way even Jo didn't, like he couldn't be uprooted. He also looked kinda flummoxed, but that was his own damned fault. He'd asked Jo to prove herself as a shaman by summoning the god, and she'd done it.

She was easiest to look at, and also kinda the most amazing. She was my best girl, had been for over a year now, and I knew her pretty well. I'd seen her working magic any number of times, and I'd seen how it filled her up and spilled out. Still, that wasn't quite the same as looking at her with the Sight and seeing how gunmetal blue healing magic washed through her like it was her blood.

Blood that was up, right now. The first time I'd met Cernunnos he'd been tryin' ta kill Jo, who'd gotten in my cab for the first time that morning. Second time I met him was when we went zombie-hunting. This morning was the third time. Best I could count, it was the third time Jo had met him, too, but maybe it was more than that, though, 'cause their connection seemed to run wilder than just a few meetings could account for. Looking at the two of 'em together was like looking into the sun. They burned my eyes, but I couldn't stop watching. I rubbed my eyes, and some of the magic Jo had put on me faded, making it easier to focus on Cernunnos.

The god was on his silver stallion, which was about the size of a draft horse with lines carved down to the delicacy of a race horse. Cernunnos was like that too: power pared down to slim limbs an' delicate bones. You could almost think he wasn't much to look at, if you weren't too bright. If you didn't notice how his shoulders thickened an' how the bone pushed at the thin skin of his temples, antlers tryin' ta get out. If you never met his eyes, you might think he was just some poor sap with some kinda genetic misfortune to his name. Me, I couldn't hold his gaze.

My Joanne, though, she couldn't look away. She was six feet of intensity, leaning in toward Cernunnos like they were drawn together by invisible wire. Most folks looking up at a god like that would seem like supplicants. Even Jo had, first time she saw him. Now it was more like she was holding herself back from pouncing. I knew the man in Joanne's life, the man she was in love with. Looking at *them* together,

I saw her love running deep, keeping her tied to the earth. Looking at her with Cernunnos, I saw how high she could fly.

An' prolly how fast she could burn, too, 'cause mortals ain't meant to soar with the gods. But nobody blamed Icarus for trying, and I thought it prob'ly took everything Jo had to say, "I can't," when Cernunnos said to her, "Come with me. Ride with me to Knocknaree and fight by my side. Let us change the future that you know. Let us defeat death in these backward days of history, and see what new world awaits us."

Joanne pressed her eyes shut like it was killing her to say no, but she shook her head. "I can't. You know I can't, Cernunnos. I've ridden with you three times already. Once more and..."

Cernunnos got a hunter's smile and leaned down toward her. "And thou'rt mine," he said softly enough I shouldna been able to hear, but I could. "Be mine, young shaman. Be mine, for thou hast *no idea* what we shall become."

I looked away, uncomfortable. I didn't belong watching these two doing their dance, and neither did Nuada.

Jo shook her head again and Cernunnos straightened in his saddle, making a face as if ta say, "*Women.*" But instead of saying it aloud he only said, "A pity," not just to Jo, but to the rest of us too. "It would have been good to challenge the troublesome one so early in his bid for earthly power, but even I will not ride against death without a force for life at my side."

Without quite meaning to, I opened my mouth and said,

"I could go."

All three of 'em said, "What?", and for a couple seconds I wondered that myself. Thing was, though, it needed doing. We'd gotten thrown to the wrong end of time, me an' Jo, an' a whole lot of things had gone wrong since we'd gotten here. A king had died, an avatar of evil called the Morrígan had cut my throat, and an avatar of good named Brigid had taken a hit for Joanne that woulda dropped her. To top it off, Brigid had realized Jo was the key to binding a death cauldron made by a guy we called the Master: somebody, or something, whose only purpose in existing was to corrupt and kill. We weren't fooling ourselves. Binding the cauldron was gonna get his attention, and that meant there was gonna be a fight. We'd been planning to get ourselves to the other side of Ireland in order to do the binding and face the fight, but our only way across was Cernunnos.

An' Jo had just made it real clear she couldn't ride with him. But we were coming from the other end of time, so we knew the cauldron got bound. It got destroyed, too, eventually. On our end of time, after the binding spell started coming loose. So the binding happened, an' that meant somebody had to go do the heavy lifting. I figured I was that somebody.

Jo, though, wasn't having any of that, from how she looked. She came right at me, like being up close would make her extra clear. "No way. Not a chance. Are you nuts? We're a million years out of time, Gary, and you want to go riding off with the Wild Hunt without me at your back? Are you crazy? Are you *nuts*?"

I shoved my hands in my pockets. "Ain't like I haven't done it before."

Joanne waved her hands in the air, voice rising as fast as they did. "With Morrison! And Suzy! And Billy! And that was in our own time! And—"

"And I didn't have the Sight," I interrupted. "And somebody's gotta go, right? There's a big fight brewing, and Brigid's gonna be waiting for us, and we got no way to get there except Cernunnos. And you can't ride with him."

I was asking a question there, and she knew it. She gave the god a desperate glance, then shook her head as she looked back at me. "I can't. I really can't. Not if I want to live my life, Gary. Not if I want to go home to Morrison. If I ride with Cernunnos again I'll never come back. He's..." She swallowed, and that time I didn't have to ask. Cernunnos was god of the Wild Hunt, master of beasts. I hated to say it, but Jo was suffering a case of genuine animal magnetism.

"All right, so you can't go, so who knows, maybe it ain't you the cauldron spell got bound to. Maybe it's me. Besides." I jerked my chin at Cernunnos, whose pointy face was smug. "Horns here ain't gonna let anything happen to me, are you? 'cause if he does, he's gonna have you to reckon with, and I don't figure that's the kind of reckoning he's looking for with you, Jo."

Cernunnos smiled, real close to a leer. Joanne growled and turned on Cernunnos. "Help me out here. Your memory works both ways. I mean, it must, right? Because we're way before you and I met the first time chronologically, but you still know who I am. So you should already remember it if Gary went gallivanting off with you in the past!"

I squinted one eye shut, tryin' ta follow her logic, then gave up. I didn't figure gods worried too much about when somethin' happened. Linear time was for humans, mostly 'cause we kept thinkin' it would help us make sense of things. After seventy-four years I knew better, but I still hadn't let go of today followin' yesterday an' chasin' tomorrow.

Cernunnos shrugged. Jo said my shrug looked like plate tectonics 'cause I had big shoulders. If I was plate tectonics, Cernunnos was the water ripplin' over 'em, smooth an' fast. "Perhaps the past I remember most clearly is one the old man did not come here in."

I grunted with offense. Being immortal meant he had to be older than me, so he had no place laying out words like old man, even if I called myself that from time to time. He ignored me and kept talking to Jo. "Of all mortals, you should realize there are paths not taken. Nothing is immutable, Joanne. Not even for a god."

Jo bared her teeth like she was gonna take him by the throat. "Okay, okay *fine*, but you're the one who said you needed a force for life—"

"He is as bright a force of life as I have seen, and never doubt that I have seen many, *gwyld*." He threw out that word on purpose. Jo an' I had looked it up ages ago. It meant shaman, or magic man, or druid, in old Irish, and Jo didn't like him using it. Most of the time he humored her, so he was drivin' home a point now. Her eyebrows pinched, sure sign she knew it, too. "More," Cernunnos said, "he carries with him a spirit of tenacity, a creature of great age and soul. He—"

"That's his *spirit animal!*" Joanne howled. "I helped him *find* that!"

"So much the better." Cernunnos sounded like a cat who'd stole the cream. "It binds you together and adds some aspect of your strength to his."

Joanne stomped a foot. I grinned at the ground, then tried to solemn up as she waved her hands again. "I said no! Just because I got you into this doesn't mean you have to go gallivanting off across time and space to—"

"Save the world, doll? Like you done a hundred times or so now?"

My girl's mouth snapped shut. I stepped up to her and put my hands on her shoulders. "I've told you I don't know how many times, Joanie. You're the best thing that's happened to me in a long time. You got me all tangled up in this crazy fantastic world of yours, and I ain't never lived like I done the past year. You keep throwin' yourself in headlong into you don't know what, and you do it every time because you're tryin' ta make the world a better place. You keep saying you want to grow up to be like me. Kid, I wish I'd been young like you."

All the fight went outta her, just like that. She had pretty green eyes and did her best to look tough most of the time, but right then her eyes softened and there wasn't anything tough about her. She was just my girl, soft-hearted and hard-headed through and through. I squeezed her shoulders. "I'm doin' this thing because it's what you'd do if you could," I told her, then winked. "Besides, this might be my one chance to kick death in the balls. You ain't gonna stop an old man from that dance, are you?"

Jo laughed. She looked like she didn't want to, but she laughed anyway, and hugged me and said what I knew she would: "Old man. I don't see any old men here. Okay, Gary, but if you don't come back..." She let me go, then repeated the threat, this time with a waggling finger at Cernunnos.

The god dipped his chin, eclipsing the setting sun and throwing the budding horns on his temples into relief. His voice went formal, making him seem just a little more alien, just a little more god-like, than he was when he sat and smirked. "You have my word, and that is not a thing I give lightly."

Joanne thrust her jaw out, staring at him, then turned back to me all sharp and business-like to shove her rapier into my hands. "All right, fine. Here. You take this. You can use it, right? I mean, hell, you can do everything else."

I took it with a chuckle and rotated my wrist, feeling its weight. The thing was balanced perfectly. I coulda held it on a fingertip and spun it around if my arms were long enough. "I'm better with a saxophone, darlin', but I'll make do. You sure, though? You might need it."

Her jaw was still stuck out. "I'm not the one proposing to go face down the man himself. You need it more than I do. Gary, are you sure? Because this is nuts."

"You can't do it, sweetheart. It's time you learn we'll go into battle for you, even if you ain't there."

"I don't want you to."

"Good generals don't." I pulled Jo close and kissed her forehead. "I'll see you on the other side, darlin'."

She backed up enough to gimme a fierce scowl. "Of time. Just the other side of time. No stupid heroics, okay, Gary? Not when I'm not there to save you."

"I promise." I gave her my best charming smile, then turned the same grin on Cernunnos. "Mind if I share your ride?"

He looked like I'd stuck him in the eye with a pin, and pointed at the boy rider beside him. "Share his. The mare is accustomed to mortal riders."

"All right. You okay with that, kid?"

The boy offered me a hand. I took it to be polite, but he showed inhuman strength in pullin' me up on the horse behind him. I shoved the rapier into a loop on the saddle and winked at Jo. "Go get 'em, sweetheart."

And then I rode off into the sunset.

CHAPTER TWO

There was nothin' in the world like riding with the Wild Hunt. Dogs, big white fellas with red-tipped ears and huge mouths, ran in front of us and bayed like bloodhounds. Grey-beaked rooks chattered and scattered in the air around us, and the horses' hooves pounded against the sky like they were running over cobblestones, loud warnings to anyone smart enough to get outta the way. Cernunnos rode in the lead, the rest of us like a flock of geese behind him, spread out in a V that shifted and mutated as we scrambled up clouds and down moonbeams. Even ridin' double with the boy, I had a grin stuck to my teeth and couldn't let it go.

Night came on full and fast, the way it does when you're flying toward it. Clearer stars than I'd seen since I was a kid burned white against the blackest sky I could remember. There was nothing to compete with the Milky Way spreading out above us, no light pollution, no air pollution, no nothin', just us and the stars and the grey-green forest way below.

For half a heartbeat I thought it'd be okay to stay here, deep in the back end of forever, but I knew I'd never do it. Jo expected me to come home on the other end of time.

The kid I rode with had a voice as clear and sharp as the stars, loud enough to be heard over howling dogs and cawing rooks and clattering hooves: "Father, this will not do. Not if we ride to battle. The mare cannot abide, so burdened."

"I ain't that much of a burden!"

"You are if we must fight," the boy said sourly. "Father." He didn't wait for Cernunnos to pay attention, just wheeled off, upward, toward the star path stretched across the sky. The dogs came our way, and then the birds, and finally the other riders. Cernunnos came after, and sent the kid a dagger glare as he took his place at the front of the ride again. I couldn't help remembering what Jo had said, back in those first days when we'd first met and had first dealt with Horns: "And a child shall lead them." Looked to me like Cernunnos might be lord of the hunt, but the kid was the boss of Pop. "Where we goin'?"

The boy said, "Home," in his clear strong voice. I caught a glimpse of longing on Cernunnos's face. Then he was ahead of us, riding fast for the stars, and the air got damned cold before I started wonderin' whether I was gonna survive going where a god called *home*.

The answer was no, a'course I wasn't, because the air got too thin an' the stars got too close, but the Wild Hunt didn't have to worry about things like that 'cause they were magic. It turned out, as we burst through the stars and crashed into a blank empty space in the sky, that for here and now, so was I. It wasn't just the Sight Jo had granted me, but also riding with the Hunt and being under the god's protection. I'd ridden with him once before, just for a couple minutes, but that was him givin' us a lift. This was real, and it went into my bones until I *belonged* with the Hunt. Until I felt the cold place between worlds edging under my skin, getting its hooks in. Until a pounding started in my heart, more than a heartbeat, more of a life pulse, the life of another world. I remembered that world, its misty forests and dew-damp meadows. I remembered the sharp smell of the sea in the air, and how the muted night colors of the ancient Ireland we'd just left behind reminded me of home. I remembered the loamy earth grabbin' at me, holding me close as I sank into it, and I remembered how laughter carried through the air like crystal, a song of its own.

I remembered all of it, an' when we burst through the walls between worlds to splash into shallow seas and ride for a silver shore, everything in my bones said I was home.

I grabbed the mare's reins and hauled up. She reared, then stomped in a circle, shaking an angry head as the rest of the Hunt swung around us, swirlin' and moving like fog. The boy took the reins back and stilled the mare while Cernunnos came out of the fog and met my eye. "What the hell are you doin' to me?"

"You are not Joanne, to demand answers from me, old man."

"Nah, I'm just her best buddy, and here to do you a favor."

He went tight around the eyes just like anybody might do, 'cept with him it did something uncanny to the horns distortin' his temples. They hadn't burst through the skin yet. Wouldn't, I reckoned, for half a year or so, but they were still there, thick and visible and making him look more dangerous than your average Joe.

The thought made me grin. Maybe more dangerous than your average Joe, but I wasn't so sure about more dangerous than my average Jo. "Knock it off," I said. "We're in this thing together, and we're both doing it for Joanne, right? So no sense in tryin' ta out-alpha each other. You got the magic mojo all over me anyway, and I know it, so lemme try again: What's happening to me?"

He clenched and loosened his jaw, but it's hard to pick a fight with a guy who's apologizing. Which was what I was doing, even if not in quite so many words. Most humans didn't like sayin' *I'm sorry* very much, and I didn't figure it got any easier if you were a god. Didn't hurt my ego any to back down, and besides, I was on his territory. I guessed Cernunnos figured all that out too, 'cause after a few more seconds of being cranky he flared his nostrils and muttered, "Two things, old ma—"

"All right, now look, Horns. You don't call Jo "little shaman" anymore, so how 'bout you stop callin' me old man? I'm a spring chicken compared to you. Call me Gary. Or Muldoon. Somethin'. Just not "Old man.""

A buncha the riders looked the other way. Or in a lotta other ways, which made me think they were tryin' not ta look at each other for fear of laughin'. Probably weren't used to people saying "No" to their boss, but hell, I didn't have much to lose, and there was nothing like being told you were old to make you feel that way.

Cernunnos said, "I shall endeavor to find something suitable to call you," through clenched, pointed teeth. I gave him a nice big smile with my own pearlies on display, and asked once more for good measure: "So what's goin' on?"

"First," he said, still through clenched teeth, "we are getting you a horse. The boy is right: in the battle that I see coming, being double-mounted would be a killing disadvantage."

"All right. And second?"

"You can ride, can you not?" Cernunnos asked. "Unassisted?"

"Been through a rodeo or two."

His expression went blank. I said, "Forget it. Point is, yeah, I can stay on a horse. What's the second thing?"

"You are not yourself an adept. A magic user, one of the connected. Therefore the Hunt cannot long abide you unless you belong to my home, to Tir na nOg. In this moment, with the Sight visited upon you, with the spirit creature living within you, you may be bound to the land because it knows she who gave you those gifts by a gift she will give it in the future. You may belong, a denizen of Tir na nOg, and as such ride with the Hunt. Welcome," he said more softly. "You are of my people now."

A sharp twist pulled at my heart. "You mean I ain't human anymore?"

Quick as that, the gentleness fled. He snapped, "All the

riders are human. All but myself and the boy, and he is half of one. Do not forget that."

"All right. All right." I raised one hand to accept it, and the boy twisted to look at me with an expression that said "Are we done now?"

I nodded. He urged the mare through the low surf up onto the damp sand. The Hunt followed, even Cernunnos, all of 'em spreading out along the shore and half-disappearing into the mist. At the back of my heart I knew the land, an' I said, "There's no stables around here," aloud.

"No, nor anywhere in this place. On your feet, Master Muldoon. Walk into the forest. You will not lose yourself there, but you may find a steed."

Feeling a lot like Jo, I muttered, "Steed. Who says things like that?" But I dismounted, gave the mare a pat on her nose, and let my feet do the walkin' up a quiet beach into a voiceless forest.

Forests sang, back home. They twittered and chirped and whistled, an' they buzzed and whispered and cracked. Here all I heard was the sound of my own feet pressing against moss that sprang back again as soon as my weight left it, and my own breath sighing in and out of my chest. Cernunnos's country was empty, lifeless, an' felt like it'd been that way a long time. I said, "C'mon, sweetheart," to the space between trees. "You out there waiting for me to ask nicely? I'm askin'. How 'bout you and me go for a ride with Horns, and kick a bad guy in the teeth?"

A nicker that coulda been a laugh bounced through grey-greenery, light enough I kinda thought it wasn't a horse at all. I couldn't say if I was disappointed when one made its way through the trees, rather than a critter with a spiral horn on its forehead. It wasn't like Cernunnos's horse, power pared down to bare lines. This one felt more human, more normal, if a grey mare coming through a misty alien forest could be normal. She walked right up to me and lowered her head, so I put my forehead against hers. She whuffed a green-smelling breath, an' I rubbed my hand under her forelock. She liked that, pressing against me, an' I had to brace to keep my feet. "You real, sweetheart, or are you like one of Jo's spirit quest animals?"

She snorted another breath, this time leavin' me wet with grass drool. I chuckled and rubbed her forehead again. "All right, then. If you're real I'll have to give you a name. How's Imelda?"

Imelda lifted her head to look at me with one big brown eye, then the other. I guessed that meant the name would do. Me and her walked outta the forest together, her pickin' her feet up high and placing them down delicate again, and carryin' her neck in a show horse's arch. She was a pretty girl, and I never knew a pretty girl who didn't like to be praised for it, so I kept my hand under her mane, rubbing and patting.

Cernunnos's riders were spread up and down the beach when we got back, most of 'em hardly more than shadows in the mist. Horns himself was waitin' on us, as was the kid, sittin' on a hunk of deadwood that shoulda been bleached of color, but was rich red like a living sycamore. He held Jo's rapier across his knees. Cernunnos glared at it, then at me.

"There you are. That was—"

The kid gave him a look, and the god's mouth puckered up like he was suckin' lemons. "That was more quickly done than I might have imagined," he admitted grudgingly. "The land senses the magic you are touched with. She will serve you well. So will this."

He tossed me a tangle of leather. For a couple seconds it didn't mean anything, but then it resolved into pieces I recognized: a double-looped belt, one loop with a long slim sheath and the other with a smaller one. Cernunnos's expression tightened up even more when I looked at him. "The shaman took my sword," he said prissily. "She failed to take its sheath and belt."

"Or the main gauche." I waggled the smaller sheathe, which was as empty as the long one. "Where'd it go?"

"The sword has never had one to match. I wore it in hopes."

"And then you lost the rapier, so no way would Nuada ever make you the knife to go with." I wanted to grin but I wasn't sure the boy's stern looks would keep Cernunnos in line if I did. Instead I said, "Thanks."

Cernunnos nodded, still scowling. "You would do well to wear armor as well."

"You don't. They don't." I nodded at the others.

"I am a god, and they have stepped beyond such mortal considerations. Dead men cannot die a second time. You, however, are vulnerable."

"Only armor I know anything about is Army helmets and flak jackets, Horns. Nobody ever meant Kevlar to stop a sword, and anything else is just gonna weigh me down."

"Find him suitable armor," Cernunnos said to the boy. "I will not explain his loss to Joanne over a matter so simply arranged. You will hardly know you wear it," he said to me, "and you will return it when this battle is done. I do not mean to make a gift of it to you as I have made a gift of that sword to Joanne Walker."

I still had a tingle at the back of my mind, one that kept sayin' this soft green land was home. Feelin' that, I muttered, "No problem, buddy. I don't need any more gifts from you right now."

Cernunnos's eyes narrowed. "Clever," he said. "Clever, that you choose not to refuse all gifts, but only those offered now."

"I'm an old dog, Horns. Most old dogs got a few tricks." I untangled the sword belt and put it on. It was made for Cernunnos, who was a fair bit narrower in the hip and waist than an old ex-linebacker, but the belt fit anyway. I chalked it up to magic, sheathed the sword, and took a few steps, getting used to the feel of it. Not bad, for a guy who'd never really worn a sword.

Cernunnos cottoned on to that, and sounded accusing: "You told Joanne you could use that weapon."

I shrugged. "I said I'd make do. I will. I learned how ta fight a long time ago, Horns. S'the difference if you're doin' it with a stick or a sword?"

"One has edges."

So did his voice. I said, "Don't worry, Horns. I can take care of myself. I ain't gonna give you anything to apologize to Jo about."

"You had best not." He whistled sharply and the dogs came to him at a run, bouncing and slobbering when they reached his side. The riders and the rooks came more slowly, apparating outta the mist already on horseback. One of 'em carried a saddle that the boy put on my mare, and she took a bridle without complaint. No bit, though. None of the Hunt's horses wore bits. I didn't figure a piece of metal in their mouths was what made 'em ride the skies anyway, so I couldn't see that it mattered. Another of the riders had the armor Cernunnos had been talkin' about. Chain mail, though it didn't seem right that a god who was around before chain mail was invented oughta have any. 'course, by that logic he shouldn't had a rapier, either. Guess even a god followed trends.

"It's cunningly made, but you will not want to wear it against your skin," he said to me, so I shrugged off my plaid shirt and tugged the mail on over my white undershirt. It weighed less than I thought it would, and didn't pinch as bad as I expected.

"What is it, mithrail?"

Cernunnos's eyes darkened like I'd offended him. "It is the very silver that sword is made of," he said sharply, "and there is no word to encompass that. It will protect you from a great deal, but I still would not advise taking a direct strike."

"Buddy, I got no plans to take a direct hit." I buttoned my shirt over the armor and clambered up on the mare. Cernunnos looked pained and Imelda blew an exasperated breath, like she thought I was making a mess of things on purpose. I grinned and patted her neck. One of the dogs howled, and half a second later we were running for the moon.

CHAPTER THREE

Somehow I expected to come out on the battle already met. Expected we'd arrive in the thick of it all, like heroes riding to the rescue, an army of wild men comin' over the ridge to save the weary soldiers. I guessed I'd been watching too many old Westerns, though, 'cause when we rode outta the sky, there was no fight going on below.

There was a big ol' mostly-flat hilltop, though. Mountaintop, I guessed, by local standards. At my end of time, it was called Knocknaree, and its claim to fame was a stone age pile of rocks called Maeve's Tomb that stood a good thirty feet tall. It wasn't here yet. Lots of others were—they were gravemarkers of some kind, called cairns, and they were all over Ireland, but Maeve's Tomb hadn't been built yet. We'd gone a long damned way back in time if a Neolithic building wasn't there yet, but that was about the last of my worries, 'cause there was somebody waiting for us, and I had a job to do for her.

Brigid, the Irish mother goddess of healing, childbirth and song. Or somethin' like that. Jo was always impressed with how much magic mojo knowledge I had, but the truth was I was barely a step ahead of her, and didn't always remember the details.

By my reckoning, it had only been a few minutes since I'd seen Brigid. She'd taken a hell of a hit, one meant for Joanne. One that woulda stopped Jo from getting to me in time to heal my cut throat, so I owed the lady one. More than one, 'cause Jo mighta died too, if Brigid hadn't gotten in the way. I wasn't traipsing around with Cernunnos just 'cause Jo didn't dare ride with him again: I had debts to pay.

I hadn't really seen what'd gone on, thanks to the aforementioned cut throat. I'd just seen the aftermath, with Brigid sinking against the *Lia Fáil* like she was dying of a wasting disease. She looked better now, her color stronger and her face not so gaunt. Red knotwork tattoos stood out on her exposed upper arms like bloody scars. Before, her copper hair had been worn loose, and her white robes had been kirtled with gold leather. Now she wore her hair in a tight braid and had a brown leather sword belt with a broad-tipped blade in its sheath. She'd seemed gentle before, but now she was fierce.

And fiercely confused, though she did a fair job of hiding it as the Hunt swept outta the sky toward her. She stood her ground as Cernunnos charged down to the earth and brought his stallion in a prancing dance around her. Brigid acknowledged him with a nod, but she was looking for Jo. Her eyes settled on me.

A guy doesn't get to be my age without being able to hear controlled fear in somebody's voice. Brigid said, "Has my sister defeated the shaman, then?" and just about managed to sound like she was only curious.

"Nah, sweetheart, Jo's fine. She just couldn't get here herself, so I came along instead."

One string of tension loosened in her. She looked from me to the swarming Hunt, then back at me again with her eyebrows lifted. "Surely one of these riders might have shared his horse with her."

"It ain't that. This is Cernunnos—"

"Yes," she said, "I know who he is."

All of a sudden I saw that she was not looking at him in the same way Joanne used to not look at Mike Morrison. I let go a silent whistle. Jo had said that Brigid and the Morrígan weren't really goddesses, even though that's what everybody called 'em in the Irish pantheon. She called 'em avatars, like they'd been imbued with the ability to act in a god's name. The Morrígan's boss was the guy Jo called The Master, and he was some kinda death god. Maybe *the* death god, the one that all our legends and myths were tryin' to represent when they gave him names like Hel and Hades and Anubis. Jo hadn't known who Brigid was answering to, but from the way she was not looking at Horns, I kinda thought she'd thrown him over in favor of whoever'd made her his avatar.

And from the way he was looking at her, I kinda thought he was in it to win her back.

Jo was gonna hate that she was missin' this.

I cleared my throat. "Right. So Jo's ridden with Cernunnos a few times now—"

Brigid's face went sharp, then slack, like she was tryin' ta hide that she'd gotten all edgy. I hurried up with what I was saying, hoping it wouldn't make things worse. "—and she says she can't ride with the Hunt again, 'cause it's too..."

As fast as she'd sharpened, Brigid softened again. She said, "Yes," a second time, an' this time it had a whole world of understanding in it. I guessed it didn't matter how she was interpreting *riding with Cernunnos*, 'cause there was no doubt she knew what it was like. "I wonder that she could refuse," Brigid said, and Cernunnos harrumphed.

"It is a talent of your line. Brigid, you are..."

"Well enough for what must be done."

He leaned down, lowering his voice. "I think not."

Brigid shrugged. She reminded me a little of Jo, facing off the god, except Jo's restraint was like sparks, and Brigid's was all inside, tied tight so nothing could get out. "We make our choices and do what must be done. I have the strength I need now, and will pay later, if I must."

"I might take the burden from you, if you would allow it."

"You know I will not. You have brought this man to me, and I need him, so I will ride with you to do what must be done. Nothing more."

"Dare you?" Cernunnos asked, and I finally realized that the rest of the world had gone away for the two of them. It didn't matter that a dozen of us were sittin' around on horses not twenty feet away at most: it was just the two of 'em alone together, in a romance that had gone all wrong. "Dare you?" he asked again. "You have ridden with me thrice already, Bríg NicFionntán. Dare you risk a fourth?"

She smiled, a tired pained smile that I'd seen too often on my own wife's face in the last days of her life. "Bríg NicFionntán was a girl in another time, with another face. I am like you now, and have only one name, or so many that none of them matter, and I might now ride with you until the end of time. My heart may still be yours, but my soul is sworn to another. You have no power over me."

Cernunnos straightened in his saddle, stripping away their intimacy and becoming the thing I'd seen him as first: a cold hard capricious bastard. "As well, then, that I do not do this only for you."

He meant it to cut, and it did. Brigid's chin came up, enough of a hit that I saw it clear as Cernunnos did. This time, though, her voice didn't betray anything but cool curiosity: "Do you not?"

"I recall a far-future memory, a reckoning with your sister's master. I have a score to settle, though in that future I have no recollection of such a mark made in my past. Perhaps we might change it all utterly, and you and I might yet pursue what we have lost."

Brigid stood silent a couple seconds, the sparks she'd buried comin' close to burning through. Then she said, "Time's passage does not alter in such a way, Cernunnos."

His voice softened the same way hers had a minute earlier. "Time's passage rarely alters that way, *cuisle mo chroí*. But even a god must try, else the long passage of the years would be unbearable with their sameness. Nothing is immutable, not even the stars. Will you ride with me?"

"I will ride with the boy."

"Of course you will." Cernunnos turned his stallion away, and the kid on the golden mare came to help Brigid mount. She thanked him, then lifted her voice, like all of us hadn't been hangin' on every word she and Horns had been saying.

"I have searched these hills while I have waited for you to come. East and north of Knocknaree lies a cavern reaching deep into the earth. There lies the cauldron which has stolen the lives of *aos sí* kings, and which will take even yours should my sister's master gain the strength he desires. Master Muldoon has come from the other end of time to help us bind it. It is a binding I know succeeds, for he also helps to destroy it, and barely a dozen undead warriors rise to protect it. Make no mistake: when the magic is made to bind the thing, my sister and her master will come to protect it. You are hunters, but I would lead you to war. Will you ride with me?"

I'd done my time in the Army. I knew how much noise a dozen men could make when they put their minds to it. The Hunt outdid that, thanks to the baying dogs and calling rooks and the horses stamping their feet and raising their voices too. The only one not shouting was Cernunnos, who looked kinda like a captain whose troops had decided to take that hill over there whether he thought they should or not. I figured we were all gonna get court-martialed in the end, but what the hell, even a soldier's gotta do something crazy once in a while or they'll all go nuts. The kid swept his mare around, Brigid's braid bouncing down her spine like a beacon, and the whole damned Hunt rode after them, cheering and waving their swords.

For once Cernunnos took up the rear. I nudged Imelda up next to Cernunnos's stallion. "You said somethin' about 'your line', meanin' Jo and Bridey there?"

He answered like a man who thought he wouldn't get any rest 'til he did. "Brigid and the Morrígan are sisters, and Joanne is the Morrígan's granddaughter, many times removed."

"You gotta be kiddin' me."

Cernunnos arched an eyebrow, wrinklin' the flesh over his budding horns. I twitched, trying not to let it turn into a shudder. "All right, so you're not kidding. Is that why you want Jo? 'cause her great-aunt turned you down?"

In seventy-four years I'd never met anybody who could do disdain the way Horns could. His lip curled and he looked at me like I was somethin' he mighta scraped off his shoe. "I hold her in higher esteem than that, and I would hope you do too."

Smug with satisfaction, I let Imelda fall back from the stallion's side. I didn't mind a god being taken with my girl, just so long as it was her, and not some cloud-chasing memory he was after.

After a couple minutes, the cloud-chased memory circled back around to me and let Cernunnos take the lead. I watched him ride forward, then gave Brigid a hairy eyeball. "Thought you were the one who knew where we were going."

"There is no hole in the earth that doesn't contain at least a few beasts, and he's the master of them all. They'll guide him there, whether they mean to or not."

"And his fragile male ego is soothed by taking point?"

She gave me a perplexed glance that turned into laughter. "Something like that, aye. Is that a turn of phrase from your time? The 'fragile male ego'? It seems appropriate."

"Shh. We hear it alla time, but we don't like to believe it. Ain't good for our egos to think they're fragile."

"And yet," she said, and I said "Shh" again. She smiled and nodded, but her smile faded faster than an old man wanted to see. "I had counted on Joanne Walker. Not that your presence isn't appreciated…"

"But I'm no magic man." I shrugged and nodded toward Horns, up at the front of the host. "He says I'm the next best thing. 'course, I coulda told him that anyway." I winked, and she laughed, quick as her smile had come. Least I could still get that out of a pretty girl, even if it was mercurial. "Jo put a whammy on me," I said a bit more seriously. "Gave me her Second Sight, an' it ain't faded yet. Dunno why, 'cause I thought it was only gonna work til sunset, but I'm still seeing straight into the bones of the world if I try to."

"And what do you see when you look at me?" Brigid wondered.

I glanced at her, tryin' ta will the depth of sight back on. Glimmers shone all around her edges. Then it was like falling into a pool: her aura, all red and gold, splashed deep inside her, but when it hit her core it turned black an' blue like somebody'd been beating on her. I blinked an' the colors got clearer, until I could see the blackness was eating her away from the inside. I took a sharp breath, and she lifted her hand to stop me from talkin'. "So you do See," she said like she'd been verifying it for herself.

"Darlin'..."

"Have no fear, Master Muldoon. I have the strength for what must be done."

"But not more."

"It will be enough."

"You saved Jo's life, didn't you. By taking that hit." The longer I looked, the easier it was to see how the magic inside her belonged to the Morrígan. It was death magic, dark an' ugly, and I didn't think an ordinary human, even one with Jo's skills, coulda survived it. "Saved mine, too, by keeping her alive. Thanks."

Brigid nodded an' changed the subject. Guess I couldn't blame her. I didn't like thinking about my own mortality, an' I was damned certain she had a lot more years to regret losing than I ever would. "You have the Sight," she said, "and I see within you the strength of a spirit protector. You may not work magic, but you are imbued with it. What else might you know that will serve us in binding the cauldron? You know its eventual fate, but do you know how it comes to its end? How it is bound? How we might ourselves cast a spell to last through the aeons?"

I rubbed a hand through my hair and thought about it. Cernunnos looked over his shoulder at us, green fire magic pounding into my skull when his eyes met mine. I flinched up straight in the saddle, scowling hard at him. "Damned if I don't. Jo and me came across a binding spell way back when this started. She don't use magic like that, no spells and chants and stuff, but I think it's 'cause she *don't*, not 'cause she can't. Anyway, this one..." Cernunnos turned away, shoulders thick like he was becomin' the stag already. "This one we set in his name."

"In his—in his name?" Brigid clawed her voice back from sounding like a fishwife and cleared her throat. "In Cernunnos's name? You know a binding spell that calls on the god of the Wild Hunt?"

"No. I mean, yeah, it does 'cause he's the one we called on. Jo told me not to say it, not even joking, but—well, hell, darlin', he was the only god I'd ever met. Who else was I gonna mention?"

"*Was he there?* At the breaking of the cauldron, *was he there?*"

"'a'course he was." It took a couple seconds to catch up on why that might matter, an' then I sat back into the saddle deep enough that Imelda pranced sideways. I said, "'a'course he was," again, except this time I wasn't feeling quite so pat. "Not when the binding was broken an' the cauldron got stolen, but yeah, he was there when Jo destroyed it. That's... that ain't coincidence, is it."

"I think it is not. And now the urgency seems greater to me than before." She shouted a name I couldn't grab hold of, some kinda harsh liquid sound that didn't leave any kinda repeatable syllables in my mind. Cernunnos reined up hard, an' Brigid snatched the reins from the boy rider's hands to urge their mare forward. She and Horns started shouting at one another. Imelda pranced uncomfortably again, and I sat there like a damned fool for a minute before kicking her forward so I could hear their argument.

Turned out I didn't get a chance. I rode up to 'em, Cernunnos roared, "*Enough!*" an' the whole of the Hunt leapt about forty miles in one step. The landscape changed, Knocknaree left far behind and low green mountains rolling up in front of me. A black pit opened up in the earth like a hell hole, and that, a'course, was where we were heading.

CHAPTER FOUR

Normal caves got a transition area, where sunlight slips through and fades until you're standin' in the dark. I rode into this one a few steps behind Cernunnos an' Brigid, and watched 'em disappear in front of me like they'd gone through some kinda portal. Same thing happened to me: one second I was in daylight, the next it was darker than night, no ambient light at all to soften the darkness. I only kept going forward 'cause I knew there were another dozen guys behind me and I didn't figure a pile-up at the cave mouth was on Bridey's agenda. She and Cernunnos musta decided the same thing, 'cause I could hear their horses on the rocky ground even if I couldn't see a damned thing.

A few more steps in I remembered Jo had magicked me, and I did that hard blink that made the Sight turn on. It was like having a super power: the dark turned colors, black light glowing in the walls and deeper midnight pulsing ahead of us. Everything felt off-kilter, like this wasn't a place living things were supposed to go, but the darker pulse was tugging at me, too. I wanted to go check it out, even when the smart part of my brain was telling me to turn tail and get the hell outta there. It seemed likely Jo spent a lotta time feeling this way, and I grinned even if we were heading for certain doom.

Cernunnos an' Brigid were like flares ahead of me, him green an' her fiery gold. I glanced at myself, which I hadn't thought to do before. I knew Jo saw my aura as silver, but it was still a shock to see my own hands kinda glowing and shining with life. White spun around the edges of silver, blurring and blending into brightness that made me wonder if the guys behind me Saw this way, an' if I was a big ol' silver lug to their eyes. Jo had been real pleased about that, when she'd triggered the Sight in me. My grey eyes had turned silver, she said, when everybody else's she'd tried it on had gone gold like hers did. Nice to know I held my own, even in mojo-land.

"It pulls at me." Brigid sounded strained.

I nudged Imelda forward a few more steps, tryin' ta catch up in the glow-in-the-darkness. "That's what it does, doll. I didn't much see the thing on my end of time, but Jo talked to me about it after she destroyed it. She said it makes you just wanna jump in. That it offers peace."

Cernunnos gave a snort. "There is no peace to be had in his grasp."

"I'm just reportin' what the lady said, Horns. How the hell did they make that thing, anyway?"

"Through the sacrifice of a willing victim," Brigid

murmured. "The cauldron is forged from my sister's soul."

I spent a couple seconds wondering how that was possible, then remembered I'd just met an elf with a living silver arm, and that that wasn't the strangest thing I'd seen by half. All I said was, "That's how it's destroyed, too, is with a willing soul. Why don't we just do that now?"

Cernunnos turned, green fire blazin' off him. "Do you wish to make that sacrifice yourself? Because I could not even if I wished to, Brigid's soul belongs to another, and my riders are dead men. You are the only one among us who could make that choice."

I clacked my teeth shut. The right thing to do was dive straight into the damned cauldron, and I knew it, but I sure as hell didn't want to. Not even knowing it might save a few lives back on my end of time. Truth was, if Jo was at my side and I could say g'bye, I'd do it in a heartbeat. But I'd promised her I'd be safe, and I hated breaking that promise. After a minute, Cernunnos, looking smug, turned away again, an' I muttered, "Son of a bitch," without meaning him at all.

"Willing is not enough," Brigid said softly. "Even I, with my soul bound to another, might crawl in it willingly to break its spell. But it calls to me so strongly I think anyone who enters it does so willingly. Not wisely, perhaps, but willingly."

I dropped my chin to my chest, remembering more clearly what Jo had said. "Innocent. Not just willing, but innocent." This time saying, "Son of a bitch," was due to relief that I hated feeling. I oughta be better than that, 'cause it might break Jo's heart, but I knew she'd forgive me for dying if I took the cauldron along with me. But while I mighta been a decent human being, I wasn't an innocent one. Not much of anybody who fights in a war is, no matter how hard you might try to keep your hands clean. And I hadn't, because you don't, not when your life and your buddies' lives are hanging on it.

"Ah." Brigid's colors went dark with unhappiness. "Innocence, of course. And to sacrifice one unwillingly would only make us into the thing we stand against. How did Joanne—" Her breath was loud even over the horses' hooves against the rocky floor. "No. Better not to wonder, and to be satisfied knowing it will one day be destroyed."

"She had help." I wasn't gonna go into it any more than that, but something in Brigid's aura relaxed, which made me feel better. A guy doesn't like making pretty women tense if he can help it.

A clatter from behind us made the three—four, counting the silent kid—of us straighten an' look back, for all that I didn't know if Bridey and Horns could see anything. The cave's mouth was a cut-away of light, still not lettin' any seep in, and the last of the Hunt's riders had just passed through it. Between one breath an' the next, the air got thicker, like I was tryin' ta breathe in coal dust.

"Now," the boy rider said. His colors were muted compared ta Cernunnos, but they were the same emeralds an' jades, overlaid with a yellowish concern. "Now we are in his realm, Father. We do not belong here. Keep me close, or risk yourself."

I was learning all kindsa interesting things. I wondered if Jo had an inkling that Cernunnos's safety was tied up in the kid's, but I bet she did. It didn't seem like the kinda thing she'd share, though. She wasn't the type to go around telling people how to hunt a god. Not unless she was the one who needed to hunt it, I guessed, but even then I wasn't sure she'd want to let everybody else know what was in her arsenal. She still had some wild ideas about keeping the rest of us safe, or doin' it all herself. I guessed that was part of why I loved her, and prob'ly part of why Mike Morrison did too, even if it made us both crazy sometimes.

"What's that mean," I asked, to distract myself. "We're in his realm now, I reckon you mean the Master, but—we ain't gone that far."

"Can you not feel it?" Brigid asked.

I could, a'course, the way the air was closing in around us an' a chill was coming up, but Jo and me had talked a lot about this Master fella and she was pretty certain he came from a lot deeper in the elemental planes than a walk through Irish countryside could allow for. On the wrong side of time or not, the country outside that cavern entrance was what Jo called the Middle World, the one ordinary folk lived in all the time. There was an Upper World, too, where she'd met a thunderbird, an' a Lower World where a lotta demons were trapped, among other things. After dealin' with the wendigo she'd told me she'd fallen through the Lower World into another level that looked a lot like Hell to her, an' *that* was a lot closer to where this Master was coming from. No way had we traveled that far, no matter how fast and wild the Hunt ran.

But in the middle of convincing myself of alla that, I tripped over the explanation. I looked around at the blackness tryin' ta eat us all up, and said a word I'd learned in Korea that didn't quite have a translation. Just as well, too. "I was thinking it looked like a hell hole when we rode up. You're telling me it really *is*?"

"One of many. There are places on this earth where he has broken through and where his denizens are vomited up into our world."

I wrinkled my nose like the image came with a smell. I wasn't sure it didn't, for that matter: the air sure wasn't right. "So you're saying it's a hellmouth. That's just dandy. I don't suppose you got Buffy on hand to help deal with it?"

Their auras went flat. I guessed I couldn't blame 'em: Jo wouldn'ta known what I meant either, and she was at least from my end of time. Sometimes I thought the girl had deliberately stayed away from all the pop culture that talked about magic. Not consciously, maybe, but deliberately. When I'd met her she'd wanted nothing at all to do with magic, but over the past year it'd become clear she'd been aware earlier on in her life that it existed. I had to hand it to her: when Joanne ran away from something, she ran but good.

"It don't matter," I said as much to myself as Brigid. "Let's get down there and lay this binding spell before any vampires claw their way outta the hellmouth to eat us."

As soon as I said 'em, I knew I was gonna regret those words forever. Maybe not straightaway, but it was the same as sayin' "At least it ain't raining," and I knew better than to say something like that. Brigid's aura sparked like she was telling me they'd known better than to say "At least it ain't raining" in ancient Ireland, too, an' then we made our way toward a dark light that started shining in front of us.

It didn't get brighter, that light. It stayed steady until all of a sudden we were in a rough-hewn round room, and the weight of the cauldron pulled us toward it. It didn't look like all that much: black iron beaten into shape with a hammer. It was big, I'd give it that, plenty big for a man to crawl into. I nudged Imelda a step toward it, then another, and each one got easier even though good sense told me they oughta be getting harder. But it was like huddling under a down comforter, too warm and heavy to throw off. Worse, I didn't want to throw it off. My shoulders sank and my eyes got droopy. Another step or two and I could tip off Imelda's back into the cauldron and nap, even if part of me was screamin' that was a bad idea. I knew it was dangerous, but it was like swimming with the current: I wanted to go where it took me an' not fight it. No wonder Jo had hated the thing. I shook myself and sat back to tell Imelda to stop. She did, her legs rigid and her body quivering like she was just waiting for the signal to get the hell outta there.

Cernunnos was even closer to the cauldron than I was, mesmerized by it. The stallion refused ta go any nearer, but the god leaned toward it, so drawn I could just about see ghostly hands inviting him in. Brigid said the name again, the one I couldn't hear right, and Cernunnos snapped upright, then full-out retreated. No other word for it, and no grace or dignity to it either. He drove his heels into the stallion's side and it jumped away, pressing itself up against a wall, as far from the cauldron as it could get.

Once Cernunnos was out of the way, the others crowded closer, led by the kid, whose face lit up with interest. Brigid finally took the reins again and guided the mare back toward Horns. She had to put her arm around the kid's waist to keep him from getting off the horse, but even so, she kept the mare between Cernunnos an' the cauldron. It made me wonder if it was easier for a mortal to resist the thing than an immortal, which didn't make sense. I'd already pushed past the limits of threescore an' ten, and the idea of crawling inside that cauldron scared the crap outta me. I reckoned if I was risking a guaranteed forever I could just about walk up and spit in its eye, but it didn't look like Cernunnos was that certain.

A'course, it'd taken a near-immortal elf to create the cauldron. Maybe the longer the life, the more restful laying down the burden seemed. I figured that made me the least vulnerable rider in this room, which was an ugly thought. That said, somebody had to step up, or we were all gonna stand around here until people started jumping into the damned pot. "Horns!"

The god of the Wild Hunt flinched, then gave me a look that shoulda peeled the skin right off me. I grinned, showing teeth. "Can you keep that kid from riding off if you put him somewhere?"

Fury flew across his face. "Of course. I may be bound to him, but he lives by my sufferance."

"Mmhnn. Kid, go stand in the..." I took a second to

think about it. Jo always had some kinda logic and pattern to how she built power circles. "In the west," I decided. "You can be the opposite power, setting sun opposing youth, which might oughta be the rising sun. An' that puts..." I thought about it again, but Cernunnos interrupted.

"Me at the rising sun? I am the eldest here, and no doubt as his father am well suited to stand across from him."

I said, "Yeah," but I didn't mean it. "Yeah, no. Because we gotta bind this thing in your name, and I'm not sure you oughta be part of the circle if we're gonna do that. Bridey, what do you think?"

From her expression, I couldn't tell what she thought, except for maybe that I was surprising her. After a thoughtful look, she shook her head. "Only four of us here are truly living. The riders have crossed beyond, and while they may someday return to mortal flesh it is not now their chosen path. The boy, myself, yourself and the lord of the Hunt must stand at the points of our compass, and Cernunnos... yes," she finally said. "Cernunnos at the east, not only to stand opposite his bloodline, but for the hope of a new day. You are correct," she said to me. "It would be best to have him stand separate, so the spell might be bound to him without mortal taint, but—"

I heard the rest of what she said, but that handful of words caught me. Mortal taint. I was willing ta bet that was why the bindings had finally failed, back on my end of time. If the cauldron coulda been bound to Cernunnos alone, maybe his doorway to forever woulda held it until the end of time. Maybe nobody else woulda had to die if we could've bound it to the god alone.

But the fact of the matter was, he had a mortal son, an' that tied him to the wheel of time too, so maybe there was never any hope of it being a permanent solution. Maybe we had to settle for good enough, an' I got into my place at the southern edge of our circle holding on to that idea. Good enough would see it through a few thousand years, and while it was lousy that anybody else would die because we could only manage good enough insteada perfect, at least it was only a few people instead of hundreds or thousands.

Brigid's command brought me back: "Begin the spell, Master Muldoon. We'll repeat it and bring what we can to it ourselves."

I grunted. "Just like that, huh?" The damned spell I'd read with Jo had a buncha nonsense about gates and things that didn't mean anything to either of us, but I reckoned if I wanted this to work I had to *make* it mean somethin'. Cernunnos was over there at the east, nothing between him and the risin' sun except a chunk of hell hole. I said, "Ah, hell," and threw myself into it as best I could.

"I call on the light to rise and bind thee. I call on the god who stands before me."

Horns got the faintest bit of a smile, which somehow made me think I was heading in the right direction. Jo was gonna be amazed, hearing I was dancing through time casting spells. Figured that could get worked in too, and did my best: "I call on time to bend before me. I call on the wind, and the earth, and the sea. I call on fire to help bind thee."

Stone cracked behind Cernunnos like it had heard me calling on it. A thin track of sunlight spilled through from way up above, lighting his ashy hair to silver and making his budding horns stand out in sharp relief. Brigid gasped and I looked her way. She held her hands out, fire blazing down from the tattoos banding her upper arms, not burning her. She was a conduit, not a martyr.

Wind howled down the crack in the stone, bringing fresh air that swept away the coal-thick taste in the cavern. The kid leaned into it with a fierce grin, and all of a sudden I heard his blood rushing like it was water on a shore. It made sense: water wore everything away, even immortality, an' the kid was what tied Cernunnos to a mortal cycle. The idea flitted away, letting me concentrate on what I had to say. The others were chanting now, repeating what I'd said, and I threw everything I had at the cauldron. "In Cernunnos' name I set this spell, and swear we four will hold it well. By these words and by our will, by our power and by our skill, we bind thee for eternity."

Power slammed out of all four of us an' crashed against the cauldron. It lit up in every color we carried, silver and white, red an' gold, an' a hundred shades of green from the god and the kid. Fire burned a pattern in it, an' water ran in crashing waves all around. Time was fluid and liquid, splashing through and over everything, an' earth grounded the thing. Then quick as a flash it was gone, but sunlight caught the cauldron's curve. In it I Saw all the magic we'd just poured in, an' I Saw how black rage boiled inside the cauldron but couldn't get out. Every one of us staggered, exhausted, but after a couple seconds Cernunnos lifted his head to bare a grin like I never wanted ta see again. I didn't notice mosta the time, but his teeth were pointed like a predator's, an' right then he looked like he was gonna go for a throat.

He didn't, though. He just grinned, and through that grin, hissed, "He comes. We must not be here when the battle meets, else he will hold the advantage. Ride. *Ride!*"

CHAPTER FIVE

We burst outta the hellmouth like the Hunt was after us, not like we were them at all, an' careened through the sky with dogs howling and birds screeching and all of us roaring from the bottoms of our souls. Roaring defiance at the dark god that was coming to mow us down, roaring triumph at having bound his cauldron into uselessness, roaring out our fear and our hope and our determination to go down like warriors. I felt like a kid again, a damned dumb kid back in Korea, usin' my voice to scare away my own fears 'cause I knew I'd never scare the enemy otherwise.

Brigid rode beside me, the boy tucked between her and the horse's neck. She wore a leather breast plate over her white robes like it wasn't worth commenting on that it had just appeared outta nowhere. But then, Jo conjured the sword I was currently wearing outta nowhere all the time, so it prob'ly *wasn't* worth commenting on. I gave a shout meant to be a question. She glanced at the kid, yelled, "It's to safety

I'll bring him now!" and peeled away from the rest of the Hunt, the gold mare thundering through the sky.

Cernunnos tried ta look like he wasn't watching them go, but I caught him glancing after them anyway. He scowled. I shrugged, and under the howl of the Hunt, said, "You gotta do what you can to keep 'em safe, Horns. It don't always work, but we gotta try."

"I do not need your understanding."

"You got it anyway." That was as much time for talk as we had, 'cause all of a sudden we were above Knocknaree, an' there was a hell of a fight going on below.

I'd run across a couple of demons in my time. Some of 'em Joanne had unloosed on Seattle, and another one we'd gone hunting. That one had been slippery, half in this world and half outta it. The army of monsters down below looked more like the first set: conjured up outta nightmares, but solid as the earth itself. I recognized a lot of 'em, just like anybody with a working knowledge of European mythology would. There was everything from minotaurs to dragons and anything you cared to think about in between: chimeras and griffins, centaurs an' trolls, giants and little people.

It was easy to tell which side was whose, 'cause the Morrígan was leading the bad guys, and I wasn't gonna forget her any time soon. Her black hair was tied back just like Brigid's, an' she wore black armor over her blue robes. Blood had been painted over the tattoos on her arms, making 'em shine purple. Only two ravens were on her shoulders, but not 'cause she'd killed one to escape Jo. The third had come back to life, or its spirit had been bound to a new shape or something, 'cause the black horse she rode was just about feathered, an' when it screamed it had a raven's voice. Every time it cried, the ranks of monsters came together a little more.

But not all the living myths were behind her. A whole bunch were on our side. *Aos sí* rode centaurs into battle. Others were just standing and fighting, blades so fast and bright I couldn't see 'em as more than a blur even with the borrowed Sight. Ichor and gore splattered all over the place. A cat-like critter with nine lashing tails, all of 'em on fire, jumped from one bad guy to another, disemboweling 'em and leaving them to die messily. A ghost-colored horse without a rider slipped through places too small for a mouse, an' kicked the brains outta the folks taking up its space when it stepped out again. I wondered if Imelda could do that, but she snorted. I took it as a no, and patted her neck right before we hit the ground and joined the fight.

There was no wasting time struggling toward the front lines. We crashed into them, horses and hounds smashing down from the air. Rooks flew at the Morrígan's ravens, dozens against two. Black feathers rose and fell on the fight's heat, birds shrieking loud enough to be heard over the sounds of swords and hooves. The dogs went through Morrígan's army like a pack of wolves, hamstringing and taking out throats, then moving on like they'd come back later for the feast. I drew Jo's rapier, and for a while the world was nothing but tryin' ta survive.

War ain't a straight picture in the mind. It ain't the battlefield they show in movies, where things make a kinda macabre sense. All it is is flashes, moments when something far away comes crystal clear, or something up close burns itself into your memory forever. It's noise, even if horses and monsters and swords made a whole different kinda noise than the guns I'd heard in Korea. The screams were still the same, and dead was dead no matter if you got killed by a bullet or an ax. A lotta the smells were the same too, blood and dirt and the purity of fresh air when wind blew some of the stink away. There was the smell of horses here, too, and nothing of gunpowder, but it was close enough to remind me of things I tried not ta think about.

I saw bits of what was going on around me. People an' creatures dying, plenty of 'em thanks to me. Every time one of 'em died I thought about the cauldron, and imagined it being unbound. If we lost, the spell we'd put on the thing would get broken, and the Master would bring every single critter who died here back to life.

It was a hell of a reason to fight, the idea we were keeping the world from getting overrun by zombies. I figured we had to win, 'cause on my end of time we weren't all zombies, but knowing that didn't make the fight any less urgent. My arm got heavy after all, even if the sword was magic, an' time and again I was grateful to Brigid, 'cause I was pretty sure she'd pulled our army together and got 'em up here on this hilltop to meet the Morrígan's army before it got to us and the cauldron. We were better off fighting in the open daylight instead of the twists and dark tunnels where the cauldron was hidden. I reminded myself of that every minute, an' breathed deep, an' once in a while felt a crazy grin stretch my face. I was on the wrong end of time fighting a battle for the future, an' I might die any time but if I did, it was a damned fine way to go out.

The riders of the Hunt spread out from each other, all of 'em finding a stretch of battlefield to call their own, but all of 'em had the same look of ferocious glee smeared across their faces. It wasn't so much joy in killing as it was joy in living on the edge.

Of all of 'em, Cernunnos was the only one without that smile. He was fighting his way back to the front, heading for the one enemy combatant that mattered. I turned Imelda to follow him, focusing hard on staying alive. More'n once I knew it was the chain mail under my shirt keeping me that way. The sword was easier to use than I expected, my arm not getting tired the way it should. I turned the Sight on the blade and saw a dull blue glow, like even through the distance an' the years, Jo's magic was holding on.

It wasn't more'n half a second I'd taken my eyes off the fight, but it was enough. A whistle caught my attention an' I looked up to see a thing about eleven feet tall and branchy like an evil Ent swinging a massive tree club at my thick skull.

A bolt of lightning stopped it. Stopped it and everything else within five yards, too. I couldn't see anything for a couple seconds, the world whited out from standing too close to the light, but the stink of burned flesh rose up, and when my vision cleared it was just me and Imelda in a smoking black circle.

Me and Imelda and Brigid.

I hadn't even seen her coming. She was only just now touching down, the gold mare carrying her and her alone. There were sparks flying off her hands, bits of lightning left over, an' for a couple seconds my heart took a break from beating. Joanne pulled down a lotta mojo, but she'd never thrown lightning, an' I didn't know if somebody human could do that at all. Made me real aware that Brigid wasn't human, even if she mostly looked it. Her horse stopped over the tree creature's ruin, Brigid with her head bowed, breath coming hard and blood dripping from her sword. She lifted her eyes, as much fire in 'em as in Cernunnos's, and she saluted me in greeting. I straightened up as tall as I could, feelin' more weight from that salute than anything I'd given or received in Korea. She looked pleased.

Then the respite was over and the fight was on us again. She was right-handed an' I was a lefty, so we covered each other's backs and hacked down everything from normal-looking people to stone-footed giants that rose right up outta the earth itself. The rapier never lost its edge, not even when it slammed into granite so hard it sent shakes up my arm. One of the giants finally came up right between us, knocking our horses away from each other. I didn't see her again after that.

All at once I was fighting behind Cernunnos, though. I got a look at him, and wanted to take another. He wasn't even pretending to be human anymore. That crown of antlers had burst through, ivory wrapping around a skull distorted way outta shape. Not quite a full-on stag, but something so close to it that the blazing green eyes were disturbing in its face. So was the way his gums pulled back from teeth that shouldn't be sharp, but were. His neck an' shoulders were thicker, and his arms brawnier. He was using the short silver sword like a machete, hackin' down everything within reach. There were too damned many of 'em, that was all. Just enough to keep him away from the Morrígan, an' I didn't think that was luck on her part.

I started feeling a grin like the rest of the Hunt was wearing stretch over my own face. I brought Imelda around so we could flank the Master's right-hand doll. Nobody was looking out for the old man on the grey mare. I slipped through the spaces up to the Morrígan as easy as I'd seen the pooka doing earlier.

Truth was, I expected it all to go to hell. I'd seen Jo fight the Morrígan She was faster and stronger than any human could be, and had a whole lotta years of practice under her belt. No way could I expect to break through her guard, and no way could somebody not have her back.

Except that was thinking like a good guy. That was thinking like someone with people to live for, instead of just a cause. That was thinking like somebody who didn't want the world to end, insteada like somebody doing her damnedest to end it. Her army was there to kill Brigid's, not to watch out for each other. Her ravens spun away across the sky, diving at some kinda choice pickings, and I seized the moment.

Maybe her black-feathered horse heard me coming. Maybe she finally saw Cernunnos and decided he was the best target on the field. Maybe a tree giant bashed into

Imelda and knocked us one step the wrong way. I dunno. But insteada Jo's rapier sliding through the Morrígan's exposed back, she was half a foot outta line with me when I struck. I scraped a chunk of leather armor an' rib flesh off her body, but it wasn't a killing blow.

An' that's when things *did* go to hell.

The Morrígan forgot about Cernunnos and turned on me, screaming like a banshee the whole while. She was bleeding pretty good, her whole left side a torn-up mess, but there was madness in her eyes and she moved like she didn't feel the pain. Her sword hammered against the rapier. Imelda's quick feet kept me from getting dead, but there were a whole lotta bad guys pressed all around and nowhere friendly to go. I ducked a sword swing and lunged with the rapier again, scoring a tiny red line that she gave back in spades. My shirt was a cut-up mess, an' only the chain mail armor was keeping me alive. Imelda backed up another couple of steps. I looked over my shoulder, wondering if I was gonna make it outta there in one piece.

When I looked back, the Morrígan was hanging off Cernunnos's sword like a side of beef. He'd run her clean through, just what I'd been tryin' ta do, except no way could I have lifted her toward the sky an' howled triumph, too. I was a tough old coot, but nothing like that. The Morrígan wasn't dead yet, still kicking and clawing at the sky as Cernunnos shook his raised arms and twisted the sword inside her.

The whole fight came to a stop under the sound of

Cernunnos's howling. It went out in a ripple around us, stillness washing over everybody. I kicked Imelda and she bounced around the Morrígan's raven-black horse, getting us nice and close to the one guy everybody was about to try an' kill. The other riders of the Hunt moved in too, 'til we'd closed ranks around Cernunnos like some kinda honor guard.

Brigid's army started cheering. Low at first, like they couldn't hardly believe what they were seeing, and then louder and louder until they were lifting the clouds right outta the sky. Back in the day, when I'd played ball, a time or two I'd made a great interception or tackle that brought the crowd to its feet. I'd thought I'd known was it was like to be worshiped, feeling that energy comin' off the fans. It was nothing, nothing at all, to the uplifting power of a triumphant army.

But the Morrígan's army stayed quiet, an' that was worse. Defeat could cry out as loud, maybe louder, than victory. Defeat was being wounded, broken in spirit, an' it had a voice to it that winning couldn't match. The Morrígan's army didn't have a voice at all, just a silence that rolled over the noise until everybody was quiet again after all. *Focused* silence, all of it concentrating on the Morrígan, dangling but not dead on Cernunnos's sword. She was still reaching for the sky, an' her whole army was looking where she was pointing.

Way too slowly, way too late, I looked too.

The blue was boiling, ruptures and bubbles letting starlight break through even in the middle'a the day. Clouds were coming together, darkening the sun, and a path of night fell outta the stars. Creatures like I'd never seen came tumbling down the path, falling like angels without wings. They cut the sky apart with screams, screams like all hope was lost an' all that was left to them was vengeance. I only knew one story that fit that kinda pain. I dragged my eyes to the front of the oncoming madness, whispering words I knew were true: "And there before them rides a pale horse. Its rider's name is Death, and Hell doth follow close behind."

CHAPTER SIX

Brigid's army scattered. Couldn't say I blamed 'em, but the Hunt held its ground while the Master came bearing down on us. Cernunnos said, "He is not," so quiet I had ta look at him. He said, "He is not your death on a pale horse, old man, not the way you mean as you say it now. He is no devil as your young faith would have him be, nor are they angels who ride with him. Broken spirits, perhaps, and lost, but there was no War in Heaven fought and lost for the love of your god. He is no more death on a pale horse than I am, and perhaps less."

"Yeah? Then what the hell is he?"

"A devourer, perhaps." Cernunnos was still holding the Morrígan up, an' his attention was all for the riders in the sky. "The devourer, perhaps—"

I muttered, "I like that," under my breath. Devourer sounded like something that might take a bite outta me, but that sat better than the idea of him being my lord and master.

Cernunnos kept talking. I shut up and listened, 'cause even with the amazing crazy life I'd led the last year, I didn't often get to hear a god wax philosophical. "—for he has tasted gods and they have failed before him. He is an ending to the souls he takes, swallowing their essence so it feeds only himself, and gives nothing back to the boundless universe."

"Ain't that kinda what death *is*?"

Cernunnos looked at me, green fire bright in his eyes. "After all you have seen at Joanne's side, Master Muldoon, do you truly believe that all I offer to those who ride with me is an eternal nothingness? That any faith which sends a guide, be it a rider or a reaper or a ferryman, to walk a soul through the veil, has nothing to offer on the other side?"

I guessed my face said it all, 'cause a sly grin curled one corner of Horns's mouth before he nodded toward the oncoming rider. "Let us face the Devourer together, Master Muldoon, and—"

"Give him a taste of his own medicine?"

"Send him mewling back to his caverns like a whipped dog," the god agreed. An eager growl rumbled through the Hunt, men an' hounds alike. I changed my grip on Jo's sword, getting ready to use it again. Cernunnos's stallion stomped a couple times an' the whole damned Hunt took to the skies, ready to meet the Devourer on his own turf. I barked a laugh, surprised even though I shouldn't have been, and bent low over Imelda's neck to keep the wind from tearing tears from my eyes. When we were good and high, high enough for Cernunnos to be sure he'd gotten the Devourer's attention, he shook the Morrígan off his sword.

Except insteada falling, she rose into the sky an' came back down at us, hands clawed like she was one of her own ravens. Blood was turning brown on her armor already, and ran in a purple streak down her blue robes, but she wasn't half as dead as I figured she oughta be. Cernunnos laughed, so I guessed it wasn't a surprise ta him, but me, I wished she'd stayed dead. Especially as she was comin' after me, even though Horns had been the one to stick a sword through her. 'course, I'd distracted her so he could do it, and—

—and she didn't have a sword of her own anymore, having dropped it on the battlefield when she got stuck. Jo's rapier had a four-foot reach. The Morrígan came at me, an' I stood in Imelda's stirrups and thrust.

The rapier flared as it smashed into the same hole Cernunnos had made. A bright flash of silver shot up her body and connected to the necklace she wore. Outlined it in blue, so I could see real clear that it was the same one Joanne wore, silver links with a quartered cross sittin' in the hollow of her throat.

Blue splashed into her skin and lit her up from inside, movie-like, so her bones shone through for a split second. All of sudden I saw Joanne between me an' the Morrígan Her eyes were wide and scared as she yelled, "*Gary!*" but then she was gone again, an' Cernunnos was knockin' the Morrígan off my blade like Mickey Mantle at the bat. This time she fell, limp and bloody, all the damned way to the ground. My sword hand was tingling, power itching through it while I tried to remember what Jo had said about that necklace. It and the sword were both made by the elf king Nuada, I knew that. That coulda meant there was just some kinda interference between one piece of magic silver and another, but the burst of blue had seemed like more than that. I was gonna hafta ask Jo about that later.

Assumin' there was a later. Cernunnos shouted something and I looked up to see the Devourer coming straight at me.

Funny thing was, I knew I oughta be scared, but all the fear flooded right outta me. I was old enough to die well, even if I didn't much want to. I'd stopped being afraid of it when my wife died. For a long time I'd just been counting the hours 'til I went with my Annie, but Joanne had changed alla that. I'd have been a better target for him before Joanne, but today I was ready to look him in the eye.

For such big guns, he wasn't much to see. Just an old man on that pale horse, just about as skinny as a skeleton. His hair was thin an' long, and his teeth were yellow, and he carried a staff instead of a sword. He wore robes kinda like the Morrígan's, and like hers, they showed off blue knotwork tattoos around his upper arms. His were faded where hers still looked bright and new, but they were the same pattern, binding them together. He lifted his staff and pointed it at me, black magic gathering in the thing so strong I could see it whether the Sight was still working or not. Feeling way too calm for good sense, I shook my sword hand and waited.

Most of a year ago, Jo had found me a spirit animal. A tortoise, a real protective kinda spirit, good for armoring up and hunkering down. Maybe not so good for quick draw fights like this was gonna turn out to be, but I had to figure a spirit animal that could protect itself could fight, even if that didn't necessarily follow in the real world. Either way, I drew the idea of that big mottled shell around me and felt the tortoise come to life at the back of my mind, ready and willing to take the hits that were comin' my way.

A tar ball of black magic blew outta the Devourer's walkin' stick and tore across the sky at me. I snapped Jo's rapier up, deflecting it as best I could. Her gunmetal blue healing power turned the blade electric, slicing through the worst of the blast and still leaving me reeling in the saddle. The air sucked right outta my lungs and stars spun in my eyes. The rapier got hot, like it'd been filled up with hate and the only way it could release it was by burning. I danced it in my fingers, but there was no way I was dropping the thing. It was my one link back to Jo. I hated ta think what might happen if it and me got separated.

The Devourer's host of riders swept around him and crashed against the Hunt. They were all kindsa amazing, awful things, not fallen angels at all. They were shimmering blues and blacks, light falling through 'em like they'd left their bodies behind a long time ago. A lot of them passed right through the Hunt and rushed for the field below, where Brigid's army was gathering again. I had to think they were going to fight, not to take up new bodies from the dead, 'cause that was a kind of sick I didn't want to know about.

I looked up again an' found myself face to face with the Master.

Cold rolled off him like he was something from between the stars. The air got thin all of a sudden. I dragged in a breath an' didn't let it out, kinda figuring I wouldn't be able to suck in another one. Imelda trembled, tryin' ta toss her head and stomp her feet, but she couldn't move any more than I could. The Master's eyes weren't any kinda color, just pale, and I felt like he was looking straight into the bottom of my soul. He didn't say a word, which was worse than talking, 'cause it gave me room to hear everything he was seeing in me, and everything he was thinking.

He didn't think the Morrígan was dead, not for a minute, but she was hurt bad enough that he had to come patch her up, and I was the mortal with the magic sword. I might not have put his Girl Friday down for the count, but I'd scraped her up with it, an' I got the idea that made me interesting. Interesting meant something for him to deal with.

He went through me like a deck of cards, lifting every part of my life up, glancing at its face and casting it away. The kid I'd been, living out in White Center, Washington before Seattle grew up big enough and absorbed it. Tinkering with cars that looked simple compared to today's machines, but at least a guy could fix 'em. The first girl I'd ever kissed, and then standing for her groom at a wedding a couple years later. The complicated pride on my ma's face when I joined the Army 'cause it was the only way I'd finish the college education she wanted me to have. The first time I saw Annie Macready, and knew I was gonna marry that girl.

He hooked onta that and spun it out so fast I couldn't follow, even after living it. Then he fell back with a death's head grin on his bony old face, said, "She will be my vengeance," and turned his skinny, arrogant back on me.

I never saw red before, not like they talk about doing, but I did then. Blood red misting over everything except the son of a bitch threatening my wife's life, an' he stood out like a lighthouse beacon, best target in a hundred miles. Imelda was moving before I even knew I'd put heels to her, and Jo's rapier was lifted like it had a life of its own. Blazing blue, connecting me to her across the years, and for one crazy second I thought it was all gonna end right there.

The Master, casual-like, threw his staff over his shoulder. A blast of power shot at me, bigger than the last and twice as fast. I couldn't get the rapier between me an' it quick enough. The last thought that rolled through my mind was *sorry, darlin'*.

A raven came up outta nowhere and took the hit for me.

Black magic exploded around it, washing off shields of white and gold. The raven tumbled wings over tail-tip, shedding feathers as it fell. I lurched for it, tryin' ta catch it, and Imelda stepped quick enough that I snagged it without tumbling from the sky myself. The bird lay in my hands, me gawking and it panting like a dog. Fast as it had lost 'em, its feathers grew back in, but bleach-white. Then it turned into something like a cave painting of a raven insteada the bird itself. Just lines, representing instead of containing. That *idea* sank into my hands, made 'em warm, and the warmth ran through me until it settled in the back of my mind. Settled on top of a tortoise shell, where it preened white feathers, gave me a one-eyed look, then tucked its head under a wing to rest.

It all took about half a breath. When I looked up, Jimmy crack corn, the Master'd gone away. Down to the fight, I thought, 'cause he probably had to pick up the Morrígan before he lit out of there, assuming he was the sort of fella who ran from a fight. I was in a hurry to go find out, but Cernunnos was in front of me, some of the stag gone from his face so more human curiosity could show through. "You are not her father, or her grandfather, but the ties that bind you—" He did somethin' with his hands that made me think of a raven's flight, then shook his head. "Be glad, Master Muldoon, that you have such affinity with Joanne. I think nothing else would have had the strength to shield you from that blow. The raven belongs to *him* as much as to her. It is a carrion-eater, after all."

"And a trickster." Sleeping or not, the bleached bird was waiting there at the back of my mind along with the tortoise. Two spirit guides, when a year ago I'd have never dreamed of having even one. Jo had told me time and again my soul was in good shape, but being backed up by a couple of spirit animals made me feel even better about it. Made me feel sharp and focused. "Reckon that's what I need as much as anything. Tricks come in handy for old dogs."

"And young shamans. The battle has all but ended. I must return you to Joanne."

"Like hell."

Horns shifted in his saddle, surprised. I guessed

not many folks gave him a flat-out no when he wanted somethin'. "We're going back to the future, buddy. I ain't letting that son of a bitch go after my wife."

Half a dozen expressions ran over his face, but there wasn't nothin' except determination on my own. I knew I oughta be tired, but there was nothing but cold anger burning in me as I wiped Jo's rapier clean and finally sheathed it. We'd done good. The cauldron was all bound up, the Morrígan was down for the count, and the Master wasn't gonna show his face again until he was good and certain of a win.

Problem was, he was counting my wife as that win. I kept staring Horns down, waiting. He looked away, deliberately, an' I tugged on the last bits of magical Sight Joanne had left me with. It barely flared, just enough to tell me Cernunnos was maybe doing something, but I couldn't tell what. His face got sour, though, like something had gone wrong, an' just then the golden mare joined us.

The boy was in the saddle again, no sign of Brigid. I grunted, curious, an' Horns shrugged. 'nuff said, so he changed the subject, sounding irritated: "I can no longer sense Joanne Walker. Not dead, I think, but out of place, perhaps travelling to one of the other realms. Until she returns to where she belongs I cannot bring you to her."

"I ain't asking you to."

"Your wife," he said, and waited.

"Two good women have happened to me, Horns. You know one of 'em. The other was Annie, an' I just brought her to that bastard's attention. I ain't gonna let that stand. If you can't get me back to Jo, then get me to Annie. I'll do the rest on my own if I gotta."

Damned if Horns didn't chuckle. "And what do you suppose Joanne would do to me if I told her I had abandoned you to him and your fate in some distant future? I can bring you to your wife, Master Muldoon, but the path is not a direct one. It will take time."

"Buddy," I said, "time is the one thing I got on my side."

CHAPTER SEVEN

Folks say history is defined by wars, by winning and losing. I thought riding through time, looking at it all from above, would show me that, especially when I was riding with the god of the Wild Hunt. Wasn't like that at all, though. I touched down through the centuries as Cernunnos brought us closer to my time, not quite living through all of it, but getting enough sense of the god, an' the riders, an' the job they did to carry it with me forever.

Cernunnos came for the souls of the dead, sure enough, and plenty of 'em were on battlefields. But a whole lot more were the ordinary folk, the ones just tryin' ta get by, living and loving as best they could. Far as I could tell, they were the ones who really made up the fabric of the world, laying down their stories, weaving 'em together and leaving a little bit of themselves behind when they died.

At the beginning there were thousands who called for Cernunnos or the Hunt at the end. Faces and names looking for him in specific, for the hounds and rooks to carry them to the other side. Time went on and they got fewer, old gods replaced by new. Horns diminished as his people died away, no joke about it: that crown of antlers he wore lost size, then barely began breaking free of his skull. At first he rode the whole year 'round, an' then got pushed back, bit by bit, season by season, solstice by solstice, until he rode from Halloween to the twelfth night, an' that was the only Christian holiday that did Cernunnos any favors. Back at the start, the twelfth night had been counted from the winter solstice, but over the years it got pushed out, until finally they counted it from Christmas. He stole a few days out of every new year from there on out, an' that was the peak of his power. Not even the failing faith of the people could take more than that away from him, and it got to where I kinda wished he could gather the flocks enough to make a stronger stand. I couldn't bring myself to like the fella, but after watching him guide his believers over the great divide a few thousand times, I learned to respect the compassion he showed.

And besides, it was a hell of a thing, riding across the stars with the Hunt. It got hard to remember I still had a fight ahead of me. Never dreamed I'd be coming at it this way, not even in the worst of the war I'd seen. There were minutes where it was easy to think I'd laid down my own burden an' was enjoying an afterlife like I'd never imagined.

An' then we rode through a cloudburst one afternoon into a remote stretch of road in California. It was Horns who knocked a pretty girl outta the road just as a truck came thunderin' outta nowhere and came half an inch from clipping her down. We were gone before she knew what had happened, but I was looking back, twisted in my saddle, to watch Annie Macready yelp and draw her feet back as the truck roared by. "So mundane," Cernunnos said a couple seconds later, "but equally unquestionable."

Annie was gone already, left in the rain, but the image of her stuck in my mind. Neat white blouse tucked into a bright yellow skirt, an' flat shoes on her feet. Blond hair hardly past her collar, but not as done-up as it'd been the night I met her. I had to swallow to get words past the tightness in my throat. "This's the late forties, Horns. Not so many cars on the road as there are today."

He said, "And yet," an' I muttered. *I toldja so* wasn't any better from a god than anybody else. 'sides, I remembered Annie tellin' me about that near miss, one night when my car overheated an' we ended up walking through a rainstorm to the nearest town. Headlights had washed over us a few times, but we'd kept walking insteada hitching. Back then it wasn't dangerous. We'd just liked keeping company in the rain. I smiled at the memory, then scowled at Cernunnos, who didn't give a damn about what happy thoughts I might be thinking.

"There was no resistance to my interference. She may not have been under attack at all, Master Muldoon. It may have only been human carelessness that nearly cost her her life today."

"Then I owe you one."

"More than one by now, I think."

Hell of a time to pick a fight, but I shook my head. "I ain't takin' that burden on, Horns. I asked for the lift through time, but you made it plenty clear that you're watching my back because of Jo, not 'cause I asked you to. You saved my Annie, and I'll repay that one if I get the chance, but I ain't starting a tab at this bar."

I'd seen the look he got a few times before, but usually it was Jo, not me, exasperating him. I guessed I'd made my point, though, 'cause he went on without belaboring it. "The more effort our enemy has put into destroying her, the more difficult you'll find it to interfere. Time is not that kind."

"Yeah." I thought of Jo, tryin' ta heal the elf king Lugh and running up against the magic of a little girl from our own time. She'd said the same thing: one big change to the time line made smaller ones pretty much impossible. "So— waitaminnit. You tellin' me I'm the goddamned Ghost a'Christmas Past? I'm gonna be stuck watching everything go to hell and not be able to *fix* it?"

Something happened in his expression, something that suggested that if I didn't know better, I might think Horns was being gentle with me. "I am telling you nothing. It's rarely wise to predict what capricious humans might achieve. I would not have said an ordinary man, even one held so highly in Joanne Walker's regard, might have struck the Morrígan a near-fatal blow, nor drawn the Devourer's attention to himself. I expect this journey with you will prove enlightening."

"That really why you're doing it? To understand how

we work?"

"I understand already," Horns said mildly. "But understanding and predicting are not the same. Pace yourself, Master Muldoon. Watch for the things that have changed, and hold those in your memory now. They will be important, if you can hold them."

"Changed, what the hell are you talkin' about, Horns? I know how my life went. It ain't gonna change."

He shook his big heavy head, an' I got the idea he was giving me as much as he could without hanging himself. It didn't seem near enough, and I thought maybe Joanne felt like this a lot, like she was working with only half of what she needed to know. I started to ask another question, but Cernunnos held up his hand, stopping me. "Watch. Remember. And act only when you are certain of your outcome, and not before, or this battle for your wife is sure to be lost."

I muttered, "I already lost it once," as Cernunnos dropped me into a college football game an' my whole life washed over me.

I always told the dolls it was the smell of wet leather and grass stains that kept me coming back to the field. Never failed to get a dimple or a laugh, like they saw fixating on scents as an intriguing sensibility. Wasn't, though. I just liked the smells, the way they filled up my chest an' got the heart pumping. They were a signal the fight was on, an' a football field was about as much fight as I was ever looking for. Getting a sacked, knocking down a long pass, jumping high for the ball. My Pop taught me to play football, but it was Ma, a ballet teacher, who made me practice pushing all the way through my toes when I jumped. Got me a few extra inches of height every time, and I caught a lotta balls—and deflected a lotta others—that the other teams didn't think I should, that way.

'course, it was a long way down to the ground when somebody tackled me at the height of a jump. Dirt an' grass an' bodies flew. The wet ball squirted outta my grip an' went bouncing end over end across the field. About eight other guys jumped on it, an' a couple more jumped on me for good measure. A whistle blew an' everybody piled off, lined up, an' started all over again.

I knew this game. It was the last college game I was gonna play for four years, an' in about two minutes I was gonna miss my last chance at a touchdown. A little fella on the other team was gonna foul me and the refs weren't gonna catch it. I was gonna eat dirt, lose the ball, and in the end, lose the game. I'd replayed it in my mind prob'ly ten thousand times over the years, the way ya do.

'f I took two extra steps sideways, though, there would be nothin' between me an' the goal posts 'cept clear air and a few thousand screams cheerin' me on, and I'd go into the Army a football hero instead of feeling like the pariah who lost the big game. Grinning like a fool, I snatched the ball when it came my way, put on a burst of power, dodged to my left...

...an' let the little guy foul me, an' fell, an' lost the game. Plenty'a complaining in the locker room later, mostly from the other guys, my pals who'd seen the foul even if the ref hadn't. "Thought you were gonna make it there, though, Muldoon," one of 'em said to me. "You looked like you knew he was coming."

"Almost saw him outta the corner of my eye," I allowed. "Just couldn't get my feet going fast enough. Shoulda been you with the ball, Smit. You got lightning feet."

He did a shuffle that made everybody laugh, an' a couple guys pounded me on the back on the way out. They knew, even if the refs didn't, an' they *didn't* know about the double-play I was living that coulda let me save the game if I'd chosen to. I watched a bunch of 'em go, waving an agreement to meet for beers an' burgers later on, then ran a towel over my head an' chased after the coach, callin', "Coach. Coach, wait up, I gotta talk to you."

Saunders was another little guy like the one who'd fouled me, 'cept not a jackass like that fella. He'd been a quarterback in his day, and didn't mind admitting he was a better coach than he'd been player. He slowed down without looking at me, studying a clipboarded playsheet instead. "Sorry about that foul, Muldoon. You know how some of these referees get if you suggest they've made a mistake. Wild horses couldn't change their minds."

"Don't matter. Ain't a life-defining moment."

He did look at me then, a grin flashing across his face. "That's what I like about you, Gary. You get your fight up when you need it, but everything else you take in stride. It makes you a good player. I'd like to see you as a co-captain next year."

"Yeah, me too." I shoved my hands into my pockets with a sigh. "But it ain't gonna happen, Coach. That's why I gotta talk to you. I'm dropping out of school at the end of the semester and enlisting."

Coach quit walking like he'd hit a wall. He'd fought in the first war, and I could see all of those memories rise up and whiten his face before he got 'em under control an' looked like he was tryin' ta sound reasonable: "What in hell would you do that for?"

I shrugged. Hands in my pockets meant I couldn't wave 'em around like I was asking for forgiveness. "The GI bill, Coach. It's the only way I can figure payin' for the rest of college."

"We can find you a scholarship—"

"Nah, Coach." I kept my voice quiet, remembering this conversation from most of a lifetime ago. "I got the grades for 'em, but it's late in the year, and other guys have snatched 'em up."

"There are private avenues, people I can talk to—"

"Coach." This one wasn't worth arguing. If I didn't join the Army, I'd never go to that USO dance and I'd never meet Annie. No way I was risking that big of a change to my life. "I don't need the special treatment, Coach. This is what I'm gonna do."

"They'll send you to war, Gary. You'll go to Korea." There was a tremor in Coach's voice I hadn't been able to hear fifty years ago, when I was young and dumb an' full of fire. The way most of me was right now, 'cause the kid was in charge an' the old man was only a voice of experience along for the ride. I wanted to make that kid say *I know, Coach. I know what it's like, I know about the sleepless nights you get for a lifetime after. I know about the faces that don't go away. I understand, and I wanna thank you for looking out for me. But this is what I gotta do anyway.*

I couldn't, a'course, not anymore than I could have when I was twenty years old and feeling a little smug about my prospects and not a bit afraid getting sent to war. Best I could do was try not to sound condescending, like I thought I knew what I was talking about, when all I said was, "I know, Coach. I'll send a postcard from Seoul, all right?"

Saunders got a tight pinched smile an' patted my shoulder. "All right, son. I wish I could talk you out of it, but if your mind's made up..."

"It is, Coach."

"Then you send me that postcard, and I'll put it with the rest." He shook my hand and we walked away, my heart bangin' with a young man's excitement and an old man's dread.

Next step I took was into the recruiter's station, though real memory told me weeks had passed, that I'd said g'bye to all my buddies, gone out drinking more than I shoulda and kissed a few girls who weren't mine to kiss. I stood up an' got measured, six foot two, two hundred ten pounds, good vision, no asthma, strong heart, all of it ticked off on boxes like I was a piece of meat being processed until I was pronounced fit for duty. Another step and I was in uniform, in Basic, turning back to give a fellow recruit a helping hand, an' the drill sergeant was in my face givin' me hell for doin' it. I said, "Sir, yes sir!" and "Sir, no sir!" like I was supposed ta, and next time gave the guy a hand again. Little skinny black fella named Andy, he told me that time. Andy from Alabama. Him and me would stay friends the rest of our lives, all the way into the next century. I wanted to say somethin' to him when I gave him a hand the third time, maybe *this is the beginning of a beautiful friendship,* but I was starting to get it then.

This was a young man's life. This was me, an' I wasn't just going through the motions. I was *living* this, living it for the first time, the way anybody would, except I had just enough awareness to know how to change things if I wanted to.

"Horns," I said out loud and a little desperate, "not every minute, buddy, or I'll go crazy. Give it to me in chunks. Lemme just touch down at the important parts—" Because if I sat in the back of my own head for fifty years, judging and second-guessing and making my older self re-think every choice I'd made as a kid, knowing I had to make the same damned choices every time anyway just to get where I was going, then I wouldn't make it through. Everybody liked to say "If I knew then what I know now," but knowin' *then, acting* on it then, would make *now* different. Nobody could do it the same way twice, live the exact same life a second time. It wasn't humanly possible.

I got the faintest idea that Cernunnos was laughing, like maybe he hadn't thought about humanly possible 'cause he wasn't human, and the idea of my life started speeding up again. He would send me through my life the same way I'd just skipped through the games and volunteering for the Army, like I was seeing the highlights reel. Big events stood out, an' some of those little moments a guy can't shake for some reason, like trippin' over my shoelace comin' around a corner during Basic. Nobody saw it except me and some birds, but a lifetime later I still got hot around the collar thinking about it.

I muttered, "Thanks," and hunkered down in my own head to watch the highlights, tryin' hard not to think too much about what I was doing when I took Andy's hand and pulled him up for the third time. Not the last, either, but he offered his own hand to me a lotta times down through the years, until neither of us could count how many or who'd done it first.

But I wasn't gonna worry about that, or anything else. I was just gonna hold on, and live...*now*.

CHAPTER EIGHT

Basic training ended with two days of leave. Me an' a buncha squirrely guys who hadn't seen a doll in weeks came outta the gates like scatter from a shotgun. Half of 'em split off right away, heading for the bars and the docks. Me and Andy and some of the others thought better of ourselves, and headed for the USO dance. I guessed it wasn't that we weren't hoping ta get lucky. It was more a matter of pride, and maybe of figuring the world wasn't gonna end if we didn't score. Not even if we got shipped off tomorrow an' didn't see another woman for months.

'sides, we were all looking pretty good in our sharp new dress greens with the seams pressed crisp an' the shoulders sitting square. Ten weeks of training got even the softest of us in some kinda decent condition, an' the guys like me who'd been athletes to start with were leaner an' harder than we'd ever been. Way I saw it, there was a dance floor full of girls who were just waiting for some fresh new Army boys to come say hi, and I hated to disappoint 'em.

The dance hall was an Eagles Club, plenty big for a city with a base the size of Fort Ord. Even with half the lights in the joint off, an eight-piece band was easy to see at the far end of the hall, 'cause hardly anybody was on the dance floor yet. The band was dressed even better'n we were, and the singer was so light-skinned he looked white. A whole group of Negro girls near the stage looked like they might be there for the band insteada the boys. Mosta the white girls were standing in little groups against the walls, though a few were dancing together and a few more were standing all alone looking forlorn.

Andy just about backed outta the room the minute he walked in. Woulda, in fact, if I hadn't been right behind him and getting my toes stomped by his spit-polished shoes. I shoved him forward. "Where you going? We just got here."

"I can't dance, Muldoon."

I grabbed him by the scruff an' hauled him off to one side so we were at least outta the way of the other fellas wanting to come in. "What the hell are you doing at a dance if you can't dance, Anderson?"

"I didn't think there'd be anybody I could dance with! I thought maybe I could watch and get an idea of what to do!"

"For cryin' out loud, Andy, Monterey's got Negros who ain't in the Army. What, you thought none of 'em were dames? An' you didn't think to ask somebody to teach you to dance?"

"Who was I going to ask—Sarge?"

That made me grin. I smacked his shoulder and he rubbed it, looking sour. "That's what would've happened if I'd asked Sarge, too."

"Yeah, forget it. Look, you go ask one of those girls down there to dance. One of 'em has gotta take pity on you, soldier."

He said, "Look," and I said, "Listen," and a pretty, petite blond walked up and said, "I'm sorry, I couldn't help overhearing that you wanted to learn to dance. I'm Anne Marie Macready, and I don't expect anybody can learn to dance until someone gets us on the dance floor," and offered me a hand.

I fell in love with her right then.

Turned out Annie Marie Macready didn't have to dance with a fella to teach him how. Instead she led me through every dance she knew at half speed or slower, making sure Andy followed along once he got himself a partner. I didn't hardly get a word in, 'cause she was concentrating so hard, but I didn't reckon I needed to. I was happy as could be, doing slow steps and admiring her teaching lessons. She was perfect as a picture in a lacy green dress with a straight neckline an' wrist-length white gloves, and it didn't matter to her that she was twelve inches shorter than me: I went where she led, so Andy could see how it was done. After a couple times around the floor, another girl tapped his partner's shoulder, and he got a couple inches taller for not looking like a fool. After a bit the floor filled up and we couldn't see 'em anymore, and Annie let me go even if I didn't much want to be. I spent the next couple hours tryin' ta catch sight of her again, and did: she never left the floor, always dancing with other fellas. I guessed I couldn't complain, 'cause I was dancing with other girls and she didn't even know my name, but I felt prickly over it anyway.

Least I did right up until she tapped the shoulder of the girl I was dancin' with, and cut in. Me and the girl were equal parts surprised, and she stepped outta the way looking like she only did it because it was the done thing. Annie stepped into my arms without missing a beat, and I grinned at her all the way around the floor.

"Private Garrison Matthew Muldoon out of Seattle," she said when the music stopped. "It's nice to meet you."

I felt like a fool, grinning so much, but she had the bluest eyes I'd ever seen and a smile that would stop traffic. "Miss Anne Marie Macready outta Monterey," I said back. "Nice to meet you too. What else did the guys tell you about me?"

"That you don't have a girl back home, and that you're all right."

"It's true I don't have a girl back home, but doll, I'm a whole lot better'n 'all right'."

Annie Macready laughed out loud, and I spent the rest of the night tryin' ta get her to do it again. Turned out it wasn't so hard. She liked to laugh, and wasn't afraid of people turning to look when she did. She only got solemn when she said somethin' about school, and I asked what she was studying. "Nursing. I'm going to be a nurse."

"Lotta long hours on your feet. Pretty girl like you could—"

"Get married straight off, instead of working? I know. I've been asked three times. Four if you count your friend Mick over there." She smiled real quick, showing off dimples, an' I made a fuss of standing up straight to look for Mick with a glower. We were off the dance floor by then, leaning in a corner and drinking fruit punch, and I gave up searching for Mick to lean again.

"So why'd you say no? I'm only asking so I know what not to do when the time comes." I kept a face straight enough to be kidding, but I thought maybe I wasn't.

Annie lifted an eyebrow high, like maybe she thought I wasn't, either, but she answered anyway. "One of them couldn't imagine a wife who went to college, much less had a job of her own. Another one liked the idea of an educated wife, but I think that was all he liked about me. I was pretty enough and smart enough. Nothing else mattered. So I didn't like him very much."

"Can't imagine why. What about the third?"

Annie looked away, soft blond curls blocking most of her expression. Then she looked up again, smiling, but her eyes were sad. "Well, I was only thirteen, and I'm sure he didn't mean it. He was my oldest brother's best friend, and he didn't come back from Europe."

"Oh, darlin'." I couldn't say why, but a pang shot through my chest. "I'm sorry. So he's why you're studying to be a nurse?"

"No." A quick shake of her head set those curls swaying again. "No, that's...my brother did come back. He'd been shot, but he was all right. And for two years he didn't say a word about the war, but he talked about his nurse. He worked, and he saved up, and he got on a boat and went back to Europe, and found her."

I put a hand over my heart. "An' they lived happily ever after?"

Somethin' wicked sparkled in Annie's eyes. "Well, no. She'd gotten married and had twin girls and another baby on the way, but that's a happy ending too. And George met another girl while he was over there, and they've gotten married since, so it was all okay. But it made me think about how a person can affect another, and how if I got married and settled right down, how I might not get the chance to be that important to someone. I'm sure I would be to my husband, of course, but it's not quite the same, is it."

"I don't reckon it is. You're a remarkable woman, Annie Macready."

"Oh, I'm Annie now, am I? Not Miss Macready, not even Anne? Annie?"

"'fraid so."

"Then I suppose you'll just have to be Gary, won't you?"

"'til the day I die, sweetheart. D'you mind? Me calling you Annie?"

She smiled again, crazy sweet smile that was gonna haunt my dreams. "Not at all. But I see Private Anderson over there stumbling over his feet with another young lady, so I think I'll go find your friend Mick and lead him through a dance or two so Private Anderson can learn them and look good."

"I'd be happy to let you lead an' teach Andy a thing or

two, darlin'."

"I couldn't have that. I wouldn't want everyone to start imagining I'm the stuck-up sort who lands a handsome soldier and then won't dance with anybody else."

"'zat mean you think I'm handsome, doll?"

She only laughed an' walked away, which coulda killed me. I watched her bring Mick out on the floor and between the two of 'em they showed Andy what to do and pretty quick he did look good again. I danced with a couple other girls whose names I forgot as soon as I heard 'em. Somewhere 'bout one in the morning I caught a glimpse of Annie getting her coat, and had one a'them moments where it seemed like my whole life was gonna hang on whether or not she was the kinda girl who liked a guy to play it cool. For a couple seconds I couldn't get my feet going right, or anywhere at all. Then I said, "Ta hell with that," loud enough to shock the girl I was dancing with, an' like a cad left her on the floor so I could chase after Annie.

I caught up with her a couple steps outside the door. She was wrapped up in a fuzzy-looking thing that was mostly collar and sleeves. I was in shirtsleeves, having run out the door without stopping at the coat check, afraid the time spent waiting there would lose me the girl for good. "Mind if I walk you home?"

She didn't even look up, much less look surprised. "Would you follow me anyway if I said I minded?"

I stopped, offended. "'course not."

"Then you can walk me home." Her heels kept clicking on the sidewalk as she looked back at me and shrugged. "A girl has to get some kind of idea of who wants to walk her home, Private Muldoon. Soldiers are usually polite, but I've already met a few who don't want to take no for an answer."

Under my breath, I muttered, "An' that's why somebody oughta be walking you home," then louder said, "Gimme a minute to get my coat?"

Her steps slowed an' I took that as a yes. Some doll at the coat check had seen me running out, and had my coat ready for me. I gave her my best grin and slung it on as I went back out the door to catch up with Annie Macready. She wasn't alone, not quite. There were other couples heading home, some driving, but a lot more walking like me and Annie. There were a few groups of girls all hanging together, which made good sense. The Eagles Club was close to a neighborhood, just far enough out that late dances wouldn't make the neighbors complain too much, but it backed up to a big wild park where anything could happen. Annie led us away from the park, into the heart of the neighborhood, and girls peeled off from their groups the deeper in we got. "'If it's anybody I know givin' you a hard time, I'll take care of 'em for you."

Her voice got syrup-sweet. "And what does that mean, Private Muldoon?"

"Means I liked it better when you were callin' me Gary," I muttered again, then, louder, said, "I donno. Talk to 'em an' knock some sense into 'em if that don't work?"

"At least you started with talking. I hate the idea of men getting into fights over me, even for the most noble of reasons."

"Thought girls liked that kinda thing."

"I suppose some of them do. They probably don't want to be nurses. Can you imagine the ignominy of having to patch up two or three of your suitors because they were fighting over you?"

"Darlin', I barely know what ignominy is, never mind having to feel it."

Annie Macready gave me a sideways look that turned into a laugh. "I don't think I believe you, Private Muldoon."

I grinned down the street. "Believe what you want, sweetheart. Not much I can do about it."

"You're a very confident man, aren't you, Private Muldoon?"

"Yeah, but I think I found a girl to give me a run for my money, Miss Macready."

Her nose wrinkled. "I like 'Annie' better."

"Then you gotta stop callin' me Private Muldoon. It makes me feel like I oughta be standin' up and saluting."

"Oh, all right. I was just teasing you anyway."

"Me too. I got a rise outta you faster, is all." I offered my arm and she wrinkled her nose again an' tucked her big fuzzy sleeve into the crook of my elbow. "How far we going?"

"In a hurry to get back?"

"Figuring how to make it last."

A giggle burst outta her. I raised an eyebrow an' she stared straight ahead, trying like the devil not to blush or laugh again. I got a grin that spread slow but wouldn't quit. "Why, Miss Macready, I think maybe you got a little bit of a dirty mind there. And you seem like such a straight-laced girl!"

Her cheeks turned bright pink and her grin was so tight I thought it might explode right off of her face if she let it go at all. "I have two older brothers and a father who are all soldiers, Mr. Muldoon," she said, prim as she could through fighting that smile. "Sometimes they say things a lady shouldn't hear."

"And then she'll keep askin' around until she finds out what they meant? Aw, c'mon, darlin', don't tell me girls don't whisper 'bout the same kindsa stuff we do," I said when she gave me a cautious look. "I got a sister too, you know."

"I didn't." She latched onto that, and I guessed I couldn't blame her. "Older or younger?"

"Older, 'bout four years older. Name's Irene. She used to give me advice about girls. Guess she still would, if I needed it."

"But you're a football hero," Annie said, which made me laugh.

"A couple seasons of college ball don't make me a hero, doll."

Her smile lit right up. "Don't spoil my fun. Football hero is how I'm telling the story, and surely a football hero doesn't need help with girls."

I grinned down the street. "You tell me."

"You're doing all right."

"Hmph. 'All right'. I'll take it, but next time I'm gonna do better."

"Next time?" Annie stopped at a driveway beneath a big

ol' leafless tree. "You expect there to be a next time? This is me."

"I sure hope so." I looked up the drive at a plain little cozy-looking house and shook my head. "Nah, sweetheart. It might be your ma, but it ain't you. Your house will be painted something bright, to match your soul."

Annie Macready said, "Oh my," and left me standing on the sidewalk and feeling like a fool.

CHAPTER NINE

I spent the whole next two days of leave trying not to fret. Me and Andy went out to see Monterey Bay, which was about the prettiest place I'd ever seen, with the calm blue water an' all sorts of little personality-filled towns around it. It was nothing like Seattle, but I guessed nowhere was ever like home. Andy seemed okay with that. I didn't know what he'd left behind in Alabama, just that he'd come out West before joining up, and I wondered just what all he'd left behind. It wasn't the kinda question a fella could ask. At any rate, we didn't have lots of time for talk anyway, 'cause I'd thought girls liked a football player, but that wasn't anything compared to being in uniform. But I kept thinking about Annie and forgetting to flirt, until Andy threw his hands up an' told me to go find the girl. I said I couldn't do that, and I thought he was gonna blow a gasket.

"I already know you're too damned dumb to have gotten her number, but you know where she lives, don't you?"

"Sure, but what kinda big puppy shows up on the doorstep without an invitation?"

"One who might get shipped out any day."

That shut me up and sent me heading across town without him, back to the street where Annie lived. A nice older lady who looked a lot like her was in the front yard, tending to a flower bed, when I walked up the street. She gave me a look up and down, then brushed her hands clean on her skirt an' got to her feet with a smile. "I guess you're Private Muldoon."

"I guess I am, ma'am. Are you Mrs. Macready?" I leaned across a low white fence an' offered my hand.

She took it with a soft grip. "I am. I'm afraid Anne's not home, though. It's Sunday afternoon. She had to head back to Oakland for school. She stays there during the week and comes home to visit on weekends."

I put my hands in my pockets an' rolled back on my heels to cast a look at Heaven, wishing Andy had kicked me into motion earlier. "That's just about the worst news I've had all week."

Mrs. Macready had dimples just like her daughter's, 'cept thirty years older. "Maybe hearing she spent all day Saturday talking about you will take the sting out. You made an impression, Private Muldoon. I might not have believed her when she said you were very handsome, but I'll have to apologize for that."

"Aw, nobody who's played as much ball as me can be all that good-looking, ma'am. Got my nose broke a couple times."

"It lends you character. Though from what Anne said you might have plenty of that already."

"Well, thanks." I caught up to what she was saying and my eyebrows went together. "'bout being handsome, I mean. I ain't sure about having so much character. Would you have a number I could call her at, Mrs. Macready? I shoulda asked her myself, but she kinda...got the upper hand somewhere along the way an' I never got it back."

Mrs. Macready took a slip of paper out of her pocket, handed it to me, and said, "You might as well get used to that, Private Muldoon. That's her number. She asked me to give it to you if you came by."

I opened the paper an' memorized the number there in a heartbeat, all the while trying not to look like a kid at Christmas. "Thank you, ma'am. And if you don't mind me sayin' so, I hope to see you again soon."

"I hope so too, Private Muldoon. My oldest boy is living in Europe now, and the younger one got married to a girl from New Jersey." She shook her head like she didn't know how that had happened. "It would be nice to see another man around the house."

"If it ain't intruding...there's no Mr. Macready?"

"Oh, there is." She said it kinda airy and light with a steel belt running below, an' I thought maybe Annie's apple didn't fall far from the tree. I also thought I knew when to not ask any more questions, nodded like I understood, an' kept my damned mouth shut, even when a cold touch ran up the back of my neck. Something seemed wrong about her answer, but I couldn't put my finger on it. Anyway, Mrs.

Macready got a crinkly-eyed look like I'd done good, and brushed her hands on her skirt again. "Care to come in for a glass of lemonade, Private Muldoon?"

I was done being a fool. "I'd love to, ma'am."

The inside of the Macready house wasn't as plain as the outside. Tidy rooms and regular furniture, but the pictures on the walls were something else. I stopped to look at one, a painted waterfall with gold mist risin' up in the shape of some kinda bird, and smiled. "Looks like magic. Somewhere you've been?"

"I'm not certain I'd want to visit somewhere that birds were made of mist and born out of waterfalls. My husband did that painting, and all the others. He's very artistic. The children inherited my pragmatic streak." She guided me into the kitchen without giving me much chance to see the other paintings, except the one that was on the wall in there. Like the waterfall, it was misty, but this one was all silvers an' greys muting far-off greenery. There were horse riders heading away from the viewer, deeper into the painting. I got no sense of urgency from 'em. They seemed content somehow, even though I couldn't see any of their faces. The fella leading 'em was on a big grey stallion, and a slender kid rode a yellow mare beside him. Most of the others were indistinct, but I could just about see the dents their horses' hooves left in the shining soft misty path.

An icy shiver ran right down my spine, like somebody'd walked over my grave, and a whisper came up at the back of my mind: *that ain't right*, it said. *I knew Annie's Pop. Nice fella, but nothing artsy about him. No way he did these paintings. Something ain't right here.* I shivered harder and shook my head, chasing the thought away.

Mrs. Macready glanced at the painting and shook her head. "It does that to everyone, but somehow it's my favorite. That's why it's in the kitchen, where I can see it. I've always thought it seemed like a path to Heaven, somehow. He calls it "The Road Home"."

"Sure is leadin' to another place. Peaceful, though, not like..." I stopped talking before I started suggesting her husband was painting pictures of Hell, an' said, "I like it too," instead. Mrs. Macready poured me some lemonade and we stood together studying the painting her husband had done. More I looked the more I saw, hints of more folks in the misty shadows, until it started to seem like I was riding with the hunters myself. After a while I gave myself another shake and stepped back. "Draws you in, doesn't it?"

"It does. Anne's favorite is one of ravens, but it's in her bedroom, so I won't show it to you. The boys have taken their favorites with them, of course. Do you do anything artistic, Private Muldoon?"

"Play the saxophone a bit," I admitted. "That's about it."

Mrs. Macready said, "Anne likes music," like it was asking about my prospects.

I started lining 'em up in my mind, then quit when they seemed kinda bleak. The idea of dying in Korea wasn't much more than somebody else's nightmare, but any soldier signing up for service had to know someplace inside of him that he might not get out of it alive. That wasn't somethin'

I wanted to think about, standin' next to Annie Macready's mother in their pretty kitchen. "Yeah? Guess I gotta try playing her a song or two, then. Maybe you'll tell me what kinda flowers she likes, too."

"Daisies. I tell her they're a weed, but she says no, Mom, they're resilient. They grow where nothing else wants to. She's always thought that way. I expect it's part of what's driving her toward being a nurse. I worked during the war," Mrs. Macready said thoughtfully. "I was happy to come home again, but I think it gave Anne ideas."

"My Ma worked, too, but she wasn't so happy to come home again. Guess it takes all types. Guess it gave me some ideas too, maybe."

She lifted an eyebrow, inviting me to keep talking. "Well, it's like this, ma'am. I'm in the military for the next four years, and I'm planning to finish college after that, on the GI bill. Way I see it, that's six years a girl's either gotta wait for me or move on. I sure like the idea of a girl who's got enough of her own things going on that she could wait an' move on at the same time."

"And had you thought all of that out before you met Anne?"

"No, ma'am, but she's sure got me thinking now. A guy's gotta have somethin' to pin his hopes on."

She smiled an' gave me a look that I thought prob'ly said *Kids. Always in a hurry*, but I couldn't argue 'bout it, either. It felt important to be chasing after Annie right now, like I might never get the chance again, an' that my whole life might turn out different if I didn't. So I thanked Mrs.

Macready for the lemonade an' bowed out, sayin, "Reckon I got a phone call to make, and some daisies to send."

"I hope to see you again, Private Muldoon. It's been a pleasure." She walked me to the door, waved me down the drive, an' I went back to the barracks to spend every last dime I'd made that week buying daisies.

Annie was wearing one in her hair when I saw her again on Saturday, an' every time I saw her again for the next four months. At dances, at movies, for walks in the park, an' if she wasn't wearing one I found one for her. I reckon she talked more than I did during those walks, telling me about school and what she was learning, while all I had to talk about was guns and drills and being bored outta my head. Bored was all right, though, 'cause bored meant I was still in Monterey and not shipping out to Korea. 'sides, corny as it sounded, I couldn't be that bored counting the hours 'til I saw her again.

We knew it was coming before they announced it, 'cause we saw the next leave window was five days long. Long enough for all the boys to head home an' say their goodbyes and then get themselves back the post. Knowing it was coming didn't make it a damned bit easier, and neither did Annie looking more beautiful than ever at the dance that night. There were names for alla the bits and pieces of her style, but I didn't know 'em. I just knew she was beautiful, an' I was the luckiest guy in the world.

Lotta other guys thought so too, one after another of 'em cutting in to ask her to dance. I mostly stood back and watched, a glass of punch in one hand and the other in my pocket, feeling the velvet box there while I watched my girl dance. She made 'em all look good, an' she smiled at me every time they turned her my way. Not much else to ask for, not as far as I was concerned.

The band finally took a break and Annie came back to me, pinks cheek from dancing so much. "I thought boys didn't like seeing their girls dance with other men, but you're over here smiling like you've got all day," she said.

I looked at some of the other guys sulking around the edges of the dance floor and scowling when their girls came back, and laughed right out loud. "Darlin', if they've got that much to worry about, I guess I wouldn't like it either, in their shoes." I winked, then cast a big look toward the dance hall clock an' came in closer to say, "Is your ma waiting up for you to come home at the stroke of midnight?"

Annie's chin came up just like I knew it would, half-pretending and half meaning it when she sounded offended. "I'm nineteen years old, Private Muldoon, and in college. I can go home when I want."

"Yeah." I kept grinning at her. "I just like seeing you get all huffy. C'mon, sweetheart." I took her hand and pulled her outta there, ducking between other couples and hurrying for the door. We were back at the Eagles Hall where we'd first met, just far enough out of the local neighborhood to let the party run late. Summer was fading out an' the woods smelled dry and dusty. Annie shivered and I pulled my coat off to put it around her shoulders. She looked like a doll in it, dressed in clothes too big for her.

"I'm lost in here!" She sounded happy, and slipped her hands through the arms, rucking 'em up until I found her fingers again.

"That's whatcha get for leaving your coat inside. Mind you, I left mine inside the first night I metcha, and you didn't lend me *your* coat."

Annie laughed. "If I'd thought you'd wear it, I might have. You'd have looked...quite astonishing, I'm sure."

"It woulda been a good color on me," I said, solemn as I could. Annie flashed another smile and tucked my coat under her to sit when we found a bench looking back at the Eagles Club. I stayed on my feet, nervous all of a sudden, an' she looked up at me with a frown starting between her eyebrows. I said, "They're sending me to Korea," fast as I could, before she could ask.

Her breath caught and she knotted her hands together, hiding 'em in the sleeves of my jacket. She looked down at 'em, biting her lip, then looked back at me. "When?"

"Saturday." Somethin' was wrong with my throat. I cleared it an' said, "We leave Saturday," again. "You gonna wait for me, doll?"

Annie Macready stood up and shook my coat sleeves back so she could stand arms akimbo and give me a look that shoulda taken my skin off. Didn't, though, 'cause there was a lotta sweetness behind it, like she was tryin' to be fierce and only partway making it. "What do you think I've been doing the last four months, Garrison Muldoon?"

Swear ta God, my knees buckled. Couldn't let myself fall down, 'cause that woulda been embarrassing, but I got a couple inches shorter for a second there and Annie's lips twitched, tryin' ta hide a smile. I said, "You're laughing at me, doll," and she said, "Yes," without a bit of apology.

"Well, all right, I guess that puts a fella in his place when he's..." My heart was slamming like a jackhammer, and I was getting dizzy with nerves. "Look, sweetheart, it ain't much, but I wanted to..." I swallowed again, wonderin' why it was so hard to get through a simple question. I muttered, "Ah, hell," and fished in my slacks pocket for that box, and held it up.

Annie's hands went to her stomach an' I thought she'd stopped breathing. All of a sudden I figured I'd better do this right, an' got down on one knee, scared as a kid sneaking into a haunted house. Annie watched me with eyes big as saucers, and she wasn't breathing, so I hurried it up, stumbling over my own words. "Well, it ain't much, but I'll getcha something better before we—I mean, *will* you, Annie? Will you marry me, sweetheart?"

The box just about flew outta my fingers when I tried opening it. Annie caught it, her hands tiny and delicate next to mine, and I turned red from the collar up. She straightened the box in my palm and put her hands over it, smiling right at me and not looking at the box at all. "Of course I will. Of course I'll marry you, Gary. I love you."

All the breath rushed outta me. Funny how thinking a girl's gonna say yes and waiting for it to happen are two separate things. "I love you too, sweetheart. Right from the first moment I saw you."

Annie tipped forward to kiss me, murmuring, "You're a

romantic," against my mouth. "Now get up before you stain the knee of your trousers."

I got up, sorta offended and mostly grinning. "Some romantic you are. Doncha wanna see the ring?"

Her dimples showed up again. "Of course I do, but I'm marrying you, not a ring." She opened it then, though, while I was back to mumbling, "It ain't much, but I wanted to have somethin', and I'll getcha somethin' better—"

"Gary." Her voice was funny an' tight. "Gary, it's perfect. It's beautiful. I forbid you to get me a different one. Put it on me?" She wasn't so graceful, either, takin' the ring outta the box, so I felt better fumbling it onto her hand with thick cold fingers. We both stood there looking at it a moment when it was on, a pretty little gold thing with pearls on either side of a chip of diamond. Annie had long fingers for somebody her size, and sensible nails that wouldn't get in the way of working, an' she was right. The ring looked perfect. I tucked my fingers under hers and brought her knuckles up to my mouth for a kiss. She laughed and threw her arms around me, the long sleeves of my coat smacking my shoulders. I picked her up and spun her around, feeling like some kinda movie star, an' put her on her feet again to give her a kiss.

"Wish I could marry you right now, doll."

"You could," she said impulsively. "Or tomorrow, at least."

"Nah." I brushed my thumb over her jaw and shook my head. "No, sweetheart, I wanna do it right. I don't wanna be in a rush. And I don't wanna—"

"Don't." She put her fingers over my mouth. "Don't even say that, Gary."

"I didn't say nothing!" But I'd been gonna, and we both knew it. I'd been gonna say I didn't want to risk leaving her a widow. I didn't want to risk leaving her with a baby and no Pop for it. I didn't wanna risk leaving her with a baby and me not being there when it was born, for that matter. But she didn't want me to say it, maybe afraid I'd jinx something if I did, so I just took her hand away and kissed it again. "And I won't say nothing," I promised. "You write to me, though, all right, sweetheart? Everything about your day, so I know what I'm comin' home to. Swear to God I'll never get bored of it. It's gonna be my lifeline."

"Are you afraid?"

That wasn't the kinda question a guy should answer truthfully, I bet. They'd been teaching us to fight, an' teaching us not to think, but anybody with two brain cells to rub together knew war wasn't safe. So it took me a minute to answer, standing out there in a park with a warm spring breeze playing with Annie's hair and making everything seem all right with the world. "Not afraid. Kinda...apprehensive, I guess. I wish there as another way, but if there was—well, I wouldn't have met you, if there was, so it ain't worth thinking about. It's gonna be fine, Annie. It's all gonna turn out all right. I'm gonna come home to you."

Her eyes were brighter than I liked to see them. "You sound so certain."

"I am. I got a feeling." I guessed maybe a lot of soldiers had that feeling at the back of their minds, saying they were coming home safe, or they might end up deserters. But mine was the one I'd heard before, telling me something was right or wrong, like Annie's Pop being an artist, even if I didn't know why it was wrong that he was. I trusted it, either way, an' brushed tears off Annie's cheeks before kissing her again. "I got a feeling," I promised. "It's gonna be okay. You wanna head back? Warm up?" I smiled. "Show off that ring?"

"Oh!" Tears or not, her smile came back. "You don't mind?"

"Mind? *Mind?* Lady, what kinda guy *minds* if the most beautiful girl he's ever met wants to tell everybody she's marrying him? A'course I don't mind! C'mon, doll." I tucked her up against my side. "Let's go tell the world."

And my father. That wasn't what she said next, but in the scheme of things, that's what seemed most important. The friends, the congratulations, Andy wanting ta know if I needed a best man already, alla that was expected. Mrs. Macready looking happy and sad all at once, I figured on that too. But excepting the paintings, there'd been no sign of Annie's pop, and he'd kinda slid from my mind. I woulda asked the old man for Annie's hand in marriage before popping the question, if I'd known he was around at all to ask, but when I said that to Annie she shook her head and said it didn't matter.

The day before I left, I found out why.

Annie didn't say much on the long drive into countryside alternating between barren rock and crop fields. I tried to start up conversations a couple of times and got the message after that. Just when I was starting to think she was gonna kill me and dump the body, and about to ask if I oughta be worried, she turned down a paved road in the middle of nowhere, and idled the car while we waited for a big set of iron gates to open up. Two words were sculpted across the gates: BELLREEVE INSTITUTION.

Hospitals were one thing. Institutions meant somethin' else entirely. I said, "Annie," real quiet, and she shook her head and wouldn't talk 'til we were parked in front of the main building. A new building, big and clean-looking, with pillars like some kinda plantation estate moved a couple thousand miles west. Grass was cut short for acres all around, with stands of trees left in place to make shade for a few folks who were out in the spring sunshine. They looked okay, for crazy people. Wearing slippers or goin' barefoot, but they were dressed in regular clothes and nobody was screamin' or tryin' ta kill anybody like they always were in books about insane asylums.

Annie put her hands on the steering wheel, looking straight ahead as she talked. "I was almost hit by a car when I was seventeen. Our car had broken down and I was walking back to town to get help, and I'd left Dad with the car. He limps. A war injury. So it was easier and faster for me to go."

I said, "Don't matter why," quiet as I could, but she wasn't much listening to me just then. Mostly she was tellin' a story that I thought ate her up inside, maybe one she was afraid I was gonna judge her for. One she was afraid was a deal-breaker for me, 'cause a crazy parent might mean she'd go nuts someday too. I wasn't gonna reassure her yet, not until she could hear me, which I reckoned might take a couple decades. I had the time.

"I was about half a mile from Dad when the car came out of nowhere. I didn't hear it coming, and I still don't know how it missed me. Something knocked me aside, and Dad..." She took a deep breath. "Dad swore he'd seen a man on a silver horse come down from the sky and tackle me."

I twitched and sat up straighter, feeling like somebody'd rung a bell nearby. Annie's jaw got tight. "After that he began to...have visions. About the man on the silver horse, and a lot of other things. He started painting them, and started telling stories about the paintings." Tears rolled down her cheeks, but she wouldn't let go of the wheel, much less look at me. "They got more and more awful, his stories. Stories about magic things happening. About demons and devils and...and sometimes about heroes, but the heroes lost a lot. And then after a while he started..."

She wiped her eyes and choked the steering wheel again. "After a while he started thinking I was important in all those stories. That the silver man had protected me because of that. And he wouldn't...let me out of the house, not even to go to school. He was trying to protect me, he said, but he started getting...violent, and it...it just got worse and worse, Gary, until finally we didn't have any choice. We're lucky," she said with all kindsa desperation in her voice. "We're lucky, because the institutions aren't like they were even just a few years ago. They treat him well. He's not dangerous as long as he thinks I'm safe, so we tell him...well, we don't tell him anything. We tell him I stay home except for when I come to visit him, and he paints, and...I should have told you. I should have told you before, but I was so afraid you'd—" She buried her face in her hands, and I finally took that as a chance to say something.

Or to pull her up against me an' hold on, which seemed smarter. I kissed her hair and let her cry while all sorts of crazy thoughts swam around my head. Same ol' voice saying *this ain't right,* while the resta me wondered what the hell it mattered if it was right or wrong. Wasn't like I could change what was, and when I thought that, the voice said *hell, what if* I'm *remembering it wrong?* and got quiet again.

Any other time and I mighta mentioned it all to Annie, mighta said I thought *I* was going crazy, but sitting in front of a nuthouse that her dad was inside didn't seem like a good time to make jokes. Instead I said, "Don't change nothin', sweetheart," against Annie's hair. "Don't mean I love you any less, and it don't mean I'm worried about our future, all right? I've seen his paintings. Your old man's an artist, and everybody knows artists are crazy. It ain't a bad thing. S'all that I'm gonna see in this, okay?"

Annie laughed, except it sounded more like a wet snort. I couldn't help laughing too, an' she laughed again in embarrassment, 'til I was belly laughin' and she was snorting like a hog in mud. Tears ran down both our faces and we leaned on each other until laughs turned to giggles and finally into wheezing sighs. I kissed her hair again and said, "Better now?", and she sat up to look at herself in the rear-view mirror.

"All except my makeup." She touched under her eyes, tryin' to wipe away mascara smears, then took a tissue from her purse and got herself tidied up again. As she folded it away, she said, "I love my dad, Gary. I wish he wasn't in here, that this hadn't happened to him, and I know it's uncomfortable, but...be nice? Please?"

"He's your father, doll. He's always gonna have my respect." We got outta the car and she took my hand, leading me into the institute. It smelled too clean and the halls echoed, but the doctors and nurses smiled hello, and called Annie by name as we went upstairs to an art studio. I hung at the door a minute, surprised to be watching half a dozen people painting and drawing. "This ain't at all like what I thought it'd be."

"It's one of the newest institutes in the country. There were reform laws passed a few years ago." Annie glanced at me to see if I knew what she was talking about, and I kinda shrugged. I remembered seeing somethin' about it in the papers and hearing it on the radios, but it hadn't affected me, so it hadn't made much impression. "They used to be very bad," Annie said. "A lot of them are still bad, but this one—a wealthy man's wife was the first patient here. He had it built for her, so she could get the best care in the country. We were lucky to live so close, so Dad could come here instead of one of the other places. That's him," she said with a nod toward an older fella with hair blonder than Annie's. He was sitting with his back to us, facing a window, but the painting he worked on didn't have anything to do with the view. All I could tell was it was a woman with dark hair, but she seemed familiar somehow.

"Will he mind if we interrupt him?"

Annie shook her head. "He paints things from his visions, not from the world, so the light never changes and the images never go away. It's fine." She tugged me forward, saying, "Hi, Dad," when we were a few feet way.

Tim Macready turned to look at his daughter, a smile already in place. But then he looked past her at me, an' the smile fell away into slack-jawed relief. He sank in on himself, hands going over his face, and dropped his forehead all the way toward his knees. The painting behind him was a green-eyed girl in her twenties, wearing her black hair so short it looked almost like my own military cut. I'd never seen a girl with hair like that, nor wearing the kinda outfit she had on: a white tank top short enough to expose her belly, jeans real low on her hips, and combat boots like my own. She had a kinda beaky nose, and a skinny scar on one cheek, and a buncha jewelry that didn't match each other: something like gold earrings, but on the back curve of her ear, not the lobe, a silver choker necklace, an' a chunky copper bracelet on her left wrist. Even weirder, she had a little purple bracer shield on one arm, and a glowin' blue sword in the other hand.

I didn't know what ta make of the painting, except looking at it was like a shot through the heart, just like seeing Annie for the first time. I stood there going hot and cold, and Tim Macready said into his hands, "It's you. Thank God it's you. You'll take care of her now."

CHAPTER TEN

Two months after I got to Korea, Annie wrote to say her dad was coming home. He'd quit painting that day, never even finishing the one he'd been working on, and the visions that had haunted him faded away. After a month, her letter said, the doctors had started being cautiously optimistic he'd recovered, and after two, they thought he was safe to go home. She'd explained to him about her being in school, and he was all right with it,

> which is so strange, after so long, that it's hard to explain, Gary. For the past three years he's been so adamant that I do nothing to risk myself, and now to have him coming home, knowing that I'm only home for the summer...my mother is worried, but trying not to show it. I only hope he'll be well enough for me to go back to Oakland in the autumn.
>
> Well, no, it's not the only thing I hope. I hope you'll come home to me soon, too, so we can be a family.

I love you.

Letters like that could keep a guy going a long time, and I got a stack of 'em every time there was a mail call. Resta the guys gave me grief, but it was envy, not meanness, that drove 'em. I took it without complaint, knowing too many of 'em didn't have anybody writing them at all.

Korea wasn't what I expected, truth be told. I couldn't have said what I *had* expected, but I guessed I had this kinda blank slate in my head for it to fill in. Except it was really blank, sorta nothing more than sand and sky, so coming halfway around the world to find out the same kinds of wildflowers grew in Korea as in my back yard in Washington kinda threw me. They spent a lotta time in Basic telling us about the enemy not being like us, but the folks I saw looked tired and afraid, and that was how me and my buddies felt a lot of the time. 'course, my commander woulda said I was looking at the South Koreans, our allies, but the only reason I could tell Northerners from Southerners was which end of the gun they were on.

One of the guys had it worse, though. He was an America-born Korean called Danny. Danny Kim, our ghost-man. He went in and out behind the lines like nobody's business, disappearing for days and weeks and coming back with intel. Mosta the time when he showed back up he tried to slip into camp quiet-like, so he could shower and get into uniform before anybody laid eyes on him. We knew what he did anyway, 'cause he wore his hair longer than reg so he could blend better with the locals. Still, it was one thing knowing and another thing seeing him come in, dusty and broody, wearin' local-style loose pants and t-shaped shirts or torn-off jeans and bare feet. I caught him coming in one night when I was on perimeter duty. I was staring out at the dark, listening to the sound of a crying baby needing help, when he came outta the trees and said, "It's not real."

For an ugly minute him and me were on opposite sides of the war, and I was the only one with a gun. The baby's crying got louder, and something wrong came through it, a kinda nails-on-chalkboard sound for real, not figuratively. "It's not real," Danny said again. "Don't go out there, Muldoon. You won't come back."

"Shit, man, I don't know if *you're* real." I waved him by, and stood my ground. After a little while the screaming faded, and I went out at dawn to have a look around. There wasn't a baby, and there wasn't any kinda sign there'd ever been one. I went back to camp feeling uncomfortable. At breakfast Danny showed up in the mess hall looking crisp as any soldier, and sat down next to me. "Thanks for not shooting me."

"Thanks for not letting me go out there. What was that screaming?"

"A demon," he said so easy I almost believed him. "It's been suckering guys in some of the other platoons, and they're going home in body bags, so don't listen to it. Not ever."

"Right." I stared at him a minute, then shuddered. "What's it like out there, all alone?"

Danny said, "Hell," reflexively, an' we both laughed. He said, "Confusing," under the laughter, though, and I wasn't surprised to hear it. It couldn't be easy spin' on your parents' people, but it wasn't something to talk about in a mess hall with a buncha officers nearby, either. So he said, "Where are you from, Muldoon?" instead, and we got to talking about the west coast and places we'd like to visit. "Assuming we make it out of here," he said, and I shrugged it off.

"You gotta assume that, Danny. All of us are gonna make it out except," and I raised my voice, "except you, Dandy, right? You're gonna end up married to three Korean wives and never go back to Milwaukee."

There was two Andies in the unit, my old pal Alabama Andy, and the newcomer Dandy Andy, who was maybe the best-looking guy I'd ever seen. Even Annie'd paused when she'd seen him the first time, and only smiled when I asked her about it, so I knew he was good-looking. He was like some kinda Viking with yellow hair and good shoulders, and a face that coulda starred in the movies. Instead he'd worked his way into and outta a lot of hearts back home, and seemed to be doing the same thing here. I guessed handsome was handsome, whether a girl was American or Korean. He said, "Three?" deadpan. "I was hoping for five or six, but I should leave some for the rest of you, huh?"

"Not for Muldoon," Alabama Andy said. "He's got Annie waiting for him." A bunch of good-natured bickering went up, but Danny leaned over toward Dandy and said, "Be careful out there. My mother and father used to tell me stories about the Korean demons who wouldn't approve of your easy way with the girls. You don't want to make them angry."

Dandy Andy grinned wide. "Yeah? How do I know if I've got one's attention?"

"You just keep an eye out for a woman so beautiful even you don't think you stand a chance, and stay away from her."

Dandy kicked back, arms folded behind his head and leaning on a wall that wasn't there. "Now that's a problem, see, 'cause there's no such thing as a girl too pretty for me."

I said, "You oughta listen to him, Dandy," without knowing quite why I said it, except that voice at the back of my head wanted to warn him, and sounded sad about it. But he didn't hear me, 'cause somebody else was saying, "Hey, you're a poet and don't know it," and another guy was finishing it up with "His feet do, they're Longfellows."

Then we got called up to fight, and for a few weeks there wasn't any joking except the gallows humor that kept us sane. Danny was with us that whole stretch, always muttering warnings that nobody took seriously 'til another one of the guys, Reckless Rick, got himself drowned when there was no water for miles from where we were. Then Dandy found the one pretty girl on the war front, and came back to the camp to die the next morning. Me and Danny stood over his body awhile, counting the bite marks, all small and perfectly round, like vampire leeches had fastened onto him. I counted more than a hundred, and finally said, "What did that to him?" to Danny.

He shrugged and said somethin' in Korean, a word I couldn't say back. "An avenger of women wronged. Like a banshee, except they suck a guy dry like a vampire. They lure men in by offering to suck, um." He trailed off, looking uncomfortable. "You probably don't want to look at his Johnson, if you know what I mean."

I hadn't wanted to in the first place, but Danny walked away an' curiosity just about killed this cat. I took a look down Dandy Andy's shorts.

Danny was right. I hadn't wanted to. Pale an' sick, I staggered off to throw up, and every damned one of us in the unit listened hard to Danny's warnings after that. I wrote letters to Annie where I told her about the strange things in the night, an' then I tore 'em up and wrote new ones not mentioning it. I hated to think she might be doing the same thing at home, picking and choosing what to tell me so I wouldn't worry, but she'd had enough heartbreak with her daddy in the institution. I didn't want to add to it.

It musta been around Christmas when Danny came out from behind the lines again and shook me awake one night. Didn't say a word, just knelt there with a hand over my mouth and a finger to his lips, waiting for my eyes to get less round and my heart to stop pounding so hard before he let me go and put his mouth next to my ear. "I need help, Muldoon. There's something out there I can't handle and you were the first one to believe me about the demons, so I've got to ask your help."

The sky was ink black beyond his head, a sliver of moon over on the horizon but not a single star shining through, though the cold said it had ta be clear. "This something I'm gonna get kicked outta the Army for?"

He sat up far enough ta flash me a grin. "Only if you get caught AWOL. No, I can cover for you. Come on. No guns. Too loud."

I rolled outta my blankets and onto my feet, leavin' the duty weapon behind and collecting a couple knives instead. My pack was only inches away, so I grabbed it too, figuring we'd get some use out of the rations if we were gonna be up all night. Danny slipped through the other sleeping soldiers like they weren't even there, an' I tried not to kick anybody hard enough to wake 'em up as I followed him.

There wasn't much distance between camp and cold raw wilderness. I looked up again, tryin' to orient myself by the stars, but I still couldn't see 'em. Once we were well outta camp I stopped to take a better look, then exhaled a steamy breath into cold air. "Danny, where're the stars?"

"That's what I need you for."

"To bring the stars back?"

"To kill the demon that's hiding them."

"Dan, there ain't—there ain't no such thing as demons." I stuttered halfway through 'cause I was thinkin' of Dandy Andy and all of a sudden wasn't so sure of myself. "What kinda demon?"

"It's called—" He looked at me and sighed. "Never mind, you couldn't say it anyway. A sky demon. It wants to eat the stars, and it starts by trying to make people forget them. It hides them under a blanket of its hair. Once they're hidden, once people begin to forget, the smallest stars become vulnerable, and—"

"Stars are giant gas balls in the sky, Dan. You can't eat 'em."

"Yeah? Can you not hide them in a clear night sky,

either?"

I said a word my Ma didn't think I should know and rubbed my eyes, hoping I'd see stars again when I was done. But I knew I wouldn't, and I was right. "Sure, buddy. How do we kill a sky demon that eats stars?"

"Cut off its head so the stars can fly back out."

"I shoulda guessed."

Dan looked surprised and I muttered, "I was joking, Danny. That was a joke. All right, how do we find this thing?"

He switched on a flashlight. "Like this."

Seemed like the whole world lit up, compared to the darkness of a starless night. I reared back, squinting. "Damn, that's bright."

"It has to be to make it think it's a star to eat."

I s'posed he had a point. We huddled together, back to back, waiting in the cold night air. When I got tired of counting the breaths I could see, I said, "Why me?"

"Because you didn't go out after the crying demon, and because you listened when I told Dandy Andy to watch himself. And your eyes are grey."

"What's that gotta do with it?"

"Silver eyes see ghosts."

"Oh, yeah, sure, a'course. Forgot about that. What the hell, Danny."

I felt him shrug. "It's what my mother used to say. I don't know if it's a Korean superstition or if it was just her own because her grandfather had silver eyes. But it can't hurt to have silver eyes along with me on this."

"There can't be a lotta folks in Korea with grey eyes."

"There aren't. Now shut up. The demon is attracted to light, not noise."

I shut up, then swung my pack around to dig out some rations, and pulled them and a flashlight out of the bag. "Hungry? Hell, I got a flashlight in here too. Should I turn it on?"

"Starving," Danny hissed, "but look. Slowly."

Just like that, I wasn't hungry anymore. My skin got cold, not from nerves and not from the air being freezing, but more like a warning of something creepy going on. I peered over Danny's shoulder.

For a second I thought hell, if that was a demon, I was all right with letting her do what she wanted. She was maybe five feet tall and Korean, 'cept her skin was white as starlight. Her lips were blood red and her eyes were black as raven wings. Her hair was amazing, black as her eyes and dancing with a life of its own, rising up toward the sky until I couldn't see what was hair and what was sky. Hiding the stars in a blanket of hair, Danny'd said, an' I didn't know how she was doing it but that's what was going on. She was wearing a midnight blue high-collared robe with sleeves so long they trailed on the ground without leaving any kind of marks. It was wrapped around her torso by black ribbon that sparkled with starlight. In that first moment of looking at her, she was the most perfectly beautiful thing I'd ever seen, like some kinda living sculpture.

'least she was until she focused on the flashlight, and her mouth opened wide enough to be bigger than her face an' to show off a bottomless pit of stars an' gleaming razor teeth. Danny yelled and threw the flashlight to one side. The demon rushed it, swallowed it down, an' just as fast spat it out again. It hit the ground with another thud, an' back-lit the demon as she spun toward us with rage pulling her already-stretched features even further outta place.

Way at the back of my mind, that voice I was getting kinda used to said *I don't remember this*. That was it, nothing more, and hell if I knew how it was supposed to remember what I was only just now doing, but I had my pick of worrying about that or worrying about the black-eyed beauty who was gonna gobble us up along with the stars. I decided on her, an' the voice got quiet again.

The demon dropped to all fours and bounded at us like some kinda big cat, clawing up the ground. Danny an' I scattered, both of us grabbin' for the knives we shoulda had out and waiting. I switched my flashlight on and she swung toward me, which was kinda what I expected if I'd been thinking it through, but not much what I wanted once I did think it through. I hit the deck and flung the light away. She leaped over me and jumped on it, but she wasn't fooled enough to try eating it this time. Still, I had time to get the knife out and roll to my feet before she turned back on me.

She pounced and Danny tackled her just before she hit me. His knife cut into her ribs, slicing the ribbon apart, an' when he pulled it away, she bled starlight. Thick shining waves of it, and drops that hung in the air instead of falling like normal blood would. She screamed a staticky sound, not like a woman's scream at all. It hissed and rushed an' made the hairs on my arms stand on end, and it did something worse to Danny, who was even closer. He looked like he was coming apart, like the sound was melting him from the outside in. I snatched up my flashlight as I ran at them, and shoved the thing down her gullet when I reached her. She hacked and spat it back up, but at least the screamin' stopped and Danny stopped looking like he was melting.

The demon skittered back. She looked less human and a lot less gorgeous, her hair tangled up and the starlight still bleedin' from her side. It was the mouth, though, that really made her a monster, 'cause it was hanging open to show all of the ugly teeth and the guts that were made up of magic instead of humanity. Danny scrambled up an' all three of us started circling each other, me and Danny working two against one.

I guessed she chose Danny 'cause he was the littler guy. I guessed she figured if she could get rid of him she could focus on me. I saw her planning it before she moved, some kinda little give-away in the way she was leaning played up by the flashlights. She went after him, but I was on her heels, not losing any time to surprise. She landed on Dan with all fours, an' I grabbed a handful of black hair that was cold as ice, hauled her head back, and slashed her throat.

Starlight exploded out, splashing toward the sky. I got knocked off my feet an' lay there watching as her hair drifted outta the sky and a million stars she'd eaten went back to their rightful places. When it finally ended, I sat up an' found out I was covered in strands of hair, 'cept they'd gone silver and brittle. They broke into snowflakes when I brushed 'em off. Danny did the same, and we got up with somethin' like snow angels on the ground behind us.

Him and me, we didn't say a word going back to camp. Didn't say a word about it later, either, and after a few years I even started wondering if Danny had been there at all, or if it'd just been me and the starlight demon alone in the Korean night.

CHAPTER ELEVEN

Three times in four years wasn't enough to see your girl in. I kept thinking how much worse it was for the fellas who had wives and kids, kids who maybe didn't know them at all, and counted myself lucky even when I was counting down the days. Annie came to meet the ship when I came home from Korea, and did it sneaky, too: I didn't know she was coming until I saw her on the docks, one of a hundred pretty girls waiting for their men to come home.

I stopped stock still an' stared a while before she'd even seen me, just looking at the way her blond hair had gotten longer an' her blue eyes were still the same. Fashions had changed too, and I guessed I knew that, but it was different seeing her in a fitted skirt an' suit jacket insteada the full skirts an' blousy tops she'd been wearing when I left. She looked grown-up an' professional, an' my heart knocked around inside of me like it was tryin' ta get out. I hadn't been nervous about coming home, not 'til I saw her, but I couldn't get my feet moving now that I had.

She finally saw me and her smile lit up bright as day at the same time she put her hand over her stomach in the same nervous way she had when I'd asked her to marry me. That made me feel enough better that I got my feet unstuck, and met her halfway when she came running. All around us guys were scooping up their girls and spinning 'em around like they couldn't contain themselves, and neither could I. Annie shrieked into my shoulder and kicked her feet, both of us laughing when I staggered to a stop and put her down again without quite letting go. "You didn't say you were coming, darlin'."

"I wanted to surprise you. A good surprise? Oh, Gary, look at you. I thought you were handsome before, but you're all grown up now. I hardly recognized you."

"You and me both, sweetheart. Nurse Annie." I grinned 'til I was fit to pop. "Congratulations, darlin'. Wish I'd been at your graduation, but at least I'll get to see you in one of those saucy little hats."

Annie laughed an' ducked her face against my chest, hiding a blush. I put my arm around her shoulders, holding her close and lowering my head to breathe in the scent of her hair. "Your letters always smelled like you. Like daisies. Didn't even know they had enough scent to linger, doll."

"I had to look a long time to find a perfume that smelled like them. I like it better than the more cultivated flower scents."

"Guess that's why you like me, too."

She rocked back so she could smile up at me. "You can't

fool me. You're hiding cultivation under a rough exterior. I remember some of the poetry you've quoted me."

"Aw, shucks, sweetheart, everybody's gotta pass English Lit if they wanna stay on the football team. 'sides," I said, solemn as I could, "what kinda guy can't call his girl the star to his wandering bark an' still call himself worth stepping out with?"

"Most of them," Annie said dryly, then laughed again and tucked herself up against me. "Come on. The car is waiting. I thought we could drive up the coast and I could meet your parents while you're on leave."

"Just the two of us? T'gether?"

"Well, I'm certainly not inviting Andy along. I like him fine, but I don't propose to share a hotel room with him!"

I got kinda dizzy. "You proposin' to share one with me?"

She dimpled, an' I spent the next couple weeks in the best kinda haze I'd ever known. I hated to go away from her again, but it was better than the first time, in some ways, 'cause the war was over. I saw some of the world, even a few places I wanted to bring Annie back to, and the day my service ended, I walked away without ever looking back.

Walked right into a big church, an' waited there with Danny and Andy and a handful of the other guys from my unit standing up for me, while Annie came through the open doors at the end of the aisle in a burst of sunlight that dazzled tears into my eyes. By the time I could see clear again she was just about at my side, her daddy walking her down the aisle like she'd hoped he could. She was soft an' pretty and perfect, an' her Pop looked like another weight was lifting off his shoulders. He never had explained what he'd said the first time we'd met, but I meant to take care of his girl the rest of my life, so I figured it didn't matter.

I didn't hear a damned word of the ceremony, nothing except the parts where I was s'posed to say *I do* an' *I will*. I got those parts out, and the rest of it I was just looking at my Annie and feelin' fit to burst. She was always beautiful, but I didn't think even Princess Grace could hold a candle to her right then. I said so on the way outta the church an' she said she'd believe me 'cause I was better-looking than Prince Rainier III, which happened to be true, so to my way of thinking, we were starting out a fairy tale.

Trouble is, fairy tales got monsters in 'em.

I was at home studyin' for the last college final when she called me from work. I'd been out of the Army and married for two years, an' in all that time I'd never heard her sound so strained or upset. I had my shoes on before I knew what was wrong, an' in the end all she could say that made any sense was, "Please hurry."

I'd been in and outta the hospital plenty of times over the past year, picking Annie up from work or just coming by to say hello. I knew a lotta the names and faces, and most folks were ready to stop and talk a minute, especially late at night like it was now. But the place was just about deserted, an' the people I saw were strained and unhappy, like somethin' might jump outta the shadows if they stopped by them for too long. I tried asking after Annie, but nobody would answer, so I took myself up to where she usually worked.

She wasn't there. I started to let myself get worried then, and grabbed a nurse who was passing by. "Where's Annie Muldoon? She usually works here."

The lady pulled away like she was afraid, instead of just annoyed at my rudeness. She whispered, "I'm not sure. They called everyone with any psychiatric experience up to the third floor a while ago. Annie went up there." She gave herself a shake and blinked like she was seeing me for the first time. "You're her husband, right? She called you before she went up. All the patients up there woke up all at once and started screaming about seeing visions. The same visions, all of them."

"Wait a minute. Woke up?"

"It's our long-term illness ward." The nurse was pulling herself together now that she had somebody to lecture about hospital regulations. "One or two of the patients up there are actually comatose, breathing on their own but surviving through IV feeds. Others are terminally ill and spend a great deal of time in medically induced comas for their own comfort."

Sounded like hell. Dying quick and getting it over with seemed like the best way to go, to me. But I kept my mouth shut, listening as the lady said, "They've all woken up, even the ones who were comatose. Nothing will put them back down, and there's something...something dreadful about their faces. Like there's no living mind inside them anymore, just some kind of anger trying to escape. I went up to help but I couldn't bear it. Almost no one's been able to stay near them for long. Anne is very brave."

I muttered, "Yeah. Yeah, she is," and bolted for the third floor. The nurse called, "She said you helped someone who had visions once! That's why she called you in!"

Annie was putting too much faith in me. I hadn't done a damned thing to help her Pa. Something else had happened that day, something I didn't understand, but it was bigger than me. And I was expecting something bigger than me was at work in the third floor hospital ward, too. All I wanted was to get Annie out of it.

About twenty feet down the hall from the ward I got a cold-skin tingle like I hadn't had since Korea. I stopped, letting that cold wash all over, an' then I backed up into one of the private rooms and looked for weapons. Not once in the two years since I'd got out had I missed having a knife or gun on hand, but right then I started feeling the lack. An IV post was something, at least, an' I crept back toward the ward with it, feeling grim.

Voices were raised in a babble, in there. Men an' women alike, all of 'em sounding like madness had taken over. Annie's pop hadn't been like that. He'd been a sane crazy person, just painting the pictures that came to his head. Didn't sound like anybody in the ward was painting anything at all.

Showed what I knew. I pushed the door open a couple inches an' ran into a body. White coat, splashed with red: one of the doctors. I knew the fella's name, but couldn't remember it. Didn't matter just then. I dropped down low, taking a quick look through the cracked-open door.

Somebody across the room was painting, making big splashes across the walls in blood. I got colder, a different kinda cold I knew from Korea. I'd felt it going into battle, knowing somebody was gonna end up dead and preparing to do everything possible to make sure it wasn't me. Killer cold, that's what it was, and I didn't like it, but I figured I'd like dying even less. I shoved the door open, stepped inside, an' took in a mess as bad as I'd ever seen in Korea.

Eight patients, all in hospital robes an' bare feet, were spread around the room. Two doctors and a nurse were on the floor, and another patient was sittin' on the nurse, scooping her eyeballs out and eatin' them. One more was the one painting on the wall, working on some kinda design I bet nobody but her wanted finished, and licking her fingers between lines. She was thin, like all of 'em, with withered muscle and skin that hadn't seen sunlight in way too long. They were moving like they'd forgotten how, stiff an' uncoordinated, but they'd moved somehow, 'cause somebody'd killed the doctors an' the nurse. One by one they started dropping down beside the bodies, and eating them raw.

The dead cold feeling I'd gotten fighting the starlight demon got stronger. A memory rose up, a memory of something I sure as hell had never seen and didn't much want to now: three dead girls spread around a park, their guts tying 'em to each other at three points of a diamond. I saw their souls rising up and being gobbled down by a black-eyed beast that got a little stronger with every bite it took.

The whole idea shifted, set down over the scene in front of me, and clicked into place. The patients weren't getting stronger with every bite they took, but something linking them together was. I couldn't see it, but I felt it taking all the warmth outta the air, and seething with rage and triumph. All that anger turned 'round and 'round, focusing itself, waiting until it was strong enough to strike.

And it was gonna strike at Annie.

She was squashed into a corner, holding a broken-off bed rail in one hand and a bedside lamp without a shade in the other. The closest dead doctor wasn't more than a couple feet from her. I thought maybe he was dead 'cause he'd put himself between her an' the patients who were now eating him. She looked half scared to death, and all determined not to die.

Took me about half a second to take all that in. I was kicking the first patient off the doctor at the door before I was even done looking around. The patient snarled an' I swung my IV pole like a bat, cracking him along the jaw. He fell back and didn't move again, which was enough for me. The second one wasn't quite eating anybody yet. I kicked him away, too, and winced when he clobbered his head on a bed leg. Dunno why that bothered me when hitting him myself wouldn't have, but he slumped, dazed, and that was all that really mattered.

The next couple of patients were women, and any other time I mighta had a problem with that, too. Guessed I wasn't so chivalrous when there were folks eating other people's eyebrows. The fourth one went down, leaving four or five more to go, but a scream rose up outta the air and the cold anger gathering pulled itself together enough to have a shape. It pulled the patients with it as it moved. Even the ones I'd knocked out slithered along the floor, dragged by the times that bound them. The demon got more solid and angrier with every step it took.

I stopped worrying about the woman painting on the wall, about all of the still-conscious patients slurping down entrails, an' vaulted two beds to slam the IV pole into the thing's back when it was barely three feet from Annie.

The thing lashed forward as it fell, scraping Annie's cheek with its nails, and burst in a wave of eye-watering heat. It was gone, fast as that. Annie screamed and twitched sideways, tryin' ta avoid my IV pole weapon. I nearly stabbed her anyway, 'cause I twitched too, both of us going to our strong side: me left, and her to the right, which meant we were both heading the same way. I let out a shout and wrenched even further sideways. The pole hit the wall an' skittered across, leaving a scar that ended in a downstroke when I hit the floor and dropped it. My heart felt like somebody was squeezing it, panic finally setting in, but I didn't know what was goin' on behind me. I rolled over, almost on my feet again when it came home that everybody in the room had dropped without a sound. Everybody but me and Annie. She flung herself against my chest and we sat down with a grunt, both of us panting and gasping. My shirt got wet from her bloody cheek pressing against my chest, but I could feelin her breathing and she could hear my heart pounding, all of it telling us we were both still alive.

The patients weren't. I didn't know what'd happened when I'd drove the metal through the thing's chest, but it had let go of the patients it'd been possessing and they'd all dropped like puppets without strings. I couldn't help wondering if the thing possessing them had been keeping them alive for a long time, or if it had only just snuck in to kick up a fuss today.

Annie put it outta my mind, though, by finally taking a deep shaky breath and speaking with more composure than I expected: "What. The *hell*. Was that?"

First off I laughed an' put my mouth on her hair. "Never heard you swear before, sweetheart."

"I've never had enough reason to," she said all primly, an' sat up with her hand still over my heart an' her poor cheek red an' bloody from the scratches. "Gary, what was that thing? And...why weren't you surprised?"

"I was surprised, doll. I was plenty surprised."

"You came in here with a weapon, took one look at the room, and handled it. You didn't seem surprised."

"That's just training, darlin'. Assessing the situation. Army taught me that." I was only telling her half the truth, though, and she knew it as well as I did. "Let's wait til we get home, all right, sweetheart? Some strange things happened in Korea. I guess I didn't wanna talk about 'em, but maybe now I better."

She gave me a good looking-over, then nodded. "All right. Gary, I have to see if anyone is alive, if there's anything I can do—" She got up, though I was shaking my head.

"There ain't, darlin'."

She said, "I know," with quiet dignity. "But I have to try."

I was never gonna stop loving this woman. I got to my feet, too, and together we righted beds, checked bodies, an' at least lifted 'em onto the beds so they were peaceful insteada thrown all over the room. Nobody was left alive except me and her. She closed their eyes as we put 'em to bed. When we'd straightened up the mess an' got ourselves to the door, she stopped and looked around. Not just at the ward of dead folks, but down the hall, like she was searching for something. "Where is everyone, Gary? Why hasn't anyone come?"

I thought about how me and Danny hadn't said one word to each other about the starlight demon, an' shook my head. "I dunno, darlin', but I don't think people come running when somethin' like this happens. I think maybe they look real hard the other way, and in the morning they tell the papers it was some kinda mysterious tragedy. We gotta get your cheek looked at before we go home."

"Something like this. What is this, Gary? What happened?"

"That scratch first, sweetheart, an' then home, an' then we talk. I don't like us hanging around here tonight. I want you home safe, all right?"

"My shift doesn't end for another two hou—"

"Annie."

She looked down, eyelashes tangling, and then she sighed. "All right. All right, Gary." She let me put her arm around her shoulders, an' I walked her outta there. We got her cheek fixed up, and on the way home I started talking. I told her about Dandy Andy an' Reckless Rick and about Danny's warnings, and about the starlight demon we'd killed, and how I'd gotten the same kinda creepy feeling at the hospital as that night. I took a deep breath an' told her about the sometimes-voice at the back of my head, the one that thought things weren't quite right, and I finally ran outta things to say and got quiet and waited.

And Annie listened through the whole thing, all the way home and to the sitting room couch, where she clasped her hands together and looked at 'em while I talked. After a while she looked up, not at me, but at the wall, and a long time after I was done, she said, "Do you think my father was crazy, Gary?"

I shut my mouth on the first answer, which was to say, "Of course not, darlin'," without thinking about it. But she was really asking, and after all I'd just said, she deserved for me to think about it a bit. Besides, as soon as I started thinking, I saw what she was really asking. There was her Pop, who'd spent a lotta years locked up for seeing visions of magic things, things that somehow revolved around Annie, and now here was her husband talking about the same kinda crazy stuff, and expecting her to believe it. Hoping she'd believe it, anyway.

"I don't know, doll. I guess I woulda said yes, before. But I don't think I am, and I guess his stories weren't any crazier than mine. I guess I gotta give him the benefit of the doubt."

"Then why me?" she asked quietly. "Is that coincidence? Can it be? That I'd marry a man who has the same kind of... visions...my father did?"

I tried a smile. "They say we marry people like our folks, sweetheart." Annie gave me a look that said she knew I was tryin' ta be funny, but my timing was lousy. I sighed and sat down to study my hands. "Let's say he ain't crazy. Let's say he was seeing the same kinda things I'm seeing now. He said when he met that I was gonna take care of you now."

"No." Annie's voice was real clear and I looked up, surprised. "No, Gary, he said you'll take care of "her" now."

I opened my hands. "Who else could he'a been talking about, doll?"

"The girl in the painting."

"Joanne." The name came outta the back of my head an' shocked us both into sitting up straighter. Annie's spine was rigid as a pipe. "Who is she, Gary? Is she our...our daughter?"

"I donno. I donno!" I put my hands on my skull, wishing I could shake some answers loose. "I donno where that came from, doll. I've never seen the girl. How could she be somebody I'm s'posed ta look after?"

"How could she be someone whose name you know?"

"She ain't." A growl came up inside me and cut loose. "She ain't, Annie. You're the one I'm supposed to take care of, til death do us part. And I'm going to. Maybe—maybe your pop passed that on to me somehow. Maybe he was carrying some kinda weight, somethin' he was never supposed to, and when we met that first time he handed it on. He started getting better after that, right? So maybe he was just...shouldering a burden for a while."

Annie looked at me a long minute, weighing whether to let the question of the girl go, and finally did. "What burden, then? And still, why me? I'm not particularly special."

"Hah!" I coughed after that laugh, tryin' ta make it less sharp, but Annie smiled anyway. "You're supposed to think I'm special, Gary. I'm your wife. But in the greater scheme of things?" She shook her head. "I can't imagine I'm all that important. Why should...magic...happen around me?"

"I guess if magic's real, darlin', why shouldn't it? But maybe it ain't about how big or important you are in the world. Maybe it's just being important enough to somebody that you're drawing it to you. Or maybe there's some kinda bigger picture we ain't seeing, or...hell, I donno, sweetheart. Maybe you're just magic. I sure think so."

She rolled her eyes an' laughed again, then got up to come huddle against my side. We were quiet a while, until she sighed. "Gary, if magic is real...what do we do about it?"

"Whatcha mean?"

"You've already fought that starlight demon, and the thing at the hospital tonight. If those are real, there must be other...other *monsters* out there, right? You're taking care of me, but who's taking care of the other people crossing the monsters' paths?"

I felt my eyebrows climbing. "What're you saying, darlin'? I finish up college like most guys do, then instead of getting a factory job or selling cars, I go out an' what, become a hunter?"

"Sweetheart," she said, an' she was teasing because she never used the nicknames I did, but there was something deadly serious in her at the same time. "Sweetheart, you weren't just hunting that thing tonight. You were a *reaper*."

"A reaper." I gave her a quick grin. "You sayin' that's what I do now? I reap monsters? I don't think that's gonna pay the bills, darlin'."

"That's all right." Annie looked as proud as she ever did, right then. "I can pay the bills."

A week later she got sick.

CHAPTER TWELVE

She was used to that. We both were. She was a nurse, working around sickness all the time. Whenever something new came in, she'd get it, just like most of the other nurses, and like most of 'em, she shook it off fast. This one, though, crept up on her and not anybody else, and insteada getting better quick, she kept getting just a little bit worse. It started in her throat like most colds, then settled in as a bright red rash in her armpits an' behind her ears. That was when *she* recognized it, an' checked herself into the hospital with scarlet fever. They hustled her up to a bed and gave her a shot of penicillin, promising she'd be a whole lot better by morning.

"You're already infected, if you're going to catch it," she told me with a kinda macabre cheer, "but there's no sense in me spreading it around more. I'll be fine in a few days. I'll feel much better in the morning, now that I've got the antibiotic in me."

"Uh huh. And I'll be sitting here until you are." It wasn't a bad bedside chair, plenty comfortable for a young guy to sack out in for a couple nights. Annie settled in and went ta sleep quicker than her light-hearted words accounted for. I watched her sleep for a long time, counting her breaths and assuring myself she was still alive, before finally falling asleep myself.

Her whimpering woke me up before dawn. Didn't have to be a doctor to tell she was worse, not better. Her skin was just about blue from paleness, all except for hot spots on her cheeks and the rash standing out like flares in every crease and crook of her body. I hollered for help and three doctors came running, along with more nurses than I could count. They loved my Annie, maybe just about as much as I did. One of the doctors went through her chart, scowling so hard his eyes disappeared. "There's nothing in here about a penicillin allergy. Do you know of anything else she might be allergic to, Mr. Muldoon?"

"Long haired cats is about it."

The doctor's eyes reappeared, sympathetic. "Probably not the cause here, but we'll keep it in mind. Nurse, can you get her an IV? She's..." He touched her forehead an' the frown came back. "Much too warm. Take her temperature every five minutes. If it's not dropping in twenty, prepare a cool bath. We want that fever to break before there's permanent damage."

I caught his arm as he tried heading out. "Whaddaya mean, permanent?"

"Very high fevers are dangerous in adults, Mr. Muldoon."

He took my hand off his arm without making a fuss about it. "If they go on long enough there can be brain damage, or other physically detrimental effects. We won't worry about it just yet, all right? Anne is young and strong, and I'm sure we'll bring her fever down with some liquids."

Half an hour later she was shivering in a bathtub, her nightgown stuck to her body an' making the rash look paler than it was. The nurses tried ta keep me out, but Annie whispered, "No, please, let him stay," and they let me through to kneel beside the tub and hold her hand. It went like that all day, in and outta the cool water, until she was looking like a drowned kitten but still flushed and hot. Somewhere 'round midnight she fell asleep, except it wasn't sleep, not properly. I stayed there, holding her hand and keeping my head down, praying and trying not to hear the nurses whispering about comas and fevers.

I figured I'd been awake about twenty-six hours when I finally figured it out, an' lifted my head to whisper, "It's the scratches. It ain't scarlet fever, Annie. It's that thing that scratched you in the ward. That wasn't..." *It wasn't an accident,* my back-of-head voice finished, even if I didn't wanna say it out loud. *That was an attack, buddy. Wish like hell I'd known that then.*

I said, "I do know it now," aloud, an' for a second I hoped Annie was gonna give me a look like I'd gone crazy, but her short quick breaths didn't even change. I leaned in anyway and kissed her hair, murmurin', "Nothin', sweetheart. I'm just worrying about you," like she was sayin' her part. Like she *had* ta say her part, because I couldn't picture my life without her. She was gonna get better, 'cause I couldn't live with anything else. *What do I do? Whaddo I do?* I asked the voice in my head, but the damned thing didn't answer. I got up an' went to the window, staring out at the night and tryin' ta think. I wished Danny was there, even if he only knew about Korean demons. It'd be something, anyway. Something more than doctors and nurses would understand.

Every damned person in that hospital ward had gone into a coma like the one Annie was in. Nobody'd said anything about 'em having a fever first, but I hadn't thought to ask about their medical history while I was trying not to get stuck by a monster. It probably didn't matter, except all of them had been on IVs an' cooling baths too. If cold didn't break the fever, then how was I s'posed to help Annie?

I didn't know if it was me or the voice saying *you sweat it out*, but the idea came through loud an' clear.

It was about the dumbest damned thing I could think of. Fevers were already hot, an' it didn't seem like raising her body temperature even more could help. But cooling her down sure wasn't, an' I remembered all of a sudden how hot the thing in the hospital ward had been. Maybe the cooler it stayed, the longer it lived in somebody, an' the longer it stayed alive the weaker the body got.

Nothin' else was working. It was worth a shot. I took Annie off the IV an' scooped her up. She didn't weigh nothing, all the water burned outta her by the fever. I bundled her up in my coat an' all the blankets I could steal from the hospital, an' drove her home to build a fire in the hearth. I dragged the kitchen table as close as I could get it an' threw blankets over the table until I'd built us a little cave in the living room, an' then I crawled inside with Annie. I lay down behind her an' tucked her against my chest to keep her warm from both sides, and started praying again.

The rash came up bright an' awful all over as she started warming up. She started shivering harder than she'd done at the hospital, bad enough I wondered right away if I was killing her instead of helping, but I had to do something, an' the doctors weren't gonna understand my crazy reasons why. I tried to close my ears to her whimpers, whispering, "It's okay, darlin', it's gonna be fine," over an' over again.

Took a long time for her to start sweating, but when she did it came on fast. Her hair went wet under my chin, an' the shivering turned to shakes and then to thrashing. I put my leg over hers an' held her tighter, still whisperin' reassurances and praying I wasn't killing my wife. I was damned near as tired as she was from holding her down when the thing finally came loose from her, an' rattled outta her chest in a coughing wheeze.

I'd seen it before at the hospital, but somehow I wasn't thinking it'd be a living moving thing again. There was a lot less to it than there'd been in the ward, but then it only had Annie, not a ward fulla folks to feed on, an' it looked weak from the heat. I reached past Annie, slow as I could, an' picked up the fire iron.

It died from the iron a lot faster than it'd done with the IV pole, an' what was left drifted up the chimney as smoke. Annie gasped in a deep breath an' rolled away from the fire with a cry, the sweetest sound I'd ever heard. I knocked the table over, bringing cooler air in, an' dropped down beside her to haul her into my arms. She was cold an' clammy and shivering again, but it wasn't a sick kinda shivering anymore.

After the longest time I picked her up again an' brought her to the bathroom, filled the tub with warm water an' got in it with her. There wasn't hardly enough room for one of us in it, never mind two, but I wasn't gonna let her go. 'sides, at least it being small meant I could reach for a cup and fill it from the sink without movin' much. Annie drank it, still without sayin' anything, and I got her another, an' another, until she finally just held it, half full, an' fell asleep against my chest. Healthy sleep, not the stillness from before. She barely even woke up with me getting us outta the tub and dried off, an' she was a warm little lump of softness at my side when I crawled into bed with her. We didn't wake up, either, not til early the next morning, when she whispered, "I'm hungry."

"That's the best news I've heard in a while, doll." I held on another minute, then kissed her hair. "All right. Bacon an' eggs or you wanna start small?"

"Porridge? I'll eat it while you're frying the bacon. And making the pancakes."

I grinned real quick. "Anything else I oughta be cooking up?"

"I think that's enough to start." She smiled an' I tried not ta see the blue circles under her eyes, or the weight that had fallen off of her in the past couple days. She looked half burned away, an' the rash hadn't faded all the way yet, bright red streaks standing out against awful pale skin.

I pulled her close again and held on a minute, finally whisperin', "Thanks for staying with me, doll. You had me scared for a while there."

"Me too. Me too, Gary, but I have to eat before I can talk about it. Before I can even think about it. Okay? Please?"

"Yeah. Yeah, doll." I kissed her again more fiercely, an' it turned out hungry an' weak as she was, there was something she needed more'n food right then. Took a while for me to get out to the kitchen, but I started ferrying food right back into the bedroom. Juice first, trying not to see how fragile she looked holding the cup in both hands and drinking with her eyes closed, an' then the porridge with lotsa cream and brown sugar while the bacon fried up. Turned out making pancakes wasn't that hard either, following a recipe from Annie's cookbook. I only burned a couple. We ate on the bed, balancing plates on our laps an' knees, just like kids sharing a Sunday morning breakfast with their folks.

I'd never seen Annie pack away so much, or been so glad to see it. Seemed like her color got better with every bite, an' after about six pancakes, a couple eggs, an' more bacon pieces than I bothered to count, she sighed an' put her fork down. "You might have to start doing the cooking, Gary. This is delicious."

"Hunger makes the best sauce, darlin'."

She nodded, then closed her eyes a minute, like she was fortifying herself. Then she looked at me, straight an' clear. "What happened?"

I explained as best as I had it figured out, watching

Annie's face grow more solemn with every word. When I finished, she asked the question she'd done before: "Why me?"

An answer came up from the back of my mind, but I choked it off before it got loose. *Because I love you* wasn't any kinda answer that made sense, and hell if I was gonna make either of us start wondering if getting married had been a bad idea. "I don't know, doll, but if something's comin' after you, then we gotta assume it's gonna come again. I'm thinking maybe we got lucky that this...poison-demon, whatever you wanna call it, that it was slow and had ta be carried inside of somebody else's body to get close enough to strike. If it had been quicker, I wouldn't have gotten there in time."

A frown pulled at the corners of her mouth. It woulda been cute any other day, but worry had claws in my guts. After a minute she got what I was thrusting at, an' put it in plain words. "Are you suggesting I learn to fight?"

"At least a little bit, sweetheart. I know you're a nurse to help people, but that thing wasn't a person. I don't wanna lose you, Annie. Let me teach you a few things."

"And what if I get a fright at work and use some of those things on an unsuspecting patient?"

"Annie, you saw that thing. Oily black smoke an' dead eyes. You really think you're ever gonna mistake something like that for a patient?"

"You said the starlight demon was a beautiful woman." She took a breath so deep it shuddered comin' out, an' murmured, "It's hard to believe I'm even saying these things out loud. Gary, this isn't *real*. Magic isn't...real."

"Ain't it? Didn't the saints fight dragons an' heal people and do miracles? Didn't Christ? I donno, Annie. Maybe it's right there under our noses an' we just don't believe it. Maybe sometimes it just crops up and bites somebody on the—" I cleared my throat. "Knee. On the knee, hard enough we can't ignore it. Maybe we just got...bit. An' maybe it ain't you, sweetheart. Maybe it's me. I'm the one your pop thought he could pass his burden on to, an' the one who killed something outta this world in Korea. Maybe you're just getting tangled up in...me."

Her frown came back, but then her mouth pursed like she was trying ta hide a smile. "We could spend the rest of our lives doing this, couldn't we? Worrying about which one of us it is. Trying to take the blame, or reassure the other, or apologize."

When she put it like that, it was kinda funny. I spread my hands. "Guess we could, yeah."

"Maybe we should just put it behind us, then. Maybe if we're going to keep having...unusual circumstances...crop up in our lives, maybe we should just accept them. Together," she said with a little emphasis. "Husband and wife. Both of us doing our parts, like God intended."

"All right, but I'm telling you if we're gonna be ready to face whatever comes along, God intended for you to learn ta use a gun, Anne Marie Muldoon."

She said, "Yes, dear," so nice and sweet that even after a while, when we went back ta sleep, I still had the funny itchy feeling I'd been fleeced.

Truth was, Annie took to shooting more naturally than I had. She didn't like pistols much, even if she saw their use, but she was a rifle sharpshooter inside'a six months. My Sarge woulda loved her, if he coulda put her on a hill with a scope. She wasn't afraid of knives, either, though she got grim at the idea of using one. "I know what they do to bodies, Gary," she said one evening. "I've helped stitch people up after knife fights."

"We ain't looking to fight people, doll. Not now and not ever."

Guessed it did the trick, or she found a way not to think about it, because she got good with the knives and then found a fencing teacher. Not the showy stuff they did for sport, but a Spanish fella who followed old swordfighting techniques and taught us both how to kill things with a long blade. "Go to Pamplona," he told me. "Run with the bulls. Fight in the ring. If you survive, you will be a man."

"He's man enough already," Annie told *him*, an' wouldn't let me go even when I said it sounded kinda exciting. She gave me one of them level looks that dames do, an' said we could discuss it when I took her to Spain. I graduated college and started playing saxophone gigs and saving up, not so I could run with the bulls, but 'cause I figured I'd surprise her something fierce on our fifth anniversary. Lotta the gigs started late and ran later, so I got into the habit of making dinner, too, so it was something Annie didn't have to do when she came off shift herself. Turned out I was a better cook than her, but insteada being upset by it she looked like the cat who stole the canary. Between that an' her dab hand at fighting, all I could figure was women were mysterious creatures.

Wasn't long before that Spanish anniversary I was planning when I came home late one night an' found Annie still up and waiting for me. She'd been crying, though she'd fixed her hair an' washed her face to try to hide it. I still saw the stains on her cheeks an' the flush of color that said something was wrong. A hundred ideas came an' went in a second, most of 'em revolving around what kinda monster she'd had ta kill. I knelt in front of her. "What is it, doll?"

"I saw a doctor today."

All the building blocks of my world went out from under me. I thumped down onta my heels, wonderin' how my hands had got so cold so fast, an' tried not to sound shaky. "How come?"

"It's been almost five years, Gary." Annie's voice wasn't like anything I'd ever heard from her, all remote an' hollow. She wasn't quite looking at me, but I wasn't sure she was looking at anything at all, the way her eyes were bruised an' empty. "We should have had at least one baby by now."

Hot an' cold rushed my face, part relief an' part terror. My heart was hammering loud enough I thought the world could hear it. "Guess I hadn't thought about it, doll. Guess I figured we had lotsa time."

"No." Just one hard word, like she couldn't make herself say anything more.

Another tremor went through me, shaking down dreams I didn't hardly know I had. Lil' boy-shaped dreams, an' lil' girl-shaped ones too. Dreams with little faces like Annie's an' big broad shoulders like mine, an' dreams with high laughing voices and stomping hurrying feet. They hardly had shapes to 'em, those dreams, until they started to fall. Then I could see 'em all clear as day, toothless grins and white wedding dresses, falling down like rain. And like rain, they hit the earth an' disappeared into sparkling splashes of nothin'.

There wasn't anything I could say, sitting there in that ruin. I got on to the couch and pulled Annie into my arms. She didn't wanna let me, staying stiff and upright, but I held on until inch by awful inch she leaned into me. Not relaxing, and feeling like she might never relax again, but at least I was holding her.

It came out in bits an' pieces over days, how the doctor said she seemed all right but that it couldn't be any surprise to a nurse that sometimes a real bad sickness, like a fever, could leave someone unable to have kids. She couldn't talk about it for more'n a minute without getting stiff and hurting again, an' all I could do was keep saying I loved her, right up until she threw a mug across the room an' screamed, "I know you love me! Don't you think I know that? Don't you think I'm afraid it's not enough?" an' collapsed into tears.

I couldn't catch her in time, she fell so fast, but I dropped down beside her an' held her again. She fought like a wildcat, hitting and screaming with a kinda horrible incoherence that made all the sense in the world. She was a nurse, she understood how it could happen to somebody else, but when it was her, when it was her own body betraying her, an' she wouldn't let me say it wasn't, 'cause to her way of thinking, it was, no matter what all her studies might say, when it was her it was unbearable. An' what if me loving her wasn't enough, if she couldn't give me babies, an' I kept sayin' it didn't matter, it didn't matter, darlin', I had her, I wasn't gonna want somebody else, but not even the tears rollin' down my own face convinced her, not for days an' weeks, until the worst of the pain had passed. I still caught it on her face some days, though, as the years went on. I'd see it when she was looking at other people's kids, an' all I could ever do was hold on an' never let go.

We had our ups an' downs over the years, an' we had our moments of the world turnin' upside-down, when some kinda magic reared its head again, but the truth was, we never had a worse time than that, not 'til the doctor told us Annie was dying of emphysema.

I had a headache start up about then, pounding at the back of my skull like a devil tryin' ta get out. I was the smoker, not Annie. Didn't seem fair she'd get the disease instead of me. Her breathing had been bad for a while and I'd cut down, started smoking outside the house insteada in it, but I threw my last pack of cigarettes away that day and wasn't ever tempted by 'em again. We sat there in silence, holding hands and listening to the doc tell us about the advancement of the disease an' treatments, but he had a look that a nurse and her husband knew plenty well. After a few minutes Annie cut him off, saying, "How long, Doctor?" with the same grace as she faced most things.

The fella sighed and looked away, then back again, preparing to give it to her straight. "The truth is, Mrs. Muldoon, I don't understand how your health has been as good as you claim for the past several years. The advanced stage of the disease suggests you should have been suffering, even bed-ridden, for an extended period of time already. If it was a cancer, perhaps, but—"

"Doctor."

"What I'm trying to say is that it's unusually aggressive, Mrs. Muldoon. If our treatments can't slow the progression, I'm afraid you may have as little as a matter of weeks."

My headache spiked, making the world go white for a minute. I couldn't have heard that right, but Annie was talking, her hands real still in her lap and her voice the kinda steady it got when she had to deliver bad news to somebody. "I've only been ill a few months. That's...difficult to accept."

"I know." The fella looked as helpless as I'd ever seen anybody, but it had nothing on the panic rising in me. A lifetime of crazy moments came back, from Annie's Pop to the fever-comas at the hospital all those years ago, from near misses in Tampa and Pamplona to the wonderful, strange months in New Orleans, and one thought came clear in my head: Annie wasn't sick.

Not a natural sickness, anyway. Not somethin' that came on the way emphysema was s'posed to. This was something more like the sick fever, something that didn't belong, that shouldna been happening to her. I was just about hearing that voice in my head again, though it'd been quiet for so long I'd damned near forgot about it. It was the one that had said *this ain't right* about a few things a long time ago, and for the first time in fifty years I was thinking the same thing: *this ain't right.*

An' the voice that'd been mostly quiet at the back of my head woke up with a roar. A whole lifetime almost like the one I'd led, only just a little different, crashed through my memories and I had just enough time to realize that voice had always been me, just me from way down the road, when it took over me and *then* became *now*—

CHAPTER THIRTEEN

My vision went double before it settled out, two of me looking through my eyes for a couple seconds. I'd been a passenger to my own life for the past fifty years, quiet and enjoying most of it, and trying ta keep my mouth shut and not make anything worse or better when I didn't, even when things I didn't remember kept cropping up. Now it was my turn, an' the fella I almost was could take his shot at sittin' in the background for a couple weeks. 'cause that was all we had, and I knew it. We hadn't had a lot of time, once the doc had diagnosed her.

And it killed me knowing Joanne Walker was only a couple miles away and three years too early to save my wife. There was nothing I could say to Jo that would change that. She was a twenty-four year old kid right now, angry at the world and a long damned way away from the girl I was gonna meet a few years down the road. I could turn up on her doorstep like some crazy old man pleading for a miracle, and it wouldn't get me one. It had to be me and Annie alone through this, and she wasn't gonna come out of it alive.

"Gary?" She and the doc had asked me somethin', and I hadn't been listening. "Gary, are you all right?"

I closed my eyes a minute, afraid to even look at her. The lady had just been told she was dying, and she was worried 'bout whether I was all right. The selfish part of me wanted to say no, but I took her hand an' bowed my head over it, still not ready to meet her eyes. "I'm okay, doll. We're gonna get through this."

She said, "Gary," again, this time with an old fondness that I missed so bad it made my hands hurt, holding hers. I dared look up, to look into blue eyes that time hadn't faded one bit, even if there were wrinkles around 'em now and her blond hair had turned snow white. I'd been looking out through my other self's eyes all this time, watching us growing old together again, but it wasn't the same as looking at her myself. I wished I knew how Cernunnos had settled me into my own self's head, and wondered what the devil had happened to my own old bones that had been riding with him for so long.

Wondering gave me a flash of mist an' greenery, a cool breath of air like comin' home, an' then I knew and understood. I was resting somewhere else, safe in the land he called home, while my consciousness took the long way 'round. More than that, I could feel my memories of riding with the Hunt settling into Tir na nOg's earth, so that the weight of what I'd seen and how it might have changed me wouldn't crush me. I'd been mostly immortal all that time, and now I was slipping back into mortal bones that weren't ready to carry so much time or so many memories. I hadn't known Horns could do that. 'course, I didn't know much about what gods could do, and didn't figure on arguing with 'em when they did it.

Annie said, "Gary," again in that same voice, and I knew she was gonna tell me what she'd said to me the first time I'd gone through this, that there wasn't any way through this one.

Only this time I said, "No." Before she said anything else, I said, "No. We gotta talk, doll. We gotta think about what's going on here, all right?"

She hesitated, then nodded. The doctor looked strained, but he got up when we did, offering support and sympathy, and encouraged Annie to start a drug regime right away. The prescriptions were waiting at the front desk. We picked 'em up on the way out, and made it to a bench on the street before Annie had to sit down and say, "Gary," again.

"Listen to me, doll." I took her hands and kissed 'em, trying not to tremble. It'd been four and a half years since I'd gotten to do that, by my count. "My girl." I'd been using those words a lot lately, meaning Joanne, but they were Annie's first. "I love you, darlin'. Don't know that I've said that enough."

Meeting her eyes, was hard. She was smiling, kinda sad and wry all at once. "You say it every day, Gary. How often do you think it needs to be said?"

"More."

"Sweetheart." She untangled her hands and put one against my cheek. "Saying it more often isn't going to make this go away. But I love you too. You know that."

"Yeah." I'd gotten sloppy sentimental the first time we'd done this, too, but not the same way. I'd been reeling from the fear of losing her, then. Now I had her back, maybe not for long, but I had her and this time I knew what we were up against. "Annie, I'm gonna start talking and you're gonna think I'm crazy, but you gotta hear me out, all right? I know you're holding yourself together and looking calm so I'll be all right, but don't worry about me. I know you're shaking and scared inside, but you gotta listen, just for a couple minutes. Can you do that for me?"

My girl took as deep a breath as she could without coughing, and nodded. "I was there when a lot of people got this same kind of bad news, Gary. I'm all right. Go ahead and say what you need to say."

"Your Pop wasn't crazy."

That came from so far outta nowhere that for a split second she looked like *I* was crazy. Then she laughed, soft an' breathless. "Thank goodness for a definite diagnosis, then. He's been dead nearly thirty years, Gary. Why does it matter now?"

"We been through some strange stuff, haven't we, sweetheart? We don't talk about it much when it ain't happening, and I guess it's died down the older we got, but... we've seen things most folks wouldn't reckon on being real, ain't that right?"

Annie smiled like I was bringing up the good times. "I suppose we have, at that. I hadn't thought about most of it in a long time. It seems like another life." Her eyes got dark, like she was rememberin' that pretty soon it would be another life.

I held her hands again, trying not to crush 'em. "Your Pop wasn't crazy, Annie. I was there the day that car almost hit you. Somebody did knock you outta the way. His name's... well, I call him Horns, 'cause his name's a mouthful, but the way I see it, sweetheart, that's where it all started."

"You were there—" Annie wet her lips, then closed her eyes a minute. I could see her trying not to dismiss what I was saying outta hand, trying not to think I *was* crazy. After a bit, she said, "Let's get my prescriptions and go home. We can discuss it there."

She was quiet in the car, an' I did my best to keep my mouth shut. Once we got home she had a look around like she'd never seen the place before. Committing it to memory, even if she was the one gonna leave. Then finally she came to sit, an' said, real mild-like, "You were there. And you never thought to mentioned that before now?"

"Darlin, I didn't...remember." I sighed and sat too, rubbing my hands over my face. "You know how you an' me, we remember different things happening at the same events? It's like that's happening inside my own head. There're things it's like I'm remembering twice, and one of those memories is seeing you by the roadside, an' Horns comin' down to tackle you outta the way."

"Who is Horns?"

I recognized the voice she was using, and looked up with a little grin. "No going all Nurse Annie on me now, sweetheart. Will you trust me if I say it don't matter who he is? That what matters is me knowing that day wasn't an accident, an' that your Pop wasn't going crazy? He did see a guy on a silver horse come outta nowhere and knock you aside, an' I can tell you that the reason it happened, the reason any of this is happening, is because of the girl in that painting he did there at the end. Joanne. Joanne Walker. She's a friend of mine, darling, or she will be, and she's got magic like you wouldn't believe."

"She *will* be?"

There wasn't no Nurse Annie in her voice anymore. It was just my girl sounding strained and about to break. I shut myself up and hugged her against me, wishing I'd known to shut up earlier. "Some of the things your pop saw were flashes of the future, huh? I got something like that going on right now too."

Her silence said more than words, but after a minute she filled it with the words, too, soft an' scared: "Do you know what's going to happen to me?"

"Yeah," I said, and for the first time in my life, deliberately lied to the woman I loved. "You're gonna be fine, sweetheart. This stupid thing is just gonna turn out to be another scare, like all the other crap that's almost gotten us through the years. An' that's what it *is*, Annie." I wasn't lying, now, and that helped sell the part that was a lie. "It ain't sickness, not the way the doctors can recognize. I guess we always knew there were monsters out there. This one's just comin' at you the best way it knows how."

"We've met monsters," Annie whispered. "They're not subtle, Gary. Why is this one? Hiding itself in sickness instead of fighting red in tooth and claw?"

"Ain't the first time it's tried sickness against you, sweetheart."

"Maybe not, but even the fever was carried by a monster. We saw it. We fought it. How can this have come from nowhere?"

I sat up straighter, still holding her but with my heart pickin' up speed. "I reckon it couldn't have. This things come on fast, sweetheart. Who's new in your life the last couple months?"

"For Heaven's sake, Garrison Muldoon," she said, prim as a school teacher, "you sound like you're asking if I'm having an affair. There was a new optometrist for my annual eye examination, two new booths at the farmers' market, a new gardener for our yard and a new yoga teacher at the studio. And I'm sure I speak to a dozen or so strangers every day, including that young doctor today. You can't possibly imagine—" She got breathless instead of indignant and collapsed against me, coughing until tears stained my shirt. Finally, a whole lot more softly, she finished, "You can't imagine we can sort through every person I've met in the last two months to determine who may be hiding a demon inside. And why me, if this Joanne Walker is a friend of *yours*? Maybe I should be asking you if you're having an affair."

I chuckled. "I wasn't askin' you that to begin with, an' from what I'm seeing of the future, the girl is too tall an' too young for me anyway. I got what I want right here. Always have. And the reason why you is simple, sweetheart. Real evil don't bother going after us. It goes after the folks we love."

"How do we fight it?"

I wasted half a breath wishing I still had Jo's magic Sight, then let it go. "We start by assuming it ain't any of the grocery store checkers or the guy who pumps your gas, or any of the other folks you only have a passing acquaintance with. How much time you been spending at the farmers' market and talkin' to the new gardener? You go to yoga all the time."

Annie's laugh wheezed in her chest. "You could make an argument for the new teacher being evil, I suppose. She's very young and very flexible. None of the old ladies like her."

"Sure, doll, but do you?"

She laughed again, stronger this time, and coughed because of it. "I'm an old lady too, but you still know how to charm a girl. Yoga's a spiritual practice as much as exercise, Gary. Surely a practitioner couldn't be evil...?"

"I don't know, sweetheart. Seems to me everybody's got potential to go bad. Being spiritual don't always mean being good."

"Then I suppose we should...what does one say? 'Hello, Darina, class on Wednesday was excellent and it's lovely to see you again, by the way, have you put a killing hex on me?'"

"No, we gotta—" I spent another half a breath wishing on Joanne's magic, then let the rest of that breath out and risked playing heavy on future memories. "We gotta find somebody who can tell by looking at 'em. There's a lady here in Seattle, a woman whose name I heard a while back. Sonata Smith. She's a medium, but she's got connections. Maybe she'll know somebody who can help us."

It was true, kinda. Me and Jo had met Sonny maybe six months ago, from the direction I was coming from. It was more like four years from now in the direction Annie was looking at it, but I figured if there was ever a time to play fast and loose with the truth, it was now. Annie didn't need to know just how much future-flashing I was talking about, and we'd use up all the time she had left if I had to explain it all anyway.

"Don't we know anyone? I know it's been a long time, but..."

"But you don't like presuming on strangers. I know, darlin', but I don't figure we do. Closest we ever came to belonging to some kinda magic underground was New Orleans, I reckon, don't you?"

For a minute she didn't look sick anymore, her whole face lighting up with a smile. "Well, if you hadn't played that jazz riff—"

"How many times I gotta tell you, I was just tryin' ta make that raven sing, is all. How was I s'posed ta know it was gonna open up a door to somewhere else?"

Annie kissed me like she always did when that jazz riff

came up, murmuring, "*Open here I flung the shutter*, Gary. Of course it opened a door."

"Hrmph." I tugged her close again to talk against her hair. "Point is, sweetheart, maybe we came close down there in the South, but up here we've never been part of that scene. We only ever dealt with what came our way. Never went looking for any of it, like some folks do. So I think we gotta ask for help this time. Lemme give this Smith lady a call, see if she can send somebody around who can read auras."

"Auras?"

"Souls. Everybody's soul's got energy, doll, doncha figure? Good energy, bad energy, and there's folks out there who can tell which is which."

Annie got a funny little frown, her eyebrows wrinkling together as she looked at me. "Where did you pick up on something like that, Gary?"

"Aww, sweetheart, you know how it is. Old dogs got a lotta tricks." I'd used that answer with Jo a bunch of times. Felt strange using it on Annie. "You sit tight. I'll see if her number's in the book." If it wasn't, I'd been to Sonny's house, but explaining that one away was more than I wanted to try. Lucky for me, Sonny was listed, and I gave her a call half-expecting to get an answering machine.

Instead she picked up on the second ring, sayin', "Hello?" in the same dryly competent voice I remembered from her. It kinda threw me, knowing she hadn't met me yet, and I spent a couple seconds fumbling an' stuttering. Her voice got amused: "Yes, this is Sonata Smith, and yes, I am a medium. I do communicate with the dead. Don't worry. I won't think you're embarrassing yourself with whatever request it is you have, nor," an' she kept the same amused tone but steel slipped into it, "nor will I hesitate to send a haunting your way if this should be another practical joker."

That bit made me laugh. I cleared my throat, promisin', "No, no, darlin', no practical jokes. I ain't sure you're the type to really send ghosts after somebody even if it was."

"Oh, probably not, but you never know." She sounded less dangerous then, like I'd passed some kinda test. "But how do you know anything about me at all?"

"Got your name from a friend, is all. Look, my name's Gary, and I'm sorry for callin' like this, outta the blue, but—"

"But you have someone you'd like to speak with, someone who's crossed over," she said gently, like she was takin' the difficulty of saying it away from me.

I chuckled. "No, ma'am, I'm afraid not. I just thought if you were the real deal you might be able to help me out with somethin' else. I need—" My heart slipped all of a sudden, missing beats and feeling like it'd fallen a couple miles down my chest. Jo wasn't ready to heal anybody yet, but she'd said something once about meeting a bunch of dead shamans after her magic had woke up. They'd been Seattle shamans, an' right now they weren't dead yet. I didn't hardly recognize my own voice, it got so tight and twisted with hope. "I'm looking for a shaman, ma'am. Somebody who can read auras and heal folks. My wife's sick, see."

Sonny Smith's voice got even gentler. "I have some

people I can introduce you to, but some illnesses can't be healed, Mr...Gary. Gary," she said again, like she was fixing it in her mind that I hadn't said my last name.

I wasn't gonna, either, 'cause she was sharp as tacks, and I didn't want her putting me together with the cabbie driving Joanne Walker around a few years down the road. I reckoned she wouldn't, 'cause she hadn't, but I wasn't gonna risk it. I already didn't know why I didn't remember talking to her, having this conversation, but either I'd been watching some kinda parallel world version of me all these years, or my memory wasn't half as reliable as I thought it was. I couldn't figure on the parallel world idea being true, not if I was still the same fella who'd left Joanne a while back and was looking to try an' save my wife, and as far as I could tell, I was. So I was betting on my memory failing me, and didn't wanna think about how or why that was gonna happen.

"Gary?" Sonata sounded real sympathetic, like she'd delivered bad news and was expecting me to be reeling from it. "I wish I could say otherwise, but it's better to have realistic expectations."

"No, ma'am, it's fine, I got realistic expectations. I knew a lady shaman once, so I figure my expectations are realistic enough to be worth trying. Thanks for the warning, though. Do you know anybody?"

"I do. Auras as well as healing, you said? I'll send the strongest aura reader I know."

"Thanks. We might gotta do some leg work with her, to meet a few people for her to read."

Sonny's voice got warm. "I like how you assume it's a woman."

"Ain't it?"

"In fact, it is. If you'll give me your address, Gary, I'll see if she's available this evening."

I gave her the address and phone number and went back to Annie, who said, "You knew a lady shaman?"

"That old lady up in the painted caves in France seemed like a shaman to me, doll." Still true, even if it wasn't who I really meant. Explaining Jo kept right on being too hard, especially when I was saying I knew a shaman, past tense, when I shoulda been using words that meant future memories.

Annie's nose wrinkled, remembering more than just the cave paintings we'd gone to visit thirty years earlier. "She seemed in need of a bath, to me."

"I reckon I would too if I'd been living up there with the cave paintings since they were made. Doesn't matter, though, does it? As long as somebody comes along. Miz Smith said she'd send somebody."

"I think I should rest before her friend arrives," Annie said quietly. "I don't suppose it really matters, Gary, if it's a typical illness or someone attacking me somehow. I'm still sick, and it's been a long day."

"All right, sweetheart. You want to go lie down in the bedroom our out here on the couch?"

She smiled. "The couch is fine. The sunshine will keep me warm. You can go tidy up the kitchen for me."

"There ain't no universe in which you left it a mess." I

got a blanket an' tucked it over her when she lay down, then trucked into the kitchen. The breakfast dishes were still in the sink, which was Annie's idea of a mess. I cleaned up and dug through the freezer to find somethin' to cook for dinner, muttering about slim pickings. By my reckoning it'd been too long since I'd cooked for my girl, and I wanted to do it right. I checked on Annie, who was sleeping, and slipped off down to the store to get a chicken for roasting. Nothin' fancy, but comforting all the same.

When I got back there was somebody walking up the drive, a tall thin woman with iron-colored hair and a long nose. She looked maybe twenty years younger than me. I parked and got out sayin', "If you're selling religion, I ain't buying."

She stopped where she was, 'bout thirty feet away. She was carrying a round leather bag with something light enough to bounce against her hip in it, and was wearing a grey hand-knit cardigan that came down to about her knees. "I'm not selling anything. My name is Hester Jones. Did you call Sonata Smith earlier this afternoon?"

"Oh, hell. I did, yeah. I'm Gary. Sorry for being rude. Thanks for comin' over, Miz Jones."

"Hester will do." She had just about the sourest voice I'd ever heard, like nothing on this earth was gonna meet with her approval. She finished comin' up the drive, gave me and my chicken a good hard look, then flicked a sharp eyebrow up. "I'd like to meet the patient."

"She was sleeping when I left her—"

"That's fine. If she can stay that way it may help.

We're trained to resist shamanic power, Mr..." Like Sonny, she realized I hadn't given her a last name, and shrugged. "Shamanic magic requires belief on the part of the patient as well as the shaman. Sleeping minds are more malleable. If it's a minor illness—"

"It ain't."

Something in my voice stopped her dead. After a couple seconds she started up again, following me, but her own voice got more sour-apples. From what she was saying, I thought she was trying to be gentle, but she had the bedside manner of a shark. Just as well Annie was gentle enough for two of most anybody. "I don't want you to raise your hopes too high. Most people only call in shamanic practitioners in desperation—"

"I'm desperate but it ain't because I don't believe. It's cause I do. A good friend of mine was a shaman, a powerful one. I know what kinda things she could do, and I'm hoping you can do somethin' similar. My wife, she don't just need healing. She needs shielding, and we gotta find out who did this to her, too."

Hester Jones stopped again, this time just outside my front door, an' touched my arm, which I didn't figure was somethin' she was comfortable with. "I may be able to help her find a spirit guide, which is as much 'shielding' as I can do. I don't even understand what else you might mean by that."

For a couple seconds things came tumbling down around me. Jo wasn't your average shaman, an' I knew that, but I didn't have much else to compare her to. Took another couple seconds to shake all of those preconceptions loose and say, "Spirit animals are great. I got some first-hand experience with that. How 'bout reading auras? I guess I donno if that's somethin' most shamans do, either."

"Sonny called me because I'm good at auras," Hester said, which made me feel like a damned fool, 'cause Sonny had said that. I guessed I might be more rattled than I was letting on, even to myself. "Let's begin with what healing I may be able to do while she's sleeping, though."

"All right. All right, thanks." I led her through the kitchen 'cause I had a chicken to put away, then went out to the living room where Annie was still huddled under the blanket. She'd never been a big lady, but she was looking real tiny and fragile, small enough to make my heart hurt. Hester went over, all business-like, an' knelt beside her.

She wasn't there ten seconds before she flinched back, color rising fast in her thin face. "There's something very dark inside her. Anything I tried outside of the safety of a sweat lodge and a power circle would risk my life as well as hers."

"I got a sauna."

For somebody with such a sour-apples face she had a pretty good smile. I figured I'd surprised it outta her, 'cause it went away again fast, but it was there for a minute. "I'm not sure I would have thought of that. Thinking outside of the box."

"The one shaman I know never even found the box. Lemme go light it up in there. Whaddya want to build a power circle with? Salt? Grass cuttings? I got all kinda stuff."

"Your sauna's separate from the rest of the house? A circle can be built around it?" Hester got up so we could talk without disturbing Annie. I led her through the house to the back yard. It was smaller an' a lot more private than the front yard, and had the sauna and a hot tub that never did much more than catch falling leaves in it. The tub was on the back deck, but the sauna was tucked up against the trees, with a glass roof that letcha see leaves moving like ghosts through the steam. Annie had never liked being hot since the fever, and never used it, but I relaxed in it a couple times a month.

Hester looked like I was some kinda genius. "The roof is perfect. Contained but also open to the sky. Salt would work well to draw the circle. You've done this before."

"A time or two. One other thing. I donno if it's how it's usually done, but I'm coming in there with you two. I ain't letting Annie be alone through whatever happens."

Hester's mouth prissed up. "I wouldn't recommend it."

"I ain't asking."

If her face got any prissier she was gonna turn into a lemon. "What would your shaman friend have done?"

"She woulda said the more the merrier." Thing was, I knew that was true. No way Jo would try keeping me, or anybody important to someone, out of a healing circle. 'course, that wasn't the answer Hester was looking for or expecting, so her face just about did turn into a lemon. But she nodded, an' I went to heat up the the sauna, asking, "How much steam you want in there?" on my way.

"The steam is less important than the heat." By the

time I got back from lightin' things up and getting the salt, Hester was losing her priss and startin' to look more serene. She took the salt and circled the sauna, mumbling some kinda mumbo-jumbo that woulda made Jo laugh, but that I reckoned set her mind at ease. She stopped when she had about two feet left open, and nodded at me. "If you'd like to get your wife now, I'll close the circle when you're both inside. Try not to wake her if you can."

"I'll try." I figured Annie would wake up the minute I touched her, but she only nestled against me when I lifted her. I hated to think what that meant for how she was feeling, and about how much she was trying to hide her sickness from me. She didn't wake up in the colder air outside, neither, and I took her into the sauna still wrapped in the blanket from the couch.

Hester came in a couple seconds later, looked at me holding Annie, and decided not to argue about it. My girl was sweating already, curls tightening up against her forehead. I kissed one of 'em and settled down to wait and watch. Truth was, Jo hardly used any of this kinda stuff. Power circles, sometimes, but never sweat lodges, so I didn't know what we were getting into, except altered states of reality. Hester finally took that bag off her hip an' pulled out a flat drum kinda like the one Jo had, only not painted so fancy. That was familiar, anyway, so I relaxed a bit as she started playing. Annie's breathing fell into rhythm with it real quick, and Hester said, "I think we'll try the spirit quest first, before any attempt at healing. It might help."

"Sure, doll. Makes sense to me."

From her face, I didn't think anybody had ever called the woman *doll* before. Not that most fellas used it these days anyway, but she looked like she'd bitten into something sour again. She kept her mouth shut, though, an' I didn't try real hard not to laugh. Way I saw it, laughter was good mojo, and Annie and me needed every bit of that we could get right now. The heat started getting worse, an' we all got quiet a while, nothing but the sound of Hes's drum and our own heartbeats keepin us company. Annie took a sharp little waking up breath, and I kissed her forehead again, murmuring, "It's okay, darlin'. We're doing a little spirit quest for you."

"Shouldn't I be awake for that? I'm hot. What's that smell, the cedar? We're in the..." She tensed up and relaxed again almost all at once. "Oh. We're in the sauna. Gary, you know I don't like saunas."

"It's just for a little while. You relax, Annie. Just close your eyes and let whatever comes wander through your mind, all right?"

"Who's playing a drum?" She sat up a couple inches, sweat rolling down her forehead, and frowned at Hester, who never stopped playing.

"I'm here to guide your quest, and perhaps try a healing later. My name is Hester Jones, and you should lie back down." She wasn't real polite about it, and Annie bristled enough to make me grin. Jo was always going on about how shamanism was mostly about change, and about getting inside of somebody's head to give 'em a moment when the world slips to the side and looks a little different. She said that's the thing that makes healing possible, having an instant when all your preconceptions fall apart. Since even the idea of a shaman was kinda mystical and soft-seeming, I figured just meeting Hester Jones threw most folks's expectations into a tailspin.

Annie, still bristling, sat up insteada lying down like a good girl. "What quest? I want to understand what's happening."

Hester gave me a look like that was somehow my fault, but I woulda bet the farm that she liked knowing what was goin' on too. Besides, I wasn't that much of a damned fool. I hadn't stayed married forty-eight years by putting words in Annie's mouth, or by taking 'em out. After a good hard glare at me, Hes answered Annie: "We're going to perform a spirit quest. Your husband is right in that there's very little you have to do except be receptive. The drum will help bring you into a trance state, and if a spirit guardian wishes to help you, it'll come to you in the trance. Usually an animal you see four times has chosen you."

"And why are we doing this?" Annie was using her professional nurse tone, the one people hopped to without thinking why.

Hes looked like she knew what was happening, but she answered anyway. "Because a spirit animal will protect and fight for you as we try a healing. It'll also make you more receptive to a healing." She added that like she thought Annie was gonna need a lot of receptivity to consider magic healing as a possibility, but I had faith in my girl.

Annie's mouth pursed up and her eyebrows bobbed a

couple seconds before she nodded and relaxed into my arms again. "All right." A heartbeat later her eyes were closed, her breathing as steady as it could be with her lungs clogged up, an' the drum was takin' us all away again.

I didn't know if it was doing anything for Annie, but after a while it brought a couple fellas I knew outta the dark. The white raven and my tortoise came in to visit, but I didn't think they were so much looking out for me as Annie. Both of 'em were looking outward, waiting on something, and every once in a while I got a glimpse of different critters ghosting their way through the dark. Once I caught sight of a crow, and once other of a buncha walking stick bugs, but my guides kept waiting, looking for something I didn't know what.

I guessed they finally saw it, even if I didn't, 'cause the raven started hopping around and flapping his wings like he was all excited, and the tortoise hunkered down feeling satisfied. The raven bounced up on the tortoise's shell and settled there, preening and shaking his feathers while we waited some more.

Seemed like about forever before Annie let go a real soft long breath and whispered somethin' I couldn't quite hear. Then she turned her cheek against my chest. "How interesting. You should try this sometime, Gary. Something actually came to me. A—"

"Don't tell us," Hester barked. She was flushed, prolly from the heat, but she was kinda agitated, too. "A spirit guide's choice is a private matter."

Annie lifted her head and gave Hes a hairy eyeball, but

didn't say anything else. I didn't figure I'd want Hes knowin' what my spirit animals were, either, even if she was helping out. "You all right to try this healing thing, then, Miz Jones?"

She nodded, but she was paying attention to Annie, not me. "I need you to understand that a shamanic healing is most effective when the person seeking healing is receptive. Without *your* belief, there's very little, perhaps nothing, that I can do."

Annie gave her a hard look. "That certainly puts the onus on the patient. Does it help you sleep at night?"

Hester's pink cheeks went pale and I tried to pick up my flapping jaw, not remembering the last time I'd heard Annie being that sharp, though I got where it was coming from. She'd spent a lotta years as a nurse, and always said a good attitude helped, but for her, medicine worked whether the patient believed in penicillin or not. I could see how the idea of laying it all on the patient would bug her right down to her bones. She started looking like she mighta regretted saying that, but she not like she wasn't gonna back down on having said it.

It took a long damned minute for Hes to find her voice. "Shamanic healing doesn't have to be at odds with modern medicine. I would encourage you and anyone else to also pursue conventional treatment. But if you're willing accept your own role in the healing process, shamanic magic may be able to help."

Annie's cheeks were pink too, like she'd helped herself to the color that'd drained outta Hes. She was as embarrassed as I'd ever seen her, an' murmured, "Of course I'm willing to accept it."

Hes nodded, so I guessed they'd sorted it out in the way women do when they ain't gonna say what they really mean. "I've had a glimpse of the illness within you. We've done a spirit quest. I think we may need to do a spirit journey, now. If we leave this plane, the illness inside you may manifest itself separately, which would allow us to fight it in physical form and drive it away. Does that make sense?"

"Not really, but I'm not sure that matters. Will it make sense as it happens?"

"It should. I'll bring you to the Lower World—"

"No." That was me, surprisin' all of us. Hes straightened up, looking like she was ready to give me a tongue-lashing, but I shook my head and kept talking. "Take her to the Upper World instead, all right? I ain't sure this thing can't just walk in and out on whatever levels it wants to, but I know the deeper you go the closer you're getting to its home territory. Reach for the sky, darling. Don't dig down deep. All right?"

Hes looked uncertain. "The Upper World's spirits are more capricious. Trying to draw this illness out for a battle there may let it escape and do harm elsewhere, if we fail."

"You can't—" I shut up before I finished asking, 'cause I already knew the answer. Jo threw magic nets around all over the place, all the time, but I'd seen her and her pal Coyote fighting together once, and it had mostly been on Jo's shoulders. Coyote was a full-out shaman, one who wasn't walkin' the warrior path that Joanne was on. He could manage some shields, but twisting magic into other shapes and catching things in it was outta his league. And Hes here couldn't even shield somebody else, so there was no chance she was gonna pull out a gimmick like Jo mighta. "I'd say it's worth risking."

"And do I get a say in this?" Annie sounded stronger, like her spirit animal was already doing some good. "What kind of harm could it do, Miss Jones?"

"I don't know. It's a strong darkness, though. Right now it's focused on you, but if it's freed to pursue weakness in others, it could reach hundreds or even thousands."

"Then there's no choice at all. My health isn't worth hundreds of others."

"Annie—"

"*Gary.* Miss Jones, if we try to examine this...darkness... in the Lower World, can you contain it?"

"It's more likely. I can reinforce our power circle there, which adds layers of protection."

"*Annie.*"

"*Gary.* No. I have not spent a lifetime nursing others simply to choose the good of the one in my last days."

"Dammit, Annie!"

"Garrison Matthew Muldoon." Annie sat up, cheeks pink and eyes flashing hot. She threw her blanket off an' got up like she was gonna stare me down. "If I am dying I am by God going to do it on my terms, and you're going to accept that."

"On a cold day in Hell, sweetheart." I stayed sitting, 'cause I was about a foot taller'n her and didn't need to stand to be damned near eye level to her. 'sides, the sauna already wasn't big enough for three anyway, if two of 'em were having a fight. "If you're dying, I'm raging every step of the way."

Annie spat, "*Though wise men at their end know dark is right*," and I stood up after all an' said, "*Do not go gentle*, Annie. You wanna try the Lower World journey first, fine, we do that, I ain't arguing. And I know you'd never forgive yourself, or me, if we did something that got other people hurt or sick, so all right, maybe we don't try the Upper World journey. But I'm never giving up, you hear me? Though lovers be lost, Annie. I'll do whatever it takes."

All the fight went outta her and she put her hand against my chest. "No, Gary. You won't. Some things we can't change. Death *does* have dominion, in the end."

"Maybe death does, sweetheart, but evil don't, and this thing that's coming at us is evil. I ain't lying down for it."

"Even if something truly terrible happens because we fight?"

"Awful things happen all the time, Annie. How're we s'posed to know if our fight makes 'em happen? How're—" Somethin' sick and cold rose up in me fast, making ice sweat stand out on my skin even though it was a hundred and five degrees in there.

There was something God-awful brewing just a couple weeks from now, something so bad it was gonna rock the whole world. I'd watched it on TV the way most folks had, and I remembered thinkin' *at least Annie ain't here to see it*. She'd died three days before, on our wedding anniversary, and even through the pain of losin' her, it had hit me like a wall.

Feeling hollow and not talking to Annie or Hester at all, I said, "It happened anyway," like somebody else might be listening. I sure as hell hadn't saved her, and it had happened anyway. That had to mean it wasn't black magic getting into souls just soon enough to make a few crazies fly airplanes into buildings. It *couldn't* be something we'd done, even if I *did* somehow save her, 'cause that kinda thing took time and planning.

'cept I was standing there outta time myself, carrying memories of the future and not remembering a whole lotta mojo that had spilled through the whole of my life. *Something* had gone wrong, *something* had changed in my life, to make me forget all of this, when the whole idea of Horns dropping me in was to try making one big change at the last minute.

An' I knew from experience, from watching and working with Joanne, that you only got one shot at changing a big event. Time mostly wanted to go the way it already *had* gone.

There was no goddamned way I was gonna stop September 11th. An' there was no goddamned way I could know if saving Annie might be the one thing giving the Master a chance to snatch back the dark magic eating up her lungs, and twist it backward in time a little to find the susceptible hearts and souls who could do something unthinkable.

I said, "But it already happened," again, an' sat down again with my face in my hands. It already happened, and I didn't see a way outta this. If I tried saving Annie an' the towers fell, I couldn't ever know if I'd helped make that happen. If I didn't and they fell anyway, I was wasting my one chance. And if I didn't an' they *didn't* fall, then my future memories were wrong too, an' I couldn't trust any of this at all.

Joanne had been real reluctant to take up her healing powers, to become a shaman, back in the beginning. She hadn't wanted to be a hero. For the first time ever, I started wondering if the girl hadn't had a point. Being a hero had a down side darker an' harder than I'd appreciated until just now.

"We do the Lower World," I finally said, feeling dull an' thick as a board. "Guess we can't risk more'n that."

"Gary?" Annie knelt when I sat, frowning up at me. "What's wrong?"

"One of them future flashes," I said, still talking into my hands. I'd seen Jo do that a hundred times over the last year. Never thought I'd be doing it myself. "Something ugly that I'd hate to learn was cause and effect working here."

"We see patterns where there are none," Hester said, all unexpected. She still sounded sharp as pins, but she sounded like she was tryin' ta be sympathetic, too. Annie and me both looked at her and she said, "Humans. We see patterns where none exist. It's a survival technique. I realize I've just warned you about potential ramifications, but you should also understand that because you see a pattern or a connection doesn't mean there is one. We would all be forever unable to act if we knew what butterfly effect our every activity might cause."

"Or our every inaction," Annie said. "Gary, you look worse than you did this morning when the doctor said I was sick. What's wrong? What did you see?"

"Nothin' anybody's gonna be able to stop."

Hester's eyebrows wrinkled together. "You're precognitive?"

"It's just a passing phase."

For about half a minute Hes just sat there, looking between me and Annie like we were something she never imagined showing up on her doorstep. Then, like she was pulling all the pieces of her curiosity back and putting 'em in line where they belonged, she said, "Shall we perform the Lower World journey?"

"Will Gary be with me?"

Hester's mouth flattened. "I don't think I could keep him out."

"All right, then." Annie finally settled back down with me, curling up in the blanket even though it was plenty warm in there. Hester went back to beating the drum, and after a minute started singing something about gates and doors and passageways. I started getting fussed about that not being the way Jo did things, then let it go. It didn't take long for the sauna to start fading in and out, an' then for a pathway to open up through one of the walls. Annie shifted, looking from it to Hes, then got up and walked into the Lower World.

CHAPTER FOURTEEN

I knew what to expect 'cause Joanne had told me about the Lower World more than once, but seeing a red sun hanging low in the sky like it wasn't ever gonna get higher was a whole lot different from knowing that's what was there. A lotta the earth was red, too. The horizons were too close and lousy with mountains. Blue clouds lingered around 'em, though above us was clear except for being a shade of yellow I'd only ever seen in Jersey. Mosta the plant life had a purple tinge, an' it was all rainforest-big, though the air wasn't that humid.

Annie stood on an orange pathway in the middle of all that, staring around in wonder. The path didn't go anywhere but backward, but I didn't guess it had to. Hester stepped past me and looked around with a click that sounded satisfied. "This will do. Are you comfortable there, Mrs. Muldoon?"

"What? Yes, I'm fine. This is...this is astonishing. You

said it's called the Lower World?"

"In the shamanic spirituality I've studied, yes. It has other names and other faces in different cultures. Here the animistic nature of all things can take on an aspect we can more easily communicate with. That's why we can fight your illness here in a way Western medicine wouldn't understand." Hester stomped a circle around Annie while she was talking, stopping four times to make some kinda little gesture. "Mr. Muldoon, I understand you want to help your wife through this, but this fight has to largely be her own. I'd like to put you in a separate protective circle. I can link them together, if you prefer, but you may not cross from one to the other."

"That sounds like a rotten plan."

"Don't be difficult, Gary."

"All right, all right. Hey, wait!" I'd been carting Jo's rapier around for a slow ride through forever, but I'd stopped carrying it when Horns had dropped me into my own story. I reckoned that shouldn't matter, especially in the Lower World, and especially since I'd seen Jo draw it outta nowhere any number of times. I concentrated on the feel of the thing, the heavy silver an' the complicated guard, and let myself think, just real quick, about the quiet misty homeland Cernunnos had brought me to for a while. A shiver ran down my spine an' back up again, resonating across a couple worlds, but the god-blessed sword glimmered an' came to life in my hands. I clutched the hilt like I was hugging it, then handed it over to Annie while trying not to see how she an' Hester were both gaping.

"This used to belong to Horns. The fella who tackled

you outta the way of the car back when you were a kid. I figure he's got your back, so maybe this thing'll do you some good."

I could see her working her way past a hundred questions, tryin' ta focus on the most important thing: "Gary, I can't use this, it's too...big..."

We were all watching when it happened. The silver kinda shriveled and shrank, melting in on itself inside of a blink, until the whole sword was about fifteen inches shorter than it'd been. My jaw flapped open. It'd never done that before, not that I could remember. A'course, Jo and Cernunnos were pretty close to the same size, an' I wasn't that much bigger, so we could all use the same-length blade. Annie hefted it a couple times now, searched for something to say, and came up with, "That's better."

Hester's eyes were near to falling out of her head. "Who are you?"

"Sorry, sweetheart, I'm just a guy. Do your thing, doll. Build me a circle. I'll stay put."

Hes ground her teeth together, but she nodded an' stomped away. Annie and me exchanged a smile, and I was looking right into her eyes when a monster burst outta her chest and attacked her.

I swore she knew it was coming. There was nothing of my surprise in her eyes. I was still gathering breath to yell and she was already falling into guard, slapping a mass of ugly away like it wasn't much more than a fruit fly. I wondered if she'd had a hint it was coming, some kinda pain inside her, but I guessed it didn't matter, at that. She and it were circling each other, keeping to the edges of the power circle, an' Hester and me were standing outside in horror. I swallowed my yell, not wanting to distract Annie. Hester vibrated with indecision, twitching forward like she'd jump in, then flinching back like she didn't wanna distract Annie either.

The thing she was fighting didn't look like any kinda monster you could name out of a book. It looked like sickness oughta: a black writhing mass of nastiness, fulla teeth an' hateful eyes and tar lashes. It looked like a bad cold felt, something heavy and ugly weighing down your chest, sucking away your ability to breath. It looked like a heart attack felt, pain running up and down your arm and pressing down on you 'til stars came into your eyes. An' all I could think, watching Annie circling around and watching it, was that at least right now it was out of her, an' that might give her a fighting chance.

I couldn't see which moved first, her or it. They were just in the middle of the power circle together all at once, blue sparks flying from Annie's sword an' bits of blackness sticking to her skin where the sickness caught hold. Even from outside of Annie's circle there was rage and hate coming off the stuff, but it kept not slowing my girl down. She just kept taking it, and fighting back, and holding her ground until the damned stuff started to falter.

Hester stepped in then, one quick smooth move that looked like they'd been planning it all along. I was used to seeing Jo's blue healing magic at work, an' it surprised the hell outta me to see Hester's hands shine bright clear yellow when she raised 'em up. The stuff faltered under that light, an' for a couple breaths I thought everything was gonna be all right. The sickness shrank, getting less dangerous-looking and somehow more scared as Annie's fighting skills and Hester's healing magic came together.

I leaned forward, not breathing, just clenching my hands and teeth and praying, when the stuff gathered itself into an arrow and punched right outta the top of the power circle.

Hester dropped like somebody'd cut her strings. Annie staggered but stayed up, an' then because she was the biggest-hearted woman in the world, she forgot about the turn-tail monster an' knelt to tend to Hester. Me, I watched the stuff head skyward until it went invisible from distance. When I looked back at the women, Hester was sitting up and holding her head. Annie was clucking and making soothing noises, and Hes looked more prune-faced than before. I guessed she didn't like that kinda fuss. "What happened there?"

"Backlash from it breaking my power circle. I think I'm lucky Mrs. Muldoon had weakened it. Where did it go?"

I pointed up. Annie and Hes both looked that way, and Hester's face got tighter still. "We've released it. Damn."

"There's gotta be some way to catch it." I didn't know who I was trying to convince, but I wasn't doing much good making myself believe it. Then I forgot about it for something more important: "Annie, how you doing?"

"Breathless!" She put a hand over her chest, smiling. "But breathless from exertion, not coughing. I feel younger here. Is that usual?"

"The spirit worlds reflect our perceptions of ourselves." Hes was still frowning at the sky. "We need to return. I have to do what I can to mitigate this creature's escape."

A beanstalk curled up outta the ground and stretched for the yellow sky.

All three of us stood there staring at it a minute. Annie rocked back on her heels to get a better look as it shot up toward through blue clouds an' reached toward the low red sun. It wasn't green itself, kinda yellowish an' ugly, but nothing had the right colors down here anyway, and it looked healthy other than being the wrong color. When we couldn't hardly see the top anymore, Annie said, "Am I right in believing that this journey is essentially...well, all about me?"

Hes, gaping like a fish outta water, snapped her mouth shut and nodded, but her gaze went right back to the beanstalk.

Annie, all business-like, dusted her hands together, said, "Well, then, I believe this should be taken as a hint," and started climbing the beanstalk. Hes and me scrambled after her. The ground fell away faster than it shoulda, partly 'cause the beanstalk was still growing and partly 'cause the world and distances were all stretched outta proportion. Then we broke through the sky and for half a second I got a glimpse of our world, but we were just passing through. We busted through that sky, too, straight into a place where the air was thinner an' the sky a lighter shade of blue.

Cold wind wanted to knock us off the beanstalk, but Annie kept climbing, even when we shot past mountaintops. After what felt like about a day, we got to the top of the stalk, where it curled up and under an' all around, with broad leaves big enough to hold us all. When Hes and me caught up, Annie was already sitting on one, knees tucked up and arms around 'em as she looked out over the whole wide forever.

I guessed if the Lower World's horizons were too close, the Upper World's were too far away. It all bent out around us like we were on some other planet, somewhere bigger'n Earth and twice as old. The beanstalk had outgrown the mountains, an' the mountains were taller than sense could make 'em. There wasn't much *besides* mountains poking up through thin clouds. There was blue below us, way below, but it looked like sky, not like water. Light didn't bounce off it, just got softer the further away it fell. In some places the mountains just stopped, falling away into cliffs that disappeared into mist, too, and no matter which way I looked the sky was cool thin blue.

Way off in the distance there were things riding the updrafts. Birds, I guessed, though I couldn't figure the size of 'em if they were visible from so far away in a world this big. Joanne had seen a thunderbird here, even brought it back to the Middle World with her, but I'd been in the hospital and hadn't seen the damned thing. She'd said it was big, though. Big enough to throw her around, and she wasn't no featherweight.

A rush of bugs came up the beanstalk, about a thousand

walking sticks that took my mind right off the birds. If they were hungry the beanstalk was gonna fall to 'em, but they didn't look interested. Instead they scrambled over Annie, who insteada shrieking like I expected, put her arms out and let 'em run over her. They just about buried her, lining up side by side on her arms and in her hair, all of 'em trying to get a look into her eyes. She just waited, until finally I got the idea they didn't find what they were looking for, and left her alone.

Surprising thing was, they came to me. Did the same thing, too, climbed all over and stared at me until I started shivering. Then they all left but one, and it sat on my shoulder. Took me a minute to realize maybe that made sense, 'cause Jo's last name, her real last name, the one she didn't use, was Walkingstick, not Walker. I shoved my hands in my pockets to keep from knocking the bug away, and took a look at Hester. She was big-eyed and looking as sweet as I'd seen her yet, like maybe there was some little bit of kid at Christmas left in her after all. I wanted to know what the devil was happening, but I was kinda afraid to ask.

The wind started taking on shapes, like clouds blowing in and making figures in the sky. I caught glimpses the same way I had in Annie's spirit quest: a whole herd of horses came running at us, parting around Annie and thundering on across the sky. They scared up a flock of fat birds 'bout the size of chickens, their wings clattering as they flew off. Some other critters were more distant, harder to name, but I saw the one that finally came to her clear as day. A big fella, a white-tailed stag that walked outta the sky as just a few wisps of cloud an' walked right into Annie and never came out again. Took me that long to figure out we were on another spirit quest after all. I shot a look at my shoulder. The walking stick was gone.

"All right." Annie's voice was real loud and clear, a shock after hearing nothin but the wind for so long. She got up, the beanstalk leaf bobbing with her weight, and she flung her arms wide. "Come and get me, you son of a bitch."

The goddamned sickness, the first dark thing I'd seen up there in the Upper World, came outta nowhere and slammed back into Annie's chest.

CHAPTER FIFTEEN

We woke up in the sauna, Annie coughing and unable to get a breath of the hot air. I picked her up and took her out in a couple long steps, crouching outside in the cool air and never letting go while she coughed herself ragged. Hester came out behind us, so worried I could feel it rattling off her. The sky had turned to twilight while we were inside, an' the last light slipped away before Annie could breathe again. She turned her face against my chest an' said, real quiet, "If you could come back tomorrow, Miss Jones? I'm very tired now, and I suppose we still have to try to find who set this illness on me."

"I'll come around ten," Hester promised, an' left without going back through the house. I picked Annie up again and brought her inside, put her on the couch, and went to make tea.

When I came back into the living room she was on her feet, looking out the window at the dark lawn. "Annie? You all right, sweetheart?"

"I spent my adult life watching people deny the truth." Her reflection was in the windows, faint 'cause there weren't many lights on inside. Made her look like a ghost, already fading. I started toward her an' she shook her head, almost a shiver, like saying *stay away*. I guessed a fellow could take offense, but I'd been married to the lady a long time. It just meant she was thinking aloud, not hardly talking to me at all, and that if I got too close she'd start feeling self-conscious and clam up. I sat down, listening insteada crowding.

"Mostly about illness, of course," she said. "Promising themselves or each other that this wasn't it, this sickness wasn't going to finish them off. Promising if they got out of there, they would change their lives for the better. A few of them were right, even when they were lying to begin with. They beat the odds, and walked out. Some of them even went on and changed their lives, or other peoples' lives, for the better. Not many, though. But that isn't the point.

"The point is I've been thinking about that ever since I started feeling poorly. About how people deny the truth that's in front of them. I suppose I'd seen a lot of it by the time we got married, and by the time I caught the fever I... well, I suppose I believed in what I saw more than in what I thought I knew. And I accepted that. I started believing there was a kind of magic in the world. I never questioned it again, which I suppose made a difference in my life. But now I'm standing here with an illness growing inside me, something that someone apparently chose to *plant* in me, and I can't help but wonder, Gary. What would have happened if I had denied it all in the first place? Would this thing not have come into me? If I had refused the world it represents, would it have lost interest? You say your future flashes suggest I'm a target because you love me, but that makes me quite the helpless victim, and I dare anyone to call me that to my face."

She wasn't so much talking to herself anymore, which meant I could chuckle without making her lose her head of steam. I didn't say nothing, though, just laughed and nodded.

Annie nodded once too, kinda sharp and brisk, and kept talking. "I chose this life, Gary. I chose the moments of madness and exhilaration that have come with discovering there are monsters beneath the bed. And if you believe there is something out there, a mastermind or an evil which wishes to destroy you because you in some way bring light into the world, then I cannot believe I'm merely auxiliary to that. I will not believe it. Even if this illness should succeed, if it kills me, it would be unforgivable for you to lay down your sword and give up the fight. So I *must* believe myself to be a target in my own right."

She faced me, eyes flashing and color high in her cheeks. "And if I'm worth that much to any agent of darkness, then I am by *God* going to give it the fight of its life. And the fight of mine."

Between one breath an' the next I had her in my arms, spinning her around and kissing her through laughter. "Darlin', I feel like I oughta be cheering. You shoulda been leading the troops, not patching them up." I set her down again, trying not to think of how light she'd been in my arms, an' brushed my thumbs over her cheeks. "And I guess you're putting me in my place, too, sweetheart. Kinda arrogant of me to figure it was all about me."

She patted my cheek. "Yes, but very male."

I snorted an' caught her hand to kiss her palm. "Mebbe so. You're right, though, darlin'. Ain't no way I'd let anything make me back down if something happened to you—*which it ain't gonna*—"

Something happened around her eyes, something that told me she thought I wasn't much of a liar, but she didn't call me on it, so I kept going. "So I shoulda seen it myself. Maybe I didn't getcha into this, darlin'. Maybe we got each other into it, but it don't matter, 'cause you're my bright star. *Would I were as steadfast as thou art*—"

She laughed all of a sudden, bright an' quick. "Why do you do that, Gary? I've known you almost fifty years and you've always used the language like you're a big dumb hunk, and then you forget yourself and quote poetry."

I said, "Girls like it," as solemn as I could, and Annie laughed again.

"I know I did. I still do. But I knew your parents, Gary. Neither of them were marble-mouthed, and they both said "isn't" instead of "ain't". I could understand it if they had, but it's an affectation and it's gotten more noticeable as you've gotten older."

Still solemn, I said, "You're only just noticin' this now? Maybe you're just gettin' pickier," and she gave me a dirty look that I smiled away. "Guess I do it more now 'cause fares like it. It fits the persona. But I guess I started it way back in college. I learned playing ball that folks underestimate you if they think you ain't too bright. Gives a guy a chance to learn a lot about what the other team's thinking and doing, if they don't worry much about chatting when you're around. S'pose I got in the habit then and never dropped it, so I gotta pull out the poets once in a while to keep my old grey cells hopping. You want me to give it a rest?"

"Could you?"

"Prob'ly not."

Annie smiled. "That's all right. I do like it. And I've wondered on and off for years. Decades. But it's a question—" She swallowed hard. "I suppose it's one of those things, it's so silly and not important, and you think you'll always have time to ask. Now I'm afraid there's not any time left, so...I asked."

"We still got all the time in the world, babe." I curled her close, wishing I could make either one of us believe me. "Silly thing to be sittin' on for forty years, though. Got anything else that's been bothering you?"

"I don't know. Do I want to know the truth about Mary Lou Stravinski?"

A guffaw burst right outta me. "There's a name I ain't thought about in a long time. I swear to you, Annie, she fell in that mud puddle just like I said. I never thought she was gonna strip her wet dress off and hand it to me once I put my coat around her, an' I swear to God she never managed to lay a kiss on me, even if that's what it looked like when you walked in. I swear I was tryin' ta get her *off* me—" I stopped, 'cause Annie's eyes were bright and her lips were pressed together like she was trying hard not to laugh. "You know alla this, doncha."

"Yes, but it's fun to watch you squirm. I never was really worried about that. You prefer blondes."

"Gentlemen do. Annie. Annie, what happened back there? Up there. You knocked that crap outta yourself, and then you..." I was pretty damned sure I knew what had happened, and why, and I hated it as much as I loved my girl.

"Took it back in. I told you, Gary. I'm going to give this thing the fight of its life. I can't do that if it's out there." She waved at the windows and meant the whole world beyond 'em. "Maybe someone did put this sickness in me, but that was on their terms. They're on mine now."

"Yeah." I closed my eyes, wishing pressing them shut would make everything she was saying go away. But I reckon I'd known just what she was doing, and there was no way she'd have ever done anything else. She wasn't gonna let somebody else suffer if she had a chance at defeating something. "You're about the bravest woman I ever knew, Anne Marie Muldoon."

"It's not going to end well, is it," she said real softly. I opened my eyes again to find her looking sad. "I'm sorry, Gary. I feel much stronger than I did earlier. I can feel the—" The sadness turned into a glower that made me laugh. "I'm telling you whether that woman says I should or not. The first animal was a cheetah, of all things, Gary. A cheetah. That's absurd. I'm not a cat person."

"Sweetheart, my spirit animal is a tortoise, so I figure they know better than we do. It ain't just about whether we got an affinity for 'em. It's about what gifts they can bring us."

Somethin' happened in her eyes, a real seriousness all mixed up with curiosity and maybe a bit more understanding than I wanted to see from her. "Your spirit animal. I didn't know you had one."

I tried not to grit my teeth, feelin like I'd blown it. "It shows up a long time from now."

That understanding in her eyes ran deeper. She tilted her head, studying me like I was some kinda new thing before sayin, real careful, "'Future flashes.'"

"Yeah, darlin'." My heartbeat was going crazy an' I was getting hot beneath the collar. I didn't know how, but I was sure she'd figured out the truth somehow. Intuition, or me being a real bad liar, or something, but I'd let too much slip and she *knew*. But I couldn't ask 'cause if it was my imagination running wild and she *didn't* know, then asking would mean the jig was up too. I was starting to blush, and I hadn't done that in thirty years.

The corner of her mouth turned up just a little. "All right, dear. If you say so. Now, what was I saying. Oh, the cheetah. A cheetah, for heaven's sake. It's something a seventeen-year-old girl would want, not a seventy year old lady. The other was—"

"A stag. I kinda saw that one, darlin'. Got a glimpse, anyway."

"Positively ridiculous," she said. "Virile and masculine.

Why on earth would creatures like that want me?"

I had a hard time pulling my eyebrows outta my hairline. Annie laughed, blushed, and laughed again. "That's very flattering, but really, Gary, I am seventy years old."

"Don't see what that's got to do with anything. 'sides, it all kinda fits together. You saw that picture your pa painted of Cernunnos, the horns on him and all. I don't figure it's a coincidence a stag came your way, is what I'm saying. You're feeling stronger, that's what matters, right?"

"Strong enough to take the fight to this enemy." The color in her cheeks wasn't from blushing anymore. It was the fire of battle getting ready to meet. "Gary, I can't just let it go out into the world, or the Upper World, wherever you want to say, and let other people be hurt by it. But if I'm strong enough to hold on a while, maybe we'll win something. Maybe if I can hold this evil inside of me just a little longer than it expects, maybe it'll mean I take one wrong thing out of the world when I go. That's worth dying for, Gary. If I'm going to die anyway, I want to make it worth something."

"You ain't gonna—"

"Everybody does, sweetheart. Whether it's tomorrow because of this sickness or thirty years from now from old age, everybody dies. I don't want to leave you, but if I have to, I'm going to take as much darkness out of the world as I can when I go."

There wasn't much I could say to that, so I didn't try. There was no arguing with the woman at the best of times, an' this was that, and the worst too. We shut ourselves in together, whispering like kids 'til way too late in the night, telling secrets about power animals and spirit journeys and doing our best to take ourselves there without anybody helping. I didn't know what time we fell asleep, but we didn't wake up until Hester knocked on the door a couple minutes after ten the next morning.

Pretty sure she thought we were too old for the state of dishevelment we came to the door in, but her sour face getting even sourer made me and Annie both laugh. I cooked everybody breakfast while Annie got herself put together.

We spent the whole day doing the rounds, everything Annie usually did. Hester's eyes went as gold as Jo's did when she turned on the mojo, which kinda surprised me. I'd figured everybody would have their own color, maybe something to do with their auras, though Jo's aura wasn't gold at all, which shot that idea fulla holes. I chuckled at myself, making both women look at me, but I shrugged it off. Explaining any more about future memories was more than I wanted to try.

All three of us got tense when we dropped into the yoga studio, figuring a spiritual center was the most likely place for a magic user, even a dark one, to hole up. Annie introduced Hester around to the teachers, an' one by one they came up clean, even the new one we'd been laying our bets on. It was coming on toward night again by then, and stronger or not, Annie was wrung out. Hester had to come home with us, 'cause she'd left her car there, but the drive back was full of her tension and apologies she wasn't making out loud. Annie finally reached between the front seats and patted Hes's knee. "It's not your fault, Miss Jones. Maybe this is a natural illness after all."

"No. I've taken a lot of people to the Lower World to battle their sicknesses, Mrs. Muldoon. No natural illness looks or fights like that." Hester's eyes were glowing gold again, like anger was turning them hot. "Shamanism says everything, even illness, has a spirit, and everything with a spirit wants to live, but this is more than that. It doesn't just want to live. It wants to kill."

I was watching her in the rear-view mirror, an' saw her realize she'd said too much. Annie went pale and turned back around to look out the side window, and Hester's mouth got thin and grim. She was already staring ahead like the Devil himself was waiting at home when we turned up the drive, but she flinched and grabbed the back of my seat as I parked the Chevy. "Who's here?"

I squinted at her in the mirror. "Nobody, far as I know. Why?"

Annie said, "Probably Myles," at the same time, adding, "The gardener," when me and Hester both looked at her. "You haven't met him yet," she told me. "He replaced Beth a few weeks ago. I did tell you that."

"Yeah, I remember. You said he was one of the new folks—" The air got a whole lot colder, raising hairs on my arms. "Hes?"

"It's like looking into a plague of locusts." She wasn't looking at either of us, but at our yard, somewhere past the curve that put the far side outta view. "His aura is overwhelmed with darkness. I can't See the colors it might once have been. He's embraced something that lends him power, but at the cost of...of everything he is." Hester Jones hadn't been uncertain for even half a heartbeat since we'd met her, but she sounded like the core of her world had been shaken. "I've never seen anything...I didn't even imagine anyone *could* do that."

"I—" I shut up on sayin *I seen it before*. I had, except not for a few years yet. Joanne had gone up against a sorcerer early on, and we'd both seen how he could get into the hearts and souls of people looking for power. Or, hell, even just looking for a way to survive. I reckoned all of that kinda power backtracked eventually to the same source, to the guy we kept calling the Master.

"It's sorcery," I said instead, which made Annie gimme another one of those *you know too much* looks, but she didn't call me on it. I didn't figure she was ever gonna.

"Sorcery—" Hester took a deep breath, trying to contain herself. "In shamanic studies, a sorcerer is a shaman who has embraced darkness. Sorcerers can do terrible things. Skinwalk. Steal someone's will. Cast curses and—"

"And cause sickness instead of healing it." I'd been on the receiving end of that, though it'd been a corrupted witch, not a sorcerer, who'd magicked me into a heart attack. "Lissen to me, Hester. Most sorcerers are gonna be at least a couple steps removed from the heart o'darkness—"

Annie, beneath her breath, muttered, "*The only thing was for it to come to and wait for the turn of the tide,*" an' I smirked but kept going. "This fella, there's a good chance he's sold himself higher up the river. Ain't nobody gonna think less of you if you walk away right now, and the truth is, sweetheart, that might be smart. The boss man in this mess, he holds a grudge, and I hate to..."

Way too late, it finally clicked. Hester Jones. Name seemed kinda familiar, yeah, because she'd been one of a half-dozen murders a few years from now. Right at the same time I'd met Jo, in fact, when a demi-god was taking his daddy issues out on the magic users in Seattle. Far as I knew, Herne hadn't been aligned with the Master, but he'd gone a long way down a road to Hell, and not much of it had been paved with good intentions. When a guy is that far off the path of righteousness, it probably ain't that hard for a worse bad guy to draw his eyes to a few particular sacrificial lambs.

An' here I was, pulling Hester neck-deep into a fight a lot bigger an' uglier than she was counting on. An' here I was knowing it was already too late, if this was all cause and effect, 'cause whether I liked it or not, she was gonna die messy in just a couple more years. *"Dammit."*

I coulda been talking the wind for all she cared. Her back was up, eyes flashing, and for a minute I liked her, sour grapes and all. "Sorcery is an abomination. It's a corruption of everything I've ever studied. It's very...chivalrous," she said, like it was a bad word, "of you to try to save me trouble, but this isn't an encounter I could ever walk away from."

"Are you on the warrior's path, doll?"

Hester was halfway outta the car when I asked, and sat back again looking genuinely surprised. "I am. How did you know?"

"From what I know most shamans ain't quite so gung-ho about fighting, is all. Healing, yeah, but I don't get the impression most of 'em are that good in a fight." I knew what I was talking about, having watched Jo's pal Coyote freeze up in a fight, and he was no minor leaguer in the mojo department. "So I figured you might be on a different path."

Hester's mouth twitched. "I'm told it's my personality. We do fight, all of us. But most of our head-on confrontation is in spirit realms, not in this world, and our battles are always on behalf of another. The few of us who follow the warrior's path are part of a more direct war. This level of corruption is so high that I'd be more afraid of some of my brethren being contaminated than I would be convinced of their ability to succeed, if they fought it in a traditionally shamanic way."

"You ain't afraid of being corrupted?"

"I'll die first."

Some folks couldn't say that without it sounding like bragging, or like it was a bit of nothing, somethin' funny that they said just to get a smile. Hester wasn't one of 'em. She coulda been a soldier just then, somebody under orders who knew she was walking into a trap but also knowing it was gonna get other people out alive so long as she held on a little while. For a minute I looked between her and Annie, cut from the same cloth even if it didn't look like it on the outside, an' when I got outta the car I saluted 'em both. I hadn't done that for anybody in a long time. Hes looked like I was maybe pulling her leg, but Annie smiled and put her hand over her heart. That settled Hester down, and the three of us went together to meet the enemy.

CHAPTER SIXTEEN

The enemy was twenty-seven, acne-scarred, and dirty to his elbows in topsoil. Nothing about him looked dangerous except maybe the idea some'a that dirt was night soil. Annie, a couple steps behind me, was repeating something she'd said when she'd hired the kid: "I met him while I was volunteering at the hospital, for Heaven's sake. He has Crohn's disease. It's been debilitating, but he achieved a remarkable recovery lately. I can't see how he could possibly be a—a carrier for evil."

"How much recovery, doll? Bedridden to walking out the door inside a day, that kinda thing?"

"Well, yes. He said he's been making dietary changes..." Annie trailed off, finally suspecting something else mighta been going on there.

Truth was, a while back I woulda thought that was nothing but good news, nothing shy of a miracle. But Joanne had watched a kid dying of cancer walk outta the hospital, too, once a sorcerer had taken up with him. I didn't figure most miracle cases were evil magic working its way in, but this time it looked mighty suspicious. The kid—Myles—straightened up like he was just now hearing us arrive. For a second he was all smiles an' good nature, just like anybody given a second chance at life mighta been. Then he saw Hester an' everything about him changed.

I'd long since lost the Sight Jo had laid on me. Didn't stop me from Seeing the kid fill up with rage like he was pulling it from the boiling core of the earth. Once in a while Jo's magic went like that, burning so bright anybody could see it, and I guessed that was what was going on with Myles. He lashed out with it. A black toothy ball of fury came tearing across the lawn at Hester, leaving burn marks behind.

For a lady who said she didn't know much about shields, she sure knew how to put 'em up for herself. Yellow and dark green shot up around her like the Northern Lights had come way down south to visit, an' a shockwave like I hadn't felt since Korea damn near rattled my teeth outta my head. Hester held her ground, and her drawing power was just as clear as Myles's had been. The earth responded to her, too, all the strong young growth of trees an' animals a quick cool rush against the core's ancient fury. She threw it right back at him, no war inside herself about whether shamanic magic was made for fighting or not. I was gonna hafta talk to Jo about that, later on.

Except I was pretty sure that conflicted or not, Jo woulda caught the kid in the teeth with her magic and knocked him head over heels into the hedges. Hester's nearly reached the kid, but another one of his tar balls flew out and swallowed Hes's magic whole. *Then* she lurched, like that was a whole lot worse than taking a hit, and I reckoned maybe it was. Bracing yourself for a beating was one thing. Getting a bite taken outta your soul's energy has gotta be something else. Hester kept her feet, but just barely, and Annie and me were both realizing somethin was gonna go wrong when the kid turned on us instead.

Turned on me, I reckoned, 'cause there was recognition in his eyes when he saw me. A sneer smeared across his face, the kinda expression I'd seen on a lotta big fellas playing ball, usually right before they went down for good. I held on to that idea and stomped forward, getting between him and the girls. "Been a while, buddy."

"*You.*"

One word, an' it sent shivers up my spine and bumps dancing down my arms. If a word could kill, I'd have dropped dead right there, but I had a funny kinda confidence holding me together. I *knew* I was walking away from this one. I had years of future memories promising that. I'd been more scared in Korea than I was right now, even if mosta the time there I'd been a lot farther away from my enemy. I looked for one of Joanne's cocky come-backs, an' said, "Me, all right. How 'bout you let that kid go and we try ta..."

Annie, a couple steps behind me, breathed, "Kill each other like civilized people?"

I laughed and muttered, "Somethin' like that, yeah, doll," back at her, and the sorcery-infested kid in our yard looked like none of this was going according to his plans. I guessed old folks weren't supposed to make jokes when they were facing certain death, though I figured old folks were better prepared for it than kids. "You ain't gonna win this one, son."

He bared his teeth in a smile. "I've already won."

I gave him a smile just as toothy in return. "*Forward, the Light Brigade,* buddy. You don't win 'til there ain't a breath left in my body to fight with."

The kid pointed a finger at me. I didn't see anything coming at me, but pain shot between my eyes, a red bolt sizzling its way through my brain. I yowled like a cat in heat an' leaned into the pain, expecting that was just the warm-up act and that things were gonna worse from here on out. The kid smiled again and swirled his hands together, calling up another ball of black magic. I liked that better'n the finger-pointing, cause at least I could see it coming.

Annie stepped right in front of me, like she was getting between me and a patient who'd gone a little crazy. "What happened, Myles? Were you given a choice? Your life for mine, or did you not even know you were making the trade?"

All the power the kid was pulling up kinda hiccuped an' stopped growing. It didn't stop swirlin' furiously in his hands, but there wasn't more of it, an' that was something. I had to hand it to my girl. A handful of words and she had the kid's attention a way I'd have never gotten it. A lifetime wasn't enough to tell her how amazing she was. She kept talking, calm and soft. "It's all right, you know. I'm not in any hurry to die, but I'm seventy years old, and you're not even thirty yet. I'd understand that choice. At my age, I might even make it too, for you, or for someone else your age. I'd make it for someone younger, a child, in a heartbeat. But life doesn't work that way, Myles. If we trade someone else's health for our own, there's usually a great cost. Kidney transplants are miraculous, but they're hard to recover from."

"I didn't need a *kidney*. I needed—I needed—"

"Time," Annie said. "You needed to be well. You needed a chance at a future, and you'd tried everything you knew how. You ate well. You exercised, when you were strong enough. You let them take parts of your intestines away, and accepted the chance you would never be able to risk the doctors rebuilding them, and that you would spend your life with a bag taped to your side."

The kid's hand went to his side. I winced. I had pals, old guys, who had to deal with crap like that, but a kid shouldn't have to. I couldn't even hold on to being angry, not with Annie sounding so calm and the kid looking so lost and unsure. Easy pickings for corruption, and Annie was there talking it all through like some kinda comprehending therapist.

"All of that, it was so much work, so much trying to survive, so much compromise and hope...and it didn't work. You're still in pain. You're still withering, and no one your age should be withering. You still can't eat without being terribly cautious, and you still weigh far less than a young man your height and age should. And then the offer comes, too good to be true, but you have nothing left to lose, and overnight you're strong again. Stronger than you've been in years. You can work outside, you can eat what you choose to. And perhaps all you have to do is visit me, though I doubt it was even that obvious. You have a green thumb, and it still makes plants respond, and now you're possessed with the strength to garden again. Possessed," she said, real quiet. "We never mean it when we say that word. But you are possessed, and it's easy enough for something evil to take your strengths and turn them to its own ends. A talent for growing things might grow illness inside someone's lungs, if it's turned to black magic."

"There's no such—!" The kid cut himself off, staring at the magic he was holding in his hands, then threw it away. Not at us, but away, like he was tryin' ta get rid of it. It crawled back toward him, climbing up his legs, writhing around him, sinking back into his skin like he'd never be able to get rid of it. His eyes snapped up again, all the fire coming back. "So what if I did? Do you know how much *trouble* he causes? If I could just get rid of him, everything could be different. I could be different—"

"It don't work that way, kid. You get rid of me and everything's gonna be different, yeah, but not the way you hope. Maybe you never get born, if you get rid of me. Maybe the world's overrun by zombies, if you get rid of me. Maybe the Dark Ages never end, if you get rid of me. But it don't matter, because here's the thing, kid. You can't get rid of me. Your master's been tryin' a long damned time, and all that's come of it is us four standin' here right now, playing out some cruel bastard's schemes. I promise you, son, killing

Annie prob'ly ain't gonna save your life, and it sure as hell ain't gonna save your soul."

"What choice do I have?"

"There's always a choice, son. There ain't always a good one, but there's always a choice."

"Dying's no kind of choice." Power exploded outta the kid's hands again, a lifetime of hurting giving way to finally being able to do something about it, even something destructive.

Annie an' I both hit the ground, a tar ball sizzling over us, and Annie turned her head to look at me. "You're going to have a great deal of explaining to do at some point, Gary."

"I know, darlin'. But not right now, all right?"

Another burst of magic came flying our way and we scattered again, rolling across the lawn and coming up grass-stained. "Really?" Annie was about as solemn an' serious as she could be, through huffing for air and scrambling around on the ground. "Really? Not now? Are you sure? Because I think now might be a good time to talk—"

I hadn't been paying any attention to Hester at all. Neither had the kid, not until she stepped up behind him an' grabbed the sides of his head with her hands. They both shouted, an' the whole world went red an' yellow around us.

Truth was, I barely saw the fight in the Lower World. We busted through and Hes got knocked away from the kid. Me and Annie grabbed each other and kept low beneath bursts of black magic exploding against Hester's yellow an' green. Annie kept right on talking to him the way she'd been doing in the yard, reminding him of who she was, of how they'd been friends, and of how he'd had it in him to fight his whole life long against his disease, and how she reckoned he had it in him now to fight this thing too.

The kid kept throwing looks toward Annie, an' every time he did, Hester got one step closer to him. The air was so thick with magic it felt like breathing molasses, like breathing tar when the power rolled outta the kid. Hester was a blaze of light against the funny-colored sky, burning brighter than I'd have thought she could. Maybe she was stepping up, maybe having an enemy worth giving it all to brought out the best in her, or maybe she was stronger in the Lower World than in ours. Maybe it was Annie pouring her own heart an' soul out, givin Hes a lift. Maybe it was me being there, a thorn in the boss-man's side and praying to take the bastard's plans apart.

An' maybe, most likely, it was that the kid had a good heart, an' that he was just so damned tired of fighting that he'd taken the chance he was given, but he couldn't live with what it meant. Nothing evil could stay rooted in somebody who wasn't willing to have it there. That was something I had to believe, and the kid had lost the willingness.

Hes stepped forward one more time an' caught the boy in her arms as he fell. Black magic ran outta him like oil, seeping into the landscape, disappearing as fast as it had come, an' the next breath we took was back at home in the Middle World. Annie scrambled to her feet and ran for the kid, shouting at me to call an ambulance. I ran for the house, wishing for the first time in my life I had a cell phone, an' called 911 while standing at the window watching the women working on the kid. I guessed he wasn't dead from how Annie kept shooting panicked looks at me, and I had a hell of a time explaining to the lady on the phone what exactly the emergency was. She got an ambulance on the way, though, and I ran back out to the yard.

Hester was giving the kid everything she had, power flaring over him in waves. Nothing about it looked or felt as strong as what Jo commanded. I wished again I could call her up and get her over here, but it was still three years too early, and nothing was gonna change that either. Annie, talkin' over Hester's head, said, "His whole system is shutting down. He'll be lucky to live until the paramedics arrive."

Hes snarled something, not even really words, just denying the truth we all saw. She kept him alive, anyway, or something did, and Annie got into the ambulance and drove away with the kid. Me and Hester sat in the grass, staring after the fading lights, until she finally said, "Your wife could have been a shaman herself."

"I reckon she coulda been. Thought you said you didn't have the chops to fight that thing."

"I didn't. Mrs. Muldoon is the one who kept him off-balance enough to let me in."

"An' all I did was sit on my duff an' watch."

"What are you, Mr. Muldoon?"

"Outta time, doll. I'm outta time." I didn't reckon she'd hear it quite the way I meant, but either way it didn't matter. Best I could hope for right then was they'd somehow saved the kid, that maybe his life was gonna turn out a little better, for as long as it lasted. I didn't see much in the way of a happier ending coming outta any of this. Annie'd done what she had ta do, but it meant I was left counting the days, and then the hours, right down to the minute she'd left me, and I was gonna hafta go through it all over again.

Hester, not knowing more than that Annie was dying, got up, put her hand on my shoulder, an' stood there a minute without tryin' ta find the right thing to say. Then she walked away, an' I never saw her again, alive or dead.

Annie came home 'round midnight, and only shook her head, telling me not to say anything, when I mighta asked about the kid. We slept late, an' when she woke up she stayed nestled beside me, taking careful breaths and listening to her own chest rattle with a clinical ear. "I'm breathing more clearly. It's easier than it was yesterday, before the spirit quests. But I can still feel the weight of it in me, Gary. I'm not going to beat this, not in the long term. You have to promise me something."

"Anything, darlin'."

"Help Myles out, if you can."

"What? He ain't dead? I thought—"

Annie shook her head. "I was too tired to talk about it last night, but Miss Jones...well, I suppose she healed him. I hope it was she, and not that...thing."

Feelin' pretty confident, I said, "If it was that thing riding him he wouldn't have come outta this alive. Pretty sure being possessed burns a fella out. I don't think he woulda recovered from it, or anything else, if Hes hadn't been there. So what'd she do, put his guts back together?

Ain't Crohn's genetic?" I'd been underestimating Hester's power, if she could do that. I wasn't sure Jo could.

Annie shook her head again. "If there's a genetic component, no one has found it yet. No, the surgical procedures are still in place, but by time I left the hospital last night none of his system was inflamed any longer. He hadn't been that healthy when he left the hospital. He'd only been in remission, but Crohn's does that. It flares and fades, so while it had been a remarkable recovery, there were still signs of it in his body. Last night the doctors couldn't find any evidence that there had ever been a reason to give the poor boy an ileostomy. So whatever's happened with him, whatever happens with me, Gary, if you can, help Myles out. This is going to be very hard for him."

"An' you think it ain't gonna be for us?" I had just enough smarts to say us and not me, but Annie saw through it anyway an' tucked herself closer to me.

"I know it will be." That was all she said. It was all either of us said about what was coming at us fast, 'cause there wasn't much else to say. She got weaker as the days went on, until I realized for the second time that she was holding on, waitin' for our wedding anniversary. I'd been slow figuring it out the first time, and was just as slow the second time around, 'cause I was trying hard not to think about anything but the last hours I had with her. We had strawberries on waffles in a room full of roses, same way we'd had 'em every morning of our anniversary since the first one, an' then, finally, she said, "I think I should go to the hospital now."

"No reason to, darlin'. Nothin' wrong with home."

"What did we do last time?"

"We went to the hospital three days ag—" I snapped my teeth together, tryin' ta eat the words I'd already said, but Annie only smiled like she wasn't surprised.

"So we've already changed it. Do you think the changes are enough? Is it going to make a difference, somehow? Will we win, Gary? Tell me what happens," she said, real soft. "Please tell me what happens, Gary. I won't be there to see it, so I want to know. We'll stay home," she promised, like promising would be the thing that would make me tell her. "We'll stay home, we won't go to the hospital, and you can tell me the future."

An' I did. It took all day, sittin' in the bed with her, holding her like I couldn't the last time through, and I told her about the next three or four years. Told her about picking up a mouthy fare one January morning, just a couple days after I turned seventy-three, an' she got a notepad outta her nightstand and wrote that down, the time and date and SeaTac terminal, and she made me put it in my wallet. "Just to make sure you'll be there," she told me, an' I smiled a bit.

"Like I could forget, sweetheart. I'd been kinda living on auto pilot up 'til then, just kinda waitin' to catch up with you. Jo...you gotta forgive me, darlin'. Jo gave me something else to live for, made me not wanna hurry dying up too much. I wish you coulda known her, Annie. She's just a kid, and she was a real mess when I met her, but you wouldn't believe the woman she's growing up into. She's our girl, Annie. She's the girl we shoulda had. So brave she's stupid sometimes, but her heart's in the right place."

"If we'd had a girl of our own all of this would be different, and you might never have met her. I don't know if things happen for a reason, but I think perhaps all of it comes around to where it's supposed to be, in the end. Tell me more. Tell me how you got the tortoise spirit animal. I can still feel this ridiculous cat in my mind, you know. It's getting ready to run. Gathering itself. I can't see its prey, but I suppose something must be out there for it to hunt. I don't think cheetahs run just for fun..."

She quieted down, an' I told her all about being witched, and how I'd known sorcery was eating away at Myles 'cause I'd seen it happen to another kid. "She didn't want anything to do with magic, Jo didn't. Not up 'til then. She just wanted a regular life."

"Not so much like us, then," Annie murmured.

I nodded. "She had a harder time taking it in. She was determined not to believe, but she had reasons. I ain't told you about her babies yet. Shh, I'll get to it. Anyway, she stepped up after the mess with the sorcerer, an' from there on out she's been...the only other person I was ever so proud to know is you, Annie. An' I gotta say, even with what we've seen an' what we did, it was small peanuts compared ta the ruckus I been getting up to with Jo. She looks just like that painting your Pop did, 'cept it don't show you how big she is. She's six feet tall, an' don't tell her I told you, but she hits like a brick wall. Not that she's been hitting me, but we shoved the top off a crypt once—"

"Was there a vampire inside?"

I laughed right out loud and kissed my girl's white hair.

"No, but we both thought there was gonna be." That got me back to the beginning, and I tried keeping the story more or less in order, but Annie kept having questions and I kept remembering bits I hadn't said before, until it was closing in on midnight an' I was finishing up the last details, telling her about the quiet ride I'd been taking through our own lives for the past fifty years.

"All that time," she whispered. "All that time and you never changed a thing."

"Couldn't risk it, sweetheart. I was bettin' everything on this last fight."

"And we're losing it. At the last minute, we're losing it. Oh! That silly cat just started running. Inside my head, Gary. I can feel it—*pulling* me. Oh. Oh no, Gary, it's hunting the stag. My stag!"

I looked for the clock. Seven minutes til twelve. That was the last minute. That was the time burned into my memory forever, 'cause that was when Annie had died. An' then the clock ticked over, six minutes to midnight, and all of a sudden we were living on borrowed time.

A shot of pain smacked me between the eyes. The same shot that the kid had taken, burning another hole through my brain, and everything started slipping away.

All the memories that had been brought back to life, the terrible gift of magic that had been part of me and Annie since the beginning. If I was stealing Annie from him, stealing time, then the Master was stealing something back. Maybe that was the whole damned reason for the kid showing up at our house a week ago at all, so he could take that shot, set some magic in my mind that would start erasing everything if somehow we held on longer than we were s'posed to.

He couldn't take the memories that were still on the way, the ones about Annie's funeral, the ones about Joanne and Cernunnos and all the other things still lying in my future, but he could take everything up 'til this minute. He could steal everything about my life that had made it something other than ordinary. My memories unraveled faster an' faster, re-weaving themselves into a life a lot like my own, except without the touches of magic. I clawed at 'em, tryin' ta hold on, *knowing* it wasn't right that Annie's Pop had been a regular fella, but not able to remember what had made him different, an' then losing hold of the idea that he'd been different at all.

It all fell apart, until the Korean War dreams were just nightmares like anybody got, until that trip we'd finally taken to Pamplona was only a vacation, and didn't have nothing to do with chasing minotaurs through cobblestone alleys. Until the secret of Annie's surviving almost being hit by a car was 'cause she'd tripped over a stone, not 'cause Cernunnos had knocked her aside, an' until every last drop of magic had been squeezed outta my life.

Every last drop but Annie. He might be able to take her away from me, but he couldn't take the magic we'd had together. Her kinda magic was the most ordinary, simple thing anybody ever had. She was the love of my life, and nothing could touch that. I held onta that as tight as I was holding her, and watched the clock click forward another minute.

The way my memory had it, she'd slipped into sleep a long while before death came knocking. But she was leaning forward, breathin' hard—clear breaths, not coughing—and her muscles were bunching and loosing like she was running with that cheetah, or maybe with the stag. I got the idea the stag was gonna win, 'cause cheetahs couldn't keep up their top speed real long, but that was laying the limitations of a real animal on a spirit guide. Whatever was going on with the power animals, they were fighting for Annie, dragging her forward. That was my girl, holding on, making this whole thing her own fight, taking it on her own terms. A bright spark of hope crashed through me. Something was changing. At the last damned minute, just like Cernunnos had said. At the last chance. That was when to make the move.

I stood up, barely knowing I was doing it, and said, "Horns," out loud, calling myself to his attention for the first time in fifty years. "Horns, I donno what's gonna happen, I got nothin', I got *nothin'*, but we're in overtime on the clock and my memories are slipping away—"

I was losing what I was saying even as I said it, sometimes wondering who I was even talking to. I sat with Annie again, folding her into my arms and whispering another prayer to the only god I knew. Half the time I didn't know what I was saying, except I knew I was holding on to hope the same way Annie was. An' seven minutes after she was s'posed to have left me, a church bell started ringing, marking out the transition into a brand new day. I put my mouth against

Annie's hair, murmuring, "'Tis the witching hour of night, doll. Everything changes in the witchin' hours."

And Cernunnos came riding, up to the old inn-door.

There was no door on this or any other earth that was gonna stop him from coming in. Truth was, I wasn't sure how he'd gotten in, poetry or no, 'cause the wall just kinda melted away as he came through. Him an' that big silver stallion, filling up our bedroom. It stamped its feet, making the floor rattle, an' I swear to God that for all of the size of the thing, all of the presence of the god, I couldn't hardly see either of 'em. They kept slipping and sliding in my vision like they were imaginary, like they were marching through a dream.

Annie saw him, though, an' gave a cry that most guys might not want to hear their girls make when another fella is in the room. All kinds of relief was in that sound, and a sob caught in her throat. I couldn't hear nothin' beyond that, 'cause a growl was rising all around, like a big cat with its back up. If Cernunnos was talking, I couldn't see it, either. There was silver light playing everywhere, an' the god's green eyes burning like fire. It was early in the year for him to be riding at all, but his horns were full like a stag's in its prime, and Annie put her hands out to him—

—and at one minute after midnight, Cernunnos pulled me outta the life I'd been leading, an' dropped me back into the heart of the Wild Hunt.

epilogue

"What *happened*? What the hell *happened*? *Horns*!" I was back to myself, sitting on Imelda's back and carryin' Jo's rapier at my side. I wasn't wearing the mithrail armor anymore, but Horns had never planned on me keeping it anyway. The Hunt was gathered in what looked a lot like my front yard, though moonlight was shining through 'em and neither the horses nor the hounds were making any kinda audible sound. Everything else was normal, except I couldn't hardly remember the past couple minutes or make sense of the mess of memory that'd been my life. "There was light, goddamn it, Cernunnos, did Annie go into the damned *light*?"

"She did." The whole Hunt was movin' around us, riders I'd known for half of forever now. The boy was on his gold mare, the two of 'em the only point of stillness in the yard. Even Cernunnos was moving, his big stallion edgy and eying me like I was something new. Horns himself was looking like the cat that got the canary, green fire burning in his eyes an' a wicked little smile curving his mouth. "She went into the light, Master Muldoon, and I think we can be assured that was not the fate the Devourer intended for her."

"Well where the hell does the light come out?" I sounded a lot like Jo, asking crazy questions that couldn't have answers, but I could barely see through the silver rising in my eyes and the sickness boiling in my belly. I'd spent the past four years remembering my whole life wrong, an' after all of it I still didn't know if I'd saved the girl. There wasn't a goddamned thing that mattered if I hadn't.

Some of the wickedness left Horns's face an' he shook his head. "I could not bring you there even if I wished to. You are not yet ready to take the final ride with me, and when you are I may be able to offer you a different path than the one you might imagine yours to take. Once I led thousands through the darkness, Master Muldoon. Now there are few who call for me in the end, but so long as they burn as brightly as you and your woman have burned, I will never fade from mortal memory."

"This ain't *about* you, Horns. Annie—you mean, Annie—" I ran outta words, my hands going numb on Imelda's reins.

"There were other spirits who might have helped her through the last days of her sickness. Others with an affinity for the sagebrush which helps to clear the lungs and is sacred to healers. But the stag is more than my creature. It is a part of my essence, and she rejected the others that came and waited for the stag instead. Of course I came for her myself, though I bent time to do it."

"We ain't supposed ta be able to mess with the time line that way." I didn't have much voice, but Horns heard me clear enough, an' looked like he thought I was joking.

"You weren't supposed to steal her a few extra minutes of life, either, Master Muldoon. We waited until the very end for just these reasons, did we not? To risk all, and to strike a blow against the Devourer just far enough out of time that he could not retaliate. She lies beyond your reach now, but that has been true as long as you have known me. You spoke words to her, earlier. A poet's words, I think, as you prepared to journey into the spirit realms."

I couldn't think what he was talking about, not for a long minute or two. All that came outta my mouth was, "You were spyin' on me?" in a voice that sounded like a sullen kid's.

"I could hardly allow you to revisit your life without my presence nearby. I had no wish to explain myself to Joanne if something should go wrong. Though lovers be lost, you said to her."

Air exploded outta me in a sigh. "Yeah. Dylan Thomas. He said—well, he said love was stronger than death, 'cept he said it better. I guess that's what poets do."

"Hold tight to his wisdom, my friend. There is no greater power, and I have known many powers in my time."

That was a little funny. Just enough funny ta start filling up the hole in my heart. I'd had a long time to mourn Annie already, after all, an' I was sitting across from a fella who was promising me that in the end, she'd gone into the light. It wasn't the ending I'd been hoping for, but at the back of my head I'd always known I wasn't gonna get that one. Even if my older memories were a mess, I trusted the ones since her death. I didn't really figure time had been gonna rewrite itself and give me those years back with her. I let that hope go, real careful-like, then let some of that laughter come up and smooth things over a little. "You tellin' me love conquers all, Horns?"

"I am."

There wasn't a trace of humor in the horned god's eyes, an' my own kinda fell away for another minute. My girl, my other girl, Joanne, she was out there, an' sometimes I was pretty certain it was love that was getting her through the day. Truth was, for the past year and some, a lotta that love had been mine. Joanne needed somebody to love her, warts and all, as much as I'd been wanting someone to love again. It wasn't ever gonna be like Annie, but I didn't want it to be. Jo needed somethin' different from me, just like I needed somethin' different from her. I guessed there were worse things to think than believin' that love conquered all.

"All right. All right, then. I guess...I guess we did all right, then. She's...Annie, I mean. She's...she's all right? Guess if I've learned anything this last year, I've learned the wheel keeps coming around. Annie's back on the merry-go-round, right? She's gonna get another chance, somewhere down the road? Old soul born to new parents? That's how it works, ain't it?"

"That is how it works, and I will guide her to her resting

place when her incarnation is ended. You've done well, Master Muldoon. You have made space for hope, and that is never a bad thing."

"Okay. All right. So we go home now." I was pushing an awful lot of thoughts an' emotions back, knowing they were gonna come back to be dealt with later. But I'd left Jo bouncing around through the wrong end of time, an' I hated ta think what kinda trouble she was getting in without me. "You figured out how to get us home yet? Back ta Jo, I mean?"

Cernunnos's lip curled. "Best you first trade your steed with one of the others. Yours has ridden a long while with us now, but she will not know Joanne's pull, when it comes. The others have met her in and out of time."

Regret caught me harder'n I expected as I slid off Imelda's back an' patted her neck. "You're a good girl, sweetheart. Hope I see you again."

She put her forehead against mine an' drooled down my shirt. I figured that was her way of saying she hoped so too, and patted her a couple more times before walking away. The rider on the brown mare—I knew his name, but there was something about the Hunt that made usin' it seem rude—he dismounted an' handed me the reins on his way to Imelda. I swung up on the mare, patted her neck too, and watched the big bearded fella ride Imelda toward the stars.

Then I looked at the house. It was starting to get that faded look, while the Hunt was getting more real around me. There was a faint trace of light through one of the dark windows, saying somebody at the back of the house was home. "I'm still in there, ain't I? Holden' her, and remembering…rememberin' somethin' that ain't quite real. Why do I remember her dying at the hospital, Horns? What the hell'd he do to me?"

"All he could." Cernunnos turned the stallion away from the house while he was talkin', and the Hunt followed him into the sky, the boy on his right an' me at his left. "I once said to Joanne that perhaps the past I remembered best, you had not come to Tara with her."

"Yeah. I remember that. So?" I looked back once more, not sure what I was hoping to see. It wasn't there, anyway: just a quiet ol' house fulla memories that I had to leave behind. Or maybe that was what I was looking for after all, 'cause after a few seconds I felt something go outta me, some kinda regret I'd been holding on to, and then I started listenin' to Horns again.

"That past is no longer the one I remember best. Now in almost all memories, you came to Tara and we fought together at Knocknaree."

"Sure, buddy, 'cause that's what happened."

"Now it is what happened. Then…" Horns shrugged, making the thick muscles in his neck flex in an ugly way. "You remember her death in a hospital because then, in those other times when you did not come to Tara, that is where she died."

"But you're saying I always came to Tara." I was giving myself a headache, an' from Horns's expression, I thought he was getting one too.

"Time opens and closes on itself, Master Muldoon. It

does not like loose ends. Your memory of her death in a hospital is—"

"An oxbow lake." I said it quick as I could, not wanting to lose the idea. "It's something that happened an' got cut out, yeah? It's maybe the one in a hundred path, and the other ninety nine went this way?"

"Yes." He lowered his big head like he'd been carrying its weight too long and I'd just lightened it a little. "You know by now that mortal minds dismiss and explain magic away even at the best of times. The Devourer caught you at the worst of them, and stole away what you had chosen to accept. The rest of it is what is necessary, nothing more. A filling of empty spaces with memories that make sense, regardless of their truth. Her death in a hospital would make sense, and is the easiest path to lying to you. You remember both deaths now because you have been at the eye of the storm, and from the eye, we see clearly."

"It happened and it didn't. We changed it an' the first way got cut out, but it's still hanging around main' an extra ripple in the current. This was easier ta understand when it was Jo messin' with time, not myself, Horns."

"Joanne has never walked so closely along her own path. This is more complex than what she has done."

"But she's the shaman!"

"And you the mortal man. Don't discount the power in an ordinary life, Master Muldoon."

I thought of Annie the same way I always did the past few years, with an ache an' a squeeze in my heart, an' I said, "Don't reckon there's much chance of that," more to myself than Horns. We'd ridden toward the stars while we were talking, but not so high as we'd gone before. The wind was soft an' warm, an' the path we followed was made of moonlight streaming across the clouds. We were moving faster than sense could make, already going 'round the curve of the world. Heading back to Ireland, so we'd be closer to where we'd left Jo.

I was about to ask Horns how we were gonna find her when the sword on my hip lit up blue an' started to fade.

Horns snarled, "Do not let it go," and grabbed hold of my horse's reins as hard as I grabbed onto the sword. The sky flickered around us once an' shut off, like we were moving through the space of a heartbeat. The Hunt disappeared, all 'cept me an' Horns, an' in the next heartbeat we were somewhere else. The sky up above was blue, an' down below was the ruins of a castle on the tallest hill for miles. Then it all went black again, another in-between heartbeat, an' when we came out it was sunset at that same castle, except it wasn't fallen-down an' the whole world's horizons were too close.

Cernunnos made a sound kinda like the one Annie'd made when she saw him, like recognition and anticipation. I started to ask, but he put his hand out to shut me up. For a second I couldn't talk, which was a lousy trick, him throwin' his weight around like that, but then the screaming started and I was just as glad I hadn't said a word.

It was like every scream I'd ever heard in Korea turned all the way up and played all at once. It went straight under my skin, making me want to run and fight back all at once. The sword yanked me toward the castle, an' the castle started falling apart, like the screams were attacking it, too. I figured if the sword wanted in there, that was where Jo was, so I kicked the brown's sides and rode for the western wall of the castle, where it was falling the fastest.

I came around the corner hard, the setting sun at my back and turning the dust from falling rock into a wall of gold that I couldn't see through. Jo's sword was pulling me so hard I could barely stay in the saddle, an' I took it out to smack one of the smaller stones outta my way.

Its light cut through the dust, lettin' me see a blond woman dressed all in white, standing with her back to me. The air was vibrating with her screams, pulsing with 'em while the building fell down around her. Joanne was a couple feet further on, barely on her feet, looking like the screams that were bugging me were about to shatter her.

The blonde never knew I was comin'. It was just a couple of long strides for the brown mare, an' I drove the rapier into the woman's back.

Her screaming cut off with a squeak, an' she slid off the sword without making any more sound. Joanne went from looking about to shatter to being rigid, the kinda rigid that said she was in more danger of falling apart now than she'd ever been before. Her eyes were wider than I'd ever seen 'em, tears rolling down her cheeks, an' she wasn't breathing. She was just staring at me, not even at the lady I'd killed, but me, like she'd never laid eyes on me before. She didn't blink while I looked down at the dead woman.

The dame was degrading like a salt sculpture in water. Her dress shriveled, an' so did her hair, an' it went faster and faster, until I figured she was prob'ly dead for good, and looked back at Joanne.

My poor girl still hadn't moved, still wasn't breathing. I didn't know what she'd been through while I'd been gone, but it didn't look like any of it had been good, an' it was gonna end with her passing out if she didn't take a breath soon. I figured I better do something, so I called up my best wicked grin, slid off the mare, an' opened my arms.

"H'lo, darlin'. Did I miss anything?"

Chronology Notes:

"The Rising Green" takes place the same weekend as MOUNTAIN ECHOES (Book Eight of the Walker Papers) but contains no spoilers for that book.

The Rising Green

The pull came from under her skin, a faint itching sensation that wouldn't go away. It reminded Suzy of the chicken pox, which she hadn't had until she was eleven, so she remembered it all miserably well. It wasn't that bad, but it was enough to wake her up. Suzy crunched her eyes shut and flung one elbow over them, rubbing her forearm with the other hand. It itched. She ignored it, or tried to. Then she lifted her elbow and looked at her clock, illuminated by a soft green glow.

A quarter to midnight. Suzy dropped her elbow over her eyes again. The green glow lingered behind her eyelids. She was supposed to be up in six hours for an early-morning study group, preparing for a test the next afternoon. She didn't *need* the study group. She was going to ace the test anyway. But study groups were the only thing Aunt Mae would let her out of the house for, ever since The Halloween Incident. It had been almost six months, and Aunt Mae still referred to it that way. The Halloween Incident.

Suzy's parents had never managed to keep her grounded for more than a weekend. Not that she was doing that thing, the *omg my parents were so much cooler than you thing,* because although it was true, it was also true that just because Suzy was fifteen didn't mean she was a complete asshole. Her aunt, her father's sister, had stepped up like crazy when Suzy's parents were murdered, and she was doing the best she could with suddenly being a parent.

It was *also* true that while her parents had been alive, Suzanne Melody Quinley had never done anything like walk out of school at the last bell, get on a bus, and head a hundred miles out of town without any kind of warning. She'd *had* to see Detective Joanne Walker. It had literally been life-and-death important. Aunt Mae would never really understand that, but then, Suzy hadn't tried very hard to make her. She'd deserved to be grounded. Maybe not for six months, but still, she'd deserved it.

And she was never going to get back to sleep with the green shimmer peeping through her elbow or her thoughts going circles on the topic of The Halloween Incident. Once she started remembering the zombies it was all over anyway. Suzy sat up with a sigh and threw the covers aside.

The room lit up, soft green with glimmers of white and gold. Suzy stared at her legs, then pulled the covers over them and lay back down, her eyes squeezed shut again.

She knew—she'd known for some time now, of course—that she was the granddaughter of a god. The daughter of a demi-god, which made her think she should be called a semi-god herself, but it didn't really matter. What mattered was that her grandfather's legacy gave her power, more power than she knew what to do with. She'd deleted someone from the time line once, with that power. Other times she'd seen dozens of futures, and had tried to help people pick the right path to the only safe one.

And every time, she'd burned, blazed, with brilliant green magic. That was the color of her power, as it was the color of Cernunnos's and of Herne's. She knew what using that magic felt like. Breath-taking. Liberating. Exciting. Terrifying.

It was *not* a gentle glow or itchiness in the middle of the night. Something was wrong. Extra-wrong, and when magic went wrong the only person Suzy knew to go to was Detective Walker. Who was in Seattle. Where Aunt Mae had forbidden Suzy to ever go again without adult accompaniment.

She tried, briefly, to envision going into Aunt Mae's room, waking her aunt up, and asking to be taken to Seattle, all while glowing like a firefly. She failed. Which meant she had to go to Seattle alone. Again. While glowing green.

She was going to be grounded for the rest of her *life*.

The whole idea made her skin itch even more. Suzy rubbed her arms ferociously, then stopped when the magic coursing under her skin brightened with the activity. It was no use panicking, she told herself as she threw the covers off again and got up to find clothes. At least she didn't have to turn the lights on. She could navigate by the glow of her skin. and wanted to bite her arms by the time she found some jeans, like she could suck the magic and the itching away as if it was poison. There was a bus at a quarter past midnight, the last one heading to Seattle. She could probably catch that. If she had an extra minute at the bus station she could even call ahead to warn Detective Walker she was coming.

She dragged her jeans on, hopping around the room when she lost her balance tugging them up. The mirror caught her attention a couple of times, reflecting an image so weird it looked like it belonged on the cover of a fashion magazine. Green highlights came from within, making her wheat-pale hair glow emerald, especially near the roots. It faded out to almost white around shoulders mostly bared by a spaghetti-strapped nightgown that wrinkled at her waist as she pulled her jeans all the way up and buttoned them. The light dimmed considerably, so her eyes were just big and dark, no longer reflecting green. She would need a hoodie to keep from attracting attention. And maybe sunglasses, because now that she'd noticed them, her eyes were starting to itch too. Suzy made a face at the mirror and turned away from it, looking for a shirt and shades.

Her fingers were two inches from the hoodie when the air shriveled up against her skin, turned cold, and pulled her backward through a hole the size of a pinhead.

There was power. That was all she could tell. Power latching on to her own magic, hauling her up a slick emerald path full of loops and twists and turns, like a roller coaster. More like a waterslide. She'd never liked waterslides. The joinings weren't smooth enough and the water wasn't deep enough, so she always fell out of the inner tubes and scraped herself up on the joints. This one was smooth, though, and fast enough that the friction made her skin burn. It burned the itch away, which helped. It also buffed her like she was a diamond—an emerald, she guessed—so that she wasn't so much glowing as shining. Like a star, if stars were green.

She ran up against another pinhead-sized hole, and got shoved through head first onto a shag carpet floor.

For a minute she couldn't see anything. There was light, lots of it, but it was all coming from her, drowning out everything else. She wasn't even afraid yet, but something was bubbling deep inside her chest. A warning, one that ran deeper than anything Suzy had ever known. A warning that up until now she'd used her magic for others, but that she had no sense at all of the depths she could plumb if it was *herself* she needed to protect. It gave her confidence, though at the same time it ran so deep it was itself a little scary. She was the child of gods, and no one in their right mind messed with gods.

Weirdly, the thought calmed the deep warning inside her. There couldn't be much that threatened gods. Joanne Walker did, but Joanne knew where Suzy lived. She would have called if she needed her, not magicked her away. Anybody else who thought they could hold even a semi-god like Suzy was either very, very powerful, or very, very dumb. She could give them the benefit of the doubt for a little bit, and assume they were dumb.

The itching had stopped. She thought that was the other reason she wasn't going absolutely crazy with fear and anger. She'd fought zombies, after all. She'd gotten through the horror of her parents' murders, and then she'd watched her birth father sluff off mortality to become the Green Man. She thought she could handle anything as long as she didn't want to scratch her skin off.

Joanne was always using her powers to discover things. Suzy's didn't work like that, or at least, she didn't think they did. But at the same time, she felt *confined* somehow, like she'd been pulled into something with a specific size and shape. She stretched out her hands and encountered resistance. A flare of her own magic shot around that sensation, exploring it in the same way Suzy had explored parks when she was little: up, down, under, over, around, in. That had been what her mother called *organic exploration,* using her whole person to learn the world. This was the same thing, except Suzy's wholeness included magic now.

She'd never explored a pentagram before, though. It surrounded her, wobbling with paltry human power. It would barely hold a mouse, much less her. Suzy laughed. Someone would have the scare of their life and end up grateful that they'd conjured a polite modern teenage granddaughter of a god into their flimsy pentagram instead of one of the much, much worse things that were out there. She would start by shattering the pentagram, just to show them how much trouble they *might* have been in. She reached out to flick it away with a fingertip.

Just before she did, a high-pitched, familiar voice squeaked, "*Suzy?*"

Suzy froze mid-motion, then moved her hand above her eyes, like shading them would help her see out of the pentagram when she was the one emitting the light. "*Kiseko?*"

"Holy crap holy crap holy crap holy cra—" The litany came in a whisper, followed by an even softer, "How do we shut this thing *down*, Rob? That's *Suzy*, holy crap it's not a *nature* god you dork it's my friend *Suzy* how did we call *Suzy* OMG WE DID MAGIC—"

The last part was overrun by a boy's intense, soft voice: "Kiseko, be *quiet* or we'll wake your *parents* up—"

"Well I told you we should've done this at your house, your parents are all big into the paranormal thing—"

"First, my parents would have noticed us raising a pentagram in the basement," the boy said very dryly, "and second, they'd ground me until I was fifteen for messing with this stuff without supervision. Kiseko, stop panicking, you're just feeding the power circle with your emotion. That's not Suzanne *Quinley*, is it?"

Kiseko blurted, "Yes!"

The unseen boy groaned and muttered something Suzy couldn't hear, then stepped up to the pentagram, putting his hands against it. Suzy could see him then, a tallish boy of twelve or thirteen, with a serious, apologetic expression. "Aunt Jo's going to kill me," he announced. "I'm really sorry. We'll get you out of there in a minute."

"Who are you? What are you—oh, nevermind. Kiseko talked you into this, didn't she?" Suzy sat down and put her face in her hands, not sure if she should laugh or cry. "Kiso, what did you *do?*"

"Oh, I just wanted to try a little magic," Kiseko said with an impatient stomp of her foot. "Robert, why won't this thing come down?"

"You're putting too much energy into it," Robert repeated. "You need to calm down."

"Kiseko," Suzy said into her hands, "doesn't do calm. She's Kiseko Anderson, Superhero." Which was nicer than super-emo, which was what Suzy's mother used to call Kiseko. She used to say that Kiseko was hysteria waiting to happen. She'd said it with a smile, but she hadn't been wrong. The first time Suzy had met her, Kiseko had been sprawled full-length on her belly, sobbing piteously into her arms. There had been no one else around. Suzy, concerned, had crouched to ask what was wrong.

Kiseko, seven years old and dripping snot, had lifted her head, discovered her parents had gone inside rather than remain on the street to observe her tantrum, and shut off the waterworks as if they'd never happened. Her face wasn't even red from crying. Kiseko had sat up, wiped her nose, and shrugged. "I don't want to live in Seattle. My parents made me move here."

"Oh! You're the new family? I watched you move in. I'm Suzy." Suzy had offered her hand like a little adult. Kiseko had burst out laughing and hugged Suzy instead. Overwhelmed, Suzanne had thought Kiseko was the strongest, wonderfulest, and most dramatic person she'd ever met. They'd made friends, *been* friends, through everything, right up until Suzy's parents and four high school students had been murdered.

Kiseko hadn't come to school for a week, not even for

the memorial services. She'd barely been able to say goodbye when Aunt Mae had come to take Suzy to Olympia. It wasn't that Suzy blamed her. It was only that she'd never seen Kiseko take the world at anything less than full tilt, and her friend's pallor and quietness still haunted her.

It wasn't in evidence now, thought. Kiseko tossed her hair proudly. "Superhero nothing. Super*witch*! I built a power circle! I still don't get why you're in it." She squinted through the brightness at Suzy. "Or why you're glowing."

Robert mumbled, "She doesn't know about y—" and then more clearly said, "If you don't know about Suzanne, why did you want to try magic in the first place? How did you know it was real?"

Kiseko stopped with arms akimbo and looked at Robert like he was about half his actual age. "The *zombies*, hel*lo*? OMG, don't tell me you didn't even notice the *zombies*—!"

"Sure, it's just most people—"

Kiseko blew an exasperated breath. "Most people are *morons*, hel*lo*! As if the *entire city* of Seattle could get turned into a film set without, like, *everybody* noticing? As if some director would think digging up my *back yard* and resurrecting my *dog* was worth the time and money? As if Suzy would just *show up* at my house to console me after we had to bury Fluffy again? Actually, Suzy, seriously, what were you doing there? I was all, like, emotional. I forgot to ask."

Suzy peered through her fingers at her best friend, who still stood arms akimbo, but now with her attention directed away from Robert and at Suzanne. As far as Suzy had known, Kiseko wholeheartedly believed Suzy had shown up at Kiseko's house a little after midnight after Halloween simply so Kiseko would have somebody's shoulder to sob on as they re-buried their beloved family pet. Not once, not *once*, had Kiseko ever suggested that she thought there was any other reason for Suzy to show up in Seattle beyond Kiseko needing her at that very moment in time. But now light was starting to gleam in her eyes. "OMG, what *were* you doing there, and does it have to do with me, like, summoning you?"

"Were you summoning me on Halloween?" Suzy asked faintly.

"No, just now! OMG! Are you dangerous?"

Suzy's response was so even, so steady, that she barely even knew it for her own voice: "You have no idea."

For the first time since Suzy had arrived, Kiseko actually went silent, her eyes round and her throat moving as she swallowed heavily. When she spoke again, it was hardly more than a squeak: "So should I, like, not let you out of there?"

"You couldn't keep me in if you tried. Kiso, what are you *doing*? Who is this boy?" Suzy's somber tone changed as she squinted again at Robert. "You're too young to be her boyfriend, right? I mean, no offense, but you look like you're twelve."

"I am. I'm Robert Holliday. My dad—"

"*Detective* Holliday? Detective Walker's *partner*?"

"Yeah." Robert looked apologetic. "If I'd had any idea she was going to summon you..."

"I wasn't summoning her! I wanted a nature god, because

it's like *April* and it's snowing and I don't want my sixteenth *birthday party* to be in a *snowstorm*—!" Kiseko broke off with a small noise of dismay. "Um, Suzy, are you a nature god?"

"No." Suzanne flicked a finger against the power circle, shattering the shields. "But my father is."

Kiseko fell over with a thud. Suzy winced and stepped out of the circle—Kiso had drawn on the carpet with chalk, her mother was going to kill her—to help Kiso sit up. "My head's ringing," Kiseko mumbled. "It feels like somebody broke a crystal glass inside it."

"I think I kind of did. Hang on, I'll get you some aspirin." Suzy stepped over Kiseko and scurried to the bathroom, which hadn't changed at all since she'd last been there. Well, the towels had probably been changed, but otherwise it, and the rest of the house Suzy glimpsed, looked the same as it had six months earlier. That was a relief. Houses should stay the same, even if the people in them changed. She came back with water and aspirin, which Kiseko took as obediently as she ever did anything. Then she gave Suzy a gimlet stare, though Suzy didn't know what a gimlet actually was, and said, "Well?"

"No, wait, first I want to know how you know Detective Holliday's son." Suzy sat down between Kiso and Robert, close enough that their cross-legged knees were all touching.

"I summoned you," Kiseko muttered. "I should get to ask the questions. We're in chess club together."

Suzy eyed Robert. "You're twelve and in high school?"

"I come over from the middle school because I can beat

everybody there too easily."

"Oh. Cool. Okay, um." Suzy pulled her hair over her shoulder and twitched into a nervous braid, then undid it again. "Um."

"Suzanne's biological father is Herne, a nature god," Robert volunteered into Suzy's nervous silence. "She didn't find out until last January, when her parents were killed. He was going to sacrifice her so he could take over *his* father's position as a wild god, but Aunt Jo stopped him. Also Suzy really, really helped with the zombies last Halloween. Like, she got her grandfather, the wild god, to ride early and save Seattle from them." He cleared his throat uncomfortably as Suzy and Kiseko both goggled at him. "Is that right?"

"Not...exactly," Suzy said faintly. "But that's...pretty close. How do you know...how did you...?"

Robert looked slightly apologetic. "Dad and Aunt Jo talked about it where I could hear, is all. And you looked like you were having a hard time getting started so I thought I'd help." His face was turning increasingly red. "Sorry."

"No, that's okay. That, um. Yeah. Pretty much." Suzy cast a tentative glance at Kiseko, whose eyes and mouth formed nearly perfect *O*'s.

"And you didn't *tell* me?" Kiso demanded in a whisper. At least she had the presence of mind to whisper. Her parents weren't going to know what to do when they woke up and found Suzy, who was supposed to be in Olympia, in their basement instead. "You didn't *tell* me?" Kiseko asked more loudly.

"It's not that easy to tell!" Suzy protested. "I wanted to,

I just, well, I mean, how? How do you say, "Hey, best friend, turns out I'm like only partly human and by the way my biological father is the one who killed everybody at the high school that day?""

Kiso went white. "What?"

"Oh, God." Suzy ducked her head and shook her hair so it fell to hide her face as she whispered, "Yeah. I guess Robert didn't mention that part. He killed my parents, too. He was crazy," she whispered apologetically through her hair. "I don't even know all of it, but he was...he was like mostly human for hundreds of years, and it kind of made him crazy. I think. And he was trying to align things so he could become a whole god, when really he was supposed to be a half-god. It was awful. He was awful. It was a mess. I didn't want to talk about it. And I can't really anyway, because who would believe it?"

"I would have!"

Suzy looked up through the curtain of her hair. Kiseko's cheeks were flushed and her eyes bright, either with offense or anger. "Would you have?" Suzy asked. "I mean, up until half an hour ago when you went crazy stupid and did *magic* and *summoned* me, would you have?"

"Well—well you could've told me anyway!"

"Aunt Jo says people work really hard at explaining magic away when it happens," Robert said quietly. "Kiseko's different to start with, because she *didn't* believe the Hollywood story about the zombies—"

"What about you?" Suzy asked. "How come you're even here?"

"My dad is a medium. He sees ghosts," Robert clarified. "Mom's a wise woman. My family's all kind of cool with this stuff."

"And Kiseko found this out how?"

"I was reading a book about magic before chess club started, a couple weeks ago. Rob said it wasn't very good if I really wanted to learn about magic. At first I thought he was kidding but he looked so serious. So then I got curious. So you're *magic*? Do something magic!"

"I don't—it's not like that. Most of my magic is seeing the future."

Kiseko lunged forward, grabbing Suzy's arms. "OMG! Can you tell me what college I'm going to? Can you tell me if I get married? How many kids do I have? No, wait, am I totally cool like Isadora Duncan and I go around having lots of kids but never getting married—"

"—and getting your neck snapped by a scarf catching on a motor car wheel," Robert mumbled.

"—oh, not like *that* part, jeez," Kiso said without catching her breath. "Can you tell me—"

"No!" Suzy held her hands up. "It doesn't work like that. The future doesn't work like that. There are millions of different ones, all based on whatever choices you make day by day. Sometimes something goes wrong and a whole lot of the futures turn bad. That's why I came up here at Halloween, I had to warn Detective Walker that her futures had all gone bad. And she managed to squeeze into the one that hadn't. So I can't, like, read your palm, Kiso. And I wouldn't want to if I could. I don't want to know what's going to happen, and I bet you don't really either."

Kiskeo stuck her chin out, then slumped back to sitting. "I guess not. Well, what good is magic you don't want to use? And why did we get you when we were trying to call up a nature god? I mean, because of your biodad, I guess, but—"

"Or maybe," Robert said worriedly, "maybe her magic responded so she could come along and protect us from *that*."

Suzy turned to see a slender earthy figure unfurling from the floor.

It didn't look evil. Not in the first few seconds, anyway. It looked quite beautiful, dark and barky, with soil spilling through the breaks in the bark. Leaves shimmered down its back like hair, and it stretched, sending the scent of new-turned earth and crushed greenery through the basement.

A deeper, older smell wafted along, too. A smell of decay, of old earth rotting and dead things falling to pieces in it. Suzy thought of zombies, and of Detective Walker's panic, and feeling very stupid, she got up and put herself between the rising green and her friends. She didn't know how to fight or protect or any of the things Detective Walker did. But she was magic, and that *had* to make her a better match for the than Robert or Kiseko were.

Robert leaned forward past her calf and slapped his hand onto the pentagram chalked onto the carpet. Suzy felt a hint of strength from him, a promise of power, but— "Kiseko!" Robert hissed. "You drew it, you have to activate it!"

"Actiwhat? Oh. Oh!" Kiseko flung herself forward too, making Suzy feel like an Egyptian god statue, flanked by two low-lying animals. Kiseko's energy sparked out, not at all organized or well-presented, but it did the job. The pentagram came to life again, still a flickering feeble thing like it had been when Suzy arrived. Suzy took a jerky step forward, lifting her hands to add her own strength to the pentagram.

The thing inside the circle lashed out, smashing a branchy arm into Suzy's chest. She staggered, but only a step. Only enough to be out of the pentagram's reach, instead of knocked aside like she should have been. Kiseko squeaked with delight, but Suzy's chest felt caved in, like she couldn't quite breathe anymore. It wasn't just the hit, either. It was the knowledge that flooded her with the ancient nature spirit's touch. Once it had been neutral, neither intentionally caring nor harming. Not anymore. Sometime, so long ago it barely remembered the neutrality, it had tasted blood. Been *fed* blood, until the earth itself was poisoned. Until the very world was riddled with spots of hate, alive with it, waiting for magic to draw it out so it could attack.

It was hungry. It wanted youth, vitality, magic, *blood*. Its spindly branch arms shot out, growing at an impossible rate, but they bypassed Suzy and went straight for Kiseko and Robert.

"*No!*" Suzy flung her hands out like she could stop the green with a word, with an action. Like she could undo the last minutes of time, because she *could*. She *had*, before, or almost. She had unraveled a man from time once before, taken the zombie corpse he had become and undone him all the way back to conception. It had been easy, like pulling a dangling thread from a shirt, and it had popped at the end, satisfying sound of the thread snapping. She couldn't do it again: something stopped her. *Time* resisted her, like it had been changed once recently and refused to be again, even for a semi-god.

Still, her magic was alive now, its own threads snapping and weaving through the air. Futures shone along them, mostly dark and deadly. Kiseko, infected by the ancient earth spirit, eyes blazing and hands becoming stretched branches like the green's. Robert falling under that attack. Suzy running, Suzy fighting, Suzy dying: she cast away a thousand futures, searching for one where they *won*. Time might refuse to listen, but the future was hers to choose. She held onto the thought, leaning hard against the earth magic's hunger. It would have everything, it said, because it was the endless turn and tide of seasons, of life. It was the rising green, and would never die.

But Suzy's power was green and rising too.

She *pushed*, pushed as hard as she knew how, using just her mind. Pushed them toward the rare and faltering futures where they survived. Only a handful among hundreds, but she wouldn't let her friends die. If the green wanted a conduit, it could try *her*, daughter of gods.

It hesitated like a living thing, tempted by her strength. Tempted by the ancient blood inside her, by that tie to something not of the world. Then its hesitation ended and it came for her. Suzy opened her arms and drew it in, tasting the most ancient scraps of earth that tied her to her demi-god father and the wild thing that was her grandfather. Herne was of this earth, as Suzy was, but Cernunnos came from far beyond, and there was something in the rising green that was as old and foreign as Cernunnos. It howled triumph as Suzy called it to herself, and it crashed into her, taking up lodging in her mind. Safe, certain, a part of her: it belonged, in a dark and frightening way.

Darkness. Utter and complete, overwhelming, and beyond the darkness, silence. Wind and breaking branches had howled and snapped a minute earlier, though Suzy hadn't heard them until they were gone. Light returned in a painful rush. The pentagram was losing cohesion, its color fading and power failing, but there was nothing left inside.

Kiseko, squealing, caught Suzy before she fell. "OMG, you banished it! OMG, how did you do that?!"

"There was a...a future where we won. I just...shoved us that way." Suzy sat down, her head in her hands. "It worked, but it...it got dark."

"No it didn't!" Kiseko bounced around Suzy, barely able to contain her delight. "You were awesome! You kicked ass! Did you see that thing, it went *fwssht!* and *zooft!* and—"

"No, it..." The green—except it wasn't green anymore, it was just the dark—it felt like it was behind her eyes now, or even deeper into her head than that. It didn't hurt, but it weighed a lot, and it throbbed in time with her heart. A trickle of it fell down from her brain to her stomach, making her want to throw up.

Kiseko, oblivious to Suzy's half-muttered protests, only ceased her praise when the ceiling creaked. All three of them froze, Suzy peeking upward and seeing Rob and Kiso doing the same thing. "*Shit*," Kiso whispered. "My *parents*. If they find a *boy* here—!"

Rob pressed a finger to his lips, then darted across the basement in a few long steps. He cranked a daylight window open, then glanced back, checking the room like he was making sure everything was okay. Kiseko flapped a frantic hand at him and he gave her and Suzy a quick, concerned smile before scrambling up to and through the window. A heartbeat later, he was gone, eaten by a suburban Seattle yard.

Suzy trembled. The wood creature would've eaten him for real, all of them. Inside her head, the darkness flared like it thought that sounded good. She clenched her hands against her temples, trying to squeeze its presence away. Green power, she told herself. Rising green, like the wood spirit had been rising green, but this was her own strength, her own magic. She didn't want a dark seed at its heart. She imagined her grandfather's vast power in her own hands, crushing the darkness away.

In an agonizing instant, it winked out. Suzy whimpered.

Kiseko was there all of a sudden, wrapping her arms around Suzy's shoulders. She was warm and sturdy, not cold and shaking like Suzy was. "You're okay, Suze. I'm here. You okay? That was crazy," she said more softly. "That was really brave, Suzy. I didn't know you had it in you. I'm sorry for messing with magic, all right? I won't do it again. I don't want to mess my best friend up. Are you okay?"

"Yeah." Suzy croaked the word. "I think so."

"Good." Kiseko sat back on her heels just enough to grin lopsidedly at Suzy. "Because we're going to have to come up with some kind of totally awesome story to explain why you're here in the middle of this mess. And then we're gonna have to convince your aunt that since you're here you might as well stay for the whole weekend, right? And—" She bounced up, bright and cheerful as always, but Suzy caught a glimpse of deeper worry as Kiseko offered a hand. The performance was all for Suzy's sake, Kiseko's way of making sure everything seemed normal.

Suzy let Kiso pull her up, then hugged her and did her best to sound light-hearted and frivolous, too. "Localized windstorm. You left the window open and look what happened!"

"That's a *terrible* cover story, Suze."

"Your parents believed the zombie movie thing, didn't they?"

"Mmrgh." Kiseko rolled her eyes. "I guess so. And so what, did the windstorm blow you in too?"

"That'd be an awfully big storm. Uh—"

"Suzy! Your aunt called!" Kiseko's parents, wearing robes and slippers, came down the stairs together and stopped, expressions comically confused at the mess spread around the basement. "She said you were coming up as a surprise for Kiseko's birthday, but we didn't expect you so soon...what happened down here?"

Suzy gave Kiseko a wide-eyed look, then smiled at her

parents. "I, um, got in way earlier tonight but I was, um, trying to surprise Kiseko so I snuck in and then we, uh, fell asleep? And then the window let in the storm and we were all like 'Oh god we have to clean this up before Mr and Mrs Anderson see,' and—but you woke up. Early. Uh. Hi!"

"It must have been the wind that woke us," Kiso's mom said to her dad, who frowned at Kiseko. "How many times have I told you to be sure the windows are closed at night?"

"I'm totally sorry, Dad. We'll get it cleaned up, okay?"

Mr Anderson nodded, appeased, and his wife smiled. "I'm glad nothing was destroyed. It's good to see you again, Suzy. I'll make you girls some strawberry waffles in the morning, but we're going back to bed now."

Kiso's parents waved and went back upstairs, leaving the two girls to blink uncertainly at each other. Kiseko finally whispered, "Your *aunt* called?"

Suzy shook her head. "No way. It's the magic, or the effect of magic. Making sense of things that don't make sense. I hope it worked on Aunt Mae, too, or I'll be grounded until I leave for college."

"Are you still gonna go to UDub?" Kiseko became light and chipper again as she looked over the wreck of the basement. "Think Mom and Dad will mind if we don't clean up until morning?"

Suzy gave her a look and Kiso giggled. "Yeah, I thought so. Okay. I'll get some towels for the water and I'll scrub up the chalk marks if you can get the branches and things." She ran off to the bathroom without waiting for an answer, and Suzy picked up the nearest branches. The window was still open, so she pushed the branches through and peered into the darkness, trying to see if Robert had escaped safely.

There was no sign of him, anyway. Instead there were stormclouds on the horizon, colored yellow by Seattle's lights. They had a dark heart, as dark as the seed she'd burst in her mine. Suzy shuddered. She knew there were other colors out there too, like Detective Walker's gunmetal silver and blue, but she couldn't see them, not even when she looked through the *other* gaze, the one that showed her the possible futures. She should be able to see them. She'd always been able to before. But there was nothing there now, just the seed of darkness.

The darkness and the shadow she cast herself, of the rising green.

Chronology Notes:

"Band-Aids and Bog-Men" takes place about a month after SHAMAN RISES (Book Nine of the Walker Papers), but contains no spoilers for that book.

Band-Aids and Bog-Men

THEN.

Auntie Sheila was a tall woman whose black hair grew wild and whose nose was as pointed as her wit. She wore skirts and strong boots, for she said knees were easier to clean than jeans and that there was no sense risking your ankles climbing up and down the mountainsides. And climb she did, up the Reek eight times a year, up Croagh Padraig, Saint Patrick's holy mountain, to say holy prayers on holy days. The strangest thing was that the Reek was always empty when Auntie Sheila went up, even if it meant there were a hundred tourists coming down and looking as if they weren't sure why.

Caitríona O'Reilly was a little afraid of her aunt, but that had never stopped her from scrambling up the loose scrim that called itself the pilgrim's path on the Reek to watch Sheila MacNamarra lay down her prayers. The same way every time, first striding North East South and West to touch the ground, and in the last year or so Caitríona had fancied that she saw a flare of white, like the aurora borealis bursting up from the earth, when Auntie Sheila finished that circle. Then she wandered the mountain's small top, avoiding the chapel at the front-center, and laid her palms against the rocky soil time and time again. Sometimes pain creased Auntie Sheila's face, and sometimes she flinched like the ground had burned her, but she never stopped. For an hour beneath the open sky each time, she laid her hands on the earth, and at the end of that hour she walked her circle the other direction to unwind it, and came back to the switchback trail leading down the mountain.

Until Caitríona was thirteen, Auntie Sheila pretended that she never saw her at all, not even when she swept by Caitríona's hiding place at the edge of the mountain. The year Caitríona turned thirteen, Auntie winked when she passed by, and all the times after that, Cat crept closer and closer to the mountaintop, trying to see more clearly. Auntie never stopped her, but nor did she tell her what it was she was doing, beyond what was clear: blessing the holy mountain, as if a site for Christian pilgrims needed a pagan's help as well.

For there was no question of that, at least. Auntie went to the mountain on the old high holy days, on Imbolc and Beltaine, Lughnasa and Samhein, and on the quarter-days as well: the solstices and equinoxes, or close enough as didn't matter. "Every day is holy somewhere, to someone," she said to Caitríona the summer Cat turned fifteen, the first words she'd ever spoken to Cat as they came off the Reek together. Caitríona, in trainers and cut-off jeans, was cold and wet to the bone after a summer storm had lashed them on the mountaintop. Sheila was every bit as wet, her denim skirt sodden and sticking to her legs, but her boots gripped the slippy mountainside more surely than Cat's trainers did, and Sheila gripped Cat's arm in turn, keeping her arright. "I like to come on the old holy days, but if I can't make it then I come as close as I can. It's what's in your heart that counts, Caitríona."

"What's in yours?" Scree shifted under Cat's feet and down she went, Sheila's grip not strong enough after all. Scrapes and bruises appeared as if by magic, but her head hit last and there were no stars to be seen, thanks be to God. She sat and turned her hands up, palms abraded, and Auntie Sheila clucked like a good maiden auntie and pulled Cat to her feet.

"All that's in me heart now is getting me auldest niece off this hill alive," Sheila said cheerfully. "Ask me again on another day and perhaps I'll tell another tale. Now I'e a plaster for ye when we get back to town, but ye mustn't take it off for three days."

"You always say that, Auntie."

"And I always mean it, and I trust ye's always listen." Auntie Sheila gave Caitríona a green-eyed glare that made her laugh and squirm at the same time, for as often as the cousins listened, they also didn't. No one could stop themselves, not with what they called Auntie Sheila's magic plasters. Auntie Sheila herself called them Band-Aids sometimes, because she'd lived in America for a time and that was the American word for plasters. Cat's youngest brother was certain the magic of Auntie's plasters was that they *came* from America, where everything was better, and so of course no matter how soon a lad took the plaster off the wound beneath was healed.

That, of all things, that was the moment that came back to Caitríona over and over as she stood at her auntie's graveside. None of the other times, none of the hunting thigh-deep through mucky bogs for ancient bodies whose spirits Auntie Sheila said needed laying to rest, not the hundred times Cat had asked again what lay inside Sheila's heart, not the digging for herbs or the winding of holly and hawthorn together for protective boughs to hang above a door. Those things *did* come back to her, sure and so, but it was the magic plasters that she couldn't stop thinking of. She had plasters in her purse now, ones she always carried so she would always think of Auntie Shelia.

And thinking of those plasters was safer than thinking about the tall lean American woman who was Auntie Sheila's daughter, and who had no tears in her eyes as she stood alone at the grave, for all that the whole family stood together. Joanne Walker still remained apart, her jaw set in a way that reminded Caitríona of Auntie Sheila, though they didn't look so much alike as all that. Cousin Joanne wore her own black hair short and had shoulders like a man, broad and strong in the black knit turtleneck that fell over faded blue jeans. She wore shoes like Auntie Sheila had favored, heavy boots for walking in, and at her throat glimmered the silver necklace Auntie Sheila had always worn.

Caitríona wanted nothing more on the earth than to

ask Joanne the story of Auntie Sheila and *himself*, the man not one of them even knew the name of. Joanne's father, who'd stolen Auntie Sheila's heart and never given it back. Cat was the oldest of the Irish cousins and only seventeen, so she had no memory of Auntie Sheila's pregnancy. It was something the sisters barely spoke of, and only when they were certain Sheila was nowhere within hearing. She'd fallen in love, they said, and come back to Ireland to bear a child when a baby out of wedlock was still a shocking and shameful thing. She'd shown not a whit of shame, they said, but before the child was born something happened, and not one of them knew what. Sheila had grown reserved and cool, given no sign of joy when her daughter was born, and in the dead of night six months later she had left Westport for America, only to return days later with no babe in arms. She'd said not a word about it, either, save that Siobhán was with her father now, and that was the end of it.

And now Siobhán, who called herself Joanne, was here, because Sheila had announced months ago that she was dying, and she'd say no more about that than Joanne's father. She called Joanne to her and they'd disappeared together, touring Europe, Caitríona's mother said. Learning to know one another before it was too late, though from the look of it they'd not known each other well enough for Joanne Walker to weep over her own mother's death.

The whole of them, all the clan who were MacNamarras once and O'Reillys and Curleys and Byrnes and some few MacNamarras still, they stood together as one, left behind by the American cousin who turned and walked away with the first fistful of dirt thrown onto the coffin, and that was that, so. The end of Joanne Walker as much as the end of Sheila MacNamarra, and the one left a hole because it left them with nothing at all of the other.

And sure, as Cat's da would say, *and sure* if Caitríona wasn't still thinking of magic plasters when she reeled off the train early on a Monday after the St Patrick's craic in Dublin town, and sure if those thoughts didn't bring her to visit Sheila's grave first, before going to the Reek herself, as she'd done a dozen times since her aunt's death.

And sure and if she didn't pass Joanne Walker on the way, and another woman, calling herself Maeve, who was the tallest thing Caitríona had ever laid eyes on, and sure and if by the end of the maddest three days any mortal had ever known, if Caitríona didn't know then that her aunt had been the Irish Mage, and that she, Caitríona O'Reilly, the oldest niece of the MacNamarra clan, was meant to take up that mantle now.

NOW.

Perfect, Caitríona O'Reilly thought, and because Joanne was on her mind, she then heard the word echoed as Joanne would have heard it: *pair-fect*. And what, Joanne would have wanted to know, was a Pair Fect? Maybe it was two people who were fecked, as if *fect* might be the past tense of *fecked*, which was already the past tense of *feck*, the Irish way of saying a word that puritanical American television always bleeped out. Unless it was an Irishman saying it, because *feck* slipped by their censors when the more Anglicized version of the word wouldn't.

Americans and Irish. Separated by a common language. Caitríona put her fingertips against the glass case encompassing the Clonycavan Man, one of the most perfectly conserved bog men to be found in Ireland. His fragile thin skin, sagging over shriveled muscles, his bones, his teeth, they were all stained rich mahogany brown from the ancient peat they'd nested in. Pickled, they were: bog acid pickled the creatures caught in it, and she'd read about each and every circumstance that improved the chances of a body being preserved instead of disintegrating. They were many, and in Ireland, they were easy to come by. Nearly sixty bog men had been found over the years, and that, Caitríona reckoned, was just the ones they'd *found*. Whole civilizations might be buried in the peat, if only they dug deep enough.

So it wasn't only herbs Auntie Sheila had been digging for in the bogs. What could be worse than being murdered and thrown into the bogs but to lie in rest for centuries before being dug up by a rumbling peat harvester with teeth so vicious that no one could be sure if the poor mummy had been cut in half before death, or if his lower half had been severed and chewed up by the peat cutter. And the Clonycavan Man, he was one of the *lucky* ones. He'd *only* been murdered, his head smashed in and so well-preserved there were still bits of brain inside his perfectly preserved skull, and they knew what his last meals had been as well. And he'd been a bit of a dandy as well, with imported hair gel in the straggly hair that remained on his head. Caitríona hoped he'd died before being chopped in half, but she could feel the poor creature's spirit still trapped within his body, the agony of his death never leaving him.

Auntie Sheila had searched out lost people like these in the bogs, and laid their spirits to rest. But these ones, the bog men brought to the museum on Kildare Street, they had been separated from their place of death before Sheila had found them, and their spirits cried and clawed at their glass coffins, a torture the anthropologists could never study. It was the memory of bog-tromping, and the thought of these glass-encased bog-men, that had brought Caitríona to Dublin at all.

Joanne, Caitríona thought, would know what to do. She'd dealt with ghosts before, though she said she couldn't see them herself. Nor could Caitríona, but she felt the captured spirit within the glass regardless, as she'd never felt it before in all the times she'd visited the museum. The bog men had been spectacles then, a breathtaking glimpse at the horror of perfectly preserved death. Now she could hardly understand how she'd missed their cries.

Joanne would start with a power circle, that, at least, Cat knew, and so that was where she was to begin as well. The bog men display was strangely suited for it, with each mummy encapsulated down a winding ramp within a border of taller walkways. She couldn't quite make a complete circle, at least not in one go, but then, there was more than one lost spirit to attend to, too.

Cat murmured, "Sorry, sorry," as she stepped around visitors. Most moved easily, more fascinated by the mummies than a living girl, but a few glanced her way in surprise. The spear, she supposed, for there was nothing extraordinary about the rest of her, except perhaps the fire-engine-red hair straight from a bottle. Still, it would be the spear that caught their attention, though in the week and some she'd carried it not a soul had mentioned it as a *spear*, but as a walking stick. A very tall walking stick, to be sure, but not one of them seemed to see the black ironwood spearhead atop a white wood haft.

Just as well, for there'd be no explaining to the guarda why she was carrying a deadly weapon through the hills of Ireland and the streets of Dublin.

There were places between the circular displays where she could slip through, build a circle that way, though there was nothing elegant about creating a power circle by way of squashing herself. If she hadn't grown two inches and gotten slimmer with it, she'd have never fit, but as it was she squeezed through, thinking resentfully of Joanne's height and slender build and the deadly white leather coat that proclaimed her cousin as a hero not to mess with. Cat popped out the other side with a whoosh of breath and stumbled over a child trying to go the way she'd come. They stopped, sharing a guilty, wide-eyed look before Cat bowed to show the boy the way. He beamed and scampered through, and Caitríona wound her way around the displays.

I'll set it on fire with me mind, she thought, and all but laughed at herself. A few months was no time to learn magic in, not without a teacher. She had no sense of what she ought to do to save captured spirits, but the first magery she had done had been simple: *I'll set it on fire with me mind,* she'd said again and again, until she *had*.

I'll free them, so, she said to herself again and again. *I'll build a circle to keep them safe as they're drawn free from their broken bodies, and then I'll release it and them, so their spirits may go where they will.* It had no skill to it, no shape or rhythm to make it a spell, but that was how the magic had been built on Croagh Padraig, and it was how she would make it today. Auntie Sheila would have had an elegance and a form to it, but that would come in time: she was young still, and had long years to learn in.

It wasn't a circle and it wasn't a shamrock that she walked. Her purse bumped her hip and the heel of the spear clacked against the ground with each step, a quiet rhythm that helped her trace a shape across the floor. It was something of an infinity loop, a never-ending figure 8. That would do, and more, the idea of it sparked delight in her heart, as if the circle wasn't the best shape for her magery anyway. As fast as delight came, it slipped away again with a pang of wondering what Auntie Sheila might have taught her, had she lived. Both those things slipped into the circle, making it one of hope and regret, and that felt right to her, for what else was she weaving but a story of that? A story of death, which was always a story of regret even when it was a good death, and a story of hope that she might release the captured spirits of the dead. And stories were the lifeblood of her people, their pride and their joy. Their weaving ran deep in the blood, and that became what she wanted to do: to tell the stories that could only be told through magery.

The power wove faster and faster, until it began to

spin tales of men she had never known: the story of a tall, handsome man with soft hands, a rich man whose bog-bound body had only two scars, little more than paper cuts on his hands. He had studied magic once himself, perhaps, feeling it deep in his blood, but none of his people had trusted him, seeing him as a giant, as a danger, as *Fir Bolg*, with his black hair and brown eyes and quick and tempting smile. The *Fir Bolg* had to die, and die badly, to keep the tribe safe from deviltry, and so holes were punctured through his arms so ropes could bind him, and pain inflicted upon his body while he screamed *no*!

And no indeed, the story whispered, no, not the *Fir Bolg*, not the dark and dire monsters of Irish folklore, but their opposites, their elfin bretheren, the *aos sí*. They had been tall, so tall, and Caitríona knew that in her bones as much as the dead man had felt magic in his, for she had met Maeve of Connacht, Queen Maebh, the Ulster Queen, and she had been born of *aos sí* blood too, and tall with it. That was the crime this man had died for: for the magic born to him as a man not of mankind, but a last and lingering soul from a dying race.

Until it wove the story of the Clonycavan Man with his gelled pompadour, and there told of a man, petty and vain, afraid his small stature made him unimportant in the eyes of his people, and so he spent what coin he had on the gel and on other bodily improvements to make himself grander than he was to catch the eye of beauty, the only thing he felt he deserved. But a woman who was not beautiful fell in love with him, and he with her. Ashamed, he began to change his ways, but her brother whom he had wronged so long ago objected, and the finely gelled head was split into pieces and his body thrown into a bog. His spirit should be bitter, but its greatest sorrow was in knowing that the woman would have thought him the small and petty creature he had once been, and that she would have died believing he had left her because he did not love her.

They wound themselves around Caitríona, these stories and others, four or five in all, until she knew them in her bones. *I'll keep them safe as they're drawn free from their broken bodies, and then I'll release it and them.* A simple spell indeed, and the first part had worked a treat. The second, though: now that she knew them, how was she to free what she'd taken into her soul?

In light, as she'd seen Aunt Sheila's spirit released. A goddess had helped then, though, and Caitríona had nothing of that power in her.

No: she *did* have that power inside her. It was Aoife's kiss that had awakened her magery. She was nothing so grand as a goddess herself, but nor were these captured spirits so badly bound as Aunt Sheila had been. Aoife's magic had burned Sheila away. Surely Caitríona needed only lift these broken souls up beyond the confines of their glass coffins to free them. Like sunshine on the water, a burst of light that rose into the sky. Now that was more poetic, sure, and Caitríona held that thought close, to make magic of it, too.

It took time, minutes or more, but a soft white light filled the museum hall, growing brighter with each moment until it erupted from each encircled body. The boy Cat had played with gave a bold happy shout and was hushed by his ma, but Cat felt the same shout rising in her. She had no great skill yet, but her ugly spells were working, and the beauty would come in time.

Faces came alive in the light, all the discoloration and distortion of mummification fading away. They might have been men of Dublin, walking the city that very day: broad faces, fair skin and light eyes. Bad teeth and thinning hair on some, but handsome cleanliness on others. Recognition and gratitude gleamed in those faces as clearly as they would on any modern man, and together they began to speak. They were thousands of years of age, and couldn't speak a word she knew. But then, neither could Maeve of Connacht, and that hadn't stopped them from speaking Irish and English both to one another. Cat bowed her head and listened, and the words came clear:

We died to feed an ancient power, bleak and cruel. Our spirits were meant for him, the Devourer, the Master, the End of All Time, and yet the bog took our souls as well as our skins. We were bound to this earth in a way that spirits are not meant to be, never to leave it without someone to grant us release.

Men of learning released our bodies from the soil: a brightness in our dark destiny. We have cried here for so little time compared to the years we lay beneath the bog, and now you have come to free our broken hearts. We are free, and in our freedom we may choose. We have been granted release, but we will not yet leave.

Call to us, Caitríona O'Reilly, Irish Mage, in your fateful hour, and we will come.

The light, the faces, the magic, faded as quickly as it had

come. Cat's knees went wobbly and she leaned her weight on the spear, suddenly knackered. The museum visitors were full of shouts and gasps and questions, their voices echoing off the walls like a band of hooligans determined to make all the noise in the world. She felt her circles unraveling beneath their feet, swift sparks of power zipping toward her as the unwinding touched them, as if each touch lent her half a breath of strength. Her shields, the daft *Star Trek* shields that Joanne had taught her to protect herself with, felt stronger as the last circle came undone, until she was herself again among the bog men and the tourists.

The mummies looked no different than before, but their cries were silenced. Their pain was gone, the suffering ended, though a sense of their presence remained. There to come to her when she called at her fateful hour, which sounded dangerous enough indeed.

A yowl broke through the thought and the boy she'd seen before appeared, a splinter embedded under his fingernail. "I wasn't supposed to touch it!" he wailed. "Mommy's going to k-ki-*kiiiillll* me!"

Caitríona laughed and crouched. "Let's see it, lad. Ootch, that looks like it hurts. It's American you are?"

"Y-ye-yeees. How'd you k-k-knoooow?"

"Ah, you're no Irishman, not with that fine Yankee accent. Here, now, let's see what I can do. I've a plaster in my bag, if you want it."

Tears spilled over the lad's cheeks, but only because he crushed his eyes into an uncertain squint. "A plaster?"

"A Band-Aid, you'd call it. Here now." Cat leaned the

spear against a wall and pushed around in her purse until she found the plaster. She held it up, then grabbed his fingertip, squeezing it hard. The boy yelped again as his fingertip turned dark red, so startled he hardly even noticed when she yanked the splinter out. Blood welled up and his eyes got rounder. She nodded and wrapped the plaster around his finger, then gave it a kiss. "There, my lad, all fixed." All she needed was the spell that Auntie Sheila had known, the one to heal the hurt. Then realization struck her and she gave his fingertip a last squeeze before setting the magic she'd known all her life: "Now it's a magic plaster, so it is, my boy. Don't take it off for three days, and the wound will be healed when you do."

His eyes widened and he nodded eagerly, then ran away again, crowing to his ma about the plaster. That was it, then, she thought: this was the life of a mage. Band-Aids and bog-men.

It sounded like a fine life indeed.

Chronology Notes:

"Twenty Years After" takes place twenty years after the Walker Papers end. The author does not consider this story to contain spoilers, but the exceedingly spoiler-shy should avoid reading it until after SHAMAN RISES, the final book of the Walker Papers, is released in December 2013.

Twenty Years After

The coolest woman I've ever known taught me that magic was real.

I don't think she meant to. No, I'm sure she didn't mean to, but she did it anyway.

I was six when she healed me of sickness brought on by dehydration. My Mom remembers it, but she thinks it was just a lucky chance that a police officer happened by with water and a soothing touch. Me, *I* remember the cool rush of strength that poured in me. It was like a drink of water in the desert—and I hiked the Mojave last autumn, so I have some idea of what that really feels like—except it didn't just soothe my throat or wet my mouth. It did line my esophagus the way a cold drink does, all the way to my belly, where it spread out nice and cool, but cold water stops there. You don't feel it wash through the rest of you, still cool and refreshing as it runs through your blood. I felt the magic through my whole body, tingling and bright and comforting. When I'm having a bad day I can still call that feeling up, the way it made my fingertips and toes buzz, and even now, twenty years after, it makes me feel better.

Then on my seventh birthday, Joanne Walker and I went down a rabbit hole in a police station and played Tar Baby with Brer Rabbit. I told her that day I was going to grow up just like her, a police officer and full of magic. Things didn't work out quite how I planned. I did four years in the military instead of becoming a cop, and it took twenty years of trying and hoping and practicing before I accepted the truth: I'm not magic.

But I'm smart.

The Yakima River started up in Cascades, fed by Keechelus Lake. It was a major tributary for southeastern Washington, providing irrigation water for the orchards, grapes and crop fields, as well as being a year-round fishing and kayaking river. The valley it fed had range lands that were used by the military for training grounds. I'd spent a few months there during my time in the Army, so it was familiar territory, but more important, it was just about in my back yard. But then, a lot of the Pacific Northwest was: I ranged down to Salem and as far north as Whistler. I'd gone out to Coeur d'Alene a few times, too, but anything big enough to draw me farther away was in Joanne's weight class, not mine.

I headed down through Snoqualmie Pass on the scent

of a rumor. That was how most things worth hunting came my way: rumors or small independent news sources. The major media had nearly collapsed under the weight of microreporting, but they'd never carried news stories about this kind of thing anyway. Boiling lakes only made the news if a scientist could explain why it was boiling. When there was no obvious cause, the news outlets shut up and pretended it wasn't happening. Most people were like that too, which I'd never even wanted to understand. As far as I was concerned, a world with active magic in it was a far better place to live than one that had none. No doubt Joanne had had a significant effect on me, but she'd had an effect on the whole Northwest, too. There was flat-out more magic now than there'd been when I was a kid, and people tried harder than ever not to see it. I didn't get it.

Keechelus Lake, held in place by Keechelus Dam, was a simmering froth. Steam billowed skyward, killing trees and sending birds to other nesting sites. No insects droned in the air and there wasn't a hint of sulfur scent or anything else that might account for boiling lakes. There was a faint scent of boiled fish. Just as well they'd dammed up Keechelus, not Kachess, one of the other lakes that fed the Yakima. Keechelus meant *few fish* in the indigenous Yakama language. That was one of a million bits of almost-useless information I'd picked up while studying anthropology and world mythologies after I got out of the military. Almost useless, but not entirely. Not if you'd chosen to hunt monsters for a living. Well, not exactly a living: it wasn't like anybody paid me to keep the world safe from things that went bump. I was a grad student in Spokane, halfway done with a degree in world mythologies. I taught two classes a semester, kept my ear to the ground for monster reports, and worked on my dissertation when I had no other option.

Where water was allowed to spill through to the river, it hissed and bubbled. I left the dam and drove downstream, taking Highway 10 and then Canyon Road, which ran closer to the river's route than the interstates did, and watched to see where the water cooled.

It didn't. All the way south, through Ellensburg and into the city of Yakima, where I turned around and headed north again. If the river boiled for ninety miles out of the headwaters, it probably boiled all the way down to the Columbia. I stopped for lunch at a diner perched on the river's edge. It was almost deserted, windows steamy and the whole place smelling heavily of fry grease.

My waitress, the only one working besides the cook, looked wrung-out and flat. I ordered two vanilla milkshakes to go with my chicken breast salad, and gave her one of them when she brought them to me. She gave it a sad smile, then went ahead and sat down with me. "Not like there's anybody else waiting on their order today."

"Yeah, I almost thought you were closed when I pulled up. Nobody in the parking lot. How long has this been going on?"

"Two or three days." Her name tag said Marnie. Marnie was in her thirties and trim in the way women who worked on their feet and didn't snack on too many french fries could be. She looked like a nice person. She wiped the back of her hand across her forehead, making almost no difference to the damp sheen there. "This is the first time in years we haven't been swamped at lunchtime. Good thing, too, because the pipes are drying up. We won't even be able to do dishes soon."

"Drying up, really? I wonder if the water's boiling out of them."

"They're not hot, just dry. I don't know why. We've had a couple geologists in, but they just wipe steam off the windows and frown at the river. They won't answer any questions. It's like it's creeping even them out. I mean, shouldn't there be news reporters down here? Big ones, I mean, not just the locals and the crazies." Her expression went guarded. "You're not one of them, are you?"

"Local, or crazy?" I smiled to take the edge off, and sipped my milkshake. There was real vanilla in it, which surprised me. "Neither. Not a news reporter, not a crazy. I bet the crazies say there's other strange things going on too, though. Because it never rains but it pours, right?"

Marnie shivered. "I wouldn't care if the crazies were saying things. That's what they do. But some of my friends say their kids, I mean good kids, not trouble-makers, you know? That they've seen some crazy things up in the mountains just the last few days. I mean, they've gone out looking, of course, who could stop them with the river all boiling up like that? And they come home saying they've seen—" She stood up abruptly, almost knocking her milkshake over. "You *are* a reporter, aren't you? And you're going to make me look like one of the crazies. You've got a camera on you somewhere, don't you? One of those micro ones you can put in earrings or hair clips." She looked at me suspiciously, but I hadn't put earrings in, and my chin-length blond hair was simply tucked behind my ears.

"Not even in my rings." I lifted my hands to show her how they were bare of jewelry, too. "Honestly, the only camera I've got is my phone, and that's in the car. I was just going to go hiking until I saw the river, and I wondered if it was even safe out there anymore." I edged a foot out from beneath the table to show her my hiking boots. "If kids have been out there hiking it's probably safe, huh?"

Marnie sat down again, still wary. "I don't know. They said there were...landslides."

"Landslides" was an obvious euphemism. I wondered what for as I made a show of letting my shoulders slump. "Aw. All the heat and steam making a mess of the underlying soil, you think? Maybe I can find someplace rockier—"

Marnie said, "No," sharply, then curled her lip. "I mean, maybe, but they said—they were up pretty high, where the treeline stopped on that snub-faced mountain, so there wasn't much soil. Rock slides, not landslides, I guess. I just don't think anybody should be out there."

"You're probably right." I finished my salad and had another sip of milkshake. "That's the best vanilla shake I've ever had."

That restored her ease and earned me a smile. "It's our specialty. We've got customers who drive out from Spokane and Olympia once or twice a month for a Sunday brunch with milkshakes." Her smile faded as she looked toward the steamy windows. "They're not going to keep coming if the river keeps boiling. I don't know what I'll do if this place closes. There aren't a lot of jobs out here."

"I'm sure it'll settle down. These things do." Another customer came in as I spoke. Marnie gave me another smile, grateful if disbelieving, and got up to say, "Sit anywhere," and offer menus. I put a twenty down on the table and left. She would think it was over-tipping of the finest degree, but to my mind, I was paying for information as well as the meal. I knew more—a little more—than I had when I'd sat down, and that was worth a lot.

In the car I pulled up a web interface and put in a search for boiling rivers, dry pipes, rock slides and supernatural origins. An unsurprisingly short list came back to me. I opened the most-likely looking pages onto the windshield and scanned them, thinking that Joanne would have skipped this step. She could afford to rush in where angels feared to tread, though. All I had was combat training and silver bullets. I'd never met anything that specifically had to die by silver, but I hadn't met much that wouldn't. Better safe than sorry.

Most of the search hits were a miss. The one that looked most promising also looked the least promising, as in "Don't be stupid, Ash: call Joanne in on this one," least-promising. Demons and godlings were out of my league. I double-checked the data from the normal channels against the undernet sites most often used by adepts like Joanne and reapers like me, and didn't come up with anything better. Either I was on the money, or the thing I was chasing was so obscure not even the connected world-wide efforts of scholars, demon hunters, and magic-users could had a database entry for it.

I cleared the windshield and muttered, "Joanne's mobile," to the car, which phoned her as I pulled out of the diner's parking lot. Her phone went to voice mail, which made me check the time. No, I wasn't calling at a bad hour, she just wasn't picking up. Fair enough. "Hey, Jo, this is Ash. I'm heading for Keechelus Lake and maybe a Sumerian demon. If you're not busy this afternoon I could probably use your help. The river's boiling and the mythology says a god killed this demon back in the day. Give me a call if you can make it." I hung up, drove back toward the lake, and pulled off the road where the bushes along the roadside were densest.

It wasn't dense enough, to my eyes. I backtracked to fluff grass up where I'd stepped on it, and to drag deadfall into more of a blockade, but I still thought the car stood out like a sore thumb. That was potentially a huge problem. This far out of town I had to worry about State Troopers, and they were the leos with the millimeter wave scanners that a lead box in the trunk couldn't trick. But there was road and there was mountainside. Not much choice in the matter. Not for the first time, I regretted driving an older vehicle: my Cadillac was three times as long as the newest electric cars. I could have buried one of those in the roadside bush without a problem.

But new cars minimal trunk space, and unlike Jo, I couldn't afford to go into battle with nothing more than my charm and good looks. She had a magic sword, for Pete's sake.

I had a grenade launcher.

I wasn't supposed to, of course. Nobody was, especially since the country-wide crackdown after the election riots when I was seventeen. That was part of why I'd gone into the Army instead of becoming a cop—it had become clear there would be advantages to having friends who worked in military supplies. As a result, the trunk of my Caddy looked like I was preparing for the zombie apocalypse, though from what I understood, zombies were extremely difficult to raise and that threat was negligible. My arsenal was meant for other, more likely scenarios, and the grenade launcher was the least of it.

Most of the grenades I carried were flash-bangs, not frags, but I had lethal capability if I needed it. I also had stun guns, pistols, knives, a garrote, and a slingshot. I'd been surprised at how loud a gun with a silencer was, the first time I shot one. Movies lied. So I'd learned how to use the slingshot for when silence really mattered, and if I thought I would be doing range-hunting, sometimes I took the compound bow out of the trunk too.

Not today, though. I packed grenades, flash-bang and frag alike. I took my space blanket, in case I was out too late and needed warmth. The brand name was something else, but the common name had stuck through the decades, even though a modern space blanket was nothing like the sheet-of-Mylar old ones. Mine didn't just trap body heat. It absorbed and re-focused solar power, and could be set to release warmth either slowly or quickly. I folded it over my backpack so it would gather heat while I hiked, then slipped my phone's tiny flat-panel subwoofers into the pack's outside pockets, muttering, "In case I'm out too late and need a party in my pocket to keep me going." It sounded like something Joanne would say, which pleased me. I strapped knives to both thighs, slid the stun guns and one pistol into the backpack along with the frags, and shouldered the pack on before sliding my Glock into the custom holster built into the pack's straps. I put a water bottle on my hip and shook my shoulders, a slosh inside the backpack assuring me the second bottle inside the pack was full, tucked snacks into pockets, and went hiking.

Asag. Sumerian demon of sickness, who, according to my undernet search, made rivers boil with his ugliness and had sex with mountains to make rock-demons to protect himself with. Rock demons and landslides had enough in common to make the link, especially with Marnie's discomfort about what the kids had reported seeing. The boiling water was a clue, too, even if I couldn't imagine what a Sumerian demon was doing in the Pacific Northwest. There'd been no reports of unusual sickness in the area, but it was possible he brought sickness, rather than followed it. With boiling rivers and drying-up wells, it was easy enough to see how sickness could come in his wake.

And he'd been defeated by a god in Sumeria. Ninurta, god of sunlight and of healing. I would probably have to wait until Joanne caught up with me to take Asag down, but at least I could locate him on my own.

Marnie had claimed the kids were up at the treeline. I doubted it. Most of the Cascades had a timberline around six thousand feet. Keechelus Lake was just south of Snoqualmie Pass, which was only about three thousand feet above sea level. If the local teens were getting hit by rock slides a couple thousand feet above the mountaintops, I was not only out of my league, but way envious of the flying teenagers.

The terrain wasn't bad. Low underbrush sprang back after I passed over it. Fir and pine trees provided cover from afternoon sunshine. Birds and squirrels scolded me for intruding on their territory, but weren't disturbed by anything stranger than me. I wasn't in the right area yet, in that case. I worked my way up the mountain, switch-backing around a few steep hills covered in huckleberry bushes. Another month and they'd be ripe. On the off chance I had time to go berry-picking, I stopped and recorded the latitude and longitude on my phone. Then I started uphill again, combating mosquitoes until I had to stop again and dig the subwoofers out and hang them on my pack. I couldn't hear the sonic buzz that vibrated the air in a way that made bugs back off, but I could feel it crawling on my skin. Hikers had been using the tech in lieu of bug spray ever since the sound industry—with some help from the military industrial complex—had turned stereo speakers into something you could roll up or put in a back pocket. They were covered with a solar screen that stored about sixteen hours' worth of low-level power usage, too, so they could be used as back-up batteries. I vaguely remembered that when I was little—when I'd first met Joanne Walker—cell phones and cameras has to be plugged in, but cars didn't. Even knowing it had been like that in my lifetime didn't make it seem any less strange.

There was a rhythm to the climb, a comfortable cadence that clearly let my mind wander. I reset my thoughts toward the data I had available, considering what I knew as I edged upward. Boiling rivers and dried-up pipes weren't making the news, but there had been a recent story about a proposition to dam the other Yakima River source lakes. I didn't know if Asag was an opportunistic demon, or the kind someone had to raise, but the threat to the free-flowing sources might tie into the signs of his presence here. All the big US rivers and a lot of the smaller ones were already dammed, and the effects of that were visible in dozens of ways all over the country. An environmentalist with his head on wrong might've thought a demon would help solve the watershed problems, but it was just as possible that demons struck where the terrain was inviting. The Cascades offered mountains for mating with, plenty of rivers, lakes, creeks and streams, and enough people that if he survived by making them sick, he'd have a steady diet of illness coming his way.

But it didn't really matter how he'd gotten here, unless someone had raised him. In that case, capturing him would give me a line back to whoever had done the summoning. If he'd simply spent the past four millennia digging his way through from Sumer and only just made it to Eastern Washington, then all I had to do was bury him again. In another four thousand years he could be someone else's problem. It wasn't the kind of solution Joanne would embrace, but I'd made my peace with what I could and couldn't do. Burying evil worked for me.

I'd climbed high enough on those thoughts that the fir trees had thinned around me. A few sturdy ones still grew higher on the mountain, but I'd reached something close enough to a tree line that I sent a silent apology toward Marnie's teens. They'd no doubt been up around this level too. I checked my phone, which told me I was at about 2600 feet above sea level. A good day's hike under ordinary circumstances, but probably nowhere near my destination. Rocks slid beneath my feet and bounced a few yards down the mountainside before settling into new beds. The mosquitoes weren't so bad this high up, but I left the subwoofers on, just in case. Then I started circling toward narrow waterfall trickles and stream rivulets spilling downhill.

I had a great view of the simmering Keechelus Lake. If my instincts were right about the causality being the demon Asag, he had to be within view of the lake himself, or it wouldn't be boiling. I didn't want to think about how many square miles the lake was visible from, because Eastern Washington would be a wasteland before I'd explored them all. But Marnie had said her kids were up on this snub-nosed peak, so that was where I had to start. I gulped down most of a sixteen ounce water bottle and stuck what was left into my pack. I had another larger bottle, too, and an unwise lack of concern about what would happen to my guts if

I drank straight from the streams. The way I saw it, they'd probably been boiled recently, and besides, my water bottles had filters that were supposed to clear the bacteria out. I hadn't gotten sick yet while on mission.

More stones shook loose as I made my way around and over boulders. I had rope in my backpack along with some very basic rock climbing gear, but if I ended up anywhere sheer I was going to have to find a way around. Being prepared for every possible contingency just weighed too much. I stopped for another drink of water, wiping sweat away and listening to rocks crack and bounce on their way down the slope.

A long gulp and a few steps later, I realized I hadn't been walking on shoaly ground for some time now, and hadn't knocked any stone loose in longer than that.

Carefully, I shrugged my backpack off, knelt, and unzipped it as I looked over my shoulder. Everything in the pack had a designated place. I didn't need to see what I was doing to find the frags, nor to gently swing the grenade launcher into place so I could load it.

The boulders just down the mountainside from me were moving. Rocking slowly, like giant eggs trying to right themselves on invisible legs. Smaller stones were crushed beneath them as they shifted, puffing into dust and bouncing into the distance. I caught signs of more movement uphill from me, and breathed carefully as I loaded the last grenades into the launcher. Then I looked up.

Stone golems were staggered across the mountainside above me. Taller and broader than me, they had visible black pits of eyes and no hands or feet, just blunt ends to their long arms and stubby legs. They had mouths, too, gaping maws like caverns built into a moving mountainside. They moved slowly and in rhythm with each other. Below me, one of the boulders cracked, egg-like again, and another golem emerged from it. The snap of a second boulder breaking apart sounded like a gunshot. I counted six, and more being birthed. I would need a blanket assault to take them all out at once, and my grenade launcher wasn't going to be enough.

A rumble started, so deep it made hairs on my neck stand up. It felt familiar, but the sensation slipped away as one of the golems below me crouched, then leapt.

I caught it in the belly with a grenade, and flung myself behind a man-sized huddle of rock to protect myself from the fragments. The roar disrupted the rumbling, but it started up again a moment later, angrier this time. The golems picked up their speed, converging on me. I waited a count of eight, long enough for the ground beneath me to vibrate hard with their running steps, then bounced up and fired again, hoping to catch more than one with the next grenade.

Two golems exploded into pebbles. I bellowed, "Hoo-ah!" and dropped again, waiting for the rest to come closer.

The stone next to me cracked open and a golem dropped its full weight on me.

Air slammed out of me in a sob. My ribs weren't shattered, but I'd felt them crack. If the golem levered itself up a few inches and dropped on me again, I'd be flattened. I couldn't afford that, and I didn't have many other options. Neither did it, though. It growled and snapped at me toothlessly, but I was certain if anything got caught between those flat gums it would be crushed. I exhaled to get the last air out of my gut so I could breathe in again, and when all the air was gone, I squirmed one arm free. The frag rifle was crushed between me and the golem, but even Joanne might think twice about setting off a grenade on her chest. Maybe not—I'd seen her take hits at least that hard and walk away—but it was a rash idea.. And I didn't have magic to back me up. I wheezed a breath past the pain, fumbled a grenade from the backpack, and swore I would never do anything this stupid again if I lived through doing it once.

Then I pulled the pin and shoved the grenade into the golem's mouth. I grabbed its lower jaw and jammed it up, closing its mouth on the grenade, and I counted eight seconds in a prayer: "Please, God, let this work. Let it work."

Stone exploded on top of me. Shards slammed into my belly. Dust penetrated my pores. A thump like being hit by the shockwave of a sound barrier breach drove me a few inches into the ground. My ears started to ring , the noise building until it had a visual of its own, rings spreading through the black behind my eyelids.

On top of that, I heard something else. An irritating vibration, enough to set the teeth that didn't feel loosened on edge. It made the air shiver, like a barrier set up around my skin.

Like a subwoofer playing a pitch to drive mosquitoes

away. Subsonics that humans couldn't hear. Subsonics that rattled the air, though, and probably the earth.

I'd led the rock golems right to me.

Maybe I wasn't so smart after all. If I'd done it on purpose it would've been clever, and it was still better than hiking all over the eastern Cascades trying to find them, but I was supposed to be the one who relied on thinking ahead. Thinking ahead was supposed to keep me from getting cracked ribs and grenade concussions.

The ringing in my ears faded a little. I had to sit up, even knowing it was going to hurt. It was going to hurt a lot. I did it all at once, rubble falling away in a noisy counterpoint to the pain crashing through my body. I didn't dare prod my ribs to see how bad they were. I could find out later, after I'd finished destroying rock golems and taking out their demon father. I rolled all the way to my feet, panting through the pain, and didn't dare stop to take stock of what other damage I'd sustained.

Four golems had been reduced to sand. There were four left, and no obvious signs of more generating. I wondered if eight was a number of significance in ancient Sumer, or if I'd just interrupted their spawning session before it reached the number I knew *was* significant, which was sixty. I had to hope so, because I didn't have enough ammo for another forty-two golems.

The four left were spreading out, acting more wary. That was anthropomorphizing: rock did not act wary, even when animated. It didn't plan, either, but *I* did, and to my eyes, it looked like they were preparing a more strategic attack. If all four picked up speed and moved in on me at once, I was done for.

At least I could even the odds. There were two grenades left in the launcher. I hefted it to my shoulder, took a breath against the oncoming kickback, and fired.

The grenade flew where it was supposed to, but I dropped. The kickback was centered against my shoulder, but it slammed the whole body at the best of times. Firing it with cracked ribs was not the best of times, and I didn't have a tripod to brace it with for the final shot. I gritted, "Hoo-ah," through my teeth this time, sat up, and fired a second time before I let myself think about it.

I blew a leg off the closest golem. It would have to do. The remaining two hesitated and I seized the opportunity to snag more grenades from my pack. Only two frags left, but three flash-bangs as well. I detonated them close enough to myself to provide cover while I crept away, an Army crawl that banged my ribs against the ground but meant not having to get to my feet again. I had dust in my teeth. Even the Mojave hadn't ground itself into me as much as this mountainside was doing.

I covered forty yards before the smoke cleared. Then I rolled on my back and stared at the sky, taking deep cleansing breaths. I couldn't manage another frag unless the golems got close enough to throw one at them, and I didn't want to let them get that close. I put the frags on my belt anyway, just in case, then quietly drew my pistol. They had eyes. Eyes were normally vulnerable. I just had to be steady enough to make the shot. I breathed, and listened, and when the cracking footsteps came clear, I rolled to my feet a second time, sighted, and fired.

The first volley was perfect. I caught one of them in the eye. Its head exploded into puffs of dust. The other one turned its face away. All the way away, so the back of its head faced me. The third one, the one I'd blown the leg off, was still down. I thanked God for small favors and got the second-to-last frag out. I knew how far I could throw it, uninjured. I figured I could manage half that distance with my ribs on fire, then knocked another three yards off to be safe. It put the detonation range dangerously close, but I couldn't risk the launcher again. Another hit like that and I'd be unconscious. And I hadn't even laid eyes on the big show yet.

That didn't bear thinking about. I watched the golem stumble over uneven ground, edging toward me with its head still on backward. They really did use their eyes, unlikely as it seemed. I flung the frag, collapsed to the ground, and tried to breathe around shooting pain while I waited for the explosion. Noise and smoke billowed after eight seconds, but it took another minute and a half to get back to my feet. The golem didn't make it to me in that time, so I knew I'd done it some damage.

Quite a lot, it turned out, though it wasn't dead yet. It was like the robot in that old sci-fi movie, pulling itself along by one arm and its grinning jaw. I didn't have an industrial metal crusher handy, so I just shot it in the eye. It died. I didn't dare sag to the earth beside it, because there had to be a creator-demon around here somewhere, and I didn't think I could get to my feet if I went down again. So I just waited. The air cooled off as the sun started sliding into the west. I could still smell boiled fish, and the frothing lake down below gave me something to focus on while I waited. Demons did not beget golem protectors just to run away while somebody went through the golems with a bunch of hand grenades.

Although now that I thought about it, that seemed like a very smart thing for a demon to do. I wondered if I'd been had. I slumped to sitting and awkwardly searched my bag for some snack bars and the rest of my water. I put the water on a rock while I ate, which hurt more than I thought it would. Light refracted in a bubble rising from the bottom of the water jug, and then in another.

By the time I realized the water was in fact *boiling*, Asag was just about on top of me.

I unloaded a clip into him, naturally. Sparks pinged off him where the bullets hit, and he rolled back, but I hadn't done any real damage. One for the notebooks: silver didn't stop demons any more than it specifically stopped anything else. I had, though, been counting on the bullets be as reliable as always, and they weren't. That was unfortunate.

He rolled forward again, having given me a chance to see what I faced but having lost almost no momentum. I expected a gorgon, something to freeze me in my tracks as well as boil water. I was a little disappointed: he was ugly, but not ugly enough to turn me to stone. He was round and multi-limbed, with a hide that looked as hard as the golems

I'd blown up. He had eyes everywhere, protruding from each of his three arms and legs. They were all of almost equal thickness, so he could cartwheel in any direction. I wished I had an elephant gun, but I didn't even have one of those in the Caddy's trunk. I'd never met anything a bullet didn't at least slow down.

I had one grenade left, but my aim was too bad to risk using it unless he was on top of me, and I'd done that once already. I was still trying to work out a line of defense when he rolled over the last chunks of stone between us, and bloomed into a Lovecraftian horror.

The hide was just that: a protective outer covering. Within it lay a silently screaming mess strewn by faces of the dead which were marked with pox and stretched long in pain. Greyish-white intestines pulsed as they strangled the dead, and tentacles popped back in from looking out of the hide, every one of them ending with a red staring eyeball. The entirety of Asag's innards dripped with acidic slime. The stench was overwhelming. Tears flooded my eyes. I coughed and threw my arm over my face, afraid the air would become toxic, and nearly fainted as the action pulled my ribs.

One of his arms unfolded. They weren't thick and stumpy after all, but multi-jointed, long, and very thin. Folded up they had to be strong as a bundle of sticks to support Asag's weight, but extended—

—extended it lashed at me like a whip, scoring a slice across the arm protecting my face. Acid burned so deeply I couldn't even cry out. All I could think was I'd have lost my eyes if my arm hadn't been in place. I could fight a demon, but I couldn't fight it blind. I curved my spine and rolled backward, narrowly escaping another lash, and waited for adrenaline to kick in hard enough to let me push past the pain in my ribs.

The crunch of hitting the ground did the trick. I'd been sitting, so it hadn't been a long fall, but it didn't need to be. Endorphins flooded my system, burning pain away so fast I knew I'd pay dearly later. But it was the only way there would be a later, so I was willing to pay. I rolled to the side, pulled a knife from a thigh holster, and braced myself for the next hit.

Ichor spurted from Asag's arm when it met the knife. A clean cut, severing the end, which fell to the ground lifelessly. The silent faces in his belly screamed aloud. I drew another gun to open fire into the tender flesh.

This time the bullets had an effect. He staggered back, reeling from one thick leg to another. Both his other arms unfolded, snapping at me almost too quickly to be seen. I tried firing once, then stopped wasting bullets: I was a crack shot, but they were slim and speeding. The knife was a better weapon against them.

The third time an arm lashed at me, I dropped the knife—I had another—and grabbed it. My hand went around it easily, and it wrapped around my lower arm like a lover's embrace. An abusive lover, because it pulled me back toward the demon's body, knocking me against rocks and yanking my feet out from under me. Still, I needed to be close if I was going to inflict the most possible damage.

Letting Asag reel me in was a more likely avenue of success than trying to dart in on my own.

When I got close enough, I shot what would be a kneecap on a human, but the bullet lodged in the stony overhide. Wrong angle, or not enough exposed flesh on the legs. I didn't have time to try again. The arm shoved me toward one of the gaping mouths. I wished I dared detonate the last frag, but there was no way I could get out of range before it went off. I shot the screaming face instead. Acid muck rained everywhere, scalding my arms. Between boiling lakes, dry pipes and the distance to the nearest hospital, I was going to come out of this one scarred.

Scarred was fine. Dead wasn't. I shot another face and came up empty on the second squeeze. The faces screamed again, but this time in triumph, and then the whole demon folded shut again.

Around me.

It was not how I'd planned for this mission to go. I didn't dare breathe. My ribs began to throb, adrenaline or no. I squirmed an arm back, trying not to think about the burns scoring my arms with each move. They'd gone beyond pain already, reaching a dull red state that would later burst into flame. Later was all that mattered.

I fumbled, tugged, and found it: the switch that activated my space blanket. Solar power radiated out, heating Asag from the inside.

He'd been defeated by a god of healing and sunlight, back in Sumer. Maybe I was smart after all.

Five seconds passed. The rotten fish stench changed

to cooking rotten fish, permeating my nostrils even when I held my breath. I gagged and bit my tongue to keep from either vomiting or breathing. Ten seconds had gone by. Normally I could make it for three minutes, maybe four, without breathing, but that was with preparation, and without cracked ribs. I figured I was good for thirty seconds, maybe forty-five, and then I was screwed.

At thirty seconds, a howl vibrated through the demon, and he erupted. I flew into the air like a geyser was propelling me, coming down hard on pointed rocks. Agony ripped through my back muscles, spasms tugging at my ribs and taking away any chance of drawing a comforting breath. I couldn't even whimper. Teeth ground together, I stared at the sky and thought *hoo-ah, hoo-ah, hoo-ah,* until a spasm released me and I could suddenly move my toes again. Nothing critical was broken, then. I was going to have a bad night exposed out here on the mountain, but at least I'd survive.

Stone slipped near my head. I twisted just enough to see what was coming at me.

The golem. The one I'd blown the leg off but hadn't killed. Stone was patient, crawling down the mountainside toward me while I fought the father demon. I closed my eyes, thought *fuck*, then whispered, "Hoo-ah," and opened my eyes again, because damned if I was going to die with my eyes closed. I had one last frag. At least I could take the bastard with me. Inch by painful inch, not much faster than the golem was moving, I tugged my backpack out from under me and dug down for the frag. When the golem was five feet away, I pulled the pin.

At the count of five, the golem disintegrated in a shower of blue.

At the count of eight, the frag did not go off. It should have. I was still staring in bewilderment at where the golem used to be. I hadn't put the pin back, or even thought to. Stones rattled, sliding and cracking against one another as footsteps pushed them out of the beds they'd settled in. I stayed on my back, clutching a grenade that should've gone off. Thin white clouds spun across the sky. If Asag had re-amalgamated and was coming back, I was in trouble. He didn't seem like the type to creep up cautiously after one defeat, though, and I was sure he hadn't destroyed his own golem.

My spine hurt.

After a minute or so a face intruded into my line of vision. Green eyes, a thin scar on one cheek. Pixie-cut hair scattered with iron grey that stood out sharply against the original black. A few lines around the eyes and mouth, but not that many for a woman pushing fifty.

When I was a kid, I'd thought she was beautiful. Now, as an adult, I could see she wasn't. Attractive, yeah, but not beautiful. Her nose was too beaky, her chin too sharp, her height too great and her shoulders too wide for anybody's idea of conventional beauty. Put it all together, though, and I still thought she was beautiful. Some of that was hero worship. Some was the power that lit her from within. But mostly it was just Joanne Walker, who had taught me there was magic in the world.

Politely, even solicitously, she said, "Mind if I take this?" and removed the frag from my death grip on it. Only when she lifted it did I see a glimmer of silvery-blue magic stuffed in the pin hole, keeping it from detonating. She gave it a casual toss that had great upper body strength behind it, and a few seconds later it exploded at a safe distance. Then she looked down at me. "I hope you don't mind me putting the kibosh on that last thing. I'm sure you could have handled it, but I was in the area. I take it you defeated the bad guy?"

I nodded.

She crouched. Her hands dangled in front of her knees, above my sternum. "Got your ass kicked doing it, too, hm?"

I nodded.

"Couldn't wait a couple hours for me to get down here to help, huh?"

I shook my head. Joanne grinned. "Yeah, I wouldn't have either when I was your age. I didn't. All the time, I didn't. I tell you, Ash, hook up with one of the Holliday kids. Get a little mojo on your side to go with the impressive martial arts skills. Clara's single."

I closed my eyes. Joanne laughed out loud and ruffled my hair. "Good news is you're only bruised all to hell and back, sweetheart. Hang on a second and let me patch you up. It'll make getting out of here easier."

The drink-of-water-in-a-desert magic rushed me. It pushed away all my aches and pains, until I could tell my spine hurt because a rock was sticking in it. My feet were numb because of the rock's location, not because I'd shattered anything. I exhaled deeply, more relieved than I wanted to admit.

Joanne curled her hands around mine and pulled me to my feet. I was four inches shorter, twenty years younger, and with far less magical aptitude than she, but she punched my shoulder like we were equals. "You okay?"

"I think so."

"Good. There's a diner with the best milkshakes in Washington about twenty or thirty miles back up the road. Let's go there and you can tell me all the ways you're more awesome than I am." She turned and slipped back down the mountainside, sending scree in bouncing waves before her. I followed more slowly, testing muscle and reflex reactions in the wake of the beating I'd taken. Nothing hurt anymore. I felt like I was fresh out of bed, ready to face the day.

I picked up a tiny stone and winged it at Joanne, catching her on the butt. She yelped, rubbed it, and turned around. "What was that for?"

"I just wanted to say if I had to slay the demon, you're buying the milkshakes."

Joanne grinned and waited for me to catch up. Then she slung an arm around my shoulders and tipped her head toward the distant diner. "Absolutely, darlin'. It's a date."

We hobbled down the hill together, and went for milkshakes.

Acknowledgements

There are literally hundreds of people to thank for NO DOMINION, but some of you have earned a special and particular shout-out:

Russ Smith, a long-time friend who was NO DOMINION's first backer

Chrysoula Tzavelas, another long-time friend who mananged to sneak in as the last pledge/upgrade

Bryant Durrell, without whom none of my crowdfunding projects would have ever happened, and who also tipped this crazy ride over the $20K mark

Erica Olson, who told me to squee more

Fred Hicks/Evil Hat Publishing, for the InDesign tutorials that helped put this book in your hands

Mary-Theresa Hussey, my Walker Papers editor, who edited NO DOMINION as well, but whose faith and interest in the project was such that she bought in

Kyle Cassidy & Charles Summerfield, for bringing Gary to life in the cover art

Tom & Rosie Murphy, my parents, who not only did beta-reading & editorial commentary on NO DOMINION, but babysat as well, which became critical as the story ballooned from a 30K novella to a 60K book

and

Ted Lee, my husband, who was serenely confident that in fact everyone would like to read Gary's story, and who was, as usual, right.

Patron Acknowledgements

Angela N. Hunt, Adrianne Middleton, agrimony, Aidan Barron, Ailsa, ajah

Alana Leahy, Alecia Ramsay, Aleis Maxim, Alice Ma, Alicia Bennett

Alis Rasmussen, Alison Marlowe, Allison Davis, Althea Clark, Amanda

Amanda Claxton, amanda Lane, Amanda Priole, Amanda Weinstein

Amber Salem, Amelinda Webb, Amy Blume, Amy King, Amy Nesbitt

Ana Ramsey, Andrea Blythe, Andy Wilson, Angela Bills, Angela Korra'ti

Angie, Anne Walker, Anne Pascale Quinty, April Koenig, arfunk

Ariane Tobin, Ariannah Wetherbee, Ashlee Thow, ashley crump

audrey salick, Axisor, Barbara Erwin, Barbara Hasebe, Becka Green Reed

Benoit Jauvin-Girard, Bernadette Constant, Beth Cato, Beth Leitman

Beverly Scrivner, Blair, Blake Gilbert, Bradetta, Brandy Terry

Breanne, Brenda Jernigan, Bretaigne Jones, Brian Nisbet

Brianna Agnew, Bryant Durrell, Buddah, CA Brandstatter

cailleuch, Cari McAskill, Carin Robertson, Carl Rigney

Carmon Williams, Carol Gabel, Carol Gagneaux, Carol Guess

Carolina Pardo, Caroline Elliott, Casey Goodwin, Casse, Cat, Cat Wilson

Catherine Fiorello, Catherine Kruta, Catherine Sharp, Catherine Stevenson

Caytlin Vilbrandt, Char Bernardin, Charlotte Calvert, Cheri Seymour

Chiray, Chris Huning, Chris Meravi, Christal Serrato, Christer Boräng

christina hightower, Christine Chen, Christine H. Lee, Christine McCann

Christine Swendseid, Chrysoula Tzavelas, Chrystin McLelland

Cindy Crawford, Claire, Coby Haas,Colette Reap, Cori Weisfeldt

Cylia Amendolara, Cyndi, Cynnara Tregarth, Cynthia Teare, Cyrano Jones

D Walther, Daisy Brown, Dan Zlotnikov, Daniel Arbuckle

Daniel Martin, Danielle Ingber, Dave Entermille, Deanna Zinn

Debbie Matsuura, Deborah Alverson, Deborah Blake

Debra Meyerson, defektesmosaik, Deirdre, Denee Zah, Denise

Denise Matthews, Denise Sanchez, Diana, Diana Morgan

Diana Rae McKinney, Diane Dupey, Diane G. Phillips

Diane Schultz, Dianne Williams, Dina Willner, Donal Cunningham

Donald McAtee, donna antonio, Donna K White, Edward Ellis

el edwards, Elektra Hammond, Elena Eddings, Eleri Hamilton

Eliel Mamousette, Elizabeth, Elizabeth B Handler, Elizabeth Cadorette

Elizabeth Spillman and Kyle Engan, Elizabeth Turner, Ella Peabody

Elli Ferguson, Emily Ervin, Emily Poole, Emily Sandoval, Emma

Emma Bartholomew, Erica L. Rodriguez, Erin, Erin Moore

Esperanza Jimenez, Evenstar Deane, FaolchuDonn

Farrell Maginnis, Flynn, Fred Hicks/Evil Hat Publishing

Freya, Gabe Krabbe, Gareth, Garrett Jones, Gemma Tapscott, Genista

Georgina Scott, Gerri Lynn, Glenn Case, Glenna Gregg, Gretchen S.

H. L. Henrikson, Harold Zable, Heather Devine, Heather Fagan

Heather Joubert, Heather Knutsen, heather longino

Heidi Berthiaume, Helen Katsinis, Holly Tidd, Ian Struckhoff

IndianaJ, Inkjade, Irish, Jacki, Jackie Powers, Jaime Deming, James Scott

Jami Nord, Jamie Bentley, Janell, Janelle Hansen, Janne Torklep, Jean Eelma

Jean Marie Diaz, Jean Tatro, Jeanie Fortman, Jeanine Rachau

Jeannette Hoffman, Jeff Linder, Jeliza Patterson, Jeni Young

jenica rogers, Jenn, Jennifer, Jennifer, jennifer adams

Jennifer Canova, Jennifer Chun, Jennifer R., Jennifer Vail

Jennifer Wiewel Westberg, Jess Hartley, Jess Westphal

Jesse Cunningham, Jessica, Jessica Lynn Qualls

Jill Valuet, Joann, JoAnne G., Joe Tortuga, Joerg Ritter, John, John Corrigan

John Johnson, Joshua, Joy Whitfield, Joyce Haslam, jppoet, Judith Cauthan

Julene Warwick, Julia Figueroa, Julian West, Julie Kuhn

Justine Birmingham, K'Lynn, kamalloy, Karen Krettler, Karolina Chmiel

Kat Bonson, Kate Jackson, Kate Kirby, Kate Larking, Kate Martin

Kate Quinn, Kate Sheehy, Kathleen, Kathleen Hanrahan

Kathleen Hopper, Kathleen Tipton, Kathryn Duffy, Kathy
Kathy Schroeder, Katie Clapsadl, katintheboots, Katrina Lehto
Kayla Lowes, Kaz D'Spana, Kell, Kelley, Kelly, Keri Hayes, Kerry
Kerry Kuhn, Kes Yocum, Kiely, Kiera Knapp, Kim, Kim Miller
Kim Wells, Kimberly Reis, Kira Noseworthy, Kori Klinzing
Kris Panchyk, Kristian Holvoet, Kristine Kearney, Kristy Moen
Kristyn Willson, Krumpff, Kyna Foster, L Welch, Lacey Ruby
Lara Amber Zia, Larisa LaBrant, Laura, Laura Anne Gilman
Laura Carscaddon, Laura Pearson, Laura Wallace, Lauren Bassett
Lauri Weaver, Laurie Gaughan, LD Steele, Leading Edge, Leah Moore
Leigh Ann Melloy, Lessa McDonald, Lexi Taylor,Lia Hunter
Lianne, linda, Linda Cox, Linda George, Linda Pierce
Lindsay Stalcup, Lindsey Snelling, Liralen, Lisa, Lisa Cali
Lisa Carlton Guertin, Lisa Cohen, Lisa Moore, Lisa Pegg, Lisa Soto
Lisa Stewart, Liz, Liza, Liza Hernandez, llwheeler, Lola McCrary
Lori Allen, Lori Long, Lori Lum, Lorri-Lynne Brown
Louise Southwick, Lydia Leong, Lyn Mercer, Lynette Miles
Lynn Mershon Calvin, Maggie Gillet, Maggie Rocheleau
Mandy Gregory Doherty, Marcia Carney, Marcia Dougherty
Maresa Welke, Margaret A. Menzies, Margaret Anderson
Margaret McGaffey Fisk, Maria, Maria Lima, Marilyn Fisher
Marjorie, Marjorie Liu, Mark Mathison, Mark O'English, Mark Sutter
Marsha Simmons, Martin Curley, Mary Agner, mary anne walker
Mary Hargrove, Mary Keefe, mary scioscia, Mary Spila,
Marytheresa Hussey, Matt Forbeck, Matthew Hunter
Maura van der Linden, Max Kaehn, melissa, Melissa Poole
Melissa Tabon, Meredeth Brewer, MeriLyn Oblad, Michael Bernardi
Michael Feldhusen, Michael Metzger, Michael Nickerson, Michael Perkins
MichaelMJones, Michelle Bennett, Michelle Carlson
Michelle Curtis, Michelle Edwards, Michelle Ossiander

Michelle Williams, Mikaela, Mike Osterman, Mindy Albright
Minerva, Moira, Morag Watson, mvshoobridge, Nancy Weston
Nanette Furman, Niall Murphy, niamhob, Nick Austin, Nicole
Noriko Shoji, Octopus Gallery, Pam Blome, Pam East, Pam Hatler
Pamela Shaw, Pat Knuth, Patricia Lockard, Patsy Tisdale, Paul Bulmer
Paul-Gabriel Wiener, Paula Stambaugh, Penni Askew, Phiala
Philip Obermarck, Piper Rainey, Poppy Arakelian, Priscilla Spencer
R Caldwell, R. Francis Smith, Rachel, Rachel Chiapparine
Rachel Coleman Finch, Rachel Gollub, Rachel Gordon, Rachel Narow
Rachel Vance, Rebecca Frey, Rebecca Studley, regis, RevBob, Robert Fisher
Robert Lynch, Robert Smith, Robin Owens, Robyn Huffman, Rolanni
Ron Chance, Rosanne Girton, Ruth, Ruth Parrott, S Hackemann
Sabine Wiem, Sam Dailey, Sam Marks, Sam Martin, Samanda Jeude
Sandra Mraz, Sandy Davis, Sandy Giden, Sara Blackmore, Sara Harville
Sarah Brooks, Sarah Lam, Scot McIntosh, Scott Drummond, Scott Shanks
Scott Tengelin, Sean Collins, Sebastien How, Shannon Scollard
Shanon Hite, Sharis Ingram, Sharon Broggi, Shawn Tumey, Sheila Lester
Shel Kennon, Shelley Shearer, Silkie & Image & the Weasels,Sherri Marx
shylydrya, Siobhain McShane-Loy, sjmathis, soapturtle, Somm
spacedlaw, Steelneko, Stephana Bekebrede, Stephanie, Stephanie
StevenM, SueAnne Merrill, Sumi Funayama, Summer Allen, Susan Baur
Susan Petroulas, Suzanne Blasi, Suzanne McLeod, Taiyo, Tammy Graves
Tania Clucas, Tantris Hernandez, Tanya Koenig, Tara F., Tara Smith
Tara Teich, Tarja Rainio, Tennille, Teresa Lessard, terrio, Therese Bui
Tiffiny Quinn, Tim Bowie, Tina Kulesa, Traci Horton, Tracie Bogart
Trudy Dowling, Valentine Lewis, ValkyrieAK, Van der Jonckheyd
Vickie Chan, Victoria Hench, virginia morris, Weirdonian, Wendy
Wolf, Yukon Beulah, Zephfire, Þorbjörg Bergmann

About the Author

C.E. Murphy began writing for publication at age six, when she submitted three poems to a school publication. The teacher producing the magazine selected (inevitably) the one she thought was by far the worst, but also told her to keep writing, which she has. She has held the usual grab-bag of jobs usually seen in an authorial biography, but writing books is better.

She was born and raised in Alaska, and now lives with her family in her ancestral homeland of Ireland, which is a magical land where it rains a lot but winter rarely actually arrives.

She can be found online at:
cemurphy.net
facebook.com/cemurphywriter
twitter.com/ce_murphy

Made in the USA
Lexington, KY
27 April 2013